"What would you do if you were mine?"

The question caught her off guard while her brain zipped off on a disorienting, romantic tangent. To be Tuck's. In his arms. In his life. In his bed.

"Sorry?" She scrambled to bring her thoughts back to the real world.

"If you were my confidential assistant, what would you do?"

"I'm not." She wasn't his anything, and she had to remember that.

"But if you were?"

If she were Tuck's assistant, she'd be in the middle of making one colossal mistake. Eventually, she would kiss her boss. She was thinking about it right now. And if the dusky smoke in his eyes was anything to go by, he was thinking about it, too.

* * *

A Bargain with the Boss
is part of the Chicago Sons series—
Men who work hard, love harder
and live with their fathers' legacies...

A BARGAIN WITH THE BOSS

BY
BARBARA DUNLOP

First Published in Great Britain 2016
By Mills & Boon, an imprint of HarperCollins*Publishers*
1 London Bridge Street, London, SE1 9GF

© 2016 Barbara Dunlop

ISBN: 978-0-263-91857-1

51-0416

Our policy is to use papers that are natural, renewable and recyclable products and made from wood grown in sustainable forests. The logging and manufacturing processes conform to the legal environmental regulations of the country of origin.

Printed and bound in Spain
by CPI, Barcelona

Barbara Dunlop writes romantic stories while curled up in a log cabin in Canada's far north, where bears outnumber people and it snows six months of the year. Fortunately she has a brawny husband and two teenage children to haul firewood and clear the driveway while she sips cocoa and muses about her upcoming chapters. Barbara loves to hear from readers. You can contact her through her website, www.barbaradunlop.com.

Thanks to Kieran Slobodin for the title.

And thanks to Shona Mostyn and
Brittany Pearson for the shoes!

One

Saturday night ended early for Lawrence "Tuck" Tucker. His date had not gone well.

Her name was Felicity. She had a bright smile, sunshine-blond hair, a body that could stop traffic and the IQ of a basset hound. But she also had a shrill, long-winded conversational style, and she was stridently against subsidized day care and team sports for children. Plus, she hated the Bulls. What self-respecting Chicagoan hated the Bulls? That was just disloyal.

By the time they'd finished dessert, Tuck was tired of being lectured in high C. He decided life was too short, so he'd dropped her off at her apartment with a fleeting good-night kiss.

Now he let himself into the expansive foyer of the Tucker family mansion, shifting his thoughts ahead to Sunday morning. He was meeting his friend Shane Colborn for, somewhat ironically, a pickup basketball game.

"That's just *reckless*." The angry voice of his father, Jamison Tucker, rang clearly from the library.

"I'm not saying it'll be easy," said Tuck's older brother, Dixon, his own voice tight with frustration.

Together the two men ran the family's multinational conglomerate, Tucker Transportation, and it was highly unusual for them to argue.

"Now, *that's* an understatement," said Jamison. "Who could possibly step in? I'm tied up. And we're not sending some junior executive to Antwerp."

"The operations director is not a junior executive."

"We need a vice president to represent the company. We need you."

"Then, send Tuck."

"*Tuck?*" Jamison scoffed.

The derision in his father's voice shouldn't have bothered Tuck. But it did. Even after all these years, he still felt the sting in his father's lack of faith and respect.

"He's a vice president," said Dixon.

"In name only. And barely that."

"Dad—"

"Don't you *Dad* me. You know your brother's shortcomings as well as I do. You want to take an extended vacation? *Now?*"

"I didn't choose the timing."

Jamison's voice moderated. "She did you wrong, son. Everybody knows that."

"My wife of ten years betrayed every promise we ever made to each other. Do you have any idea how that feels?"

Tuck's sympathies went out to Dixon. It had been a terrible few months since Dixon had caught Kassandra in bed with another man. The final divorce papers had arrived earlier this week. Dixon hadn't said much about them. In fact, he'd been unusually tight-lipped.

"And you're angry. And that's fine. But you bested her in the divorce. We held up the prenup and she's walking away with next to nothing."

All emotion left Dixon's voice. "It's all about the money to you, isn't it?"

"It was to her," said Jamison.

There was a break in the conversation, and Tuck realized they could easily emerge from the library and catch him eavesdropping. He took a silent step back toward the front door.

"Tuck deserves a chance," said Dixon.

Tuck froze again to listen.

"Tuck had a chance," said Jamison, his words stinging once again.

When? Tuck wanted to shout. When had he had a chance to do anything but sit in his executive floor office and feel like an unwanted guest?

But as quickly as the emotion formed, he reminded himself that he didn't care. His only defense against his father was not to care about respect or recognition or making any meaningful contribution to the family business. Most people would kill for Tuck's lifestyle. He needed to shut up and enjoy it.

"I knew this was a bad idea," said Dixon.

"It was a terrible idea," said Jamison.

Tuck reached behind himself and opened the front door. Then he shut it hard, making a show of tromping his feet over the hardwood floor.

"Hello?" he called out as he walked toward the library, giving them ample time to pretend they'd been talking about something else.

"Hi, Tuck." His brother greeted him as he entered the dark-hued, masculine room.

"I didn't see your car out front," Tuck told him.

"I parked it in the garage."

"So you're staying over?"

Dixon had a penthouse downtown, where he'd lived with Kassandra, but he occasionally spent a day or two at the family home.

"I'm staying over," said Dixon. "I sold the penthouse today."

From the expression on his father's face, Tuck could tell this was news to him, as well.

"So you'll be here for a while?" Tuck asked easily. He loosened his tie and pulled it off. "What are you drinking?"

"Glen Garron," Jamison answered.

"Sounds good." Tuck shrugged out of his jacket and tossed it onto one of the deep red leather wingback chairs.

With a perimeter of ceiling-high shelves, a stone fireplace, oversize leather chairs and ornately carved walnut tables, the library hadn't changed in seventy years. It had been built by Tuck's grandfather, Randal, as a gentleman's retreat, back in the days when gentlemen thought they had something to retreat from.

Tuck didn't fill the silence, but instead waited to see where his father and brother would take the conversation.

"How was your date?" his father asked.

"It was fine."

Jamison looked pointedly at his heavy platinum watch.

"She wasn't exactly a rocket scientist," Tuck said, answering the unspoken question.

"You've dated a rocket scientist?" asked Jamison.

Tuck frowned at his father's mocking tone.

The two men locked gazes for a moment before Jamison spoke. "I merely wondered how you had a basis for comparison."

"First date?" Dixon queried, his tone much less judgmental.

Tuck crossed to the wet bar and flipped up a cut crystal glass. "Last date."

Dixon gave a chopped laugh.

Tuck poured a measure of scotch. "Interested in the game with Shane tomorrow?" he asked his brother.

"Can't," said Dixon.

"Work?" asked Tuck.

"Tying up loose ends."

Tuck turned to face the other men. "With the penthouse?"

Dixon's expression was inscrutable. "And a few other things."

Tuck got the distinct feeling Dixon was holding something back. But then the two brothers rarely spoke frankly in front of their father. Tuck would catch up with Dixon at some point tomorrow and ask him what was going on. Was he really looking at taking a lengthy vacation? Tuck would be impressed if he was.

Then again, their father was right. Tucker Transportation needed Dixon to keep the corporation running at full speed. And Tuck wasn't any kind of a substitute on that front.

Amber Bowen looked straight into the eyes of the president of Tucker Transportation and lied.

"No," she said to Jamison Tucker. "Dixon didn't mention anything to me."

Her loyalty was to her boss, Dixon Tucker. Five years ago, he'd given her a chance when nobody else would. She'd been straight out of high school, with no college education and no office experience. He'd put his faith in her then, and she wasn't going to let him down now.

"When was the last time you spoke to him?"

Jamison Tucker was an imposing figure behind his big desk in the corner office on the thirty-second floor of the Tucker Transportation building. His gray hair was neat, freshly cut every three weeks. His suit was custom-made to cover his barrel chest. He wasn't as tall as his two sons, but he more than made up for it in sturdiness. He was thick necked, like a bulldog. His brow was heavy and his face was square.

"Yesterday morning," said Amber. This time she was telling the truth.

His eyes narrowed with what looked like suspicion. "You didn't see him last night, sometime after the office closed?"

The question took her aback. "I… Why?"

"It's a yes-or-no answer, Amber."

"No."

Why would Jamison ask that question, and why in such a suspicious tone?

"Are you sure?" Jamison asked her, skepticism in his pale blue eyes.

She hesitated before answering. "Do you have some reason to believe I saw him last night?"

"*Did* you see him last night?" There was a note of triumph in his voice.

She hadn't. But she did know where Dixon had been last night. He was at the airport, boarding a private jet for Arizona. She knew he'd left Chicago, and she knew he wouldn't be back for a very long time.

He'd told her he'd left a note for his family so they wouldn't worry. And he'd made her promise not to give anyone more information. And she was keeping that promise.

Dixon's family took shameless advantage of his good nature

and his strong work ethic. The result was that he was over-worked and exhausted. He'd been doing an increasing share of the senior management duties at Tucker Transportation over the past couple of years. And now his divorce had taken a huge toll on his mental and emotional state. If he didn't get some help soon, he was headed for a breakdown.

She knew he'd tried to explain it to his family. She also knew they refused to listen. He'd had no choice but to simply disappear. His father and his lazy, good-for-nothing younger brother, Tuck, were simply going to have to step up.

She squared her shoulders. "Are you implying that I have a personal relationship with Dixon?"

Jamison leaned slightly forward. "I don't imply."

"Yes, you do. You did." She knew she was skating on thin ice, but she was angry on her behalf and Dixon's. It was Dixon's wife who had cheated, not Dixon.

Jamison's tone went lower. "How dare you?"

"How dare you, sir. Have some faith in your own son."

Then Jamison's eyes seemed to bulge. His complexion turned ruddy. "Why, you—"

Amber braced herself, gripping the arm of the chair, afraid she would be fired on the spot. She could only hope Dixon would hire her back when he returned.

But Jamison gasped instead and his hand went to his chest. His body stiffened in the big chair and he sucked in three short breaths.

Amber shot to her feet. "Mr. Tucker?"

There was genuine terror in his expression.

She grabbed the desk phone, calling out to his assistant as she dialed 911.

Jamison's assistant, Margaret Smithers, was through the door in a flash.

While Amber gave instructions to the emergency operator, Margaret called the company nurse.

Within minutes, the nurse had Jamison on his back on the floor of his office and was administering CPR.

Amber watched the scene in horror. Had his heart truly stopped? Was he going to die right here in the office?

She knew she should get word to his family. His wife needed to know what had happened. Then again, Mrs. Tucker probably shouldn't be alone when she heard. She probably shouldn't hear news like this from a company secretary.

"I need to call Tuck," Amber said to Margaret.

All the blood had drained from Margaret's face. She dropped to her knees beside Jamison.

"Margaret?" Amber prompted. "Tuck?"

"On my desk," Margaret whispered, as if it was painful for her to talk. "There's a phone list. His cell number is there."

Amber left for Margaret's desk in the outer office.

While she punched Tuck's cell number, the paramedics rushed past with a stretcher. The commotion inside Jamison's office turned into a blur.

"Hello?" Tuck answered.

She cleared her throat, fighting to keep from looking through the office door, afraid of what she might see. She thought she could hear a defibrillator hum to life. Then the paramedics called, "Clear."

"This is Amber Bowen," she said into the phone, struggling to keep her voice from shaking.

There was silence, and she realized Tuck didn't recognize her name. It figured. But this wasn't the time to dwell on his lack of interest in the company that supported his playboy lifestyle.

"I'm Dixon's assistant," she said.

"Oh, Amber. Right." Tuck sounded distracted.

"You need to come to the office." She stopped herself.

What Tuck really needed to do was to go to the hospital and meet the ambulance there. She searched for a way to phrase those words.

"Why?" he asked.

"It's your father."

"My *father* wants me to come to the *office*?" His drawling tone dripped sarcasm.

"We had to call an ambulance."

Tuck's voice became more alert. "Did he fall?"

"He, well, seems to have collapsed."

"*What?* Why?"

"I don't know." She was thinking it had to be a heart attack, but she didn't want to speculate.

"What do you mean you don't know?"

"The paramedics are putting him on a stretcher. I didn't want to call Mrs. Tucker and frighten her."

"Right. Good decision."

"You should probably meet them at Central Hospital."

"Is he conscious?"

Amber looked at Jamison's closed eyes and pale skin. "I don't think so."

"I'm on my way."

"Good."

The line went silent and she set down the phone.

The paramedics wheeled Jamison past. He was propped up on the stretcher, an oxygen mask over his face and an IV in his arm.

Amber sank down onto Margaret's chair, her knees wobbly and her legs weak.

Margaret and the nurse emerged from Jamison's office. Margaret's eyes were red, tears marring her cheeks.

Amber rose to meet her. "It's going to be all right. He's getting the best of care."

"How?" Margaret asked into the air. "How could this happen?"

The nurse excused herself to follow the paramedics.

"Do you think he has heart problems?" Amber asked quietly.

Margaret shook her head. "He doesn't. Just last night…" Another tear ran down her cheek.

"Did something happen yesterday?" Amber assumed Margaret had meant yesterday, maybe late in the afternoon.

"He was in such a good mood. We had some wine."

"You had wine in the office?"

Margaret stilled. Panic and guilt suddenly flooded her expression, and she took a quick step back, glancing away.

"It was nothing," she said, focusing on some papers in her in-basket, straightening them into a pile.

Amber was stunned.

Jamison and Margaret had been together last night? Had they been *together*, together? It sure looked like it.

Margaret moved briskly around the end of her desk. "I should… That is…" She sank down in her chair.

"Yes," Amber agreed, not sure what she was agreeing to, but quite certain she should end the conversation and get back to her own desk.

She started for the hallway, but then she paused, her sense of duty asserting itself. "I'll call the senior managers and give them the news. Did Jamison tell you about Dixon?"

Margaret looked up. "What about Dixon?"

Amber decided the news of Dixon leaving could wait a couple of hours. "Nothing. We can talk later."

Margaret's head went back down and she plunked a few keys on her keyboard. "Jamison had a lunch today and a three o'clock with the board."

Amber left Margaret to her work, her mind racing with all that would need to be handled.

Dixon was gone. Jamison was ill. And that left no one in charge. Tuck was out there somewhere. But she couldn't even imagine what would happen if Tuck took the reins. He wasn't a real vice president. He was just some partier who dropped by the office now and again, evidently giving heart palpitations to half the female staff.

A week later, Tuck realized he had to accept reality. His father was going to be weeks, if not months, in recovery from his heart attack, and Dixon was nowhere to be found. Somebody had to run Tucker Transportation. And that somebody had to be him.

The senior executives seated around the boardroom table looked decidedly troubled at seeing him in the president's chair. He didn't blame them one bit.

"What I don't understand," said Harvey Miller, the finance director, "is why you're not even talking to Dixon."

Tuck hadn't yet decided how much to reveal about his brother's disappearance. He'd tried calling, text messaging and emailing Dixon. He'd had no response. And there was nothing to go on except the cryptic letter his brother had left for their father, saying he'd be gone a month, maybe even longer.

"Dixon's on vacation," said Tuck.

"Now?" asked Harvey, incredulity ringing through his tone.

Mary Silas's head came up in obvious surprise and chagrin. "I didn't hear about that."

She was in charge of human resources and Tuck knew she prided herself on being in the know.

"Get him back," said Harvey.

Instead of responding to either of them, Tuck scanned the expressions of the five executives. "I'd like a status report from each of you tomorrow morning. Amber will book a one-on-one meeting for each of you."

"What about the New York trade show?" asked Zachary Ingles, the marketing director.

Tuck's understanding of the annual trade show, a marquee event, was sketchy at best. He'd attended a couple of times, so he knew Tucker Transportation created and staffed a large pavilion on the trade-show floor. But in the past he'd been more focused on the booth babes and the evening receptions than on the sales efforts.

"Bring me the information tomorrow," he said.

"I need decisions," said Zachary, his tone impatient.

"Then, I'll make them," Tuck replied.

He might not have a clue what he was doing, but he knew enough to hide his uncertainty.

"Can we at least conference Dixon into the meetings?" asked Harvey.

"He's not available," said Tuck.

"Where is he?"

Tuck set his jaw and glared at the man.

"Do you want a full quarterly report or a summary?" asked Lucas Steele. He was the youngest of the executives, the operations director.

Where the others wore custom-made suits, Lucas was dressed in blue jeans and a dark blazer. His steel-blue shirt was crisp, but he hadn't bothered with a tie. He moved between two worlds—the accountants and lawyers who set strategic direction, and the transport managers around the world who actually got things from A to B.

"A summary is enough for now." Tuck appreciated Lucas's pragmatic approach to the situation.

Lucas raised his brows, silently asking the other men if there was anything else.

Tuck decided to jump on the opportunity and end the meeting.

"Thank you." He rose from his chair.

They followed suit and filed out, leaving him alone with Dixon's assistant, Amber.

He hadn't paid much attention to her before this week, but now she struck him as a model of fortitude and efficiency. Where his father's assistant, Margaret, seemed to be falling apart, Amber was calm and collected.

If she'd wandered out of central casting, she couldn't have looked more perfect for the part of trustworthy assistant. Her brunette hair was pulled back in a tidy French braid. Her makeup was minimal. She wore a gray skirt and blazer with a buttoned white blouse.

Only two things about her tweaked his interest as a man—the fine wisps of hair that had obviously escaped the confining braid, and the spiky black high-heeled sandals that flashed gold soles when she walked. The loose wisps of hair were endearing, while the shoes were intriguing. Both could have the power to turn him on if he was inclined to let them.

He wasn't.

"We need to get Dixon back," he told her, setting his mind firmly on business. His brother was priority number one.

"I don't think we should bother him," she replied.

The answer struck Tuck as ridiculous. "He's got a corporation to run."

Her blue eyes flashed with unexpected annoyance. "*You've* got a corporation to run."

For some reason, he hadn't been prepared for any display of emotion from her, let alone something bordering on hostility. It was yet another thing he found intriguing. It was also something else he was going to ignore.

"We both know that's not going to happen," he stated flatly.

"We both know no such thing."

Tuck wasn't a stickler for hierarchy, but her attitude struck him as inappropriately confrontational. "Do you talk to Dixon this way?"

The question seemed to surprise her, but she recovered quickly. "What way?"

He wasn't buying it. "You know exactly what I mean."

"Dixon needs some time to himself. The divorce was very hard on him."

Tuck knew full well that the divorce had been hard on his brother. "He's better off without her."

"No kidding." There was knowledge in her tone.

"He talked to you about his wife?" Tuck was surprised by that.

Amber didn't reply right away, and it was obvious to him that she was carefully formulating her answer.

He couldn't help wondering how close Dixon had become to his assistant. Was she his confidante? Something more?

"I saw them together," she finally said. "I overheard some of their private conversations."

"You mean you eavesdropped?" Not exactly an admirable trait. Then again, not that he was one to judge.

"I mean, she shouted pretty loud."

"You couldn't leave and give them some privacy?"

"Not always. I have a job that requires me to be at my desk. And that desk is outside Dixon's office."

Tuck couldn't help but wonder exactly how far-reaching her duties had become when Dixon's marriage went bad. He took in her tailored clothes and her neat hair. She might be buttoned down, but she was definitely attractive.

"I see…" He thought maybe he did.

"Stop that," she snapped.

"Stop what?"

"Stop insinuating something without spitting it out. If you've got something to ask me, then *ask* me."

Fine with Tuck. "What were you to my brother?"

She enunciated carefully. "I was his confidential assistant."

He found himself easing forward. "And which of your duties were confidential?"

"All of them."

"You know what I'm asking."

"Then, ask it."

Despite her attitude, he liked her. There was something about her straightforward manner that he admired very much. "Were you sleeping with my brother?"

As he looked into her simmering blue eyes, he suddenly and unexpectedly cared about the answer. He didn't want her to be Dixon's mistress.

"No."

He was relieved. "You're sure?"

"That wouldn't be something I'd forget. My car keys, maybe. To pick up cat food, yes. But, oops, having sex with my boss just slipped my mind?" Her tone went flat. "Yes, Tuck. I'm sure."

He wanted to kiss her. He was suddenly seized by an overwhelming desire to pull her close and taste those sassy lips.

"You have a cat?" he asked instead.

"Focus, Tuck. Dixon's not coming back. At least not for a while. I know you've had a cushy run here, but that's over and done with. You've got work to do now, and I am not letting you duck and weave."

Now he really wanted to kiss her. "How're you going to do that?"

"Persuasion, persistence and coercion."

"You think you can coerce me?"

"What I think is that somewhere deep down inside you must be a man who wants to succeed, a man who actually wants to impress his father."

She was wrong, but he was curious.

"Why do you think that?" he asked.

"You strike me as the type."

"I never imagined I was a type."

Truth was he didn't want to impress his father. But he did want to impress Amber, more than he'd wanted to impress a woman in a very long time.

Unfortunately for him, she wasn't about to observe him in the part of suave, worldly, wealthy Tuck Tucker. She was about to watch him fumbling around the helm of a multimillion corporation. He couldn't have dreamed of a less flattering circumstance.

Two

Amber was torn between annoyance and sympathy.

For the past week, Tuck had arrived at the office promptly at eight. He seemed a little groggy for the first hour, and she'd fallen into the habit of having a large coffee on his desk waiting for him. She could only guess that he hadn't yet modified his playboy nights to fit his workday schedule.

She'd moved from her desk near Dixon's office to the desk outside Tuck's office. Tuck didn't have his own assistant, since he was so rarely there, but now he was taking on Dixon's work. He was also taking on Jamison's. Margaret had been out sick most days since Jamison's heart attack, so Amber was keeping in communication with directors and managers and all of their assistants, trying to be sure nothing fell through the cracks.

This morning, voices were raised behind Tuck's closed door. He was meeting with Zachary Ingles, the marketing director. They were two weeks from the New York trade show and deadlines were rapidly piling up.

"*You* were tasked with approving the final branding," Zachary was shouting. "I sent three options. It's all in the email."

"I have two thousand emails in my in-basket," Tuck returned.

"*Your* disorganization is not *my* problem. We've missed the print deadline on everything—signs, banners and all the swag."

"You need to tell me when there's a critical deadline."

"I did tell you."

"In an email that I didn't read."

"Here's a tip," said Zachary. But then he went silent.

Amber found herself picturing Tuck's glare. Tuck might be out of his depth, but he wasn't stupid, and he wasn't a pushover.

A minute later, Tuck's office door was thrown open and Zachary stormed past her desk, tossing a glare her way. "Tell your boss he can pay rush penalties on every damn item for all I care."

Amber didn't bother to respond. She'd never warmed up to Zachary. He was demanding and entitled, always running roughshod over his staff and anyone else below him in the corporate hierarchy. Dixon put up with him because he was favored by Jamison, and because he did seem to have a knack for knowing how to appeal to big clients with expensive shipping needs.

Tuck appeared in the office doorway.

"Lucas will be here at ten," she told him. "But your schedule is clear for the next half hour."

"Maybe I can read a few hundred emails."

"Good idea."

He drew a breath, looking like he wanted to bolt for the exit. "What am I doing wrong?"

"Nothing."

"I'm behind by two thousand emails."

"Dixon was very organized."

Surely Tuck didn't expect to rival his brother after only a single week. It had taken Dixon years to become such an effective vice president.

Tuck frowned at her. "So everyone tells me."

"He worked very long and hard to get there."

Yes, Tuck was arriving on time. And really, that was more than she'd expected. But Dixon had taken on far more than his fair share of early mornings and late nights working out systems and processes for covering the volume of work. Tuck seemed to expect to become a boy wonder overnight.

Tuck's tone hardened. "I'm asking for some friendly advice. Can we not turn it into a lecture about my sainted brother?"

"You can't expect to simply walk through the door and be perfect."

"I'm not expecting anything of the sort. Believe me, I know that Dixon is remarkable. I've heard about it my entire life."

Amber felt a twinge of guilt.

Tuck did seem to be trying. Not that he had any choice in the matter. And it didn't change the fact that he'd barely bothered to show up at the office until he was backed into a corner. Still, he was here now. She'd give him that.

"Zachary should have given you a heads-up on the branding," she said. "He should have pointed out the deadline."

"I shouldn't have missed it," said Tuck.

"But you did. And you're going to miss other things." She saw no point in pretending.

"Your confidence in me is inspiring."

She found herself annoyed on Tuck's behalf, and the frustration came through in her voice.

"Tell him," she said. "Tell them all. Tell them that it's *their* job to keep you appraised of critical deadlines, and not just in an email. Make it a part of your regular meetings. And make the meetings more frequent if you have to, even daily. I mean, if you can stand to see Zachary every day, that is."

Tuck cracked a smile.

It was a joke. But Amber shouldn't have made it. "I know that was an inappropriate thing to say."

He took a couple of steps toward her desk. "I don't have a problem with inappropriate. It's a good idea. I'll send them an email."

"You don't have to send them an email." Her sense of professionalism won out over her annoyance at his past laziness. "I'll send them an email. And I can triage your in-basket if you'd like."

His expression brightened and he moved closer still. "You'd read them for me?"

"Yes. I'll get rid of the unimportant ones."

"How will you do that?"

"I have a delete key."

He leaned his hands down on the desk, lowering his voice. "You can do that? I mean, and not have the company fall down around my ears?"

Amber found herself fighting a grin. "With some of them, sure. With others, I'll take care of them myself, or I'll delegate the work to one of the unit heads. And I'll flag the important ones for you."

"I swear, I could kiss you for that."

It was obviously a quip. But for some reason his words resonated all the way to her abdomen.

Her gaze went to his lips, triggering the image of a kiss in her imagination.

She caught the look in his eyes and the air seemed to crackle between them.

"Not necessary," she quickly said into the silence.

"I suppose the paycheck is enough."

"It's enough."

He straightened, and a twinkle came into his silver-gray eyes. "Still, the offer's open."

She considered his handsome, unapologetic face and his taut, sexy frame. "You're not like him at all, are you?"

"Dixon?"

She nodded.

"Not a bit."

"He doesn't joke around."

"He should."

Her loyalty reasserted itself. "Are you criticizing Dixon's performance on the job?"

"I'm criticizing his performance in life."

"He's been through a lot."

She didn't know how close Tuck was to his brother, but she had seen firsthand the toll Kassandra's infidelity had taken on Dixon. Dixon had been devoted to his wife. He'd thought they were trying to start a family while she had secretly been taking birth control pills and sleeping with another man.

"I know he has," said Tuck.

"He was blindsided by her lies."

Tuck seemed to consider the statement. "There were signs."

"Now you're criticizing Dixon for loyalty?"

"I'm wondering why you're so blindly defending him."

"When you're an honest person—" as Amber knew Dixon was "—you don't look for deceit in others."

Tuck's gaze was astute. "But you saw it, too."

Amber wasn't going to lie. "That Kassandra had a scheming streak?"

"Aha." There was a distinct ring of triumph in Tuck's tone.

"I saw it, too," she admitted.

He sobered. "I don't know what that says about you and I."

"Maybe that we should be careful around each other?"

"Are you out to get me, Amber?"

"No." She wasn't.

She didn't find him particularly admirable. An admirable man would have shown up to help long before now. But now that he was here, she'd admit he wasn't all bad.

"Are you going to lie to me?"

"No."

"Will you help me succeed?"

She hesitated over that one. "Maybe. If you seem to deserve it."

"How am I doing so far?"

"You're no Dixon."

"I'm never going to be Dixon."

"But you seem to have Zachary's number. I can respect that."

It was a moment before Tuck responded. "How'd he get away with that crap with my dad?"

"He didn't pull that crap with your dad."

"He's testing me."

"We all are."

"Including you?"

"Especially me."

But Tuck was faring better than she'd expected. And she seemed worryingly susceptible to his playboy charm. She was definitely going to have to watch herself around him.

At home in the mansion, Tuck found himself retreating to the second floor, spreading work out in the compact sitting room down the hall from his own bedroom. Stylistically, it was different from the rest of the house, with earth tones, rattan and stoneware accents. He found it restful.

The big house had been built in the early 1900s, with hardwood floors, soaring relief ceilings, elaborate light fixtures and archways twenty feet in height. It was far from the most welcoming place in the world, full of uncomfortable antique chairs and somber paintings. And right now it echoed with emptiness.

Last week, they'd moved his father to a specialized care facility in Boston. His mother had gone with him to stay with her sister. His mother had asked her trusted staff members to come along for what looked to be an extended stay.

Tuck could have replaced the staff. But he was one man, and he had no plans to do any entertaining. Well, maybe a date or two, since he didn't plan to let his responsibilities at Tucker Transportation keep him celibate. But the house still had two cooks, two housekeepers and a groundskeeper. He couldn't imagine needing any more assistance than that.

For now, he headed down the grand staircase to meet his college friend, Jackson Rush, happy with both the opportunity for conversation and the break from office work. While Tuck had studied business at the University of Chicago, Jackson had studied criminology. Jackson now ran an investigations firm that had expanded around the country.

"I hope you have good news," said Tuck as Jackson removed his worn leather jacket and handed it to the housekeeper.

"Dixon took a private jet from Executive Airport to New York City," said Jackson.

"But not a Tucker Transportation jet." Tuck had already checked all the company records.

"Signal Air," said Jackson.

"Because he didn't want my dad to know where he went."

"That seems like a solid theory."

The two men made their way into the sunroom. It was dark outside, not the perfect time to enjoy the view through the floor-to-ceiling windows, but the sunroom was less ostentatious than the library.

"So he's in New York." As far as Tuck was concerned, that was good news. He'd worried his brother had taken off to Europe or Australia.

"From there, it looks like he took a train to Charlotte."

"A train?" Tuck turned his head to frown at Jackson. "Why on earth would he take a train? And what's in Charlotte?"

"Secrecy, I'm guessing." Jackson eased onto a forest-green sofa. "He wouldn't need ID to buy a train ticket. You said your dad tried to stop him from leaving?"

Tuck took a padded Adirondack chair next to a leafy potted ficus. "Dad was terrified at the thought of me actually working at Tucker Transportation."

"Then, I guess things didn't work out so well for him, did they?"

"Are you making a joke about his heart attack?"

"I didn't mean that the way it sounded. From Charlotte, our best guess is Dixon went on to either Miami or New Orleans. Anything you know of for him in either of those cities?"

Tuck racked his brain.

"A woman?" asked Jackson.

"He's barely divorced from Kassandra."

Jackson shot Tuck a look of incredulity.

"She was the one who cheated, not him. I doubt his head was anywhere near to dating again."

"Well, we're checking both cities, but so far he's not using his credit cards or hitting any bank machines. And there's no activity on his cell phone."

Tuck sat back. "Does this strike you as bafflingly elaborate?"

"Your brother does not want to be found. The question is, why?"

"He doesn't know about my dad," said Tuck. "He doesn't know he's abandoned Tucker Transportation to me alone. If he did, he'd be here in a heartbeat."

"Anything else going on in his life? Any chance he's got an enemy, committed a crime, embezzled from the company?"

Tuck laughed at that. "Embezzle from himself? He's got access to all the money he could ever want and then some."

"An enemy, then. Anybody who might want to harm him? Maybe the guy who slept with Kassandra?"

"Dixon's not afraid of Irwin Borba."

"What, then?" asked Jackson.

"He said he needed a vacation."

Tuck wanted to believe that was the simple answer. Because if Dixon was at a beach bar somewhere drinking rum punch and watching women in bikinis, he'd be back home soon. It had already been two weeks. Maybe Tuck just had to hang on a few more days without sinking any ships—either figuratively or literally—and he'd be off the hook. He sure hoped so.

"There's a major trade show coming up in New York," he told Jackson. "And we're launching two new container ships in Antwerp next week. Surely he'll return for that."

"He's expecting your dad will be there." Jackson restlessly tapped his blunt fingers against his denim-covered knee.

That was true. Dixon would assume Jamison would represent the company in Antwerp.

"Have you checked his computer?" asked Jackson. "Maybe he's got a personal email account you don't know about."

"Maybe." Tuck wasn't crazy about the idea of snooping into Dixon's business, but things were getting desperate.

"Check his office computer," said Jackson. "And check his laptop, his tablet, anything he didn't take with him. It looks to me as though he's traveling light."

Tuck had to agree with that. "What's he up to, switching transportation in two different cities?"

"He's up to not being found. And he's doing a damn good job of it. Any chance he's got a secret life?"

"A secret life?"

"Doing things that he can't tell anyone about. He does travel a lot. And he runs in some pretty influential circles."

"Are you asking if my brother is a spy?"

Jackson's shrug said it was possible.

"If there's one thing I've learned in the past week, it's that Dixon couldn't have had time for anything but Tucker Transportation. You wouldn't believe the amount of work that crosses his desk."

"Don't forget you're doing your dad's job, as well," Jackson pointed out.

"Even accounting for that. I'm starting to wonder…"

Tuck wasn't crazy about saying it out loud. But he had to wonder why they hadn't asked for his help before now. Was he truly that inept?

"You're a smart guy, too." Jackson seemed to have guessed the direction of Tuck's thoughts.

"I don't know about that."

"Well, I do. Your dad and Dixon, they probably got into a rhythm together early on. And you never seemed that interested in working at the company."

"I tried." Tuck couldn't keep the defensiveness from his voice. "In the beginning, I tried. But I always seemed to be in the way. Dad definitely didn't want me around. Dixon was his golden boy. After a while you get tired of always barging your way in."

"So you're in it now."

"I am. And it's scaring me half to death."

Jackson grinned. "I've been in the thick of it with you before. I can't picture you being afraid of anything."

"This isn't the same as a physical threat."

"I'm not just talking about a barroom brawl. Remember, I'm running a company of my own."

"That's right." Tuck perked up at the thought of getting some free advice. "You are. How big is it now?"

"Four offices, here in Chicago, New York, Boston and Philly."

"How many employees?"

"About two hundred."

"So you could give me a few tips?"

"Tucker Transportation is on a whole different scale than I am. You're better off talking to your friend Shane Colborn."

"I'm better off finding Dixon."

"I'll fly to Charlotte in the morning."

"You need a jet?"

Jackson cracked a grin. "I'm not going to say no to that offer. Sure, hook me up with a jet. In the meantime, check out his computer."

"I'll get Amber to help."

"Amber?"

"Dixon's trusty assistant."

An image of Amber's pretty face came up in his mind. He wasn't normally a fan of tailored clothes and no-nonsense hairstyles. But she seemed to look good in anything.

And then there were those shoes. She wore a different pair every day, each one sexier than the last. Something was definitely going on beneath the surface there. And the more time he spent with her, the more he wanted to figure out what really made her tick.

When Tuck strode into the office Monday morning, Amber's hormones jumped to attention. He was dressed in a pair of faded jeans, a green cotton shirt and a navy blazer. His dark brown hair had a rakish swoop across the top, and his face had a sexy, cavalier day's growth of beard.

He definitely wasn't Dixon. Dixon's confidence was never

cocky. And Dixon had never made her heart pump faster and heat rise up her neck.

"I need your help," he stated without preamble.

Amber immediately came to her feet. "Is something wrong?"

"Come with me." His walk was decisive and his voice definitive.

She experienced a new and completely inappropriate shiver of reaction.

This was a place of business, she told herself. He wasn't thinking about her as a woman. He sure wasn't thinking the same things she was thinking—that his commanding voice meant he might haul her into his office, pin her up against a wall and kiss her senseless.

What was wrong with her?

Tuck headed into Dixon's office and she forcibly shook off her silly fantasy.

"Do you know his password?" Tuck asked, crossing the big room and rounding the mahogany desk.

"His password to what?" she asked.

"To log on to the system." Tuck leaned down and moved the mouse to bring the screen to life.

She didn't answer. Dixon had given her his password a couple of months back on a day when he was in Europe and needed her to send him some files. She still remembered it, but she knew he'd never intended for her to use it again. What she technically knew, and what she ought to use, were two different things.

Tuck glanced up sharply. "Tell me the password, Amber."

"I…"

"If you don't, I'll only have the systems group reset it."

He made a valid point. As the acting head of Tucker Transportation, he could do whatever he wanted with the company computer system.

"Fine. It's ClownSchool, capital C and S, dollar sign, one, eight, zero."

Tuck typed. "You might want to think about whose side you're on here."

"I'm not taking sides." Though she was committed to keeping her promise to Dixon. "I'm trying to be professional."

"And I'm trying to save Tucker Transportation."

"Save it from what?" Had something happened?

"From ruin without my father or Dixon here to run it."

"What are you looking for?" she asked, realizing that he was exaggerating for effect and deciding to move past the hyperbole.

Tucker Transportation was a solid company with a team of long-term, capable executives running the departments. Even from the top, there was a limited amount of damage anyone could do in a month.

"Clues to where he went," said Tuck.

Then Tuck seemed to have an inspiration. He lifted the desk phone and dialed.

A moment later, a ring chimed inside Dixon's top drawer.

Tuck drew it open and removed Dixon's cell phone, holding it while it rang.

"How does it still have battery power?" he asked, more to himself than anything.

"I've been charging it," said Amber.

His attention switched to her, his face crinkling in obvious annoyance. "You didn't think to *tell me* his cell phone was in his desk drawer?"

Amber wasn't sure how to answer that.

"And how did you know it was there anyway? Were you snooping through his drawers?"

"No." She quickly shook her head. She was intensely respectful of Dixon's privacy. "He told me he was leaving it behind."

Tuck's piercing gray eyes narrowed, his brows slanting together in a way that wrinkled his forehead. "So he told you he was leaving? Before he left, you *knew* he was going?"

Amber realized she'd spoken too fast. But now she had no choice but to give a reluctant nod.

Tuck straightened and came to the end of the desk, his voice gravelly and ominous. "Before you answer this, remember I'm the acting president of this company. This is a direct order, and I don't look kindly on insubordination. Did he tell you where he was going?"

Dixon had given her an emergency number. And she'd recognized the area code. But he hadn't flat-out told her where he was going.

"No," she said, promising herself it wasn't technically a lie. "He needs the time, Tuck. He's been overworked for months, and Kassandra's betrayal hit him hard."

"That's not for you to decide."

She knew that was true. But it wasn't for Tuck to decide, either.

"He doesn't even know about our father," said Tuck.

"If he knew, he'd come home."

Tuck's voice rose. "Of *course* he'd come home."

"And then he'd be back to square one, worse off than he was before. I know it must be hard for you without him."

"You *know*? You don't know anything."

"I've worked here for five years." It was on the tip of her tongue to say that it was a whole lot longer than Tuck had worked here, but she checked herself in time.

"As an *assistant*."

"Yes."

"You don't have the full picture. You don't know the risks, the critical decisions."

"I know Dixon."

Tuck's tone turned incredulous. "You're saying I don't?"

Amber's voice rose. "I'm saying I've been here. I watched how hard he's worked. I saw how much your father slowed down these past months. I watched what Kassandra's infidelity did to him. He was losing it, Tuck. He took a break because he had no other choice."

Tuck gripped the side of the desk, his jaw going tight.

Amber mentally braced herself for an onslaught.

But his voice stayed steady, his words measured. "My father was slowing down?"

"Yes. A lot. Margaret was funneling more and more work to Dixon. Dixon was scrambling. He was staying late, coming in early, traveling all over the world."

"He likes traveling."

"You can't constantly travel and still run a company. And then Kassandra."

"Her behavior was despicable."

"It hurt him, Tuck. Yes, he was disgusted and angry. But he was also very badly hurt."

Tuck rocked back on his heels, his expression going pensive. "He didn't let on."

Amber hesitated but decided to share some more information. If it would help Tuck understand the gravity of the situation, it would do more good than harm.

"There were times when I heard more than I should," she said. "I know Dixon was ready to be a father. He thought they were trying to get pregnant. Instead, she was taking birth control pills and sleeping with another man."

It was clear from Tuck's expression that Dixon hadn't shared that information with him. He sat down, and his gaze went to the computer screen. "He still needs to know about our father."

She knew it wasn't her place to stop Tuck. "Do what you need to do."

He glanced up. "But you're not going to help me?"

"There's nothing more I can do to help you find Dixon. But I'll help you run Tucker Transportation."

"Finding Dixon is the best thing we can do to run Tucker Transportation."

"I disagree," she said.

"Bully for you."

"The best thing you can do to run Tucker Transportation is to *run* Tucker Transportation."

Tuck was silent while he moved the mouse and typed a few keys. "You should have told me."

"Told you what?" She found herself moving around the desk, curious to see what he would find on the computer.

"What he was planning," said Tuck as he scrolled through Dixon's email. "That he was secretly leaving."

She recognized the headers on the email messages, since they automatically copied to her account. "I'm Dixon's confidential assistant. I don't share his personal information with anyone else."

"There's nothing here but corporate business," said Tuck.

Amber knew that would be the case. Dixon was always careful to keep his personal email out of the corporate system. And he'd been doubly careful with the details of his secret vacation.

Tuck swiveled the chair to face her. "What would you do if you were mine?"

The question caught her off guard while her brain zipped off on a disorienting, romantic tangent. To be Tuck's. In his arms. In his life. In his bed.

He rose in front of her. "Amber?"

"Sorry?" She scrambled to bring her thoughts back to the real world.

His voice was rich and deep, laced with an intimacy she knew she had to be imagining. "If you were *my* confidential assistant, what would you do?"

"I'm not." She wasn't his anything, and she had to remember that.

"But if you were?"

If she was Tuck's assistant, she'd be in the middle of making one colossal mistake. Because that would mean she was sexually attracted to her boss. She'd want to kiss her boss. Eventually, she *would* kiss her boss. She was thinking about it right now. And if the dusky smoke in his eyes was anything to go by, he was thinking about it, too.

She plunged right in with the truth. "I would probably make a huge and horrible mistake."

The lift of his brows told her he understood her meaning. And he slowly raised his hand to brush his fingertips across her cheek. "Would it be so horrible?"

"We can't," she managed to respond.

He gave a very small smile. "We won't."

But he was easing closer, leaning in.

"Tuck," she warned.

He used his other hand to take hold of hers, twining their fingers together. "Professionally. On a professional level, given the current circumstances, what would you do if your loyalty was to me?"

She called on every single ounce of her fortitude to focus. "I'd tell you to go to the New York trade show. It's the smart thing to do and the best thing to do for the company."

"Okay."

His easy answer took her aback.

She wasn't sure she'd understood correctly. "You'll go?"

"We'll both go. I'm still going to find Dixon. But until I do, I'm the only owner this company has got. You're right to tell me to step up."

Amber moved a pace back and he released her hand.

New York? Together? With Tuck?

She struggled for a way to state her position. "I don't want you to get the wrong idea. I'm definitely not going to—"

"Sleep with me?" he said, finishing her thought.

"Well. Okay. Yes. That's what I meant." She hadn't planned on being that blunt, but that was it.

"That's disappointing. But it's not the reason I want you in New York. And I promise, there'll be no pressure on that front." He smoothly closed the space between them and leaned down.

She waited, her senses on alert for the kiss that seemed inevitable.

But he stopped, his lips inches away from hers, his voice a whisper. "I really like your shoes."

She reflexively glanced to her feet, seeing the jazzy, swirling gold-and-red pattern of her high-heel pumps.

"They'll look good in New York." He backed off, his voice returning to normal as he took his place in front of the computer screen. "Let's stay at the Neapolitan. Book us on a flight."

Once again, she fought to regain her emotional equilibrium. She swallowed. "Do you want an airline ticket or should I book a company plane?"

"What would Dixon do?"

"Dixon never flies commercial."

Tuck grinned. "Then, book us a company plane. If I'm going to take Dixon's place, I might as well enjoy all his perks."

Amber wanted to ask if he considered her one of Dixon's perks. But the question was as inappropriate as it was dangerous. Her relationship with Dixon was comfortably professional. By contrast, her relationship with Tuck grew more unsettling by the day.

Three

Tuck knew he had no right to be cheerful. Dixon was still missing and Zachary Ingles was unforgivably late arriving at the JWQ Convention Center in midtown Manhattan. Add to that, thirty Tucker Transportation employees were working with the convention center staff to assemble the components of the company's pavilion, with less organization than he would have expected.

Still he couldn't help but smile as he gazed across the chaos of lights, signs, scale models and scaffolding. Amber was at the opposite end of their allotted space, watching a forklift raise the main corporate sign into position. Her brunette hair was in a jaunty ponytail. She wore pink-and-black checkerboard sneakers, a pair of dark blue jeans and a dusky-blue pullover. It was as casual as he'd ever seen her.

"Mr. Tucker?" A woman in a navy blazer with a convention center name tag on the lapel approached him through the jumble. "I'm Nancy Raines, assistant manager with catering and logistics."

Tuck offered his hand. "Nice to meet you, Nancy. Please call me Tuck."

"Thank you, sir." She referred to the tablet in her hand. "We have the east-side ballroom booked for Friday night, a customized appetizers and hors d'oeuvres menu with an open bar for six hundred."

"That sounds right," said Tuck.

He'd read through the company's final schedule on the plane and he understood the general outline of each event. Out of the corner of his eye, he saw Amber coming their way.

"We understand that there was a last-minute booking of a

jazz trio, Three-Dimensional Moon," said Nancy. "Are they by any chance an acoustic band?"

"An acoustic band for six hundred people?" Tuck found the question rather absurd. How would anyone ever hear the music above the conversation?

"The reason I ask," said Nancy, "is we have no arrangement in place for a sound system."

"There's no sound system?"

That was clearly a mistake. Aside from the music, there were three speeches on the event schedule and a ten-minute corporate video.

Amber arrived. "Can I help with something?"

"This is Nancy. She says there's no sound system for the reception."

"There should be a sound system," said Amber. "And three projection screens."

But Nancy was shaking her head. "There was no tech ordered at all."

"Someone from the marketing department should have handled that. Have you heard anything from Zachary?" Tuck asked Amber. He needed to get to the bottom of this right away.

"I've texted, emailed and left a voice mail, but he's not returning."

Tuck withdrew his phone from his pocket. "We'll need the tech setup," he said to Nancy. "Can you take care of it?"

She made a few taps on her tablet. "I can try. It will have to be rush, and that'll mean a significant surcharge." She looked to Amber. "Do you have the specs?"

"I'll get them to you," said Amber, pulling out her own phone. "I'll track someone down."

Nancy handed her a business card. "You can send them to my email. I'll call a couple of local companies."

"Thanks," said Amber.

Tuck pressed the speed dial for Zachary.

Once again, it rang through to his voice mail.

"Maybe his flight was delayed," Tuck mused.

Amber held up her index finger. "Melanie? It's Amber. We need specs for a sound system for Three-Dimensional Moon. Can you find their web page and contact their manager?" She paused. "In the next ten minutes if you can."

Tuck checked his text messages, and then he moved to his email interface.

"I've got a new message from Zachary." He tapped the header.

He read for a minute and felt his jaw go lax.

"What?" Amber asked.

"It's a letter of resignation."

"No way." She moved to where she could see his small screen.

"It says he turned in his keys to security and asked them to change his password."

Tuck had no idea what to make of the message. Zachary had been with the company for a decade, rising through the ranks to his current, very well-paid position.

"Why would he do that?"

Excellent question.

Tuck's phone rang. He saw that it was Lucas Steele.

Tuck took the call, speaking without preamble. "Do you know what's going on?"

"Zachary walked," said Lucas.

"I just got his email. Do you know why?"

"Harvey went with him," said Lucas.

"Harvey, too? What on earth *happened*?" Tuck couldn't keep the astonishment from his voice. Two long-term directors had quit at the same time?

Amber's eyes widened while she listened to his side of the conversation.

"Peak Overland made them an offer," said Lucas.

"Both of them?"

"Yes."

The situation came clear in Tuck's mind. "Without Dixon, we look vulnerable."

"Yes, we look vulnerable. Nobody knows anything concrete, so there are theories all over the place. I'm hearing everything from he's been thrown in jail in a foreign country to he was killed skydiving."

"He's in New Orleans," said Tuck. "Or maybe Miami."

There was a silence.

"You don't know where he is." Lucas's voice was flat.

"He's on vacation. He needs some time alone."

"The divorce?" asked Lucas.

"That's my best guess."

"Okay," said Lucas, his tone growing crisp again. "You need me to come out there?"

"Yes. But I also need you in Chicago. And I need you in Antwerp."

What Tuck really needed was Dixon and there was absolutely no time to waste. His next call would be to Jackson.

Lucas gave a chopped chuckle. "Where do you want me?"

"Can you hold the fort in Chicago?"

"I can."

"Talk to security. Change the locks, change the system passwords. Make sure they can't do any damage."

"Will do."

"Is there an heir apparent to either Zachary or Harvey?"

"Nobody comes instantly to mind. But I'll think about it. And I'll ask around."

"Thanks. Talk to you in a few hours."

Tuck's lack of knowledge and experience with the family company suddenly felt like an anvil. He needed his brother more urgently than ever before.

"I'd choose Hope Quigley," said Amber.

"Who?"

"She's a manager in the marketing department. She's been on the social media file for a couple of years, but she's incredibly organized."

"You want me to promote a blogger to marketing director?"

Amber frowned. "It's a lot more than just blogging."

"That's a huge jump in responsibility."

Her hand went to her hip. "And you'd know this, how?"

Tuck did not want to have to make this decision on his own. "I'm calling Jackson. No more messing around. We're turning over every possible rock to find Dixon."

Something shifted in Amber's expression. "You don't need Dixon back."

What an absurd statement. "I absolutely need Dixon back."

"You can promote Hope. And there are others who can step in."

"The company needs a strong president. Look around you. We've got two days to pull this thing together. The reception is already in trouble, and there are thirty private meetings set up with the *marketing director*."

"You take the meetings."

"Yeah, right." As if he was going to speak knowledgably about Baltic Exchange indices and intermodal freight transport.

"Take Hope with you. Give her a new title. She's got two days before the meetings. She can come up to speed on the specific client accounts."

"I've never ever met the woman."

"Then, take Lucas with you."

"Lucas has to keep our current freight moving across the ocean."

"You're right." Amber pursed her red lips, folding her hands primly in front of her. "It's all hopeless. We should just give up and go home."

He didn't have a comeback for her obvious sarcasm. He knew what she was doing, and he didn't appreciate it.

"Are you this insubordinate with Dixon?" How had she kept from being fired?

Tuck dialed Jackson.

"I don't need to be insubordinate with Dixon. He knows what he's doing."

"Well, I…" But there was no retort for that. Tuck didn't know what he was doing. And that was the problem.

Jackson answered his phone. "Hi, Tuck."

"You need to pull out the stops," said Tuck. "Do whatever it takes."

"But—" Amber began.

Tuck silenced her with a glare. "I just lost my marketing director and my finance director."

"Did you fire them?" asked Jackson.

"They quit. Rumor has it they got an offer from a rival, and with Dixon out of the picture—"

"People are getting nervous." Jackson filled in the thought.

"It seems I'm not seen as a strong leader."

"You've barely gotten started."

Tuck knew that was no excuse. Maybe he should have barreled past his father's objections years ago. They might have been able to stop him from having any power at Tucker Transportation. But they couldn't have stopped him from learning. This was his fault, and he had to fix it.

"Find him," he said to Jackson.

"I'm in New Orleans."

"Do you think he's there?"

"I don't know that he's not. There's no evidence that he left."

"Is there evidence he arrived?"

"Maybe. It could be nothing. Can I get back to you?"

"Don't take too long." Tuck's gaze met Amber's.

She gave a slight shake of her head.

He knew she wanted him to leave Dixon alone and do it all himself. But there was too much at stake. He didn't dare try.

Tuck looked fantastic in a tuxedo. But then Amber had known that all along. She'd been seeing pictures of him in the tabloids for years, mostly at posh events or out on the town with some gorgeous woman. His ability to work a party had never been in question.

The Tucker Transportation reception was ending, and the

last few guests trickled out of the ballroom. Amber made her way to the main doors, grateful to have the evening at an end. Her feet were killing her, though that was her own fault. She'd knowingly worn two-hour shoes to a five-hour party.

But she hadn't been able to resist. This was by far the fanciest party she'd ever attended. And she'd never even taken the silver lace peep-toe pumps out of the box. They had a crimson stiletto heel and she'd done her toenails to match. Her feet looked fabulous, setting off her rather simple black dress.

The dress had cap sleeves and a slim silhouette. Its one jazzy feature was the scattering of silver sequins at the midthigh hemline. She'd worn it at least a dozen times, but it was tried and true, appropriate to the occasion.

Tuck appeared beside her, lightly touching her waist. "You promised me a dance."

"Your dance card seemed full," she answered him.

"Women kept asking, and I didn't want to be rude."

Amber kept walking toward the elevator. "You forget the point of hosting such a lavish reception was for you to make business contacts, not to collect phone numbers."

"You sound jealous."

She wasn't jealous. She refused to be jealous. She was merely feeling critical of his wasted opportunities.

"That was a business observation, not a personal one."

"No?" he asked.

"No."

Though, at the moment, it felt intensely personal. His hand was still resting at her waist. The heat from his body called out to her. And his deep voice seemed to seep through to her bones.

"Dance with me now."

She steeled herself against the attraction. "The band is packing up."

The only music was the elevator kind emanating from the small hotel speakers on the ceiling.

"We can go somewhere else."

"It's late. My feet are killing me. And I don't know why I'm giving you excuses. No. I don't want to go somewhere else and dance with you. I want to go to bed."

He let a beat go by in silence. Then there was a lilt in his voice. "Okay. Sure. That works for me."

They came to the elevators. "Tell me you didn't mean that how it sounded."

He pressed the call button. "That depends. How did it sound?"

"You can't flirt with me, Tuck."

"Am I doing it wrong?"

"That's not what I—"

"It was a great party, Amber. Against all odds, we got our pavilion up and running in time. The crowds have been super. And the party came off without a hitch. We even had a good sound system. Thank you for that, by the way. Can we not let our guard down and enjoy the achievement for just a few minutes?"

"I work for you."

She needed to nip his playboy behavior in the bud. It didn't matter that he was a charming flirt. And it didn't matter that he was sharp and funny and killer handsome. This wasn't a date. It was a corporate function, and she wasn't going to let either of them forget it.

"So what?" His question seemed sincere.

"So you can't hit on me."

"Is that a rule?"

"Yes, it's a rule. It's a law. It's called sexual harassment."

"I'm not seriously asking you to sleep with me. I mean, I wouldn't say no to an offer, obviously. But I'm not making the suggestion myself. Except, well, you know, in the most oblique and joking way possible."

Amber was stupefied. She had no idea what to say.

The elevator door opened, but neither of them moved.

"You're my boss," she tried.

"Dixon is your boss."

"You know what I mean."

"Are you saying I can't even ask you on a date? That's ridiculous. People date their bosses all the time. Some of them marry their bosses, for goodness' sake."

The door slid closed again.

She couldn't seem to stop herself from joking. "Are we getting married, Tuck?"

He didn't miss a beat. "I don't know. We haven't even had our first date."

She blew out a sigh of frustration. "What I'm saying, what the law says, is that you can't in any way, shape or form hint that my agreement or lack of agreement to something sexual or romantic will impact my job."

"I'm not doing that. I'd never do that. How do I prove it? Is there something I can sign?"

She pressed the call button again. "Tuck, you have got to spend more time in the real world."

"I spend all my time in the real world."

The door slid back open and they walked inside the elevator.

She turned to face the front. "If you did, you'd know what I was talking about."

"I do know what you're talking about. All I wanted to do was dance."

The door slid shut and they were alone in the car.

He was right. She didn't know how the conversation had gotten so far off track.

"We don't have time to dance," she told him. "You need to focus on tomorrow's meetings. You have the list, right? Did you study the files?"

"I looked at them."

"What does that mean?"

"I scanned them. I know the basics. Besides, you agreed to be there with me."

"You can't defer to your assistant when you're meeting with owners and executives of billion-dollar companies."

"I've been busy. I had to work some things out with Lucas. And then I took your advice and interviewed Hope."

"You did?" Amber was glad to hear that.

"Yes. I liked her. I'm going to give her more responsibility."

"That's good."

"So forgive me if I didn't find time to memorize the details of thirty client files."

Amber was tired, but she shook her brain back to life. Thank goodness she'd said no to the second glass of champagne.

"We'll go over them tonight," she told him.

He glanced at his watch.

"Unless you want to get up at 4:00 a.m. and go over them in the morning."

"Four a.m. is a late night, not an early morning."

"You're starting with a breakfast meeting."

"I know. Who set that up? Breakfast meetings are evil. They should be banned."

The elevator came to a stop on the top floor.

"Let's get this over with," Amber said with resignation.

Together, they walked the length of the hall to Tuck's suite. She'd been in it yesterday, so she knew it wasn't a typically intimate hotel room.

The main floor was a living area, powder room and kitchenette. You had to climb a spiral staircase to even get to the bedroom. According to the floor plan sketched on the door, there was a whirlpool tub on the bedroom terrace, but she had no intention of finding out in person.

As she set her clutch purse down on a glass-topped table and slipped off her shoes, her phone chimed. Curious as to who would text her at such a late hour, she checked the screen.

She was surprised to see it was her sister.

Jade lived on the West Coast and only contacted Amber if she needed money or was having an emotional crisis. It was uncharitable, and maybe unfair, but Amber's first thought was that Jade might be in jail.

"Are you thirsty?" Tuck asked, crossing to the bar.

Amber sat down on a peach-colored sofa. It was arranged in a grouping with two cream-colored armchairs in front of a marble fireplace.

"Some water would be nice," said Amber, opening the text message.

"Water? That's it?"

"I'd take some fruit juice."

I just hit town, Jade's text said.

"You're a wild woman," said Tuck.

"I'm keeping my wits about me."

Which town? Amber answered her sister.

"In case I make a pass at you?" asked Tuck.

"You swore you wouldn't."

"I don't recall signing anything."

Chicago.

What's wrong? Amber typed to her sister.

Nothing all good. Well, dumped boyfriend. Jerk anyway.

"Amber?" Tuck prompted.

"Hmm?"

"I said I didn't sign anything."

She glanced up. "Anything for what?"

He nodded to her phone. "Who's that?"

"My sister."

"You checked out there. I thought it might be your boyfriend."

"I don't have a boyfriend." She absently wondered what she'd ever said or done to make Tuck believe she had a boyfriend.

I'm in New York City, Amber typed to Jade.

"Good," said Tuck in a soft tone.

A shimmer tightened her chest.

I was hoping to crash with you for a couple of days, Jade responded.

Amber's fingers froze and she stared at the screen.

"What does she say?" asked Tuck, moving closer.

"She wants to stay with me."

"Is that bad?"

"She's not particularly...trustworthy."

Jade was constantly in and out of low-paying jobs, and in and out of bad relationships. The last time she'd stayed with Amber her sister had prompted a noise complaint from a neighbor, drunk all of Amber's wine and left abruptly without a goodbye, taking two pairs of Amber's jeans and several of her blouses along for good measure.

I'll call you when I get back, Amber typed.

"Oh?" Tuck took a seat on the other end of the sofa.

Thing is, Jade returned, I kind of need a place now, tonight.

Amber swore under her breath. It was coming up on midnight in Chicago, and her little sister had nowhere to go. She didn't delude herself that Jade would have money for a hotel.

"What is it?" asked Tuck.

"She needs a place now."

"Right now?" He glanced at his watch.

"I'm guessing she just got in from LA." Amber wouldn't be surprised if Jade had hitchhiked.

Hotel? Amber wrote.

Can't afford it. Jerk took all the money.

Of course the jerk boyfriend took Jade's money. They always did.

"I take it cash flow is an issue," said Tuck.

"That's a polite way to put it."

"Send her to the nearest Aquamarine location."

Amber raised her brow in Tuck's direction. The Aquamarine was a quality, four-star hotel chain.

"Tucker Transportation has a corporate account," said Tuck.

"I know Tucker Transportation has a corporate account."

"You can tell her to use it."

"I can't misuse the company account for my sister."

"You can't," he agreed. "But I can."

"I won't—"

"I need your attention," said Tuck. "I need you off your cell phone and I need you not worrying about your sister. The way I see it, this is the cheapest way forward."

"That's a stretch."

Tuck's tone turned serious. "Tell her. Let me make that an order."

Amber wanted to argue. But then she didn't particularly want to send Jade to her town house, nor did she want to rouse a neighbor at this hour to give her a key.

"I know you respect orders," said Tuck. "You are the consummate professional."

"You're messing in my personal life." Amber knew she shouldn't take him up on it, but she was sorely tempted.

"Yeah," he said. "I am. Now send her to the Aquamarine."

Amber heaved a sigh.

Before she could send the message, Tuck scooped the phone out of her hand, typing into it.

"Hey!"

"You know it's the best answer."

She did know it was the best answer. And she'd been about to do it herself. Further protests seemed pointless.

"She says great," said Tuck.

"I'll bet she does."

He set the phone down on the coffee table. "You're a good sister."

"In this instance, I think you're the good sister."

"Never been called that before."

"Neither have I."

Tuck chuckled, obviously assuming she was making a joke. She wasn't.

Four

Tuck was pretty good at handling late nights, but even he was starting to fade by the time he and Amber shut down the last client file. She looked exhausted, her cheeks flushed, makeup smudged under her eyes and her hair escaping in wisps from the updo.

"That's as ready as we can be," she said.

They were side by side on the overstuffed sofa, a lamp glowing on an end table, the lights of the city streaming through open curtains on the picture window across the room.

Tuck had long since shrugged out of his suit jacket and loosened his tie. His shirtsleeves were rolled up, but he was still too warm. The thermostat might be set too high. More likely, it was his attraction to Amber.

She was intensely sexy, every single thing about her, from her deep blue eyes to her rich brunette hair, to the delicious, sleek curves revealed by her fitted dress.

"Do you feel confident?" she asked, tipping her head to look at him.

He realized he'd been silently staring at her.

And he was still staring at her. He was overwhelmed by the urge to kiss her, kiss her deeply and thoroughly, taste those soft, dark red lips that had been teasing his senses all night long. He knew he shouldn't. Her earlier reluctance was reasonable and well founded. Anything romantic between them was bound to be complicated, today, tomorrow and into the future.

"Tuck?" she persisted, clearly confused.

He lifted his hand, brushed the stray hairs back from her cheek.

She sucked in a quick breath and her eyes closed in a long

blink. When they opened, they were opaque, misty blue with indecision.

It wasn't a no, he told himself. She wasn't ordering him to back off. She was tempted, just like him.

He knew there had to be a whole lot of reasons not to do this, but he couldn't seem to come up with them at the moment. So he leaned forward instead, slowly and steadily.

She could stop him, run away from him, pull back from him at least. Whatever she decided, he'd accept. But he had to at least try.

She didn't do any of those things, and their lips came together, his bold and purposeful, hers heated, smooth and delicious. He altered the angle and his arms went around her. He kissed her once, twice, three times, desire pulsing through his mind and electrifying his body.

She kissed him back, tentatively at first. But then her tongue touched his, tangled with his. Her body went malleable against his, her softness forming to his planes. He eased her back on the sofa, covering her from chest to thighs, tasting her mouth, inhaling her scent, feeling her back arch intimately and her heartbeat rise against his chest.

He wanted her bad.

He kissed his way down her neck, pushing the cap sleeve of her dress out of the way, leaving damp circles on her bare shoulder. He thought about her zipper, imagined pulling it down her back, the dress falling away, revealing a lacy bra, or her bare breasts, that creamy smooth skin that was silken to his touch.

"Tuck?" Her voice was breathless.

"Yes?"

"We…"

He stilled. He knew what came next, though every fiber of his being rebelled against it.

"Can't," she said, finishing the thought.

He wanted to argue. They could. They really could, and the world wouldn't come to a crashing halt.

But he'd never coerced a woman into his bed before and he wasn't about to start with Amber.

"You sure?" he asked.

He could feel her nod.

"I'm sorry," she said.

He eased back. "No, I'm the one who's sorry. I shouldn't have kissed you."

"I should have said no."

"I'm glad you didn't."

"I'm… Oh, this is not good." She struggled to sit up.

He moved out of the way, offering his hand to help her up. Neither of them seemed to know what to say.

Tuck broke the silence. "I guess we're ready for the meeting."

"Tuck, I—"

"You don't have to explain."

A woman was entitled to say no for any reason she wanted. And he did understand her hesitation. She worked for him, at least temporarily. She was smart not to let it get complicated.

She rose to her feet. "You're an attractive guy. But you know that."

He stood.

"I'm sure most women would—"

"I don't like where this is going." He didn't.

"I know you don't often get turned down."

"Now, how would you know that?"

"I read the papers."

His annoyance grew. "You believe the tabloids?"

"They have pictures." Frustration crept into her tone. "You can't deny you have gorgeous girl after gorgeous girl on your arm."

"Is that what you think of me? I didn't kiss you because you're beautiful, Amber."

"I *know* that. I'm not comparing myself to them."

"Comparing yourself?" He didn't understand her point.

"I'm not suggesting I'm one of your bombshells."

"Good."

She was so much more than that. He might not have known her long, but he knew there was more depth to her than a dozen of his Saturday-night dates combined.

Her shoulders dropped. "I'll just say good night."

"You didn't do anything wrong."

He didn't want her to leave. He wanted to keep talking, even if they were arguing. He liked the sound of her voice. But he also wanted to kiss her again and carry her off to his bed. He couldn't do that.

"It's late," she said. "We're both tired. Let's not say or do anything we're going to regret."

"I don't regret a thing."

"I do."

The words were like a blow to his chest. "I'm sorry to hear that."

"I'm your employee, Tuck."

"You're Dixon's employee."

"Tucker Transportation's employee. And you're a vice president."

"In name only." He found himself parroting his father's words.

"You need to change that, Tuck. You really do."

"Are you lecturing me on my corporate responsibility?"

"Somebody has to."

He was about to retort that they already had. But then he realized it wasn't true. Neither his father nor Dixon had lectured him. They'd never pushed him to become more involved in the company. They'd barely suggested he show up. But he wasn't about to admit that to Amber.

He had to stop himself from taking her hands in his. "How did we get here?"

Her eyes narrowed in puzzlement. "We were prepping for the client meetings."

"I meant in the conversation. We were talking about us, and suddenly we're on to Tucker Transportation."

"There is no us."

"There was almost an us."

It was barely there, but he could tell she stifled a smile.

It warmed his heart.

"I'm leaving now," she said.

He reflexively grasped her hands. "You don't have to go."

"I do have to go."

"Stay." He gave himself a mental shake, backing off. "I'm sorry. I never do that. I never try to convince a woman to sleep with me."

She arched a brow. "They normally throw themselves into your bed?"

They did. But he knew how that sounded.

"I like you, Amber."

"I'm not going to sleep with you, Tuck."

"That's not what I'm asking."

"It's exactly what you're asking. It's 2:00 a.m., and I'm in your hotel room." She hesitated. "That was my mistake, wasn't it? What was I thinking?"

"You didn't make a mistake."

She tugged her hands from his. "I didn't think this through. I just assumed you wouldn't misunderstand."

"I didn't misunderstand. I didn't plan this, Amber." He'd taken her behavior at face value. He knew she was only trying to help him get ready for the meetings.

She held up her palms and took a couple of backward paces. "Time for me to say good night. Don't forget the breakfast meeting." She took her purse from the table. "Don't be late."

"I'm never late."

"True," she allowed as she retrieved her shoes and strode toward the door. "But I always expect you to be late."

"Why?"

"I'll see you tomorrow." And then she was gone.

He wanted to call her back. He *wished* he could call her back. But he'd made enough mistakes for one night. He realized that if he wanted Amber to let him get anywhere close to her, he had to back off until she was ready.

Back in Chicago two days later, Amber dreaded meeting up with Jade. She was happy her sister had dumped whatever loser boyfriend she'd hooked up with this time, but she also held out no hope for the next one, or the one after that. Bad boyfriends and heartache had been Jade's pattern since she'd dropped out of high school.

Amber tried to harden her heart. Jade was an adult and responsible for her own behavior. But Amber couldn't help remembering her sister as a lost little girl, younger, who had struggled even more than Amber with their mother's addiction to alcohol.

She made her way from her car up the stone pathway to the lobby of the Riverside Aquamarine. Jade was going to meet her in the coffee shop. But since it was shortly after noon, Amber wasn't going to be surprised to find her in the lobby lounge. It was sadly ironic that Jade had turned to alcohol to combat a childhood ruined by alcohol.

The hotel lobby was bright and airy, decorated by white armchairs and leafy plants. The lobby lounge was central, but Amber didn't see Jade at any of the tables. She moved on to the coffee shop that overlooked the pool and quickly spotted Jade at a booth.

As Amber approached, Jade slid from the bench and came to her feet.

Amber's jaw nearly dropped to the floor.

Jade was pregnant. She was very, very pregnant.

"What on earth?" Amber paced forward, coming to a stop in front of her sister.

"Seven months," said Jade, giving a wry smile as she answered the obvious question.

"But…when? How?"

Jade's expression sobered. "Seven months ago. And the usual way. Can we sit down?"

"Oh, Jade." Amber couldn't keep the disappointment and worry from her tone. Jade was in no position to be a good mother.

"Don't 'oh, Jade' me. I'm happy."

"How can you be happy?"

"I'm going to be a mother." Jade slid back into the booth.

As she took the seat across from her, Amber noted she was eating a salad and drinking a glass of iced tea. "You're not drinking, are you?"

"It's iced tea," said Jade.

"I don't mean now. I mean *at all*. You can't drink while you're pregnant, Jade."

"Do you think I'm stupid?"

Stupid, no. But Jade's judgment had always been a big question mark.

"That's not an answer," Amber pointed out.

"No, I'm not drinking."

"Good. That's good. You've seen a doctor?"

"Yes, I saw a doctor in LA. And I'll find a clinic here in Chicago, too."

A waitress appeared and Amber ordered a soda.

She stared at her sister, noting the worn cotton smock and the wrinkled slacks. Jade's cheeks looked hollow and her arms looked thin. Amber hated to think her sister might not be getting enough to eat.

All the way here, she'd been hoping Jade's stay in Chicago would be brief. She'd dreaded the idea of having her move into the town house for days or weeks. Now she realized that was exactly what had to happen. Jade needed stability, a warm bed, good food.

"Have you been taking care of yourself?" Amber asked.

Jade gave a shrug. "It's been okay. Kirk was getting more and more obnoxious about the baby. He said he didn't mind, but then he started talking about putting it up for adoption."

Amber's opinion of this Kirk person went up a notch. "*Have* you thought about adoption?"

Jade's expression twisted in anger. "I am *not* giving away this baby."

"To a good home," said Amber. "There are fantastic prospective parents out there. Loving, well educated, houses in the suburbs—they could give a baby a great life."

Jade's lips pressed together and her arms crossed protectively over her stomach. "Forget it."

"Okay," said Amber, letting the subject drop for now. "It's your choice."

"Damn right it's my choice."

"Yours and the father's."

"There is no father."

"You just said Kirk wanted to give the baby up for adoption."

"Kirk's not the father. That's why he wanted to give the baby away. It's not his."

The revelation took Amber aback. Kirk dropped back down in her esteem. "I don't understand."

"I was pregnant when I met Kirk. He said he didn't mind. He said he loved kids. But then…" Jade gave another shrug.

"Who's the father?" asked Amber. Maybe there was some hope for financial support. Heaven knew Jade was going to need it.

"It was a one-night thing."

"You didn't get his name." Amber shouldn't have been surprised.

"Only his first name. Pete."

Amber tried not to judge, but it was hard.

"He was a sailor."

"You mean in the navy?"

Jade nodded.

"Well, did you try to find him?"

"It was weeks before I knew I was pregnant."

"What about DNA? After the baby's born. The navy must have a database."

"He was Australian."

"Still, did you contact—"

"Amber, I am not going to track down some Australian sailor and ruin his life over a one-night stand."

"Why not? He ruined—"

"Don't you *dare* say he ruined mine. He seemed like a really nice guy. But I went into it with my eyes wide-open, and it was my choice to carry on with the pregnancy. I'm having a baby, my son or daughter, your nephew or niece, and I'm going to take care of it, and I'm not going to drag some poor man kicking and screaming into an obligation he didn't sign up for."

Jade's words and attitude were surprising but in some ways admirable. Amber wasn't used to her taking such personal responsibility.

"Okay," she told her sister. "You can come and stay with me."

Jade was silent for a moment. "Thank you."

"We'll figure this out together."

But Jade was shaking her head. "I'm not looking for you to take over my life."

Who'd said anything about taking over?

"It's only temporary," Jade continued. "I'm studying. I'm going to write my GED. Then I'm going to get a proper job."

Amber could barely believe what she was hearing. "You're working on your GED?"

"I've been working on it for months now."

The surprises just kept on coming. "Seriously?"

"Why would I joke about that?"

"That's fantastic." Amber was beyond impressed. "I'll help you. We can—"

"Whoa. You need to dial it down."

"I didn't mean to dial it up."

"Giving me a place to stay is great, *really* great. But that's all I need right now."

Amber forcibly curbed her excitement. But it was the first time Jade had shown an interest in anything but partying, and Amber's hopes were running away with her. A baby was an enormous responsibility. But other single mothers had pulled it off. If Jade could keep up this new attitude, she might have a fighting chance.

Amber couldn't help but smile at the possibilities, even as Jade came back with a warning frown.

"I thought we'd have him back by now," Tuck said to Jackson.

It was late-afternoon Tuesday, a week after the New York trip, and the rain was streaming in sheets down the picture window overlooking the river. The two men lounged in the armchair group in the corner of Tuck's office. Tuck's desk was piled with paper and his email in-box was approaching the breaking point. Most of it was bad news, and he was anxious for Dixon's return.

"I thought so, too," said Jackson. He had one ankle over the opposite knee, his legs clad in black jeans topped with a steel-gray T-shirt. "Your brother's wreaking havoc with my reputation."

"I know I'm losing faith in you," said Tuck. "And I'm beginning to consider the wild rumors."

"That he's a spy?"

"That there's at least something going on that I don't know about." Tuck didn't believe Dixon had a secret life. But he was all out of reasonable explanations. It had been nearly a month since his brother had disappeared.

"Is there anything we could have missed?" asked Jackson. "Some paper record, a secret email account, a different cell phone?"

"I've searched his office. I've looked through the mansion. I even called Kassandra."

"You *called* Kassandra?"

"You didn't?"

"Of course I did. But it's my job to chase down every lead."

"It's my company," said Tuck. "And it's going rapidly downhill without Dixon."

"What was your take on Kassandra?" asked Jackson.

"That's she's a selfish, spoiled princess who gambled and lost." Tuck couldn't help a grim smirk at the memory. Clearly, his former sister-in-law had expected a hefty financial settlement.

"She's holding a grudge," said Jackson. "Do you think she'd harm him?"

"She probably wants to. But that would require risk and effort. She's lazy."

"Yeah," Jackson agreed. "I'm starting to wonder if he was kidnapped."

Tuck frowned. He'd been picturing Dixon on a tropical beach somewhere. If his brother was in trouble, then Tuck's anger at him was completely misplaced.

"Maybe he was forced to write that letter to your dad," said Jackson.

"Tell me you're not serious."

"Who saw him last?"

Tuck nodded to his closed office door, his thoughts moving to Amber. She'd kept him carefully at arm's length since the night in New York, but he was practically obsessing over her.

"His assistant, Amber," he told Jackson. "He was in the office for a few hours the day he left."

"Can you call her in?"

"Sure." Tuck came to his feet. "But I've already pumped her for information. She's the one who gave me his password. He didn't tell her where he was going."

He crossed to the door and drew it open, walking into the outer office.

Amber was at her desk, profile to him as she typed on the keyboard.

"Can you join us?" he asked.

She stopped typing and glanced up, her blue gaze meeting his. There was a wariness there, which he chalked up to the kisses in New York. Could she tell he wanted to do it again?

He was dying to do it again. He feared it was written all over his expression every time he looked her way.

"Sure." She smoothed out her expression and pushed back her chair.

As usual, her outfit was straitlaced, a navy blazer over a matching pleated skirt and a white blouse. Her spike pumps were bright blue with a slash of white across the toe. They appeared simple by Amber-footwear standards, but they still struck him as sleekly sexy. Or maybe it was only his fevered imagination.

As she rose, he caught a glimpse of lace beneath the neckline of her blouse and his desire went into hyperdrive. He warned himself to bide his time until Dixon returned. When things were back to normal, he'd try approaching her again. Amber would no longer be working for him then.

"What do you need?" she asked as she passed by him.

"Jackson has a couple of questions." Tuck fell into step behind her.

"What kind of questions?"

"About Dixon."

She twisted her head, pausing just outside the office door. "What about Dixon?"

Did he detect guilt in her eyes? Was she nervous?

"The usual questions." He found himself scrutinizing her expression.

"What are the usual questions?"

"Shall we find out?"

"I've told you everything I know."

"You say that in a way that makes me wonder."

"Words strung into a sentence make you suspicious?"

"You're jumpy," he said.

"I'm annoyed."

"You have no reason to be annoyed."

"I've got work to do."

"So do I. And none of our work gets easier until Dixon is back."

Her eyes narrowed. "He shouldn't be your crutch."

"He's everybody's crutch. Do you know where he is?"

"No."

He gestured her forward. "Then, let's go talk to Jackson."

Amber squared her shoulders and moved into the office.

Jackson rose. "Nice to see you again, Amber."

"Why do I feel like this is an interrogation?" she asked.

"I have that effect on people," said Jackson.

"You should stop." She took one of the armchairs in the grouping.

"I'll keep that in mind."

For some reason, the exchange grated on Tuck. Jackson wasn't flirting with her. But he was joking with her and Tuck didn't like it.

"Your questions?" he asked Jackson.

Jackson caught his gaze and looked puzzled.

"Sure," said Jackson, obviously waiting for Tuck to sit down.

Tuck perched on the arm of a chair. He folded his arms over his chest.

It took Jackson a moment to move his attention back to Amber.

"I'm sure you'll agree," he said to her, "that Dixon has been gone longer than any of us expected."

"How long did we expect him to be gone?" she asked.

"Did he tell you how long he'd be gone?"

Amber glanced fleetingly at Tuck. "His letter said a month."

"It's been a month."

"Almost."

"No phone call? No postcard?"

"Who sends a postcard these days?"

"People who want you to know they're having a good time and wish you were there."

Amber's gaze hardened. "I doubt he's having a good time."

Tuck could almost hear Jackson's senses go on alert.

"Why?" Jackson asked.

"You know about his ex-wife." Amber wasn't asking a question.

"I do."

"Then you know he's recovering from her treachery."

"Treachery?"

"What would you call it?"

"Infidelity."

"Okay."

Jackson paused. "What was your relationship with Dixon?"

"Hey," Tuck protested. "Amber's not on trial."

Jackson shot him a look of astonishment. "Should I be doing this without you?"

"He was my boss," said Amber. "Full stop. And if one more person insinuates it was something inappropriate, I'm walking out the door."

"Who else insinuated that?"

"Back off," said Tuck. This was getting them nowhere. It was only annoying Amber, and rightly so. He didn't blame her for being ticked off.

"Who else?" asked Jackson.

"Tuck." She slid him an angry glance.

He held up his hands in surrender. He hadn't considered anything of the sort for quite some time now.

"And Jamison," said Amber.

Jackson's tone slipped up in obvious surprise. "Jamison thought you were having an affair with his son?"

"Only because Jamison was having an—" Amber snapped her mouth shut.

Jackson blinked.

Tuck rose to his feet.

Amber stiffened her spine.

"You're going to have to finish that sentence," said Tuck.

She shook her head.

"I insist."

"We all know what she was going to say," Jackson said.

"I didn't say it," said Amber.

"My father was having an affair?"

She glared at Tuck. "Let it go."

"With who?" he demanded. Tuck's first reaction was that it couldn't be true. Then again, it absolutely could be true. Lots of high-powered, self-gratifying people cheated. Why not his father?

"It's not for me to say," Amber responded. "I found out by accident. In fact, I don't even know for sure."

"Who do you suspect?"

Who it was might have no bearing on Dixon's situation. Then again, it might. Had Dixon known about the affair?

"That would be gossip," said Amber.

"My father is in the hospital. My brother is *missing*. Gossip already."

She glanced from Tuck to Jackson and back again. "Can I swear you two to secrecy?"

"Amber," Tuck all but shouted.

This wasn't a negotiation. There were no conditions. She was answering the question.

"Yes," said Jackson. He glared at Tuck. "We'll keep it to ourselves. As you say, it's speculation. It would be wrong for us to act on hearsay."

"Margaret," said Amber.

"His Margaret?" Tuck asked.

"Who is Margaret?" asked Jackson.

"His assistant," said Amber.

"But—" Tuck couldn't wrap his head around it. Margaret Smithers could best be described as matronly. She was middle-aged, slightly overweight, her hair was partly gray and her clothes were polyester.

"Expecting a blond supermodel?" asked Amber.

Tuck wasn't about to admit that was true. "I was expecting him to be faithful to my mother."

"Did Dixon know?" asked Jackson, his thoughts obviously moving along the same lines as Tuck's.

Dixon had just been a victim of infidelity. Finding out about their father might have angered him enough to leave. Tuck couldn't help but wonder if he planned to stay gone.

"No," said Amber.

"How can you be sure?" asked Tuck. It would at least have been some kind of explanation.

Amber had to think about it for a moment. "I'm as sure as I can be. I didn't figure it out until the heart attack. And Dixon never acted as if he knew."

"How did you figure it out?" asked Jackson.

"The way Margaret acted when Jamison collapsed," said Amber. "She mentioned they'd had wine together the night before. Then when she realized what she'd said, she panicked."

"You were with Jamison when it happened?" asked Jackson.

"I was in his office. He was upset, grilling me about Dixon. When I wouldn't tell him anything, he got really angry." She fell to silence, and her shoulders drooped. A cloud came over her eyes. "Maybe I should have told…"

Tuck looked to Jackson. Both men waited, but she didn't elaborate.

"Should have told what?" Jackson prompted in a soft voice.

Amber refocused on him. "Nothing."

"What was he asking?"

"Where Dixon went."

"But you didn't tell him."

"No."

"Tell us."

She drew back. "I don't know."

"You just admitted that you did," said Tuck.

She shook her head in vigorous denial.

"You said maybe you should have told him, but you didn't tell him."

"That's not what I—"

"No," said Tuck. He kept his tone carefully even, but inwardly he was furious. She'd been lying to him. She'd watched him struggle all these weeks. She'd pretended to help him, when all the while the solution had been at her fingertips.

"You can't walk it back," he said. "You know where Dixon went. Tell me. Tell me right this second."

She compressed her lips, staring at him, her expression a combination of guilt and defiance.

"That's an order," he said. "Tell me, or you're fired—"

"Tuck," Jackson cut in.

"No," said Tuck. "She's sat back and let Tucker Transportation fall down around my ears. She doesn't get to do that and keep her job."

"I can't," she protested.

"Then, you're fired."

Five

Tuck's final words echoed inside Amber's ears.

She put her compact car into Park outside her town house, set the brake and gripped the steering wheel. She was home an hour early, and it felt surreal. The sun was too high in the sky and kids were still playing in the park across the street, whooping it up on the slide and the jungle gym.

Fired. She'd been fired from Tucker Transportation. She had no job. She had no paycheck. Her savings might take her through the next month, but she had mortgage payments, utility payments, phone bills and food bills.

She cursed the new shoes on her feet. She'd worn them for the first time today and she couldn't take them back. Then again, they were gorgeous and they'd been on sale. And, really, how much would a refund help? It would barely fill up her gas tank.

She couldn't waste time worrying about might-have-beens. She had to get it together. She had to start job hunting right away.

The front door opened and Jade stood there, looking out, her rounded belly pressing against an oversize plaid shirt. Amber was reminded that she also had Jade and the baby to worry about. Not that it changed her plans.

She'd update her résumé tonight and get out job hunting first thing tomorrow. It would have been nice to have Dixon as a reference. She sure couldn't use Tuck.

She turned off the engine, trying unsuccessfully to banish his image from her mind. He'd been angry. That much was certainly clear. But he'd looked hurt, too, seeming disappointed that her loyalty was to Dixon. She wished she could have given Tuck what he wanted, but she couldn't serve them both.

She stepped out of the car and waved to Jade as she walked up the stepping-stones. The sage and asters were barely hanging on. The other blooms had faded away, and only the leaves remained. October was not exactly a cheerful month.

As she approached the door, she pasted a smile on her face. "How are you feeling?"

"Huge."

Amber widened her smile at the joke.

"I made an appointment at the community clinic," said Jade, as she stepped back from the doorway.

"That's good." Amber had been insistent that Jade get proper medical care. "When is the appointment?"

"I told them my due date and they got me in tomorrow."

Amber glanced at Jade's stomach. "I guess they know there's no time to waste."

"Being pregnant is not an illness."

"But you want a healthy baby."

"Oof." Jade's hand went to her stomach. "This one's healthy, all right. It's got a kick like a soccer player."

"I can drive you to the appointment," said Amber. She'd be happier if she heard firsthand what the doctor had to say.

"I can take the bus."

Amber dumped her purse and headed for the living room. "It's no trouble. I can afford to take a little time off."

"Are you sure?"

"Positive."

Amber would be taking more than just a little time off. But she didn't see any need to say so immediately. Hopefully, she'd have a new job lined up before she had to share the news about losing this one.

"Are you hungry?" she asked Jade.

"I made macaroni casserole."

Amber couldn't hide her surprise. "You cooked?"

Not that macaroni casserole was exactly gourmet, but Jade

had never been handy in the kitchen, nor particularly self-motivated when it came to household chores.

Jade grinned proudly as they walked to the kitchen. "It's all ready to pop into the oven."

"That sounds delicious. Thanks."

Jade turned on the oven while Amber set out plates and cutlery and let her optimism build. She had five solid years of work at Tucker Transportation. She'd built up her administrative skill set, and surely that would be transferable to any number of companies. Maybe she could gloss over her reasons for leaving. She might even be able to use Margaret as a reference.

She hoped Tuck wouldn't be vindictive and spread word around the company that she was fired. But she really had no idea how he'd handle it. He was pretty angry right now.

There was a sudden knock on the front door.

"Expecting someone?" asked Jade.

"Not me. You?"

"Nobody knows I'm here."

Amber went for the door, suspecting it was a neighbor, maybe Sally Duncan from next door. She was on the townhouse council and loved to complain. Perhaps old Mr. Purvis was barbecuing on his patio again.

Amber had voted to repeal the prohibition on barbecues at the last council meeting. Sure, the smoke was annoying. But who in their right mind would ban hot dogs and hamburgers?

She swung open the door, startled to find Tuck standing on her porch. He was frowning, eyes narrowed. Worry immediately clenched her stomach.

"What do you want?" she asked him.

"To talk."

"I have nothing else to say."

"After you left, Jackson pointed out the error of my ways."

She didn't want to hope. But she couldn't help herself. Was Tuck offering her job back?

"I came here to give you another chance," he said.

She waited.

"You being gone helps neither of us," he said.

She had to agree with that. But she doubted he cared about helping her.

"Another chance to what?" she prompted.

"What can you tell me about Dixon?"

"I've told you everything—"

"Well, hello there." Jade arrived, breaking in with a breezy tone. "Are you one of Amber's neighbors?"

Tuck's brow shot up as he took in the pregnant Jade.

"He's my boss," said Amber, instantly realizing it was no longer true. But before she could correct the statement, Jade was talking again.

"Really? Very nice to meet you. I'm Amber's sister, Jade." Jade stuck out her hand.

"Jade, this really isn't a good time."

"Tuck Tucker," said Tuck as he shook Jade's hand.

"Are you hungry?" asked Jade.

"No, he's not," Amber quickly responded.

"I need to borrow your sister for a few minutes," Tuck said to Jade.

"Does she need to go back to work?" asked Jade.

"No," Tuck and Amber answered simultaneously.

"I just need to speak with her," said Tuck.

"Oh," said Jade, glancing between them, obviously picking up on their discomfort. "Then, I'll leave you two alone."

As Jade withdrew, Amber moved onto the porch, pulling the door closed behind her. It was cold outside, but she wanted to get this over with.

"The job market's very tight out there," said Tuck.

"Are you trying to frighten me?"

"I'm asking you to be realistic. I need to talk to my brother."

"I promised him I wouldn't tell a soul. That included his family."

"So you admit you know where he is."

"I don't know with any certainty where he is."

"Why are you talking in riddles?"

She reached behind herself for the doorknob. "I've told you what I can."

"I can't imagine Dixon wants you to be fired."

"I can't imagine he does, either."

Dixon had always given her top-notch performance evaluations. He'd praised her work, often saying he didn't know how he'd live without her. She liked to think he wouldn't want her fired.

"Don't make me do it," said Tuck.

"I'm not *making* you do anything."

"Ignoring an order is gross insubordination."

"Betraying a confidence is worse."

He leaned in. "Circumstances have changed since you made that promise."

She knew they had. But she also knew Dixon's doctor had told him to get away from the pressures of Tucker Transportation.

"Amber." Tuck reached out, his hand encircling her upper arm. "I *need* this, please."

His touch brought a rush of memories—the strength of his embrace, the taste of his lips and the scent of his skin. Suddenly, she was off balance, and she felt herself sway toward him. Her hand moved to steady herself, her palm coming up against his chest.

He groaned deep in his throat. "I don't want to fight with you."

She jerked her hand away, but he was faster, engulfing it in his own, pressing it firmly back against his chest.

His tone was gravelly. "Don't make me fight with you."

She battled the desire rising in her body. She wanted nothing more and nothing less than to collapse into Tuck's arms and kiss him until every other thought was driven from her brain.

She met his gaze. "I've told you everything I can."

His expression turned mocking. "And you *still* claim there's nothing going on between you and Dixon."

"I'll claim it as many times as it takes. It's the truth."

"Yet you'll give up your job for him?"

"I'll give up my job for a principle."

He tugged her closer, voice going quiet. "You sure about that?"

She enunciated each syllable. "Positive."

He kissed her.

She was so surprised that she didn't fight it. Her lips were pliable under his—soft, welcoming—and, for a second, she kissed him back. Her brain screeched at her to stop. But his embrace was oddly comforting. His kiss was tender. And the warmth of his chest seemed to make its way into her heart.

Then reason asserted itself. She forced herself to push against him, staggering back and thudding against the closed door. They stared at each other. Her chest rose and fell with labored breaths.

"I had to be sure," he said.

"Sure of *what*?"

"That you're not in love with my brother."

"Go away." She scrunched her eyes shut to block him out. "Just go away, and stay gone. I think I might hate you."

He didn't make a sound.

After a moment, she opened one eye. His back was to her and he was halfway down the path, striding toward a sleek black sports car.

Thank goodness he was leaving. Thank goodness he was out of her life. She could get a new job. She *would* get a new job. The last place on earth she wanted to be was working for Tuck.

The door opened behind her.

"Amber?" Jade's voice was hesitant.

"Yes." Amber shook some sense into herself.

"Your boss is your boyfriend?"

Amber turned. "What? No."

"You just kissed him."

"That?" Amber waved it away. "That was nothing. He was being a jerk, is all. He fired me."

"He *what*?"

"We had a disagreement. No. More a difference of opinion. I'd call it a difference of principles and values. He's not a man I want to work for." Amber paused. "I'm fine with the way things turned out."

She was fine. At least she would be fine.

"What will you do?" There was worry in Jade's expression.

Amber linked her arm with her sister's and moved them both inside. "I'll get another job. This was a good job, but it's not the only job. I have skills and experience. Maybe I'll even make more money."

"You sound confident."

"I *am* confident."

Maybe her leaving Tucker Transportation was inevitable. Jamison had most certainly planned to fire her before his heart attack. If she looked at it like that, she'd actually been granted an extra month with Tuck at the helm. But it was doomed to end one way or the other.

Dixon would eventually come back and he'd probably take her side. But Jamison was the president of the company. Eventually, he'd recover fully and overrule Dixon. And with Tuck now on Jamison's side... Well, this was definitely the time for her to move on.

Tuck's workload had gotten completely out of control. Without Amber as the gatekeeper, he was inundated with problems, big and small. He had a temporary assistant, Sandy Heath, borrowed from the finance department, but she mostly just asked him a lot of questions, slowing him down instead of speeding him up.

Jackson had followed a new dead-end lead to Cancún, and another manager had resigned this morning. They were bleeding employees. His father's recovery was going more slowly than expected. Jamison might not return to work at all.

"Sandy?" Tuck called through the open door.

"Yes?"

He could hear her stand and move to the door.

"Is Lucas Steele on his way up?"

Sandy paused in the doorway. "I don't know."

Tuck took a beat. "Could you find out?"

"Sure."

Tuck glanced at his watch to confirm the time. "Did you tell him ten?"

"I believe so. I mean, I called when you asked me to. But I got his voice mail."

"Did you try his assistant?"

Sandy paused. "I'll do that now."

"Great." Just great. Tuck couldn't even get his operations director into his office when they only worked three floors apart.

He came to his feet. "Never mind."

She looked puzzled. "You don't want Lucas?"

"I'll go down."

"I can—"

"I'll find him."

"I'm sorry."

Tuck relaxed his expression. "Don't worry about it."

There was no point in being annoyed with Sandy because she wasn't Amber. Only Amber was Amber, and she was ridiculously good at her job.

He went to the elevator and rode down to twenty-nine. The hallway on that floor was linoleum rather than carpet. The offices were smaller than on the executive floor, and there was far more activity. It was the nerve center of the company, where every company conveyance was tracked on a series of wall-mounted screens, with information on every single shipment available with a few keystrokes. Tuck had come to like it here.

Lucas's office was at the far end of the hallway. It was large but utilitarian, its numerous tables cluttered with maps and reports, keyboards and screens. Tuck knew Lucas had a desk in there somewhere, but he wasn't sure the man ever sat down.

"Hey, boss," Lucas greeted from behind a table.

One of his female staff members was working beside him, clicking keys and watching a set of three monitors.

"The *Red Earth* is back on schedule," the woman said without looking up. "They'll make their 6:00 a.m. port time."

"Good," said Lucas. "Need me?" he asked Tuck.

"You didn't get Sandy's voice mail?"

Lucas glanced guiltily at his desk phone. "We've been slammed this morning."

"Not a problem," said Tuck. "Got a minute?"

"Absolutely. Gwen, can you make sure we get the fuel agreement signatures sent? We have until close of business in Berlin."

"Will do," said Gwen, again without looking up.

Lucas led the way out of his office, turning immediately into a small meeting room along the hall.

"What's up?" he asked Tuck, closing the door behind them.

"I feel as if we should sit down for this," said Tuck.

"Bad news?" Lucas crossed his arms over his chest. "Are you firing me?"

Tuck scoffed out a laugh at the absurdity of the statement. "I'm promoting you."

"Yeah, right." Lucas waited, alert.

"I'm serious," said Tuck.

"Serious about what?"

"I'm promoting you."

It took Lucas a beat to answer. "Why? To what? There's nothing above director."

"Nothing in operations," said Tuck.

"Right," said Lucas, as if he'd just proved his point.

"Vice president," said Tuck.

"Are you running a fever?"

"I need you upstairs."

"I'm no vice president." Lucas gave an exaggerated shudder. "You think I am?"

"Yes."

Tuck pressed his lips together. "Only because they gave me the title."

"You're nuts."

"I'm serious."

"Okay." Lucas braced his feet slightly apart. "Vice president of *what*?"

"I don't know."

"I can see you've really thought this through."

"Executive vice president."

"That's *your* title."

"I'm acting president."

Lucas's arms moved to his sides. "I suppose you are."

"I'm drownin' up there. Dixon's completely dropped off the planet, and Dad's recovery is pushed back. I know it's not your first choice, but what am I supposed to do?"

"Hire someone."

"I'm hiring you."

"Hire someone else."

"I will. For your job."

"You don't need to hire anyone for my job. Gwen can do it. She can probably do it better than me."

Tuck didn't feel any need to respond to the statement. Lucas had just made the next argument for him.

"Yeah, yeah," said Lucas. "I know what you're thinking."

"What am I thinking?" Tuck asked.

"That you can pick me up and plunk me into some fancy office, and the operations department won't even notice I'm gone."

Tuck fought a smirk. "Your words, not mine."

"They're true."

"That's good."

"I wouldn't have the first idea of what to do upstairs," said Lucas.

"And you think *I* do?"

"You're a Tucker."

"You're the last one left," said Tuck.

"The last one of what?"

"The last director. The others quit."

"Not Oscar?"

"Yesterday. The rumor mill now has Dixon pegged as an

embezzler who will bring down the company, and the head-hunters are out in force."

Lucas frowned. "There's no chance he actually...?"

Tuck was astonished. *"You, too?"*

"No. Not really. What would be his motivation? Plus, you'd have noticed the missing millions by now and reported it. Law enforcement would be crawling all over this place."

Tuck couldn't help but admire Lucas's combination of faith and hard, cold analysis. "He has no motivation. And he didn't do anything illegal."

"I gotta agree," said Lucas.

"Doesn't mean I won't knock his block off."

Lucas pulled out a molded plastic chair and sat down at the rectangular meeting table.

Tuck took the seat across from him.

"You're serious," said Lucas.

"Completely. While Amber was here, it was doable, marginal but doable. Without her, I can't keep it going. We've lost three major accounts since Zachary left."

"You think he's poaching them."

"I know he's poaching them. What I don't know is how to make it stop. I mean, maybe I can make it stop, if I can find the time to make some calls and build up some relationships. But I don't even have time to breathe. I need Dixon, and I need him now."

"I thought Jackson was looking."

"He hit a dead end. It's dead end number eight, I think."

"Hire another investigative firm."

"There's nobody better than Jackson. If only—"

Tuck's thoughts went back to Amber. Usually, when he thought about her, it was about their kisses, particularly that last kiss. A woman didn't kiss like that, especially not in the middle of a fight, if she didn't have a thing for the man. Amber had to be attracted to him on some level, and the knowledge made his skin itch.

"If only what?" asked Lucas.

"She knows something. She can get Dixon back for me."

"Who?"

"Amber."

Lucas pulled back in his chair, a speculative expression coming over his face.

"Not like that," said Tuck. "Not at *all* like that. She was his confidential assistant and he confided in her."

"What did he tell her?"

"She's not talking. I ordered her. Then I fired her. But she's not talking."

"Bribe?" asked Lucas.

"She just gave up her job over integrity."

"Blackmail, then?"

"With what? She's as straight up as they come. The only thing outrageous about her is her shoes."

"Her shoes?"

"You've never noticed?"

Lucas shook his head. "Can't say that I have."

"I don't see how I blackmail her over red glitter stilettoes." Though Tuck would love to have pictures of them.

"Can't believe I missed that."

Tuck forced his mind back to the job. "Will you do it?"

Lucas curled his fingertips against the table. "Temporarily."

Tuck felt a rush of relief. "I hope that's all I'll need. Even together, we can't replace Dixon."

"No, we can't."

"I'm going to find him."

"You should definitely bribe her."

"She'll never go for it."

"You don't know that until you ask."

"Yes, I do."

If Amber was willing to trade ethics for money, she'd never have let him fire her.

Amber sat down at her kitchen table, taking up where she'd left off scrolling through an employment website. Jade was across from her, writing her way through a practice math exam. The coffeepot was between them and their breakfast dishes were piled in the sink.

Jade had offered to clean up later while Amber made the rounds of some more major companies in the city. Surprisingly, after three weeks in Chicago, Jade was still following her new life plan. She was rising every morning with her alarm, eating healthy and studying for the GED test she hoped to pass before the baby was born.

By contrast, Amber's new life plan was completely falling apart. She'd applied for dozens of jobs, had landed only three interviews and had so far been beaten by other candidates on two of them. Every morning, she told herself not to lose hope. But she'd already dipped into her savings to make the month's mortgage payment. Other bills were coming due, including Jade's appointments at the community clinic.

"You look nice today," said Jade. "Very professional." She nodded approvingly at Amber's blazer and skirt.

"Focus on the test," said Amber.

"I bet you get an offer."

"That would be nice." Amber wasn't going to let Jade see her worry.

"Ooh." Jade's hand went to her stomach. "That was a good one."

"I bet it's a boy," said Amber. She copied and pasted a promising-looking job ad into her open spreadsheet.

"Girl," said Jade. "But a soccer player."

"Boy," said Amber. "A placekicker for the Bears. Big money in that."

"You think we'll need Junior's money?"

Amber was beginning to think they'd need it before Junior even started preschool.

"I doubt we will," said Jade. "We're both going to get jobs—good jobs, high-powered jobs. We'll get promoted up the ladder and make fortunes."

Amber couldn't help but smile. She liked it when Jade was optimistic. "Dreamer."

"I am," said Jade. "For the first time in my— Ouch. I think that one went through the uprights."

The phone rang. Amber couldn't control the lurch of anticipation that hit her stomach. It could be another interview, or possibly a job offer from Pine Square Furniture. Please, let it be a job offer. Pine Square Furniture paid quite a bit less than what she'd made at Tucker Transportation, but she'd jump at anything right now.

As Amber started to rise, Jade leaned back and lifted the receiver.

"Hello?"

Amber held her breath.

"Oh, hi, Dr. Norris."

Amber's disappointment was acute. She turned to hide her expression from Jade, rising and pretending to check the printer for paper.

"Okay," Jade said into the phone.

Amber reminded herself these things took time. She could make it a few more weeks, even a couple of months. She hadn't really expected to find a job the next day, had she?

"Which test?" There was worry in Jade's tone.

Amber turned back.

"Is that a problem?" Jade's worried gaze met Amber's.

Amber quickly returned to the table, sitting down in the chair beside Jade.

"That sounds scary," said Jade.

"What is it?" Amber whispered.

Jade's eyes went glassy with the beginnings of tears.

"What?" Amber said louder. "What's wrong?"

Jade unexpectedly pushed the receiver at her, nearly dropping it between them.

Amber scrambled to get it to her ear. "Dr. Norris? This is Amber."

"Hello, Amber. Is Jade all right?"

"She's upset. She's okay. What did you tell her?"

"I have a concern with her blood pressure."

Amber had known that. "Yes."

They'd talked about Jade taking some medication to keep it down in the last few weeks of her pregnancy.

"I'm afraid the follow-up tests aren't encouraging."

Amber rubbed Jade's shoulder. "Is everything okay with the baby?"

"So far, yes. Jade has a condition called preeclampsia. It's serious. I'm recommending you bring her into the hospital."

The hospital? "How serious?"

Jade sniffed and reached for a tissue.

"I'd like to monitor Jade's health and the baby's health."

"Overnight? Until the medication kicks in?"

"Until the birth, I'm afraid. We can't take this condition lightly. There are risks to the placenta, organ damage for Jade, even stroke."

Amber squeezed Jade's hand. "How soon should I bring her in?"

"Is she still having headaches?"

Amber moved the phone from her mouth. "Headache?" she asked Jade.

"It's not bad," said Jade.

"Yes," Amber said to the doctor.

"Then, let's not wait. This morning if you can."

"We can," said Amber.

"My office will make the arrangements."

"Thank you." Amber ended the call.

"So I have to go back?" asked Jade.

"Yes. The doctor says they need to monitor you. She wants you in the hospital."

"The *hospital*?"

"She's worried about your blood pressure."

"But they said there was medicine."

"We can ask more questions when we get there." Amber couldn't help feeling a sense of urgency.

"How long will I have to stay?"

"It might be for a while. We don't want to take any chances. This is what's best for you, and what's best for the baby." Amber stood. "Let's go pack a few things."

Jade gestured to her books. "But I'm studying."

"I'll bet you can study in the hospital. In fact, it might be the perfect place to study. There'll be nothing else for you to do. They'll cook for you. They'll clean for you."

"Hospital food?"

"I'll smuggle you in a pizza."

Assuming Jade was allowed to eat pizza. Amber drew Jade to her feet.

"I can't do this," said Jade. "I can't just up and leave for the hospital at a moment's notice."

"Sometimes it works that way."

Jade glanced around the kitchen. "How can I, what can I— Oh, no." She grasped tightly onto Amber's arms.

Amber's heart leaped. "Is something wrong?"

"The money."

"What money?"

"The *money*, Amber. This is going to cost a fortune. Where will I get the money?"

"Don't worry about that."

"I have to worry about it."

"Worrying won't help anything. Not you, and definitely not the baby." Amber would have to do the worrying for them.

"But—"

"We'll borrow it. Then we'll pay it back." Amber struggled to put confidence in her voice.

"I'm so sorry."

"This isn't your fault. You're doing so well." Amber motioned to the books. "You've been studying. You've been eating right. You're here. You need to keep doing everything you can to give your baby the best possible chance."

"I'm scared." But Jade started to move.

"I know. I'm not saying it isn't unsettling. But it's going to be fine. Everything is going to be fine."

Amber would get Jade to the hospital, and then she'd talk to her bank. She had some equity in her town house and a decent credit rating. Once she found a job, she would qualify for a loan. So she'd find a job. She'd find one fast. She'd flip burgers if that was what it took.

Six

Tuck knew a losing hand when he was dealt one. But he also knew he couldn't walk away from this. For better or worse, and so far it was definitely worse, the company was his responsibility.

It was Saturday afternoon and he'd parked down the block from Amber's town house, waiting for her car to appear. The block was neat and bright, lawns trimmed, gardens tended, with kids playing in the park and people walking their dogs. The homes were compact, four to a building, with very little traffic passing on the street out front.

He figured he'd have the best chance if he tried to reason with her in person. It was too easy for her to hang up a phone. And he doubted she'd answer a text or email. Plus, her expression might help him, give him a signal as to which tactic might sway her and which was a nonstarter.

He knew it wasn't about self-interest for her. And he couldn't imagine she'd have one iota of sympathy for him. But maybe she'd care about the other employees. Maybe she would care that the demise of Tucker Transportation would be job losses and financial ruin for the families of her former coworkers. The way he saw it, that was his best hope.

He spotted her silver hatchback pull up in front of the town house, and he quickly exited his sports car. While she hopped from the driver's seat he approached from the side.

Dressed in a pair of navy slacks and a striped pullover with a matching blazer, she was lithe and graceful as she moved across the sidewalk. Her hair was in a neat braid, while her low-heeled boots were a sexy purple suede. She was compellingly beautiful in the cool sunshine, her profile perky, her skin smooth as silk.

She hadn't seen him yet, so she had a smile on her face. He supposed he'd change that soon enough.

It didn't take long. She caught a glimpse of him, squinted at him and then frowned.

"Hello, Amber," he said, covering the last few paces between them.

Her glance flicked behind him as if seeking context. "What are you doing here, Tuck?"

"Been out shopping?" he asked conversationally. It seemed like a reasonable guess for a Saturday afternoon.

"I've been visiting—" She stopped herself. "What do you want?"

"I need to talk to you."

"I don't have time to talk." She started for the walkway that led to her front door.

"It won't take long."

She turned. "Then, let me be more blunt. I have all the time in the world, but I don't care to spend any of it with you."

"You're still angry."

"What was your first clue?"

"I didn't want things to go this way."

"Goodbye, Tuck." She took a backward step.

"Dixon is still missing."

She shrugged.

"It's been over six weeks. I'm getting worried."

"He can take care of himself."

Under normal circumstances, Dixon could take excellent care of himself. But these weren't normal circumstances.

"Who takes a six-week vacation?"

"Lots of people."

"Not my brother."

Even if their father had been healthy and at the helm, Dixon would never have left for this long, especially not without contacting them. Tuck's focus had been on Tucker Transportation, but he was becoming genuinely worried about his brother.

"Maybe you don't know him as well as you think you do," said Amber.

"Clearly, I don't. Why don't you enlighten me?"

"Why should I know him any better than you?"

"You know him."

It was in her eyes.

"You knew why he left," said Tuck. "And you know where he went." Tuck believed there was no romance between her and Dixon. But there was something—a closeness, respect, confidence.

"He doesn't want to talk to you?"

"He's got nothing against me."

Tuck and Dixon might not be the closest brothers in the world. But they weren't estranged. They weren't fighting. There was no particular animosity between them.

Tuck stepped forward. "Things have gotten worse since you…left."

"You mean since I was fired."

"Yeah, that." He didn't know why he'd tried to soften the words. They both knew what had happened. "We're losing accounts. We're losing staff. We've gone from high profitability to a projected loss for next month."

There was no sympathy in her blue eyes. "You might want to do something about that."

"I'm worried about the employees," he said, ignoring her jab. "If this goes on much longer, people could lose their jobs."

"What does that have to do with me? Considering I already lost mine."

"I'm appealing to your basic sense of humanity."

"While I'm still standing on my basic sense of ethics and values."

He eased closer. "Where is he, Amber?"

"I don't know."

"What do you know?"

She raised her chin. "That he didn't want me to tell you anything."

"That was weeks ago."

"I haven't heard anything to contradict it."

"So you haven't heard from him?"

She drew back in obvious surprise. "No."

"Does he know how to contact you?"

"He'd probably try to call me at my desk."

"Touché."

"He knows how to contact you, too, Tuck. If he wanted to talk to you, he'd call." She turned to go.

"What about an emergency?" Tuck called out. He could taste failure, bitter in the back of his mouth. "Can you get a message to him? That's all I'm asking. Get a message to him. You can name your price."

She stopped. Then she pivoted, gaping at him in clear astonishment. "My *price*?"

"Anything you want." He could feel his last chance slipping away. "What do you want?"

To Tuck's immense relief, she actually looked intrigued.

"You'd pay me to get a message to Dixon."

"Yes."

She seemed to think about it. "What would you want me to say?"

"You'll do it?"

Had Lucas actually been right? Was money going to sway her?

"What would you want me to say?" she asked again.

"Tell him about my father's heart attack and tell him I'm destroying the company."

She looked a little surprised by the last statement. "You want to make certain he comes home."

"I want to make certain he knows the cost of staying away."

"I'm not going to lie for you."

"It's not a lie."

"It is. You're not destroying the company. You've hit a rough patch, sure, but—"

"You haven't been there."

It was every bit as bad as he was making it sound.

"You're exaggerating," she said.

They could have this debate all day long and get nowhere. He had a toehold on a yes here, and he didn't want to give her a chance to back out.

"What'll it cost me?" he asked.

"You're talking about a flat-out cash bribe?"

"If that's what works."

She looked skeptical. "And I'd only have to tell him about your father."

"And that I'm destroying the company."

"I'm not using the word *destroy*."

"Then, tell him I've projected a loss for next month." Tuck knew that would come as a colossal shock to Dixon. He'd be on the first plane home.

He could see the debate going on behind her eyes.

"How much?" he asked.

What would she ask for? Five figures, six? He'd pay whatever she wanted.

"My job back," she said.

He hadn't been prepared for that. And he was shocked she'd be willing. "You want to work for me again?"

"I want to work for Dixon again."

"Job's yours," he said. He'd be thrilled to have her back. In fact, he felt guilty that her request was so modest. He moved a little closer. "You have to know you've got me over a barrel?"

"Do you want me to ask for something more?"

He did. If nothing else, he was curious. "Yeah. Go wild."

She hesitated.

He raised a brow, waiting.

"All right." She withdrew a paper from her purse, unfolding it. "Since you insist."

"What's that?" He tried to look, but she pulled it toward her chest.

"You can give me a signing bonus."

"How much?"

"Twenty-eight thousand, two hundred and sixty-three dollars."

Now she really had him curious.

"Where did that number come from?"

"None of your business." She refolded the paper and stuffed it back in her purse.

"Seriously. What are you paying for?"

"Seriously. None of your business."

Tuck told himself to shut up and take the victory. "You'll call him."

"I will."

"I mean now."

"Right now?"

He gave a sharp nod.

"I suppose." She turned again for the front door.

He followed and she twisted her head to look at him.

"You don't trust me?"

"I do. I don't." No, that wasn't true. He couldn't imagine she'd lie about making the call. "I do trust you. But I want to see what happens."

She unlocked the front door, pushing it open. "I don't know for sure where he is. I didn't lie to you about that. But he did leave an emergency number."

Tuck wanted to ask exactly how bad things had to get before she decided it was an emergency. But he didn't want to start another argument.

He stayed silent, and she dropped her purse on a table in the small foyer and extracted her phone, dialing as she moved into the living room.

"Did he get a special cell phone?" Tuck asked. That made the most sense.

Amber shook her head, listening as the call obviously rang through.

She sat down on a cream-colored loveseat and crossed her legs. Tuck perched on an end of the sofa at a right angle to her. It faced a gas fireplace and a row of small watercolor seascapes.

"Hello," said Amber. "Can you connect me to Dixon Tucker's room?"

A hotel, obviously. Tuck wanted to know where. He wished he could see the area code.

"He's not?" asked Amber, her tone sharper.

Tuck focused on her expression.

She was frowning. "I don't understand. When did he do that?"

Tuck didn't want to be suspicious, but he couldn't help but wonder if she was playing him. Was she going to pretend she'd tried to get Dixon but failed?

"That's less than a week. Did he say where he was going?" She met Tuck's eyes, sitting up straight and bracing her feet on the carpet. Either something was actually wrong, or Amber had a great future in acting. "Yes. I understand."

"What?" he asked her.

"Thank you," she said into the phone. "Goodbye."

"What did they say? Who was that? Where's Dixon?"

Amber set the phone onto the sofa cushion beside her. "He left."

"Left *where*?"

"Scottsdale."

"Arizona?"

"It's called Highland Luminance."

It struck Tuck as an odd name. "A hotel?"

"A wellness retreat."

The words weren't making sense.

"What's that?" Tuck asked. "And what was he doing there?"

"Getting well. At least he was supposed to be getting well.

But he left." Concern furrowed her brow. "He left after only a few days. Why would he do that?"

"Why would he go there in the first place?"

Sure, Dixon's divorce had been ugly. But people went through ugly divorces all the time.

"For help," said Amber. "They have a spa, yoga, fresh air and peace, organic food, emotional and physical therapy."

"You're trying to tell me that my brother took off to Arizona for organic food and yoga."

"I'm not *trying* to tell you anything."

Tuck searched his brain for an explanation. "None of this makes sense."

"He was exhausted," said Amber. "Upset by—"

"Yeah, yeah. You've told me all that. But it's not credible. Dixon's a smart, solid, capable man."

Amber's voice rose. "You worked him into the ground."

"I didn't do a thing."

"Exactly," she said with finality.

He glared at her. "You're saying this is *my* fault?"

"Yes. Yours, your father's, Kassandra's, all of you."

He opened his mouth to defend himself, but no good argument formed inside his brain. Was it his fault? Why hadn't Dixon come to him? They could have talked. They could have worked things out. He'd have been happy to support his brother.

"Dixon is very private," Tuck explained to Amber.

"If I was you," she responded in a flat tone, "I'd stop worrying about why he went to Arizona. I'd worry about where he went from there."

She had a point. She had a very good point.

He pulled his phone from his shirt pocket and dialed Jackson.

"Hey" was Jackson's clipped answer.

"Dixon went to Arizona," said Tuck.

"You sure?"

"Scottsdale. A place called Highland Luminance. He

left there about five weeks ago, but we can pick up his trail. I'll meet you—" Tuck looked at Amber. "*We'll* meet you in Scottsdale."

Her eyes widened and she shook her head.

"I'm in LA," said Jackson. "I can be there in the morning."

"We'll be there tonight," said Tuck.

"No way," said Amber.

Tuck ended the call. "You obviously know my brother better than I do. You work for me again and I need you in Scottsdale."

"I really can't."

"Yes, you can." As far as Tuck was concerned, this was not negotiable.

Amber slipped quietly into Jade's hospital room, not wanting to disturb her if she was napping.

But she was sitting up in the bed reading a textbook, and she smiled. "Did you forget something?"

"No," Amber answered.

Jade wore a large yellow T-shirt and a pair of stretchy green pants visible though the open weave of her blanket.

"Is everything okay?" she asked.

"How are you feeling?"

"Good. I'm fine. But I'm feeling guilty just lying around here."

"You're studying." Amber rounded the bed, pulling a bright orange vinyl chair up closer.

"Not as hard as I should."

"That's okay. Your main job is to stay healthy and grow that baby for a few more weeks."

Jade's cheeks were rosy, her face puffier than usual, but her eyes looked clear and bright. She put a hand on her budging stomach. "The baby's getting bigger by the hour."

"That's what we want. I have some good news."

"I can go home?" Jade hesitated. "Well, to your home."

"No, you can't go home. Not yet. But I did get a job."

Jade started to smile, but for some reason she sobered, looking sad. "You're so good. You're amazing."

Amber wondered if her sister's hormones were messing with her mood. "It's just a job, Jade."

"No, it's not just a job." Jade looked like she might tear up.

"Hey." Amber reached for her sister's hand, worrying this might be a sign something was wrong. "What is it?"

Jade blinked. "It doesn't matter what I do, how much trouble I cause. You always take such good care of things."

"You're not causing trouble. I'm your big sister. Of course I'm going to help you."

Amber wished she didn't have to leave town right now. She knew Jade was an adult, and she knew the hospital would take good care of her. But she still felt guilty.

"Do you remember Earl Dwyer?" asked Jade.

The name took Amber by surprise. "You mean Mom's old boyfriend?"

Jade nodded, sniffing and dabbing at her nose with a tissue. She gazed for a moment at the reflection in the window. "I was thinking about him last night."

A picture of the man came up in Amber's mind and her neck prickled at the memory. "There's no reason to think about him."

"You remember how he yelled at us all the time?"

"You should be thinking happy thoughts for the baby."

"Do you remember?"

"Yes, I remember. But I'm surprised you do. You couldn't have been more than five when he moved out." Amber remembered Earl's snarling face, his booming voice and how she'd locked herself and Jade in their bedroom whenever an argument had started between him and their mother.

"I remember everything about him," said Jade, her voice going small.

Amber moved to the bed, perching on the edge to rub Jade's shoulder. "Well, stop. He's long gone."

"Do you remember the fire?" asked Jade.

"Yes." Amber couldn't figure out where Jade was going with this.

Was Jade worried about her own choices in men? Maybe she was worried about how her future boyfriends might impact her baby.

"Mom used to tell Earl not to smoke on the sofa," said Jade. "She yelled at him about it all the time. She said he was going to pass out, light the place on fire and kill us all."

"He nearly did." Amber shuddered at the memory of the acrid smell, the billowing smoke, the crackling flames rising from the sofa stuffing.

"That's how I knew it would work." Jade's eyes seemed unfocused.

"How what would work?"

"He passed out that night," said Jade, twisting her fingers through the blanket weave as she spoke. "Mom was in her bedroom. I remember Janis Joplin was playing on the radio." Jade sang a few bars. "You were asleep."

"So were you," said Amber.

But Jade shook her head. "I was awake. I went into the living room. I was so scared he'd wake up. I pictured it over and over, like an instant replay, those pale blue eyes opening, his stinky breath, his scabby hands grabbing me."

Amber went cold all over.

"But he didn't wake up," said Jade.

Amber let out a shuddering breath of relief.

"So I took his lit cigarette from the ashtray. I took the newspaper off the table. I crumpled a corner, just like I'd seen them do on that wilderness show. You remember? The one with the park ranger and the kids in Yellowstone?"

Amber couldn't answer.

"I tucked it all between the cushions, and I went back to bed."

"Oh, Jade," Amber rasped, her hand tightening on her sister's shoulder.

"I lit the fire, Amber." Tears formed in Jade's eyes. "I lit the fire and you put it out. It wasn't until years later that I realized I could have killed us all."

"You were five years old." Amber couldn't wrap her head around such a young child conceiving and executing that plan.

"Do you think I'm evil?"

"I think you were scared."

"I knew it would work," said Jade. "I knew if Earl set the sofa on fire that Mom would kick him out and we'd never have to see him again."

Amber drew Jade into her arms, remembering her as such a small child. "It was a fairly brilliant plan," she whispered against Jade's hair. "Another time, you might want to have a plan for putting the fire out."

"I was thinking last night," said Jade.

"You need to stop thinking about this. It's over."

"I was thinking that's how it's been my whole life. I've been starting fires, and you've been putting them out. And now I'm pregnant. And I'm sick."

"You're going to get better."

"But you have a new job. So my baby and I won't starve on the streets."

Amber's chest tightened painfully. "You're going to be just fine. We're *all* going to be just fine."

Jade's voice broke. "Thank you, Amber."

"You are so very welcome."

"I'm going to do better."

"You're already doing better."

"I'm going to get a job and I'm going to pay you back. And somehow, some way, I'm going to be the one helping you."

"Sure," said Amber. "But, for now, I have more good news."

Jade pulled away and looked up. "What more could there be?"

"I got a signing bonus. And it's enough to cover your hospital bill."

Jade blinked, her eyes clearing. "Are you kidding me?"

"I'm serious."

"Why? How? What's the job?"

Amber wasn't going to lie. "It's my old job."

It took Jade a moment to respond. "You're going back?"

"I'm going back."

Jade looked worried. "To Tuck? To the guy who kissed you?"

"To his brother. Dixon. Dixon will be back soon and I'll work for him again."

"He's the nice one, right?"

"He's the nice one." All Amber had to do was find him and get everything back to normal.

"What about Tuck?" asked Jade.

"What about him? He's barely ever there. Once Dixon's back, I'll never even have to see him."

Jade frowned. "But you kissed him."

"He kissed me."

"You kissed him back. I saw it. You kissed him back, which means you must be attracted to him."

Amber gave a shrug. "Maybe a little bit. He's a good-looking guy. And he's smart and funny. You should see the string of women lining up to date him. But nothing more is going to happen between us. He'll never really be interested in me."

She'd thought a lot about Tuck's kisses, concluding they were a power play, or a test like he'd said, or maybe it was just his habit to kiss any woman who happened to be around. If the tabloids were anything to go by, he did a lot of kissing with a lot of different women.

"You have to be careful of men," said Jade.

Amber didn't disagree, especially thinking about Earl and her mother's other boyfriends. Not to mention the stories about some of Jade's exes.

"Even when things start out well," said Jade, "they usually end badly."

Amber shifted from the bed back to the chair. "You and I agree on that."

"But lust is a funny thing."

"This isn't lust." Maybe it was curiosity, maybe sexual attraction, but what Amber felt for Tuck didn't rise to the level of lust.

"I've dated guys I knew were bad for me."

"You knew?"

"Yes, I knew. But it didn't keep me away. In fact it made them even more attractive."

"I'm not you," said Amber. She couldn't imagine herself setting aside good sense and taking up with a man who was clearly trouble.

Jade looked unconvinced.

"I have some other news," Amber said briskly, determined to move on. "I have to go away for a few days. It's for work."

Jade's eyes narrowed critically.

"For Dixon," Amber quickly added. She definitely didn't want Jade worrying about her. "He has a thing in Arizona, and I need to go out there. Do you think you'll be okay?"

"I'll be fine. I'm only going to lay here and study."

Amber congratulated herself on successfully switching the topic away from Tuck.

"Good." She came to her feet. "Because I have to leave tonight."

Jade's smile faded, but she gave a brave nod. "Are you sure you don't think I'm evil?"

Amber gave her sister a hug. "You're tough and brave, and a little bit brilliant. Take care of yourself. Feel good. And don't study too hard."

"Enjoy Arizona. Is Tuck going with you?"

Amber didn't have it in her to tell an outright lie. "Probably. For part of it anyway."

"Don't fall for him."

"I won't."

"He'll look sexy, and you'll want to. And I saw the way he looked at you. He wants to sleep with you."

An unwelcome wash of longing swept through Amber. "Too bad for him."

"Just say no."

"Well, I'm not going to say yes."

Amber wouldn't say yes. In fact, she doubted he'd ask again. He'd flat-out told her she wasn't as attractive as his usual dates.

Deep down inside, she knew she wasn't going to get another proposition from Tuck. He had far too many options in his life to even give her a second thought.

Seven

Tuck still wanted Amber. He wanted her very badly, and his desire was growing by the minute.

She was radiant in front of him, curled up in a padded rattan chair in the Scottsdale hotel courtyard. The gas fireplace flickering between them gave her face a gorgeous glow. Floodlights decorated the palm trees and rock garden behind her, while stars winked above them in the blackened sky.

"Do you have any ideas?" she asked.

There were any number of great ideas pinging around inside his head. But he doubted Amber was anywhere near his wavelength.

She was a picture of openness in a midnight blue knee-length dress and a cropped cardigan sweater with the sleeves pushed up. Her spiky sandals were dropped carelessly on the concrete patio in front of her. After her second glass of wine, she'd tugged her hair loose, and it flowed over her shoulders.

"I'm his brother," said Tuck, knowing she'd understand he was talking about their earlier conversation at Highland Luminance. "There must be someone who can authorize a release of information to me."

"The receptionist didn't seem encouraging." Amber referred to the woman who had asked them to leave the wellness resort.

"I can't imagine his yoga participation requires the same confidentiality rules as, say, an STD diagnosis."

"She did tell us the date he left."

"More than five weeks ago."

Amber took another sip of her wine, dark against her lush lips. Her face and shoulders were creamy and smooth. He remembered her taste, her scent and the feel of her lithe body enclosed in his arms.

"We should brainstorm about Dixon," she said.

Tuck shook himself out of a fantasy that had him kissing a shadow next to her collarbone. "What do you mean?"

"What do you know about him? Any unfulfilled dreams, secret desires?"

"He doesn't tell me his secret desires." Nor did Tuck confide in Dixon. And he was especially keeping quiet about his feelings for Amber.

"Toss out anything," she said. "What about when you were young, while you were growing up?"

"My desires have changed since I was young. I imagine his have, too."

"Play along," said Amber. "What else have we got to do?"

Tuck didn't dare voice his ideas.

The slight breeze rustled her hair and she brushed it back from her cheek. "Funny thing, I was reminded earlier today that childhood events can impact our entire lives."

He forced the sexy images from his mind. "You think Dixon is reacting to his childhood?"

"I think he's reacting to exhaustion and a cheating wife. But how he reacts could be influenced by his core self-perception."

"Core self-perception. Is that from the Highland Luminance brochure?"

"No." Her tone turned defensive. "It's from a documentary. But it's valid. It just means who you think you are."

"Who do you think you are, Amber? What's your core self-perception?" He was more interested in her than in Dixon.

"That's easy. I'm organized, a caretaker. I can't leave people to their own mistakes."

Tuck couldn't help but smile at the answer. "You left me to my own mistakes."

"Only after you fired me. Up until then, and against my own better judgment, I was helping you."

He knew that she had. "I was grateful."

"I could tell."

"I hired you back," he pointed out.

"Only because you needed me."

"True. But here you are."

"What about Dixon?"

"Don't you want to know about me?" Tuck knew the question sounded a bit needy, but he couldn't help himself.

"I already know your self-perception."

"Do tell."

"Talented, successful and good-looking. You know you're talented because so many things come easy, and the rest is reflected back in the mirror."

Her assessment was wholly unflattering.

"So I'm conceited?"

"I think you're singularly realistic."

"I was born into a rich family that had few expectations of me."

She didn't disagree.

"But that doesn't make me feel talented and successful," Tuck continued. "It makes me feel spoiled and useless."

Her expression turned decidedly skeptical. "Yet you don't do anything to change it."

He refused to argue. If she hadn't noticed how hard he'd been working lately, pointing it out to her wasn't going to change a thing.

"I'm here, aren't I?" he asked instead.

"To get back to the status quo."

"For the benefit of Tucker Transportation."

She seemed to consider that for a moment. "You're doing a pretty good job, you know."

At first he thought he must have misheard. "Excuse me?"

"You heard me. Don't fish for compliments."

"You took me by surprise with that."

She leaned slightly forward. "You're doing a pretty good job. This desperation to find Dixon is about you getting away again, not about the health of the company."

"You're wrong." Tuck might have been reluctant to come on board, but he was actually glad he had. He'd felt more useful in the past six weeks than ever had before in his life.

"I'm right," she said. "But we could go back and forth on it all night long."

Tuck bit back an all-night-long quip. He really had to get his craving for her under control.

"This is about Dixon," said Amber, her tone going crisp. "In the past, when he was young, what made him happy? What made him angry?"

"I made him angry," said Tuck.

She broke a grin at that. "Why does that not surprise me?"

"Because I'm the villain in this story."

"How did you make him angry?"

"I stole Nanny Susie's candies," he told her. "She kept a jar of them in the pantry as treats for good behavior. I dragged a kitchen chair into the pantry and piled a step stool on top, then I climbed up and filled my pockets. Dixon was freaking out. He was sure we'd be caught."

"That's bizarrely ironic."

"That I stole the good-behavior treats?" He grinned. "I get that now. I didn't get it then. They were delicious."

"Did you get caught?"

"No."

"Did Dixon eat the candies?"

"Yes. He held out for a while, but eventually he gave in. Maybe the experience scarred him? Should we be canvassing the local confectionaries?"

She rolled her eyes. "What else have you got?"

"I used to sneak out my bedroom window and meet girls in the middle of the night."

"Did Dixon sneak out with you?" she asked.

"No. By then, I guess he held firmer to his convictions. Or else he was loyal to his girlfriend. Which, now that I think about it, he really was. He only had two of them before Kassandra. Bettina Wright and Jodi Saunders. They were both gorgeous, but they also struck me as boring and a little stuck-up."

"You have different tastes than your brother."

Tuck let his gaze rest on Amber. "I do."

He knew that if he'd been working side by side with her for five years, married or not, his loyalty would absolutely have come into question.

The air seemed to thicken and heat between them. If he'd been closer, he'd have reached for her.

"So Dixon is dependable," Amber said into the silence. "He's honest, loyal and hardworking."

"You sound like my father."

"Even in the midst of an emotional crisis, first he tries to get your father's permission to leave. Then he leaves your father a letter of explanation and me as a fail-safe."

"You weren't much of a fail-safe."

"I told you I thought you could handle it. I still believe you could handle it if you'd apply yourself."

"Apply myself with no knowledge or experience to the running of a multinational conglomerate?"

"Whose fault is it that you have no experience?"

Tuck wanted to say his father's. He wanted to say his brother's. But he knew it was also his own fault. He'd sat back and allowed this to happen.

Had he always chosen the shortcut? Steal the candies instead of earning them? Make out with the girls without dating them?

"Do you think people can change?" he asked.

"I think we can try."

He felt the magnetic pull between them again.

Her expression turned guarded and she rose to her feet. "I should really go to bed."

He stood with her. "Any chance that's an invitation?"

"Tuck."

He immediately regretted the joke. "I know."

She looked up at him, eyes deep blue, cheeks flushed, the

breeze teasing her hair. Her lips were slightly parted and they looked so incredibly kissable.

"Is your flirting reflex really that strong?" she asked.

"It's not a reflex."

"Then, what is it?"

"It's you, Amber. It's all you."

"I'm not trying to send signals."

"You're not trying, but I know you feel it, too."

"Can you make it stop?" she asked, her voice a rasp.

He slowly slipped his arm around the small of her back, settling it there. "Why?"

She leaned slightly away, but she didn't break his hold. "Because it won't end well."

"We don't know that."

"One of us does."

"You can't predict the future."

"I can predict the next sixty seconds."

He gave a cautious smile. "I'm afraid to ask."

"You're going to kiss me, Tuck."

"That's a relief." He tightened his hold on her and leaned in. "I thought I was getting a knee to the groin."

"And then we'll—"

"Then nothing," he said. "Kissing you will take at least the next sixty seconds."

The sixty seconds passed, and then another and another. Tuck's lips were firm, his body taut and his embrace was sturdy and sure. The fire brought a glow to her skin, and the heat of passion built inside her.

She knew they had to stop. But she didn't want to stop. She didn't want to step away from the cradle of Tuck's arms or from the tendrils of desire weaving their way along her limbs. She decided she could risk a few more seconds, relish a few more moments of paradise.

They were both unattached, consenting adults. They could hug and kiss and generally test the limits of their endurance without bringing the world to a screeching halt. They were on a public patio, screened only by cactus plants and a latticework of vines. It wasn't as if things could get too far out of hand. Could they?

Tuck broke the kiss and dragged in a strangled breath. He buried his face in the crook of her neck. His palms slid lower, cupping her rear, pressing her into the V of his legs. His body was firm and aroused. The realization should have worried her rather than thrilling her.

"What happens next?" he asked between labored breaths.

She knew she had to get herself under control. It was time to say no, time to remind them both of who they were, time to politely retreat to her room and regroup for tomorrow.

"I thought I knew," she said instead.

"You don't?"

"I do," she said against his chest. "I should. I thought I did."

He drew back just far enough to look at her. "You're overthinking."

"I'm underthinking." If she was even contemplating letting things go further, she wasn't giving it anywhere near enough thought.

"That sounds promising."

"Tuck." She sighed, leaning against his strength for one last moment.

"I have a marvelous room," he responded, his voice rumbling deeply. "A huge bed, an enormous tiled shower and I bet room-service breakfast is fantastic. And I'm willing— no, *eager*—to share it all with you." But then his hold on her loosened and his tone changed. He drew back even farther. "But when a woman has to debate this long about whether or not to make love, the answer is already there."

She wanted to disagree. But he was right. And he was being such a gentleman about it.

It was chivalrous and admirable, and she was deeply disappointed. What had happened to the bold Tuck who'd stolen candies and sneaked out his bedroom window?

"You're saying no."

"I'm saying *hell yes*. But I don't want you to regret anything. And you would."

He was right again.

"You're nicer than people think," she said.

"I'm smarter than people think."

"Is this you being smart?"

"Responsible. This is me being Dixon. I've always known he was the better man."

"Yet you're here. And he's missing."

"Life is full of ironies."

She forced herself to take a step back, out of Tuck's embrace. "I'm really sorry."

He gave a self-deprecating shrug. "That you don't want to sleep with me?"

"That I let things get away from me. I didn't mean to lead you on."

"I'd rather have the shot than not." He reached out and smoothed her hair. "Kiss me any old time you like. And take it as far as you want. I can handle the disappointment. Who knows, maybe one day you'll be sure about what you want."

It was on the tip of her tongue to agree. But she didn't dare voice it. If she wasn't careful, she would convince herself she wanted him now, right now.

"Don't look so scared," he said.

"This isn't like me."

"It's called *chemistry*, Amber. It doesn't have to mean anything."

Her chest went hollow. Reality brought with it intense disappointment. "So you've felt this before? You've done this before?"

"All the time."

And it meant nothing to him. Good that they'd cleared that up. Jade was right. Getting involved with the wrong man inevitably ended badly.

"I'll never be sure." Then she realized it sounded as though she was waffling. "I mean, I'm already sure. The answer is no, and it's going to stay no. I'm here to work. I'm here to find Dixon. And that's all. Full stop."

"You want to add an exclamation point to that?"

"You're mocking me."

"I am. You have to admit, it was a quick turnaround."

"It took me a minute to get my head on straight. That's all. Good night, Tuck."

"Good night, Amber." The mocking tone was still in his voice.

She struggled to leave things on a professional note. "Jackson will be here in the morning?"

"You think Jackson will protect your virtue?"

"I'm thinking about finding Dixon. I've moved on."

She had. No more kissing Tuck. No more touching Tuck. No more flirting with Tuck.

She would keep her distance and keep it professional.

After a sleepless night fantasizing about Amber, and repeatedly asking himself why on earth he'd behaved like a gentleman, Tuck wasn't in the mood to care about corporate sales. But Lucas was on the phone asking, and Lucas was right. Robson Equipment was an important client and Tuck was only half an hour from Phoenix.

"Tell them yes," he said to Lucas. "Jackson showed up with a couple of guys. I'm sure they can spare me for a few hours."

Robson Equipment was hosting a black-tie business event and Lucas had arranged an invitation. It would be a chance to Tuck to touch base with the corporate brass and head off any moves Zachary Ingles might be making to poach the account.

"Take Amber," said Lucas.

"Jackson needs her help."

"Tell him he needs to share."

After her stance last night, Tuck couldn't imagine Amber agreeing to attend a dinner. "I don't need a date."

"She's not your date. She's your assistant. She knows the

account inside out and I'm beginning to think she's smarter than you."

"Ha-ha."

"That wasn't a joke."

"I doubt she'll agree," Tuck told him flat out.

"She's there to work, isn't she?"

Tuck didn't want to explain the complexity of their relationship, not that he was even sure how. The chemistry between them was combustible. He'd lied to her last night. What he'd felt with her didn't happen all the time. He'd never experienced anything like it in his life.

He could vow to keep his hands off her. But he was too smart to trust himself. He might have decided to behave more like Dixon, but it was definitely going to take some practice.

"Tuck?" Lucas prompted.

"She'll be working all day already."

"So pay her overtime."

"I'm not sure—"

"What did you do?"

"What do you mean?"

"You did something to upset her."

"I did not. Okay, I did. But it's not what you think."

"What do I think?"

"That I made a pass at her."

"That's exactly what I think. I bet she said no. And I hope you remember that for next time."

"She didn't say no. Far from it." Tuck checked his ego, but not quite in time.

There was a pause. "What did you do?"

"Nothing. But it's complicated."

"Uncomplicate it," said Lucas.

If only it was that easy. "You're such an armchair quarterback."

"Do I need to quote the Robson sales figures for last year?"

"No." Tuck knew they were significant.

"Are you going to argue that she doesn't know the portfolio?"

"I'm not." Tuck knew he was being cornered, but there wasn't a thing in the world he could do to stop it.

Lucas was right on all counts. Lucas was looking out for the best interests of Tucker Transportation, which is exactly what Tuck needed to be doing.

A knock sounded on the hotel room door.

"Get it done," said Lucas.

"I will."

"I'll talk to you after." Lucas ended the call.

Tuck finished buttoning his shirt as he crossed the living room of the suite. It was southwest in character, lots of rusts, browns and yellows, creating a warm atmosphere. The bed had been extraordinarily comfortable, the room temperature perfect with a fresh, fragrant breeze coming in from the desert side.

He'd returned here last night to find chilled champagne and chocolate-covered strawberries. Nice touch, but it was impossible to enjoy them by himself. He'd longed to invite Amber over to share, only to talk, just to listen to her voice, watch her expressions.

He blew out a cold chuckle as he reached the door. He wasn't kidding anyone, least of all himself. He wanted Amber in his bed, naked, smiling, welcoming him into her arms without a single mental reservation.

He answered to find her in the outdoor breezeway, Jackson by her side. Even without a smile, she was gorgeous, totally perfect.

"We've checked hospitals, morgues and police stations," said Jackson, heading directly into the room.

Tuck dragged his gaze away from Amber. "I take it you found nothing."

It wasn't a question. If there was bad news, Jackson's manner would be quite different.

"No leads from airlines, private or public. We've checked trains, buses and rental cars."

"Buses?" Tuck couldn't bring himself to believe Dixon would take a bus. "Have you *met* my brother?"

Amber marched into the room, expression schooled, her manner all business. He inhaled her subtle scent as she passed, feeling pathetic.

"He could have bought a car," she suggested.

"That would be more like him," Tuck agreed.

"We'll check to see if anything was registered in his name or in the company's. In case he stayed here in the Scottsdale area, we're also checking hotels, motels and resorts."

"Surely, he wouldn't buy a house," said Amber. She still hadn't looked directly at Tuck.

"Depends on how long he's planning to stay," said Tuck, willing her to meet his eyes.

"I suggest we have breakfast," said Jackson. "Then Amber and I will walk through everything she remembers."

"What about Highland Luminance?" Tuck asked.

"Their records are confidential."

"I know, but maybe you could—"

"Probably best if that's the last question you ask on that front," said Jackson.

"Got it." If Jackson was up to something less than legal, Tuck didn't want to know.

Amber looked puzzled. "What are you planning to—"

Both men shot her warning looks.

"Right," she said and shut up.

Tuck stuffed his wallet into his back pocket and located the room key. "Let's get started on what Amber remembers."

"It'll be better if she and I do it alone," said Jackson.

Tuck fought a spurt of jealousy. "No."

"She needs to be relaxed."

"She is relaxed. She will be relaxed."

"Given your history…" said Jackson.

Tuck couldn't believe she'd told him about last night. "Our *history*?" he challenged.

"You fired her."

"That?"

"Yes, that."

"I need to hear what she has to say," said Tuck.

"She doesn't want you there."

Tuck tried to catch her gaze again. He willed her to reassure Jackson, but she didn't.

"She might prompt a memory, remind me of something from our childhoods."

"You're going to use that against me?" Amber challenged.

"Do you or do you not believe Dixon's background might be relevant?"

Her blue eyes narrowed.

"It's not as if you're going to be naked."

"Oh, *that's* helpful," Jackson mocked.

"He's just being ridiculous," said Amber.

"She's right," Tuck agreed. "But I don't want to miss something because neither of you recognize its significance."

There was a beat of silence. "He's also right," said Amber, her shoulders dropping a notch.

Tuck would take the win.

"Don't gloat," she said to him.

"I'm not."

"You're such a liar." She started for the door.

"I'm going to need her tonight," Tuck said to Jackson.

Both Amber and Jackson swung their gazes his way.

"Robson Equipment is hosting a corporate event in Phoenix. Lucas said, and I'm quoting here, Amber has to attend because she's smarter than me, and we can't afford to lose the account."

"Fine by me," said Jackson.

Amber opened her mouth, but Tuck cut her off. "Double overtime. You'll be well compensated."

She hesitated. Then she nodded and turned for the door.

Tuck was surprised, shocked even. Money had swayed her again? This was starting to seem too easy.

Eight

Amber had dredged up every possible memory about Dixon's plans. Jackson was very good at his job, leading her down pathways that would have seemed insignificant to her, but clearly helped form the picture of Dixon's state of mind.

Tuck had been quiet throughout the conversation, excusing himself afterward without comment. She couldn't tell if he was pursuing a new lead or if he was annoyed with something she'd said. Jackson had immediately left to meet with his team, leaving Amber with some time to call Jade.

The news from the hospital was all good. Jade's blood pressure was stable and there were no other worrisome signs. They'd done an ultrasound and the baby still seemed fine. The technician had given odds on it being a girl.

Amber had also discovered that her signing bonus had been deposited into her bank account. It was a huge relief to know she was able to pay the hospital bills as they arrived.

Up next was the Robson party. After their kiss last night, she was nervous about spending the evening alone with Tuck. But she reminded herself that this was what she'd signed up for. Finding Dixon was one thing, but she also had to help Tuck keep the company running.

Lucas had said the Robson party would be formal—evening-gown and black-tie formal. She had a sleeveless, black crepe dress at home that would have worked. But she'd traveled light, with nothing but business and casual clothes in her suitcase.

Fingers mentally crossed, she navigated the hallway to the lobby shops, hoping the hotel boutique had something suitable.

She stopped at their display window, taking in a sublimely

beautiful cobalt blue dress. The cap sleeves were sheer netting and appliqué, with a fitted, crisscross bodice of supple, lightweight tulle. The dress was finished with an elegant, full skirt that glittered under the display lights.

It was perfect. It was also ten times Amber's price range.

She wandered inside, checking out the few formal gowns among an eclectic women's collection that ranged from hats and purses, to beachwear and jackets. She found a couple of dresses that would work without breaking her bank account and the saleslady directed her to a compact fitting room.

She started with an unadorned navy gown with three-quarter-length sleeves and a V-neck. It was neutral, and she could see how it would fit well on many body shapes. She moved out of the cubicle to look in the full-length mirror.

"A bit uninspiring," said a male voice behind her.

She turned to find Tuck, a plastic suit bag slung over his arm.

"Great minds think alike," he said, holding up what was obviously a newly purchased outfit for the evening.

She turned back to the mirror. "It's not bad. It's not as if I have a lot of choices."

"I do like the shoes."

Fortunately, Amber had tossed in a pair of silver spike heels that had just enough rhinestones to make them interesting. They weren't perfect with the navy dress, but she could get away with them.

"I've got a pair at home that would work better with this dress."

"I have no doubt that you do."

She peered at him in the mirror, trying to determine his level of sarcasm.

"Don't look so suspicious. Your extensive shoe collection is one of my favorite things about you."

"Nice save."

"It wasn't a save. I'm saying you need a different dress."

"There's not much to choose from."

He pointed over his shoulder at the display window. "What about that one?"

The saleslady was quick to pounce. "We do have it in her size."

"Great," said Tuck.

"Wrong," said Amber. She hated to be crass, but she didn't see any point in pretending. "It's too expensive."

"It's a business function," said Tuck.

"I know that."

"She'll try it on," he said to the saleslady.

"No, she won't."

"I'm not asking you to pay for it."

"You're sure not paying for it."

He was her boss, not her boyfriend. A few kisses notwithstanding, they didn't have the kind of relationship that allowed him to buy her clothes or anything else for that matter.

"Not me, Amber. Tucker Transportation."

"That's not how it works."

"That's exactly how it works. You're here on business. I'm compelling you to attend a *business* function. Your wardrobe is the company's responsibility."

"Did the company buy your suit?" she challenged.

"Yes."

"You're lying."

"Corporate credit card." There was a distinct note of triumph in his voice. He gestured to the navy dress. "You're not going in that."

"Yes, I am."

"Like it or not, Amber. Part of your function tonight is to be a billboard for Tucker Transportation's success."

She could barely believe he'd said it. "A *billboard*?"

"Don't get all high and mighty. It's part of the gig."

"You're saying I'm visual entertainment for your boardroom cronies? Do you want me to jump out of a cake, too?"

The saleslady had just returned with the dress and her mouth dropped open at Amber's jibe.

"It applies to me, as well," said Tuck. "Thanks." He smiled at the saleslady and took the dress from her arms. "I can't show up in a cheap suit."

"I don't imagine you own a cheap suit."

"Don't pretend you don't understand my point. You know full well what I mean. You and I both have to look the part tonight."

Amber hated that she did, but she got what he meant. And he wasn't wrong. She glanced at the rich cobalt blue dress. The irony was that it would be perfect with her shoes.

She looked for a graceful way forward. "Tell me this isn't the first time Tucker Transportation bought somebody a dress."

"This isn't the first time Tucker Transportation bought somebody a dress."

She gave him a skeptical frown.

"I think," he added. "Okay, I don't care. My rationale is sound." He glanced at his watch. "And we're running out of time. You might want to do something with your hair."

"What's wrong with my hair?"

The saleslady piped up. "We have a lovely salon in the hotel."

"Can you get her an appointment?" asked Tuck.

"Right away."

"This is ridiculous," Amber muttered. But she scooped the dress from Tuck.

It would be, by far, the most luxurious thing she'd ever worn. But if the man was determined to drop that much money for a single evening, who was she to fight him?

In the opulent ballroom, Tuck had to struggle to keep from staring at Amber. He'd expected the dress to transform her from her usual librarian look. But he'd had no idea the effect would be this dramatic.

The salon had styled her hair in an updo, wispy around her temples, showing off her graceful neck and highlighting her amazing cheekbones. Her makeup was subtle, but deeper and richer than she normally wore. Her thick, dark lashes and artfully lined eyes reflected the deep blue of her dress.

At the moment, he was trying hard to concentrate on Norm Oliphant's description of his newly evolving supply chain, but he was torn between watching Amber and glaring at the dozens of men checking her out. Didn't they realize she was with him?

Dinner was over and a music ensemble was filing into the room. Lighting was being subtly adjusted, dimmed around the perimeter, slightly brighter to highlight the polished wood dance floor.

"I hope there's some good news about your father," said Norm.

Tuck checked his wandering mind and told himself to behave like Dixon. Kassandra had been gorgeous as well, but he was certain his brother had never let that detract from business discussions.

"We're all encouraged," Tuck said to Norm.

"So you've seen him recently?" asked Norm's wife, Regina.

Tuck wasn't sure how to answer that. Truth was he hadn't seen his father since they'd move him to Boston. But how was that going to sound?

Amber smoothly and unexpectedly stepped in. "Tuck has become so pivotal to the day-to-day operations, Jamison is insistent that he focus on the company. Jamison has his wife with him, of course. She's been a stalwart support every day during his recovery. But he gathers peace of mind knowing Tuck is at the helm."

Tuck could have cheered. It was all lies, of course, made up on the spot, which made her explanation all the more impressive.

"Where's Dixon in all of this?" asked Norm.

Amber stepped slightly closer to both Norm and Regina, lowering her voice, throwing Norm off balance with the intensity of her gaze. "I'm sure you heard what happened. With Dixon's wife?"

"We did," said Regina, leaning in.

Amber nodded. "Tuck insisted Dixon take some time to himself. He left a contact number, but we haven't wanted to bother him. You know how brothers can be when one is betrayed. They value loyalty above everything."

Regina glanced at her husband.

"Loyalty," Norm agreed with a nod.

"In business as well as life," said Amber.

Her words were bang on, the inflection perfect. Tuck had to glance at her to convince himself she'd done it on purpose.

He caught her gaze and realized she had. She had skillfully and adroitly reminded Norm of his long-standing business arrangement with Tucker Transportation. She was frighteningly good at this.

Then Amber gave the man a dazzling smile.

Norm raised his glass to Tuck in a toast. "Good of you to come tonight."

"Good of you to invite us." Tuck took a drink with him.

The small orchestra came up with opening bars on the opposite side of the hall.

"We'll be in touch next week," Norm said to Tuck. "I hear Zachary Ingles moved on."

"I'm afraid he thought the grass was greener," Tuck said with a disapproving frown, deciding to stick with the loyalty theme.

"Don't like to see that," said Norm.

"I've promoted Lucas Steele to vice president. Good man. He's been with us for over a decade."

"Worked his way up through the ranks?" asked Norm, looking pleased by the notion.

"Absolutely," said Tuck, though he had no idea exactly how far through the ranks Lucas had worked his way up. "Corporately, we like to nurture talent."

Tuck was tossing things out on the fly, but it seemed like a vague enough statement to be true of most companies.

"Have Lucas give my guys a call," said Norm.

"First thing Monday," said Tuck.

Norm smiled at Regina. "Shall we dance, dear?"

"My pleasure, darling."

Tuck and Amber watched the two walk away.

"You were good," she said. "Very confident, very much in charge."

"Me? You're the one who deserves an acting award. My father gathers peace of mind knowing I'm in charge?"

"I'm sure he does. Or he would. If he knew what I know."

Tuck arched a brow. "Dixon left a contact number?"

She gave a sly smile. "He did. It didn't work in the end, but he did leave a number."

"Remind me to listen very carefully to how you phrase things."

"You don't already?"

Tuck started to smile, but then he caught another man eyeing Amber and sent him a withering stare.

"We should dance," he said.

"Why?"

Because she might not be his date, but she'd arrived with him. He wasn't used to having women poached from under his nose, and he wasn't about to start now.

"It'll look good," he said, taking her hand.

"To who?" But she came easily as he started walking.

"Norm and Regina."

"You think?"

"Sure."

Why wouldn't it look good? It was a perfectly acceptable excuse. They made it to the dance floor and Tuck turned her into his arms.

She fit perfectly. Of course she fit perfectly. And she smoothly matched his rhythm. Within seconds, it was as if they'd been dancing together for years. He immediately relaxed, drawing her closer.

"Thank you for all that," he said into the intimacy of their embrace.

"Just doing my job."

"You're doing it extraordinarily well."

"I guess that's what you get when you pay double overtime."

Tuck smiled at that. "You're a mercenary at heart."

She was quiet for a moment. "Money makes life easier."

"It can," he agreed. "But it can also be a burden."

Right now, Tuck felt the weight of every employee who depended on Tucker Transportation.

Her tone turned teasing. "Spoken like a man who just spent a mortgage payment on a dress."

"In order to ensure hundreds of other people can make their next mortgage payment."

"Do you have any idea how that feels?" she asked.

"To make a mortgage payment?" He wouldn't pretend he did. "The house has been in our family for a couple of generations."

"To worry about making your mortgage payment. To worry about paying for food, clothes, medical bills."

"You know I don't."

They danced in silence. He could tell she was annoyed with him. He didn't really blame her. From the outside looking in, his life must seem like a walk in the park.

Then it hit him, what she might be saying.

"Do *you* earn enough money?" he asked.

She glanced up in obvious surprise. "What?"

"Should I give you a raise?"

"Where did that come from?"

"It sounded as though you were having money problems."

"You pay me fairly."

He searched her expression. He could tell the conversation was hitting very close to home for her. If it wasn't now, then when? When had she been worried about meeting expenses?

"Your childhood?" he suggested.

"This isn't about me."

"Your childhood?" he repeated.

"Fine. We were poor. My mom was single. She drank. A lot."

He digested the information. "I'm sorry you had to go through that."

The orchestra switched songs, but he kept on dancing.

"It was a long time ago," said Amber. "Truth is, it impacted Jade more than it impacted me."

"How so?"

"She had a hard time settling into life. She quit school, left town. Then she bounced from job to job. She always picked the wrong men."

Interesting, but Tuck was far more curious about Amber than he was about Jade. "And you? Did you pick the wrong men?"

She gave a little laugh. "I didn't pick any men at all. Well, not many. I had a boyfriend in high school. But then I graduated and started working. I took a lot of night-school courses at community college, so there wasn't much time for a social life."

"You don't date?" Tuck couldn't help but contrast his own active social life.

"Occasionally. Casually." She glanced around the opulent ballroom. "I have to say, this is the most extravagant event I've ever attended. I guess I should thank you for the experience."

"Anytime." He was serious.

His brain ticked through the information she'd just given him. He liked the idea of what he thought she had to mean.

"So you're saying…" He tried to frame the question. "How do I put this…"

"Don't you *dare* ask me about my sex life."

As if anything on earth would stop him. "Tell me about your sex life."

"Shut up."

He gave a brief chuckle. "I'll tell you about mine."

"I've read about yours."

"Not the details."

"Nobody wants the details."

"I disagree. Reporters ask me about them all the time." He maneuvered them around the crowd to a quieter spot on the dance floor.

"Do you answer?"

"No. If I did, they'd be disappointed."

"Did you just tell me you're a bad lover?"

"What? No. I meant that I'm not as practiced as people assume." He hesitated, then went for it. "Not that you'd have a basis for comparison."

"You're outrageous." But her tone was laced with amusement.

"I won't argue with that. But I'm also available. You know, if you're in dire need of—"

The end of her fist connected sharply with his shoulder, startling him.

"Ouch."

"You better believe, *ouch*," she sniffed with mock offense. "I had a boyfriend."

"Not since high school."

"And I've had offers since then."

He knew that was true. "At least a dozen tonight alone."

She looked puzzled.

"You're not paying attention, are you?" he asked.

"To what?"

"To all the men in the room eyeing you up."

She seemed surprised. "It's the dress. And maybe the hair. Probably the shoes."

"It's all of that," he agreed. "But it's more than just that."

He couldn't help himself. He splayed his hand across her back, urging her close, molding their bodies together.

"Tuck."

"I won't pretend I'm not attracted to you."

The word *attracted* was the understatement of the century. He was wild about her, burning hot for her, growing more so by the hour.

"Jackson's here."

It took a moment for her words to make sense. He'd pictured their conversation taking an entirely different turn.

She signaled the direction with a nod and Tuck easily spotted Jackson in the crowd. He stood out in blue jeans, a white T-shirt and a worn leather jacket. It was easy to tell from his expression that he had some news.

Tuck quickly escorted Amber from the dance floor, meeting up with Jackson at the edge. The three of them made for the double doors that led to a quiet foyer.

"Dixon bought a car," said Jackson when they emerged into the relative privacy of the long, high-ceilinged, glass-walled room.

"When?" asked Tuck.

"Five weeks ago, a three-year-old Audi convertible. He paid cash."

"Is he still in Scottsdale?"

"Didn't stay here long," said Jackson. "We tracked the car to a marina in San Diego."

Tuck's anticipation rose. "Did you find Dixon?"

"There, he bought a sailboat."

Tuck waited for Jackson to elaborate.

"Forty-footer. Paid cash."

The situation was getting stranger by the second.

"I thought you were watching his bank accounts," said Tuck.

"We are. Does your brother normally carry that kind of walking-around money?"

Tuck didn't know. But that did seem like a lot of money to have at his fingertips. How long had Dixon planned this little adventure?

"Did you find the sailboat?" asked Amber.

"It left the marina weeks ago and hasn't been back."

They all stared at each other in silence.

"I doubt he sank," said Tuck. "There'd have been a distress call. We'd have heard from the authorities by now."

"Probably," said Jackson.

"Was it equipped to sail solo?"

"It was."

"Something's not right," said Amber.

"No kidding," Tuck agreed. There were plenty of things not right in this.

"When he headed for Scottsdale," she said, "even though it was a secret, he left a letter for your dad, and he left a number with me. He was that careful. There's no way he'd sail off into the Pacific without telling anyone at all."

"That's exactly what he did," said Tuck.

His worry about his brother was rapidly turning to annoyance. What had Dixon been thinking?

Amber was shaking her head. "Not without any word at all. I can understand that he didn't like it at Highland Luminance. And clearly he can afford a nice boat. But he's not irresponsible. He's trying to clear his head so he can do a good job at Tucker Transportation. He's not trying to harm it."

"Trying or not," said Tuck, "that's exactly what he's doing." He really wished Amber would stop defending Dixon.

"He…" She snapped her fingers. "That's it."

"What's it?" asked Tuck.

"Jamison," she said. "Dixon would have contacted Jamison. He didn't know anything about the heart attack. As far as he's concerned, your dad's still running the company. We searched through Dixon's accounts. And we've been monitoring Jamison's work email, but not his personal email."

Jackson swore under his breath. He was instantly on his phone giving instructions to one of his staff.

Tuck had to admit it was possible. It was even likely. It certainly made more sense than anything else right now. For weeks now, Dixon could have been operating under the assumption they knew his plans. He thought Jamison was running the show. He had no idea Tuck was making a mess of it.

Dixon was still gone. And Tuck still had to find him. But at least it made a little bit of sense now.

* * *

It was late into the night, and the three of them were back in Tuck's hotel suite when Jackson received a copy of an email from his investigator. The original had been sent by Dixon to Jamison's little-used personal email address. Amber was relieved they'd found an answer and happy there was a logical explanation for Dixon's behavior.

"It was sent from an internet café the day he left San Diego," said Jackson from where he was sitting at the round dining table. "He says he plans to spend a few weeks sailing down the Pacific coast. He apologizes but tells your dad to have confidence in you. He knows you can do it."

Tuck shook his head. "Not under these circumstances."

He'd parked himself in an armchair beside the flickering gas fireplace.

Amber had chosen the sofa. She'd kicked the shoes off her sore feet and curled them beneath her. The cushions were soft under her body, while the heat from the fire warmed her skin. Her brain had turned lethargic at the end of such a long day and she would have loved to let herself fall asleep.

"Can you answer Dixon's email?" Tuck asked Jackson.

"Easy. But he'll have to stop somewhere and log on in order to see it."

"He might not check," said Amber. "The point of the whole exercise was to get away from everything."

"He's been away from everything," said Tuck. "It's time for him to come back."

"Before he's ready?" she asked. She understood Tuck's frustration, but Dixon had a right to take some time to himself.

Tuck sat up straight and his voice rose. "How much time does the guy need?"

"You tell me." Her annoyance gave her a renewed shot of energy. "You're the expert. You've had nothing but time to yourself for years now."

He frowned. "Not by choice."

"They held a gun to your head?"

Jackson rose, closing his laptop. He muttered something about having work to do as he headed for the suite door.

Tuck didn't react to him leaving. His attention remained focused on Amber. "They did everything possible to keep me at arm's length."

She found that hard to believe.

"You think I'm lying," he stated.

"I know you had an office. You had keys to the building. Dixon invited you to meetings."

"Meetings where my father took great pleasure in setting me up for failure."

"How?"

"By cornering me with arcane questions to prove I didn't know anything."

"*Did* you know anything?"

He glared at her and she regretted the question.

"I mean," she said, attempting to backtrack, "you could have studied up, surprised him, turned the tables on him."

"That seemed like a lot of work to impress a guy who only wanted me gone."

"Why would he want you gone?" Tuck might be a bit of a rebel, but what father wouldn't be proud to have him as a son?

"Because he liked Dixon better. Parents aren't all perfect, Amber. They don't automatically love their children."

"Your father loves you."

Even as she uttered the statement, Amber realized she had no idea how Jamison felt about Tuck. She was under no illusions about automatic parental love.

She shook her head, regretting her words. "I'm sorry. I don't know that. I don't know anything about it."

Tuck blew out a breath. "It's okay."

She gave a little laugh. "I don't even know whether my own mother loved me."

His gaze turned sympathetic.

Uncomfortable, Amber sat up a bit straighter, attempting to explain. "I'm not sure my mother knew how to love anyone.

She said she loved us. I even think she wanted to love us. But she was so incredibly self-absorbed, she couldn't see past her own needs and desires."

"And your father?"

"Long gone before I had any memory of him."

"Did he support you at all? Financially?"

Amber couldn't help but cough out a laugh. "I'd be surprised if he stayed out of jail. My mother had extraordinarily bad taste in men."

"Where is she now?"

"She died. It happened while Jade and I were still teenagers."

Deeper sympathy came up in Tuck's eyes, softening his expression, making him look approachable, sexy. This was not good.

"How are we talking about me?" she asked.

They needed to get back to arguing.

"You helped raise your sister?"

"She was sixteen when it happened. I was eighteen. There wasn't much raising left to do." And by that time there hadn't been much of an opportunity to change any of Jade's habits.

"That's when she dropped out of school?" he asked.

"She took off after a few months. I didn't hear from her for a while."

Tuck rose and helped himself to a bottle of water, holding one out for her.

She nodded and accepted it.

He sat down at the opposite end of the sofa. "What did you do?"

"I graduated from high school and got a job." She twisted the cap and broke the seal. "With Dixon. He took a chance on me."

"That's surprising," said Tuck.

"I worked hard. I promised him I would, and I did."

"I believe you." Tuck stretched one arm along the back of the sofa. "No wonder you have no patience for me."

"I wouldn't say—"

"It's way too late to protest now. From where you're sitting, I had it all, every advantage, every privilege. My education was paid for, and I walked straight into a VP job in Daddy's company."

"I've never complained about my employment." She'd been grateful for it. "Well, up until you fired me anyway."

"You're back."

"I am."

He seemed to ponder for a moment. "You think I squandered my birthright."

"Those are your words, not mine."

"Then, give me your words."

She took a minute to come up with an answer. "I think you've always had a lot of options. And most of them were very pleasant options. It's not hard to understand why you'd choose the easiest path."

"Ouch."

"Who wouldn't?"

"Apparently not you."

"That's because I never had any easy options." The memories of her teenage years brought a knot to Amber's stomach. "I could work my butt off and only just get by, or I could give up and spiral down like my mother."

She took a drink, letting the cool water bathe her throat.

"Some might say spiraling down would be the easy path," said Tuck.

"To a point. But after a while, it gets a whole lot harder." The thought of living like her mother—the drinking, the smoking, crappy housing, used clothes, the carousel of shabby men—made her physically ill. She took another sip.

"What would you do?" he asked. "If you were me? If you had what I have?"

"I'm not trying to tell you that I'm morally superior."

"What would you do?"

Her instinct was to continue arguing the point. But instead, she considered the theoretical question. "Then or now?"

"Then. No, hindsight is too easy. Now. What would you do now?"

"If I were you," she said. "I'd go home. I'd leave Dixon alone, and I'd go home, work hard and prove to my father that he was dead wrong."

"Because that's the hardest path?"

"Because that's the most satisfying path."

Tuck stared into her eyes for a long time.

She grew uncomfortable, worrying she'd made him angry.

"Will you help me?" he asked.

The question surprised her. But there was only one possible answer. And she meant it sincerely. "I will."

"Will you like me?" As soon as he'd uttered the words, he looked away. But he wasn't fast enough to hide the uncertainty in his eyes.

She realized he'd made himself uncharacteristically vulnerable with the question. She knew she had to be honest. "I already like you."

His posture seemed to relax. "You're one in a million, Amber."

He couldn't be more wrong about that.

"I'm incredibly average," she said. "Thing is, in your world, you don't often come across incredibly average."

A knowing smile came across his face. "Stand up."

The request was abrupt and she wondered what she'd done wrong. Did he want her to leave? He didn't look angry. But then, it was getting late.

She stood.

"Put on your shoes."

She slipped her feet into the delicate high heels. But as she made to head for the door, he gently grasped her shoulders, turning her away, propelling her in the opposite direction.

"What are you doing?"

Before he answered, they were through a set of open double doors and into the bedroom.

"Look," he said, turning her toward a full-length mirror.

"What?"

There was nothing to see. The dress still looked great and it still went with the shoes. But her hair was coming loose and her makeup had faded. Her cheeks were rosy from the earlier wine and maybe from debating with Tuck. Her eyes were slightly shadowed with exhaustion. She really did need to get some sleep.

He brushed his fingertips across her shoulder, his tone going deep. "Is there anything about you that is remotely average?"

His words sent a tingle down her spine.

"You're amazing, Amber. You're flat-out amazing. You're gorgeous and smart as a whip. You're insightful and funny." He brushed her hair from the side of her neck. "And I can't get you out of my mind."

He eased slowly forward until his lips connected with the crook of her neck. They were soft and hot as she gazed at his image in the mirror. He kissed her again, lips wider this time, leaving a circle of moisture behind.

He planted a chain of kisses along her shoulder while his palms slipped down her bare arms. She watched his dark head, felt the air cool the moisture on her skin, let desire and arousal throb to life inside her. Then his hands came to rest on her waist, his blunt fingers splayed on her stomach, dark in relief against the glittery blue of the dress.

She leaned back against him. He was solid, a tower of muscle and strength. Their gazes met in the reflection, midnight blue and pewter gray. She let him in, not flinching, absorbing his obvious passion and returning it with her own.

He reached for the zipper at the back of her dress, watching her reaction closely as he drew it down. The air brushed her back and she quivered with the mix of sensations. He brushed aside the fabric and kissed her shoulder. His fingers delved into her hair, tugging at the clip and releasing thick waves.

She gasped in a breath and her hands curled into fists. It was the point of no return. No, it wasn't. She'd already passed no return when she'd met his eyes in the mirror. Her and Tuck, for now, at least for this small moment, were inevitable.

She shrugged her shoulders and the dress slipped down, the fabric cascading over her breasts, past her hips, pooling on the thick carpet.

His eyes darkened, his gaze pausing on her pink satin bra. It swept over her navel to the tiny matching panties, down the length of her legs to the sparkling shoes.

"One in a million," he whispered in her ear.

His hand closed over her breast and he kissed that first spot on her neck.

She knew she should look away, close her eyes and safely drown in the sensations of his touch. But she watched while he unhooked her bra. He set her breasts tumbling free. Then he let his fingertips roam from the curve of her hip, to the indentation of her naval, to the mound of her breast and her pearled nipples.

He touched and fondled while her temperature rose and her lungs dragged in air. When his hand dipped under her panties, urgency overwhelmed her. She turned in his arms, meeting his lips, tangling her limbs around him while his hand drove her to heights of passion.

"You are incredible," he rasped between kisses, peeling off the flimsy panties.

She pushed off his jacket, then struggled with his tie.

He tore off the new shirt and they came together, skin on skin, finally. He embraced her, held her tight, strong arms wrapped firmly around her as he explored every nuance of her mouth.

Then he lifted her and carried her to the big bed, yanking back the covers to deposit her on the crisp sheets. She lay on her back, watching as he stripped off his clothes.

When he was naked, he gazed down. He took in her disheveled hair, his eyes moving over her breasts to the shadow of her thighs, down the length of her legs. Then he smiled.

She realized she still wore her shoes.

She couldn't help but grin sheepishly in return.

"One of the things I love best about you," he said, coming to lie next to her on the mattress.

He renewed his exploration of her body, and she returned the favor, reveling in the taut muscles of his shoulders and arms, his washboard stomach and the strength of his hips and thighs. She kissed her way over his salty skin while he found her sensitive and erotic spots, the crook of her knee, the inside of her thigh, the tips of her nipples.

Then he rolled on top, his solid weight pinning her satisfyingly to the mattress. He took a second with a condom, then stared straight in her eyes.

She flexed her hips upward and felt him sliding inside. Her head tipped back and her eyes fluttered closed. Her world contracted to the cloud of sensation that was Tuck. His scent surrounded her. His heat enveloped her. His fingertips were magic and his lips were delicious.

His rhythm was slow and steady. First her bones melted to nothing. Then her limbs began to buzz. His pace increased and she couldn't contain her moans. Wave after wave of passion washed over and through her.

She couldn't move. She couldn't breathe. Her mind had gone into a free fall. And then the world burst open, and she cried out his name, hanging on tight, never wanting to let go.

Nine

Tuck knew that making love couldn't have been an easy decision for Amber. But for him it had been the easiest path, and definitely the most pleasurable path.

He eased onto his side, taking his weight from her and gathering her close. "I'm sorry," he whispered.

"For?" she whispered back. "Was that not your best work?"

He wanted to laugh, but he was afraid it would be the wrong reaction. "I know you weren't sure."

She turned her head and looked questioningly up at him.

"About making love," he elaborated.

"Did I not seem sure?"

"I guess you did."

"Should I have made you wait?"

"That might have killed me. I've been desperate for you since day one."

She smoothed her hand across his chest. "I've been resisting you for a while now."

He let his ego absorb the compliment.

She curled herself into a sitting position.

"What are you doing?" He wanted her to stay exactly where she was.

She moved to the edge of the bed. "Now that we've got that out of our system."

"Whoa, what?" His system was just getting started.

She rose and crossed the bedroom. "I realize it was inevitable. It might be nothing but chemistry, but it's still pretty powerful stuff."

Nothing but chemistry?

Okay, sure, he remembered saying that. Problem was he couldn't remember why.

She slipped into her panties, turning to face him while she dressed.

For some reason, he'd expected her to be shy. He wasn't sure why, maybe because of the clothes she usually wore.

He sat up, draping his legs over the edge of the bed. "You don't have to leave."

She stopped in the midst of fastening her bra, looking surprised. "We need to get to sleep. I assume we'll be leaving first thing in the morning."

"There's no rush."

They were flying in a Tucker jet. They could leave any old time they wanted. It didn't even have to be tomorrow.

"We've got a ton of work to do," she said. "I said I'd help, and I will. I'll do as much as I can. But you've got to do your part, Tuck. Dixon could be back soon. You might not have much time and you need to start proving yourself."

Wait a minute. "We *want* Dixon back."

"Sure we do. But not right away, not if you want to show your father you've got what it takes to run the company."

Tuck came to his feet. "I don't have what it takes to run the company."

Amber dropped the dress over her head, pushing her arms through the flimsy cap sleeves. "Maybe not yet."

"I don't know what you think I can do."

"You can start by hiring some new executives. Lucas needs help." She turned and presented him with the zipper.

He didn't want to zip her up. He wanted to strip her down again. He wanted her naked again, in his bed, in his arms, making love until neither of them could move and then sleeping until noon.

"I can't hire new executives."

"Zip me up. Yes, you can."

"That's a permanent decision. I'm temporary."

"You're a Tucker and you're in charge. Make a decision."

This was the first time Amber had struck him as being cavalier. She was normally careful and methodical.

"Is there something wrong with my zipper?" she asked.

"You don't have to go yet."

She reached back and zipped herself, making it most of the way up. Then she turned and gave him a quick kiss. "I'm exhausted."

"Sleep here."

She stilled, a stricken expression crossing her face. Just as quickly, it disappeared. "That's not going to happen."

"Why not?"

"This was a bad idea. I mean, it was a good idea, because it had to happen. But at its foundation, it was a terrible idea. We need to forget about it and move on."

"Move on to *what*?"

He didn't want to forget about what had just happened between them. It was the greatest sex of his life.

"Haven't you been paying attention?" she asked. "You're going to run Tucker Transportation. It goes without saying, but I'm saying it anyway, absolutely no good can come from a fling between us. It'll compromise your credibility and it'll destroy my career. You've fired me once. I'm not about to give you or Dixon or your father a reason to fire me again."

"Nobody's going to fire you."

She shook her head. "That's the *only* sure thing that happens when assistants get involved with their bosses."

"You can't know that."

She took a deep breath, squaring her shoulders. "Do you want to do this?"

He didn't dare hope she meant make love again. "Do what?"

"Do you want to *try*? Or do you want to spend the rest of your life as a self-indulgent playboy and a vice president in name only?"

"Those are my only two choices?"

"Yes."

"Then, I'm willing to try."

At least he could still spend time with her. And maybe he could manage to impress her. And maybe, if he was very lucky, their chemistry would rear its head again and she'd come back into his arms.

In the breezeway outside Tuck's hotel suite, Amber sagged against the wall. It had taken everything she had to pull off the act, to pretend that making love with Tuck hadn't thrown her for an absolute emotional loop.

She might not have been able to stop herself. But she knew she'd made one of the world's biggest mistakes. She had hopped into bed with her boss. She'd hopped into bed with her boss, and it was fantastic.

At least it had been fantastic for her. Who knew what it was for him? Maybe he had sex like that every Saturday night.

Maybe she'd been mediocre. Maybe he'd been disappointed. She forcibly stopped her brain from going there.

She wasn't going to do that to herself. If it hadn't been good for him, too darn bad. He'd have to get past it, maybe move on to someone else. She was moving on. She was definitely moving on.

She straightened from the wall, putting one foot in front of the other. Her room was along the courtyard and up one flight of stairs. She was going to shower and sleep, and then she was going back home to focus on Jade, the baby and Tucker Transportation.

Tonight was a lark. It didn't have to define her. It didn't even need to define her relationship with Tuck.

"Amber?" Jackson's voice came from a pathway at a right angle.

She stopped. Her heart sank and her stomach contracted into a knot of embarrassment and guilt.

She forced herself to turn and face him. "Hello, Jackson."

"I'm glad I caught you." His expression wasn't condemning, nor was it judgmental.

Maybe he hadn't guessed what had just happened.

She should play it cool. She could have taken her hair down for any number of reasons. From this angle, he couldn't see her zipper was partway down. She made a mental note to keep her back away from him.

"Did Dixon ever mention a woman?" he asked.

Amber forced herself to stay calm and collected. "What kind of a woman?"

She fought off the urge to smooth her hair. It would only call attention to the mess.

"Someone other than Kassandra."

"You mean a girlfriend?" She knew that wasn't possible.

"Yes."

"Dixon wasn't fooling around. He was as honorable as they come."

"I know you're loyal to him."

"That's not loyalty talking," said Amber. "Jackson, he didn't cheat on Kassandra."

"What about after they separated?"

"Nobody I ever heard about."

Jackson showed her his phone with a photo of a pretty blond woman. "Recognize her?"

"No. Who is she?"

"Is there any chance, any chance at all, that Dixon left Chicago to be with another woman?"

"He wouldn't leave Chicago to do that. His friends would be cheering from the rooftops. He wouldn't hide it."

Jackson was obviously deep in thought.

"What's going on?" she asked.

"I'm covering all the bases."

"Where did you get the picture?"

"She might be connected to the sailboat. We're tracking it down the coast."

"There might not be so much of a rush now."

Amber was warming up to the idea of Tuck proving himself to his father. He'd obviously spent his whole life riddled with self-doubt. She knew he'd feel good if he succeeded. And she knew he had it in him. He just had to apply himself.

Jackson's brow rose. "Why do you say that?"

"Tuck's going to run the company. It's the first chance he's ever had. This might even turn out to be a blessing in disguise."

Jackson didn't respond, but skepticism came into his eyes.

"You think it's a bad idea." She wished she hadn't come to respect Jackson's opinion.

"I think it's not Tuck's idea."

"It was. Kind of." She struggled to remember the exact details of the conversation. "He's always felt inadequate."

Jackson looked amused. "He's been too busy having fun to feel inadequate."

"You're wrong."

"You've known him how long?"

"A few weeks," she admitted.

Jackson gave her an indulgent smile. "He's not what you think he is."

"Don't patronize me."

"Then, let me put it another way. He's not what you want him to be." Jackson's sharp eyes took in her messy hair and what had to be smeared makeup.

In that second, she knew she was caught. And it was humiliating. Jackson thought she was going after Tuck. He thought she wanted to domesticate Tuck. She could only imagine he thought she was one of a long line of gold diggers out to become Mrs. Tuck Tucker.

She had to get out of here. "Good night, Jackson."

"I like you, Amber."

She gave a chopped laugh of disbelief.

"You're too good for him," said Jackson.

"I don't want him."

Jackson's smile was indulgent again. "You want him to be a better him."

She opened her mouth to deny it.

But Jackson spoke overtop her. "There's only one reason a woman wants that."

"There could be a hundred reasons why a woman wants that."

"You might not know it yet. But you're falling for him. Don't fall for him, Amber. You'll only get hurt."

"Advice to the lovelorn, Jackson?"

"Advice from a guy who knows Tuck."

"Well…" She had no good comeback to that. She truly didn't know what to say. All she knew was that she wanted the heck out of this conversation right now. "Thank you."

She turned sharply away, then realized he'd seen her partially undone zipper.

She swallowed. She lifted her chin and squared her shoulders. He'd obviously already guessed. He'd come to all the wrong conclusions afterward, but he knew full well that she'd just slept with Tuck.

When she looked up and saw Amber, Jade closed her textbook and pushed the wheeled bed tray off to one side. "Welcome back to the real world."

"I'm on my way to the office," Amber told her, moving closer. "We landed about an hour ago."

Taking a private jet to Scottsdale and back had been a surreal experience for Amber, but there was no disputing the convenience.

"How was it?" asked Jade with enthusiasm. "Warm? Great? I looked up the resort—*nice*."

"We were pretty busy working." Amber had struggled all night long, then especially during the flight back, to keep focused on the work and not to think about Tuck.

Jade gave a mock frown. "You didn't spend hours at the spa?"

"I'm afraid not."

"I was hoping to live vicariously through you."

"I could lie," Amber offered.

"Would you? That would be nice. I'm so bloated and tired and achy, I'd kill for a massage or a few hours in the hot springs."

"The weather was great," said Amber. "The hotel was gorgeous, the food, rooms. The beds were really comfortable."

"Was that a Freudian slip?"

Amber didn't understand Jade's point.

"Beds," Jade elaborated. "Plural?"

Amber realized it was a joke, but embarrassment made her mind go momentarily blank.

Jade's eyes went wide. "Wait a minute."

"It was a figure of speech," said Amber.

Jade's surprise turned to concern. "Tell me you didn't."

"I didn't do anything." At least nothing that was Jade's business, nothing that was anybody's business, except hers and Tuck's. And they were forgetting all about it.

"You *slept* with him?"

Amber didn't want to lie, so she didn't answer.

Jade reached for her hands. "Oh, Amber. You're usually so smart."

"It wasn't stupid."

"I don't want you to get hurt."

"I'm not getting hurt. It just…happened." Amber realized how trite that sounded. "It was only the once."

"He's your boss."

"Only for a little while. Dixon will come back and then it'll all be over. Tuck barely shows up at the office."

When Dixon got back, Amber fully expected Tuck to return to his previous life. He might want to impress his father, but he wasn't likely to give up the parties and vacations in order to work his butt off.

Last night she'd had a few moments of optimism. But she knew Jackson was right. Tuck liked his life exactly the way it was. Last night Tuck had told her what he thought she wanted to hear. He probably always told women what he thought they wanted to hear.

She lowered herself onto the bedside chair. "I don't know what I was thinking."

"You were thinking he was a superhot guy. At least, that's what I'm usually thinking."

Amber gave a helpless laugh. "He was. He is. Oh, man, he was good."

For the first time since it happened, she let the full bloom of their lovemaking rush through her mind. It had been amazing. And she wanted to do it again, so badly.

"At least there's that," Jade said softly.

"You say it as if it's a good thing."

"It's not?"

Amber straightened in the chair. "No, it's not. It would have been better to be disappointed."

"So you didn't want to do it again," Jade said with sage understanding.

"What is *wrong* with me? I'm no better than Margaret."

"Who's Margaret?"

"Tuck's father's secretary. Turns out she's having an affair with him."

"He's married?"

"Yes."

"Tuck's not married," said Jade.

"He's still my boss."

"True. But that makes it risky, not immoral. Those are two totally different circumstances."

"It was a mistake," Amber said, more to herself than to Jade. "But I'm over it. I can do that. I'm tough." She drew a bracing breath. "Now, what about you? Is everything still looking good?"

Jade's hand moved to her stomach. "She's kicking less. I bet it must be getting crowded in there."

"Is that normal?" Amber's gaze rested on Jade's bulging stomach.

"The doc says it often happens that way. My back is absolutely killing me." Jade moved and stretched in the bed.

"I'm sorry."

"And I've got heartburn and an overactive bladder. I'll be so glad when this is over."

"It won't be much longer," said Amber, feeling sympathetic. "I've been thinking I better get shopping. Have you thought about what you'll need? Can you make me a list?"

"You don't have to buy me things."

"You're going to need a crib and diapers."

"There's a secondhand store on Grand. We could check there after I get home."

"Sure," said Amber, knowing the least she could do was to buy her new niece a crib. She didn't want to make Jade feel bad about her financial circumstances, so she'd figure out the necessities on her own and get them ready.

"I should head for the office," she said, coming to her feet.

She wasn't looking forward to it, but she was confident that the more time she spent around Tuck in the office, the easier it would be to keep her feelings in perspective.

"In a way, it's reassuring," said Jade, a look of contentment on her face.

"What is?"

"To know you're not perfect."

"Who ever said I was perfect?"

"Mom, me, you."

"Me?" Amber couldn't imagine when or why she would have said that.

"You don't remember the straight As?"

"I didn't get straight As."

"You got a B plus in tenth-grade math."

"See?"

Amber remembered it well. It was a blight on the report card, as if someone had painted a black, hairy spider in the middle of a butterfly collage.

"You set your alarm for six fifty-three every morning."

It had made perfect sense to Amber. "I liked to lay there for two minutes before getting out of bed."

"You knew all the food groups. You talked about them at every meal."

"We didn't always have them."

"We never had them. But you knew what they were. I remember Mom giving us each five dollars for candy. She was drunk, of course, in an 'I love you, kids' mood."

Amber didn't like to remember her sloppy, tearful mother professing her love for them. It was inevitably followed by a monologue of self-pity, then a rant about how they didn't love her back. Then she'd vomit and pass out in the bathroom. More often than not, leaving a mess for Amber to clean up.

"Don't go back there," she said softly to Jade.

"I spent it all on chocolate," said Jade. "You bought chewable vitamins. I was baffled."

"I don't remember that," said Amber, searching her memory for the incident.

"You were perfect," said Jade.

"You make me sound pretentious and superior." What could Amber have been trying to prove?

"You didn't want us to die of scurvy."

But they hadn't been on the verge of malnutrition.

"We had juice with breakfast most mornings," said Amber.

"I hate to admit it, but part of me is glad you jumped into bed with your boss. If you're not all good, then maybe I'm not all bad."

"You're not bad, Jade."

"I'm pretty bad."

"No. And anyway, you're getting better."

"I'm trying."

"I'll try, too," said Amber.

"Try to do what? Be worse?"

"Be, I don't know… Normal, I guess, less uptight and judgmental. Those are not attractive qualities."

Jade grimaced as she shifted her back to a new position. "I realize now that you were trying to hold chaos together with your bare hands."

"Maybe I should have let it go."

Maybe if she had, Jade wouldn't have run away. Maybe if she hadn't been so morally superior, they could have worked together.

Then it came to her that she should do the same thing now—let things go. It was none of her business what Tuck did or didn't do with Tucker Transportation. Dixon's decisions were similarly his own. Why did she feel an obligation to control the situation?

"I can't see you doing that." Jade looked amused.

"A month ago, I wouldn't have been able to picture you writing your GED."

"Those are opposites."

"Not really."

"Don't change, Amber. I need you just the way you are."

For some reason, Amber's eyes teared up. She quickly blinked.

"I won't change," she promised. At least not so that Jade could see. But she wasn't going to badger Tuck anymore. Nobody needed that. She was surprised he'd put up with it this long.

Jamison's eyes were closed, his expression lax, and his wrinkled skin was sallow against the stark white of the hospital sheets. Machines whirred and beeped as Tuck moved cautiously toward the bedside, screens glowing and colored dots of LED lights blinking in different rhythms. There was an oxygen tube beneath Jamison's nose and an IV line in his arm.

It was odd seeing him like this. Tuck half expected him to open his eyes, sit up and bellow out orders.

"Dad?" Tuck said softly.

Sounds from the hallway drifted through the glass door and windows: a phone ringing, a nurse's voice, a cart wheeling by and the ping of an elevator.

"Dad?" he repeated.

Jamison's pale blue eyes fluttered open, looking cloudy instead of sharp.

"Hi, Dad," said Tuck.

He felt as though he ought to squeeze his father's hand or stroke his brow. But they didn't have that kind of relationship. There was no tenderness between them. Wary suspicion interspersed with crisp cordiality was more their style.

"Dixon?" Jamison rasped, then he coughed and grimaced with the effort.

"It's Tuck," said Tuck.

Jamison squinted. "Where's Dixon?"

"He's still away."

"Away where?"

"Sailing," said Tuck.

"On the lake?"

"Off the coast of California." Tuck paused. "I've been taking care of things while he's gone."

Jamison's frown deepened. Then he waved a dismissive hand, the IV tube clattering against the bed rail. "Where's your mother?"

Tuck pulled in a chair and sat down. "She's with Aunt Julie."

"Why?"

"Dad, you know you're in Boston, right?"

Jamison looked confused for a moment, then his brow furrowed deeply and he looked annoyed. "Yes, I know I'm in Boston."

"And you understand that you had a heart attack." Tuck was growing concerned with his father's apparent level of confusion.

"You must be feeling pleased with yourself." Jamison's voice seemed stronger. He gripped on to the bed rails.

"How so?"

"You got rid of me. And you've sent Dixon off somewhere. What have you been up to without us?"

Ah, yes. Tuck's father was back.

"I didn't give you a heart attack, Dad."

"I want to see your brother."

"Get in line," said Tuck. Then he regretted the sarcasm. "Dixon can't be reached right now."

"Of course he can. Call him."

"He's out of cell range."

"Then, send somebody after him, write a letter, use a carrier pigeon for all I care."

Tuck spoke slowly and clearly. "Dixon is gone. I can't find him and I can't get him back. That's why I'm here."

"This is nonsense," Jamison growled. "Just because I'm here in this hospital bed doesn't mean you can lie to me."

"I'm not lying to you."

"The business can't run without Dixon."

"It is running without Dixon, Dad. It's been running without Dixon for nearly two months."

Jamison opened his mouth, but Tuck kept on talking. "I'm here for your proxy."

Jamison's eyes bugged out. "My *what*?"

"I've held off as long as I can. But I need to make some decisions. I need to hire new executives and I need a proxy vote for your shares."

"It'll be a cold day in hell before I give you control of Tucker Transportation."

"It's only temporary."

"Where's Dixon?"

Tuck leaned slightly forward. "Dixon's gone. He left on his own and he hasn't come back."

"What's going on? Why are you doing this?" Jamison groped for the nurse call button and pressed it.

Tuck pushed back the chair and came to his feet. "I'm not *doing* anything. I'm jumping in to run your precious company."

"You don't know how to run the company."

"You're right about that."

The two men stared at each other.

A nurse breezed into the room.

"Mr. Tucker?" she asked. "Is something wrong?"

"Yes, something is wrong," Jamison stormed. "My son is telling me lies."

The nurse looked to Tuck and he gave a slight shake of his head.

"Are you in any pain?" The nurse checked his IV.

"I'm not in pain. My other son, Dixon, can you bring him here? I need to talk to him."

"I'm going to check your blood pressure." As she spoke, the nurse wrapped Jamison's arm in a blood-pressure cuff.

"Dad," Tuck began again, "you're in no condition to attend a board meeting."

Jamison tried to sit up.

"Oh, no, you don't," said the nurse, placing a hand on his shoulder. Her tone was calm but firm. "Your blood pressure is slightly elevated."

"Is that dangerous?" asked Tuck, wondering if he should leave.

"Only slightly," said the nurse. She frowned at Jamison. "You try to stay calm."

"I'm perfectly calm."

The nurse moved to the foot of the bed, making notes on the chart.

"Harvey Miller resigned," Tuck told his father.

"We have no finance director?"

"No."

"What did you do?"

"Nothing. He moved to a different company. People do that sometimes."

"Where did he go?"

"That's irrelevant. The important point is that I need to replace him. To do that, I need to formalize my position as interim president. So I need your proxy to vote your shares."

"You can't be president."

"Okay," said Tuck, thoroughly tired of this argument and every other one he'd had for the past decade. "I won't be president." He turned to leave.

"Dixon can be interim president."

"Sounds good," Tuck called over his shoulder. "Let me know how it all turns out."

"Bring him here," Jamison shouted out.

"Calm down," said the nurse.

Tuck stopped and turned back. "I'm sure he'll show up eventually. Until then, well, Tucker Transportation will have to survive without a finance director and without a president. I'm sure it'll be fine. After all, anything's better than having me in charge, isn't it?"

"Insolent," said Jamison.

"So you always say. I'm here. I'm offering to help. Take it or leave it. It's entirely up to you."

Jamison glared at him while the machines beeped his vital signs, the hospital hallway buzzed with activity and the nurse refilled his plastic water jug. Tuck almost felt sorry for his father—almost. Even when the man was all but desperate for Tuck's assistance, he'd only grudgingly accept it. How was that supposed to make a person feel?

"I'll give you my proxy," said Jamison. "Time limited."

"Fine," said Tuck.

He reached into his inside jacket pocket as he returned to the bed, producing the letter his lawyer had crafted. "We can both initial on an end date."

He approached the bed and maneuvered his father's tray into position. Then he jotted down a date one month away and stroked his initials next to the addition.

"I need my glasses," Jamison muttered.

Tuck spotted the glasses on the bedside table and handed them to his father. Then he handed over the pen and watched while Jamison signed over formal control of the company. Butterflies rose up unexpectedly in his stomach.

He didn't want this. He'd never sought it out. But now that he had it, he found he didn't want to fail.

Ten

"This was all your doing," Tuck said to Amber as he gazed at the aftermath of the party in the huge, high-ceilinged living room of his family's home.

Though staff had been ubiquitous throughout, she could see the mansion showed the effects of hosting two hundred people. The midnight buffet was being cleared away by the catering staff and the few glasses left on side tables were being dispatched to the kitchen.

"It doesn't look that bad," she responded.

He pulled at the end of his bow tie, releasing the knot. "I'm not blaming you for the mess."

"Then, what?"

He gestured to an armchair next to the marble fireplace.

Grateful, she sank down on the soft cream-colored leather. It was a relief to get off the four-inch heels.

Tuck sat in the opposite chair. "You convinced me I could do it."

"Throw a party?"

Tuck was nothing if not a party guy. She had to assume he'd thrown dozens, if not hundreds, of parties himself over the years.

"I meant run the company. If you hadn't pushed me to start making decisions, I never would have gone to see my father."

"And if you hadn't gone to see your father."

"I wouldn't have hired Samuel and Gena."

"I like Samuel and Gena."

"So do I. I'm not sure how my father's going to feel about them."

"Because they're too young to have such responsible jobs?" The two were both in their early thirties.

"I'm sure they won't fit his image of an executive."

"Do you think clients will care that Samuel wears blue jeans?" asked Amber.

"Lucas wears blue jeans."

"Operations and marketing are two different functions."

"True," Tuck agreed. "Thirsty? You want some ice water?"

"Sure."

Amber expected him to rise and pour some water at the bar. Instead, he subtly raised a hand and a staff member was instantly by his side.

"Yes, sir?" said the neatly dressed waiter.

"Can you bring us some ice water?"

"Right away, sir." The man withdrew.

Amber could only stare at Tuck for a moment.

"What?" he asked.

"Even knowing you were so rich, I didn't picture all this."

He gazed around at the soaring ceilings, wooden pillars and expensive oil paintings. "It is rather ostentatious."

"Flick of a finger and the ice water appears."

"I thought you were thirsty."

"I thought we'd pour it ourselves."

"Aah. You're uncomfortable with the household staff."

"I'm baffled by the notion of household staff."

"It's a big house," said Tuck.

"That doesn't mean you can't pour your own water."

"Are you calling me spoiled?"

"I always call you spoiled."

To her surprise, he shrugged. "Fair criticism. If it helps, I often pour my own water, and my own whiskey. I even go so far as to open my own beer bottle."

She couldn't help but grin. "Then, I take it all back. You're obviously a self-sufficient man."

The waiter returned, setting down a silver tray with two glasses and a pitcher.

"Shall I pour, sir?" he asked.

"We'll be fine, thanks," Tuck answered with a wry grin. The man left.

"Okay, now you're just trying to impress me," said Amber.

Tuck sat up and leaned forward. "Is it working?" He poured them each a glass, handing one to her.

"Be still, my beating heart."

"You do know it's not always like this."

"Always like what?"

"This many staff members, hanging out in the living room, dressed in a tux." He tugged off the tie and undid his top button. "Other parts of the house are a lot less formal."

She found herself glancing around again. "I would hope so. I'd be jumpy if I had to live in this 24/7."

He took a sip of his water. "Want to know a secret?"

"Has anyone ever said no to that question?"

He chuckled. "I guess not."

"Then, yes, do tell me your secret." She took a long drink, realizing she was very thirsty after a martini and two glasses of wine.

"The place makes me jumpy, too."

"Yeah, right." She continued drinking the water.

"I never liked this room. Or the library. You should see the library. Talk about pretentious and forbidding. My dad's fortress. It's positively gothic." He lowered his tone. "Nothing good ever happens in the library."

"Now you really have got me curious."

"You sure you're brave enough to see the library?"

"Oh, I'm brave enough. Besides, your father's not here."

"Check out the lion's den while the lion's away." He set down his glass. "You're very smart. That's what I like about you."

She gave a saucy grin at the compliment, but it also warmed her heart. It was nice to think that Tuck considered her intelligent. She'd certainly gained great respect for his reasoning and judgment. She'd also come to respect his hard work.

The past two weeks, she'd found herself wondering if he'd always been industrious, but simply focused on things other than Tucker Transportation. There was no doubt he'd raised the bar on being Chicago's preeminent playboy bachelor.

He came to his feet. "Let's go."

She rose and grimaced as her shoes pinched down on her swollen feet.

"Something wrong?" he asked.

"Would it be terribly rude if I took off my shoes?"

His mouth broke into a mischievous smile. "Shoeless in the library. You're a maverick, Amber, no doubt about it."

"Good thing your father's not around to see this." She peeled off the shoes and dropped them to the carpet.

"I may send him a picture."

"And get me fired?"

Tuck headed across the room and she fell into step beside him.

"Nobody's going to fire you," he said.

"You did."

"I was mistaken. And I've learned my lesson."

"Jamison was about to fire me. Dixon's the only one who hasn't wanted to send me packing."

"What do you mean Jamison was about to fire you?"

"When he had his heart attack," she admitted. "When I wouldn't tell him anything about Dixon. I swear the next words out of his mouth would have been *you're fired*."

"But he had a heart attack instead."

"I wasn't glad," she hastily told him, assailed by a wave of guilt. "I mean, even to save my job, I would never wish a heart attack on anyone. Maybe I should have told somebody. I guess that would have been you. Should I have told you? Or... Oh, no, do you think it was my fault?"

"Wow." Tuck came to a stop in the hallway, canting his body to face her. "You just did a whole big thing there all by yourself."

He seemed unusually tall, unusually imposing and unusually impressive.

"I really hadn't given it enough thought before," she said. "The man had a heart attack because I refused to help him. I'm not sure I deserve to keep my job."

"My father had a heart attack because of one too many rib eyes, and a fondness for chocolate truffles and Cuban cigars. Don't beat yourself up." Tuck put his hand on the knob of a dark paneled door. "Are you ready?"

"I'm not sure I'm through feeling guilty."

"Yes, you are. Of all the stressors in his life, you'd be ranked near the bottom. If you want to blame anyone, blame Dixon."

"Dixon *had* to get away."

"Yeah, yeah. We all know your opinion on that. Then, blame me. Or maybe blame Margaret. Keeping his affair a secret had to be stressful."

Amber couldn't argue with that. Tuck pushed the door and it yawned open.

As she walked in, antique lamps came up around the perimeter of the rectangular room, giving it a yellowish glow. The ceilings were arched, the woodwork dark and intricately carved and the books were lined on recessed shelves, secured behind fronts of black metal latticework.

There were clusters of armchairs with worn leather upholstery. And in the center of the room was an oblong table, set on two massive pedestals and surrounded by eight antique chairs, upholstered in burgundy damask.

"I can picture him here," she said, her voice sounding small in the imposing space.

"I try not to," said Tuck. Then he unexpectedly took her hand. "Come here."

"Why?" A flutter of reaction made its way up her arm, crossing into her chest. She was instantly aware of Tuck as a man, her attraction to him and the fact that they were completely alone.

"I want you to sit."

"Why?"

"Here." He pointed to one of the armchairs.

"What are you doing?" She didn't know what he had planned, but something in his voice was arousing her.

"Sit," he said softly.

She did.

"I want to picture you there," said Tuck. "With no shoes." He unexpectedly reached around her and unclasped her hair, letting it fall around her face. "Perfect," he said.

Then he paused, his gaze squinting down.

"What?" She felt suddenly self-conscious.

"One more thing." He reached out again, sliding his index finger under the spaghetti strap of her silver-and-ice-blue cocktail dress, dropping it down off her shoulder.

Her arousal ramped up, sending pleasure impulses along her thighs. She gazed up at him, unable to speak.

He took a step back. "*That's* what I'm going to remember in this room."

Her entire body heated under his gaze.

He watched her intently for a full minute, his eyes dark and clouded with obvious desire.

"You want to see my favorite room?" he asked.

She knew she should say no. It was the only reasonable answer. His question could mean anything and everything.

But her lips stubbornly formed the word *yes*.

Amber looked surprised when they entered the second-floor sitting room. Tuck could only imagine that she'd expected something bigger and grander. She gazed at the earthy rattan furniture, the watercolors on the walls and the stoneware vases atop pale maple tables.

"Not what you were expecting?" he asked.

"Not even close." She ran her hand over the back of the sofa, moving farther into the room.

With her bare feet, loose hair and the spaghetti strap still drooping over her shoulder, she seemed to belong here. She'd looked great in the library, the juxtaposition of such a feminine woman in such a masculine room. But here she looked fantastic. He wanted to close the door, lock out the world and maybe keep her here forever.

"It keeps me grounded," he told her.

"I've never thought of you as being grounded." Her pretty smile took some of the sting out of the words.

"What do you think of me as being?"

"Indulged, cosseted, lucky."

"I suppose I'm all of those things." He saw no point in denying it.

"It's more complicated than that." She looped around and came back to him.

"Nice of you to say so."

"I'm only being honest."

"Then, nice of you to notice," he said.

"It took me a while to notice." She stopped in front of him, all fresh faced and adorable. Her skin was satin smooth above the dress, lips a perfect pink, her hair just mussed enough to be off-the-charts sexy.

He remembered her naked. He remembered every single nuance of her body, the curve of her hip, the swell of her breasts, the blue of her eyes as passion overwhelmed her.

"Took me about half a second to notice you," he said gruffly.

"What did you notice?" She was so close, it was about to drive him crazy.

The slightest movement of his hand and he'd be touching her waist, feeling the pulse of her skin. If he leaned in, just a few inches, he could kiss her. Or at least find out if she'd let him kiss her. He picked up the scent of her hair. His fingertips twitched with the memory of her skin.

"Your eyes," he said. "Your shoes and your sassy mouth."

"Somebody has to keep you in line."

He eased slightly closer. "You want to keep me in line?"

She didn't answer, but her eyes darkened to indigo.

"Know what I want to do to you?" he asked softly.

Her lips parted.

He moved closer still, twining one hand with hers. He brushed back her hair, leaned in close to her ear.

"Kiss you," he whispered. "Pull you into my arms. Peel that dress from your body and make long, slow love to you."

"That wasn't…" Her voice went breathless. "What I was expecting."

"No?" He placed a kiss on her shoulder, reveling in the sweetness of her skin.

"I'm lying."

He kissed her again, closer to the crook of her neck. "Yeah?"

"It was exactly what I was expecting."

"But you came up here with me anyway?" His lips brushed her skin as he spoke.

"Yes." Her palms touched his chest, warm and intimate. "I want you, Tuck. I keep trying to ignore it."

He drew back to look into her eyes. "I can't ignore it."

"I feel as if we need to…" She toyed with a button on his dress shirt.

"Make love?"

"Set some ground rules."

He tenderly kissed her lips. "Sure. Whatever you want."

"This can't impact our working relationship."

He cradled her chin with his palm, kissing her again. He didn't see how that was possible, but he wasn't about to disagree. "Okay."

"You can't fire me, or promote me, or give me any better or worse treatment because I'm…"

"Completely and totally blowing my mind?"

"Tuck."

"I'm not going to fire you."

"Or promote me."

"Maybe. Probably. I think I pretty much already have. You want a new title?"

"You're not listening."

He kissed her again. "You're very distracting."

She pressed against him, her body molding to his. "We have to get this straight."

"Keep the boardroom out of the bedroom." He wrapped his arms around her, sighing in complete contentment. Up against him, wrapped around him, that was where she belonged. That was where he wanted her to stay.

"Right." She sounded surprised.

"Then, shut up, Amber. We're a long way from the boardroom."

He kissed her and passion roared to life within him.

She kissed him back, coming up on her toes, her arms winding around his neck. He tipped his head to deepen the kiss, pressing the small of her back, arching her body, inserting his thigh between her bare legs.

She groaned his name. Then she went for his belt, his button, his fly, her small hand all but searing him with need.

"Amber, don't." He could feel his control slip away.

"I can't wait," she rasped. "I've waited, and I'm done waiting."

She didn't have to wait.

He reached beneath her dress and stripped off her panties. Then he dropped into a chair, sitting her straight and square in his lap. She loosened his slacks and eased herself down. She was hot and tight, and each inch was a straight shot to paradise.

He bracketed her hips and pushed himself home.

She braced her hands on his shoulders. Her head tipped back. "Oh, yes," she whispered.

"You're amazing," he told her. "Fantastic. Spectacular."

Her nails dug in and her thighs tightened around him. He lost track of time as their pace increased. His world contracted and then disappeared. There was nothing but Amber. He didn't end and she didn't begin. They were fused to one and he needed to hold on to that forever.

She cried out his name and the sound pierced straight through him. Her body contracted and pulsed, and he followed her over the edge in a cascade of heat and sensation. He dropped back on the chair, cradled her face with his hands, pulled her down for a kiss, tasting her, breathing her, feeling life pulse through her, willing the euphoria to last forever.

Then he cradled her close, thinking how perfectly she fit against him.

"Stay," he murmured in her ear. "I want you in my bed. I want you in my arms. The night in Arizona was sheer torture after you left me."

Her chest rose and fell against his, the sound of her deep breaths echoing through the silent room.

"Okay," she finally said.

He drew back. "Okay?"

She nodded.

"Okay," he said, his body relaxing with relief. "Okay."

Amber's ringtone woke her from a sound sleep. She was instantly aware of Tuck's naked body wrapped around her, the faint sandalwood scent of his sheets and the sound of a fan whirring above the big bed. The phone rang again.

She pushed up on her elbow and groped for the bedside table. Tuck groaned and moved beside her. A moment later, the room was flooded with light. Her phone rang a third time as she blinked to adjust her eyes.

"Did you find it?" he asked.

"Yes. It's here." She fumbled with her cell as she answered, clumsy with sleep. "Hello?"

"Amber Bowen?" The woman's voice was crisp.

"Yes. It's me."

"This is Brandy Perkins calling. I'm a nurse at Memorial Hospital."

Amber sat straight up. "Hi, Yes." She had met Brandy a number of times. "Is something wrong?"

"Can you come into Maternity right away?"

"Yes, of course." Amber swung her legs to the side of the bed. "Is Jade all right?"

Tuck sat up beside her.

"Her blood pressure has taken an unexpected spike."

Tuck's hand cradled her bare shoulder, his voice deep and soft. "Something wrong?"

"The baby has gone into distress, and we're performing an emergency C-section."

"I'm on my way." Amber rose from the bed as she ended the call.

Tuck's voice was sharper, more alert. "What's wrong?"

"I need to get to the hospital. It's Jade." Amber tracked down her panties, stepping into them and locating her bra.

He rocked to his feet. "I'll drive you."

"No. That's okay. I've got my car."

"You're upset. You shouldn't drive yourself." He was dressing as he spoke.

"I don't know how long I'll be."

"So what?"

"So I want to take my car."

Her dress on, she headed for the bedroom door. Her shoes were still down in the library. She was pretty sure she remembered the way back.

Tuck followed. "What happened?"

"It's her blood pressure. The baby's in distress and they have to do an emergency Caesarean. I knew there was a chance, but things were looking so good. I didn't expect…"

She knew Jade's condition could be life threatening, for both Jade and the baby. But she hadn't wanted to face that possibility. She'd been too optimistic, too cavalier about the potential danger.

She should have paid more attention to how Jade was feeling. Maybe if she'd spent more time at the hospital instead of throwing a party and sleeping with Tuck. What if she'd left her phone in her purse downstairs and didn't hear it ring? What if the battery had died overnight?

"Jade's already at the hospital?" Tuck asked as they took the stairs.

"She's been there for two weeks."

"Why didn't you say something?"

"Say what?"

Amber's personal life was another thing she was keeping separate. Tuck had barely even met Jade.

"Tell me something that big was going on in your life."

"Why?" She entered the library.

Luckily, the lights were still on, and she quickly located her shoes.

"Oh, I don't know," said Tuck. "Because we see each other every day."

"Only because we work together."

She marched toward the living room. Her car keys were in her purse. She was maybe thirty minutes from the hospital, twenty-five if traffic was light, which it ought to be at 3:00 a.m.

"Right," said Tuck, a strange tone in his voice. "We work together. That's all."

She paused to take in his expression. "I have to go to my sister right now."

"I'll drive you."

"No, you won't. Good night, Tuck."

"It's morning."

She didn't even know how to respond to that. She left through the front door, taking the long driveway past the brick entry pillars and onto the street.

Traffic was blessedly light and she was able to find a good parking spot at the hospital. She rushed through the lobby, going directly to Jade's room. She knew her sister wouldn't be there, but she hoped the nurses could give her some information.

Brandy was at the nurse's station.

"How is she?" Amber asked, realizing she was winded.

"Still in surgery," said Brandy.

Amber didn't like the look on the woman's face. All the way here, she'd been telling herself it was going to be fine. Jade was going to be fine. The baby was going to be fine.

Amber swallowed. "How bad?"

Brandy came around the end of the counter. "She had a seizure."

Amber felt her knees go weak.

Brandy took her arm. "Let's sit down."

"Is she…" Amber couldn't bring herself to ask the question. "What about the baby?"

"They're doing everything they can." Brandy led her toward a sitting area in a small alcove.

"I don't like the sound of that." It was not at all reassuring.

Brandy sat next to her on a narrow vinyl sofa. "The baby is very close to term."

"So she has a fighting chance."

"Very much so," said Brandy.

"And all I can do is wait."

"I know it's hard."

Amber nodded. She was sitting here wondering if her sister and her niece were going to live or die.

"Can I get you something?" asked Brandy. "There's coffee in the corner or water?"

"I'm fine."

"Would you like to freshen up?"

Amber glanced down at her dress and realized how she must look. She hadn't removed her makeup before tumbling into bed with Tuck. It was probably smeared under her eyes. Her hair had to be a fright.

"That bad?" she asked the nurse.

Brandy gave her a smile. "You'll be able to see Jade once she wakes up, not to mention hold the baby. You don't want to scare them."

"Yes," said Amber. "Let's think positively."

A woman in scrubs came through a set of double doors.

Brandy took Amber's hand and Amber's heart sank through the floor.

They rose together.

"Dr. Foster, this is Jade's sister, Amber," said Brandy.

"Jade is weak," the doctor said without preamble. "We had to restart her heart."

Amber's legs nearly gave way.

"She's in recovery," said Dr. Foster. "Her vital signs have stabilized and her blood pressure is under control."

"She'll be all right?" Amber felt the need to confirm.

"We expect her to make a full recovery."

"And the baby?"

The doctor smiled. "The baby is healthy. A girl."

"I have a niece?"

"She's in the nursery. You can see her if you want."

Amber gave a rapid nod, her eyes tearing up. Worry rose up from her shoulders and she felt instantly light.

Eleven

As soon as Amber had left the mansion, Tuck realized he'd been a total jerk. Her sister was having emergency surgery. What did it matter if he and Amber's relationship was up in the air? They could talk about it tomorrow, or the day after that, or the day after that.

She'd made love with him. Then she'd spent the night with him. He'd reveled in holding her naked in his arms, joking and laughing with her. He'd looked forward to breakfast together, mentally filing away another image of her in his family home.

Instead, he'd showered and changed, stopped to pick her up some coffee and a bagel and made his way to the hospital. She had to be exhausted, and distressed, and he was determined to make up for his behavior. She needed his support right now. She didn't need him arguing with her.

It took some time to locate the maternity wing. But once there, he was told visiting hours didn't start until seven and he had to wait in the lobby. He gave in and drank both cups of lukewarm coffee, finally getting on the elevator with the blueberry bagels for Amber.

As he approached the room, he could hear her voice. It was melodic and soothing.

"She's incredible," she was saying.

"Isn't she?" Jade responded, her voice sounding slightly weak.

Tuck paused to brace his hand on the wall, relief rushing through him. He hadn't realized he'd been that worried.

"Thank you," said Jade. "For being here. For helping us."

"Don't be silly," Amber responded. "Of course I'm here, and of course I'm helping."

"You always do."

"She has your eyes," said Amber.

"I thought of a name."

"You did?"

"After you. I'm going to name her Amber."

For some reason, Tuck's chest went tight.

"I don't know," said Amber.

"We owe you so much."

"I'm her aunt. It's my job, and she doesn't owe me a thing. Look at that face, those blue eyes, that tiny nose."

There was a silent pause.

"I think," Amber continued, "that she's her very own little person. She deserves her very own name."

"You think?" asked Jade.

"I'm sure. Thank you. Really, it's a wonderful thought."

There was a pause and Tuck took a step forward.

"What about Crystal?" asked Jade.

"Another rock?" There was a trace of laughter in Amber's voice.

"You're solid as a rock," said Jade.

"So are you," said Amber.

"And she will be, too."

"Crystal. I love it. It's perfect."

Tuck knew he should either walk away or announce himself, but something kept him still and silent.

"Do you think the three of us can become a family?" asked Jade, a catch in her voice. "The way we never were."

"Yes," Amber said softly. "You, me and Crystal. We can do that."

"No creepy boyfriends."

Tuck found he didn't like the sound of that. He wasn't creepy. Then again, he wasn't a boyfriend.

"No unreliable men," Amber stated firmly.

Did she think of him as unreliable? She probably did. She probably thought Dixon was more reliable, which wasn't fair, given the current circumstances.

He gave himself a mental head slap. If he didn't want to keep hearing things he didn't like, he needed to stop eavesdropping.

"She's never going to be frightened," said Jade, as Tuck moved for the door. "Or hungry, or lonely."

"We'll keep her safe."

"I'll get a job," said Jade.

"Not today, you won't."

He knocked softly on the open door. "Hello."

Amber looked up. She was sitting in a chair at the bedside covered in a pale green hospital gown, a pink bundle in her arms. He couldn't see the baby's face, but she had a head of dark hair—a brunette like her aunt.

Jade was propped up in the bed, looking exhausted, her face pale, her hair flattened against her head.

"Tuck." Amber was obviously surprised to see him.

"I wanted to make sure everything was okay." He glanced at the paper bag in his hands, realizing he should have brought flowers or maybe a teddy bear.

"Hi, Tuck," said Jade. She seemed less surprised and gave him a tired smile.

"Congratulations, Jade." He moved to get a better view of the baby. "She's beautiful."

"Isn't she?" asked Jade.

"Are you okay?" he asked, giving in to an urge to squeeze her hand.

"Sore. But I'm going to be fine."

"I'm very glad to hear that."

His attention went back to Amber and the baby. She looked good with a baby in her arms, natural, radiant.

"How did you know I was here?" asked Jade.

Amber's eyes widened.

Tuck paused to see how she'd answer.

She didn't.

"Were you with him last night?" asked Jade.

She was very quick on the uptake for someone who'd just had surgery.

"It was a corporate party," said Tuck.

"We spent the night together," said Amber.

Her answer thrilled him. Yes, they'd spent the night together. And he didn't care who knew it.

"Sorry to interrupt," said Jade, glancing between them.

Tuck grinned with amazement. "You had to have one of the best excuses ever."

Jade chuckled and then groaned with obvious pain.

"I'm sorry," he quickly told her.

"Don't apologize for being funny."

"I didn't mean for it to hurt."

Crystal let out a little cry.

"It does," said Jade. "I hate to whine, but it hurts a lot."

"Do you need me to get the nurse?" he asked.

Crystal wiggled in Amber's arms, emitting a few more subdued cries.

"Maybe you should," said Jade, holding out her arms to take Crystal. "I want to try to feed her again. You should go home," she said to Amber.

"No way."

"Get some rest. Take a shower."

"I don't need to rest."

"Yes, you do."

Amber hesitated.

"I can drop you," said Tuck.

"I have my car." She stood to hand the baby to Jade. "Okay, but I'm coming back."

"I would hope so."

Tuck started for the corridor to find a nurse.

Amber's voice followed him. "Goodbye, sweetheart."

He knew she was talking to the baby, but he loved the word anyway.

He located a nurse and then met Amber in the hallway.

"You look exhausted."

"I am *so* relieved." She pulled off the gown, revealing last night's dress. "Her heart actually stopped."

Tuck automatically reached for Amber, pulling her to him. "How can I help?"

"I'm fine. I was terrified, but I'm fine now."

"Let me take you home."

"There's no need."

"It'll make me feel better. I need to do something useful."

"You're very useful. You signed up four new accounts last night."

"I mean useful to you."

"You're keeping the company afloat, keeping me in a job, helping me pay my bills."

Tuck drew back, a bolt of comprehension lighting up his brain. "Twenty-eight thousand, two hundred and sixty-three dollars."

"Huh?"

"Jade was already in the hospital when you came back. That was the amount on her bill. You asked for a signing bonus. You agreed to help me. You did it all because of her."

He could tell by Amber's expression that he'd hit the nail on the head. Then he wondered what else she'd done because of her sister.

He backed off. "Is that why you're helping me with the company?"

"In part, yes. I need a job right now, Tuck. More than I've ever needed a job in my life."

He loosened his hold on her and drew back. "And the rest?"

Her expression narrowed. "The rest is the rest." She didn't elaborate and he didn't jump in. "I hope you're not asking if I slept with you to protect my job and support my sister."

He was. No, he wasn't. He wasn't, but he couldn't help but worry that her behavior with him was laced with complexities.

"Don't worry about it," she said.

"Don't worry about *what*?"

"I'm going home to change." She glanced down at her dress. "I look ridiculous. I'll see you at the office tomorrow."

She tossed the hospital gown in a nearby bin and turned for the elevators.

He wanted to call her back. He needed to understand where she was coming from, what she was feeling for him, what last night had meant to her. But he couldn't let himself be selfish again. She'd had a rough night. Jade needed her. And Tuck was simply going to have to wait to find out where he stood among everything else in Amber's life.

They might have spent the night together...well, half the night together. But everything Amber knew about Tuck remained true. No matter how tempting it was to let him drive her home and comfort her, she couldn't let herself pretend they were in a relationship. He was her boss, not her boyfriend. At best, they were having a fling. At worst, she was a two-night stand.

She had Jade and she had her new niece, Crystal. They were her family, her personal life, her emotional support. It wasn't Tuck.

In the office Monday morning, she steeled herself to see him. She dropped her purse into her desk drawer and plunked down on her chair. She told herself they'd worked the party together like a practiced team, picking up on each other's cues, making clients laugh and agree and, most important, closing the deal.

That had to be enough. It was *going* to be enough. She scrunched her eyes shut and gritted her teeth. She wasn't going to allow herself to want more.

"Good morning, Amber." Dixon's voice nearly startled her out of her chair.

"Dixon?" she squeaked, her eyes popping open.

He looked tanned and toned and totally relaxed.

"I'm back," he said simply.

"Where? How?"

Dixon wasn't the hugging type, so she didn't jump up to embrace him.

His smile faded. "I heard about my dad. I flew straight to Boston yesterday and then I came here."

"Welcome back." She was happy to see him.

She told herself it was an enormous relief to have him here. Things could get back to normal now. She could stop juggling so many problems and Tuck—

She swallowed. Tuck could get back to normal, too.

"He in there?" Dixon cocked his head to Tuck's closed office door.

"I think so."

"Great." Dixon's intelligent gaze took in the clutter on her desk. "Looks as if you're busy."

"It's been busy," she agreed.

"But you'll move back to my office?"

"Of course I will. Right away."

"Good."

"How was your trip?"

"Enlightening."

"You feel better? You look better."

"I feel better than ever. I can't wait to get back to it."

"Great. That's great."

Tucker Transportation would be in experienced hands once again.

Just then, Tuck's office door opened. He appeared in the doorway and instantly spotted Dixon.

From behind her desk, Amber could feel Tuck's shock. His expression seemed to register disappointment. But then it quickly went to neutral.

"Dixon." Tuck's tone was neutral, too.

"Tuck," Dixon answered evenly.

"You're back."

"You're about the twenty-fifth person to say that."

Tuck glanced at Amber.

"I said it, too," she said into what felt like an awkward silence.

"You know about Dad?" Tuck asked.

Neither man moved toward the other, and she was struck by the wariness of their attitudes. Dixon had to be wondering if Tuck was angry. She couldn't tell what Tuck was thinking.

"I saw him yesterday," said Dixon.

"But you didn't call? Didn't think to give me a heads-up?"

It was Dixon's turn to glance at Amber and then at Tuck. "Should we step inside your office?"

Tuck crossed his arms over his chest. "I don't know why. You seem to like to keep Amber more informed than you keep your own brother."

Dixon seemed taken aback.

"She didn't give you away," said Tuck, finally taking a step forward.

Amber found herself glancing anxiously down the hall, worried that other staff might overhear their argument.

"I fired her," said Tuck. "And she still wouldn't tell me your secrets."

Now Dixon looked confused.

"Where you were," Tuck elaborated. "Where'd you go?"

"*Why* would you fire Amber?"

"Insubordination."

"No way."

"To me, not you."

Amber couldn't stand it any longer. "Tuck, please."

Tuck gave a cold smile. "The loyalty's returned just like that." He snapped his fingers. "I guess it never really went away."

"Amber's as loyal as they come," said Dixon.

She moved from behind her desk. "I'm going to let you two talk." She nodded at Dixon. "Maybe an office or the boardroom?"

"Good suggestion."

"She's full of them," said Tuck.

"Has he been treating you like a jerk?" Dixon's question was for Amber, but he stared at Tuck as he asked it.

Amber met Tuck's gaze. "Not at all."

Tuck stared back. "Except when I fired her."

Dixon seemed to pick up on the tension between them. "How'd you get her back?"

"Money," said Tuck.

"A signing bonus," said Amber.

Dixon grinned at that. "Well, there's no doubt she's worth it. If she'd been permanently gone, you'd be answering to me."

Tuck's jaw tightened. "As opposed to you explaining *to me* where the hell you've been for two months?"

"I suppose I owe you that."

Amber moved again, determined to leave. "You have a ten o'clock with Lucas," she told Tuck.

"Maybe," he responded.

What did that mean? Was he heading out the door before 10:00 a.m.? Now that Dixon was in the office, would Tuck simply walk out?

Good.

Great.

It really didn't matter to her either way.

With the two men sizing each other up, she quickly made her way down the hall. She'd set herself up outside Dixon's office once again. Tuck could come and say goodbye or not. It was entirely up to him.

Tuck stared at his brother across the table in the meeting room.

"I told him I needed to get away," said Dixon. "He wouldn't listen."

"I heard." Tuck didn't see any point in hiding anything. "I overheard the two of you talking in the library. I heard what he said about me as a vice president."

"Were you surprised?"

Tuck hadn't been surprised. But he had been disappointed.

"Nobody wants their father to have such a low opinion of them."

"We're talking about Jamison Tucker."

"He likes you just fine."

"Yeah," Dixon scoffed. "Well, we all know why that is."

"Because you're the anointed one."

"I mean the other."

"What other?"

Dixon stared at him in silence and obvious confusion.

"I have no idea what you're talking about," said Tuck.

"The affair."

"With Margaret?"

Dixon drew back. "Who's having an affair with Margaret?"

"Dad."

"What?" Dixon was clearly shocked. "What on earth makes you say that?"

"Because it's true. Margaret gave it away to Amber."

"It's not like Amber to gossip."

"She wasn't gossiping. Wake up, man. Do you know what you've got in Amber? The woman will practically take a bullet for you. She has more character than you can imagine."

Dixon's intelligent eyes sized him up. "Got to know her pretty well while I was gone?"

Tuck was not about to give away anything that might embarrass Amber. "Got very frustrated with her at one point." Then his mind jumped back in the conversation. "What affair were *you* talking about?"

"Mom's."

"Whoa. No way."

"You knew about it."

Tuck knew no such thing. "Who thinks Mom had an affair?"

"Dad."

"What? When? And he's living in a glass house, by the way."

"Three decades ago."

"Clearly that's relevant." Tuck knew their father's affair had gone on right up to his heart attack.

Dixon carefully enunciated his next words. "Thirty years ago. In the months *before* you were born."

Everything inside Tuck went still. "Are you saying?"

"How do you not remember that huge fight we overheard?"

"Are you saying I'm not Jamison's son?"

"You are his son. He did a DNA test years ago."

"Then, how is that the thing? Why would it make him hate me?"

"He doesn't hate you."

"He has no use for me."

"My theory," said Dixon, "is that he looks at you and remembers you could have belonged to someone else."

"That's really messed up."

Dixon scoffed out a cold laugh. "Up to now, you thought we were a normal, functional family?"

Tuck came to his feet as everything became clear. He'd never had a chance. He'd been fighting for something he couldn't possibly win. He had to get out of here, leave the company, maybe leave the city. Maybe he'd leave the state and the money behind and find his own life and career.

There was a brisk knock on the door before it opened to reveal Lucas.

Lucas didn't miss a beat when he saw Dixon. "You're back."

"I'm back."

"Good. Tuck, Gena wants to join us at ten."

"Who's Gena?" asked Dixon.

"Our new finance director."

"Why do we have a new finance director?"

"Harvey quit," said Tuck.

"Why?"

"He missed you."

"What did you do?" Dixon's tone was decidedly accusatory.

"Nothing," said Tuck, heading for the door. "Hasn't that always been the problem?"

"I'll try to get him back," said Dixon.

Tuck halted, a flash of anger hitting him. Dixon intended to reward Harvey for his disloyalty?

Tuck opened his mouth to protest, then decided not to waste his breath. Dixon was back. Tuck's father was never, *ever* going to accept him. And what Tuck liked or didn't like no longer had any relevance.

"Whatever," he said without turning. To Lucas he said, "Dixon can take the ten o'clock."

Twenty paces down the hall, he came to Amber at her old desk outside Dixon's office. She was setting out her things, settling in.

"So that's that?" he asked, struggling to come to terms with his life turning so suddenly and irrevocably upside down.

"My boss is back." She didn't pretend not to understand.

"You bailed quick enough."

"He asked me to move here."

"And what Dixon wants—"

Amber glared at Tuck.

He wanted to tell her she couldn't, that she should march back to her desk at his office to work with him, not with Dixon. He wished he had the right. He wished he had the power. Against all reason and logic, he wished his brother had never come home.

"What about you?" she asked, adjusting the angle of her computer screen.

Unlike her, he did pretend to misunderstand. "My office has been in the same place for years."

"And what are you going to do in it now?"

"Nothing."

He could take a hint. Well, maybe he couldn't take a hint. But he could understand the bald truth when it was thrown up in his face. He wasn't wanted here. And there was nothing he could do to change it. He might as well have been born to a different father.

Two months ago, it probably wouldn't have mattered. But

it mattered now. Maybe it was pride. Or maybe he liked the sense of independence and accomplishment. Or maybe he just liked Amber.

He was going to miss her.

He wasn't sure he could leave her.

"You're walking away," she said.

"I am." He had to stifle the urge to explain.

He knew she understood dysfunctional families, and he knew she'd understand what he was going through. But he couldn't presume they had a personal relationship. She'd made that clear enough at the hospital yesterday morning. She was his brother's assistant, and that was all.

"I won't be your boss anymore," he said, determined to give it one last shot.

"We both knew that would happen."

That wasn't a hint one way or the other. She wasn't giving him any help here.

"We could," he said. "You know…"

She raised her brows and looked him in the eyes.

"Date," he finally said, wondering what the heck had happened to his suave, sophisticated style.

"Each other?"

Okay, now he was just getting frustrated. "*Yes*, each other."

"Is that a good idea?"

"I'm suggesting it, aren't I?"

"You're free now, Tuck. And you're practically running for the front door. And that's fine. I understand. You never said or did a thing to suggest otherwise. And you don't need to now. Dixon's here. You have your life back."

Tuck stared at her in silence.

That was how she saw him? Well, at least he knew the truth. Even after all they'd done together, how hard they'd worked to save clients and accounts, she thought he'd only been biding his time until he could go back to the party circuit.

"I'm free," he agreed between gritted teeth.

"Then, no reason to linger."

He stared hard into her eyes. "No reason at all."

Unless he counted how he felt about her, how much he wanted to be with her, how hard he wished she'd see something in him besides an irresponsible playboy.

"I'm going to be busy with Dixon," she said airily. "And with Jade, and with Crystal."

"I'm going to be busy getting my name back in the tabloids." As he said it, he willed her to call his bluff.

She didn't even hesitate. "Good luck with that."

"Thanks."

There was nothing left to say. But the last thing he wanted to do was leave.

He wanted to hug her. He wanted to kiss her. At the very least, he wanted to thank her for the help and for the amazing memories.

Instead, he left without a word.

Twelve

Amber missed Tuck, and the hurt was beyond anything she could have imagined. Each day she arrived at the office and promised herself it would be better. She'd think about him less, stop imagining his voice, stop thinking every set of footsteps in the hallway might be his. She was going to get past it.

Jade was home from the hospital and Crystal was adorable. Though the baby wasn't the best sleeper in the world. Amber told herself that living in a state of mild sleep deprivation had to be contributing to her depression. Surely, one man couldn't be the cause of all this.

Dixon had slipped right into the familiarity of his old job. He was definitely in a more upbeat mood, but he was just as efficient as always, no matter what the crisis.

It was coming up on eleven and the phone had been ringing almost constantly. There was a storm in the Atlantic and a major rock slide across one of the main rail lines between Denver and Salt Lake City. Everybody was rerouting and rescheduling.

"The Blue Space file?" Dixon called through the open door of his office.

Amber knew the Blue Space file was in Tuck's office. She'd been avoiding going in there, worried about triggering memories. Not that anything specific had ever happened in his office. They hadn't kissed and they certainly hadn't made love there. Thank goodness, at least, for that.

"I'll get it," she called back.

"They're phoning right after lunch," said Dixon.

"On my way."

She took a bracing breath and stood. She was going to do

this. In fact, she wanted to do this. Maybe it would be a turning point. Maybe she'd built it up to be something it wasn't. She could probably walk in there, get the file, walk back out and realize it was just another room.

She headed down the hall.

Tuck's office door was closed. But she refused to slow down. She reached out, turned the knob, thrust the door open and walked inside.

There, she stopped, gasping a breath, picking up his scent, her brain assailed by memories. Tuck laughing. Tuck scowling. His brows knitted together in concentration.

She could hear his voice, feel his touch and imagine his kiss.

"Amber?" Dixon's voice startled her.

"I'm sure it was on the desk," she said, pushing herself forward.

There was a stack of files on the corner of the desktop and she began looking through them.

"I'm meeting Zachary for lunch," said Dixon.

"Zachary who?" She tried to remember if there was a Zachary connected with Blue Space.

"Zachary Ingles."

She looked up. "Why?"

Dixon moved closer. "I'm trying to get him to come back."

"Why would you do that?"

"Because he's good. And he took a bunch of accounts with him when he left."

"There's nothing good about that."

She'd never liked Zachary. She didn't trust him and she'd been glad to see him leave. The new guy, Samuel Leeds, was much more professional. He was young, but he seemed to be learning fast.

Dixon chuckled. "I know Zachary's not the warmest guy in the world."

Amber continued sorting. It wasn't her place to criticize, and she didn't want to insult Dixon.

"Samuel's a bit too laid-back," said Dixon. "He's inexperienced. A director position isn't the place to learn the ropes."

"He's enthusiastic," said Amber.

"A little too enthusiastic."

Dixon had said the same thing about Gena, the new finance director. He hadn't replaced her yet, but Amber knew he'd been in contact with Harvey.

"Are you going to undo everything Tuck did?" As soon as she asked, Amber immediately regretted the question.

"You mean, am I going to undo the damage?"

She practically had to bite her tongue.

"It must have been bedlam around here." Dixon crossed his arms over his chest.

"Who says that?"

"Harvey, for one."

"Consider the source."

Dixon didn't respond and Amber realized she'd gone too far.

"What did that mean?" asked Dixon, a clear rebuke in his tone.

Amber straightened and squared her shoulders. She was loyal to Tucker Transportation and she'd been appropriately loyal to Dixon. She now found herself feeling some of that loyalty toward Tuck.

"Tuck worked hard," she said.

"I've no doubt that he did."

"He not only worked hard—he succeeded. Yes, Harvey and Zachary bailed. But you should ask yourself what that says about them."

"They couldn't work with Tuck."

"Or they *wouldn't* work with Tuck. Zachary stole your clients. He *stole* them. He was disrespectful to Tuck. He was disloyal to you. He was downright dishonest. And, by the way, he hits on your female employees. Tuck, on the other hand, came in here without the first idea of what to do. He could have bailed. He could have turned and run the other way. But he didn't. He dug in. Even knowing what your father thought of him, and how he'd been treated in the past, and how overwhelming the learning curve turned out to be, he stuck it out. Did you thank him? Did your dad thank him? Did anyone thank him?"

"We paid him."

"He didn't do it for the money. And he didn't do it to save the company. He has pride, Dixon. He had purpose. We won back half the clients and we signed up some more. He worked eighteen-hour days, threw his heart and soul into making sure the company didn't fail while you were off sailing. He hunted far and wide to get Gena and Samuel. Yes, they're both young. But they're well educated. They have some experience. And they're bringing new energy to the company. And that's thanks to Tuck, who was thrown in here without a lifeline."

Amber stopped talking. As she did, the magnitude of her outburst hit her.

"Amber?" Dixon began, clearly baffled by her behavior.

She was instantly overcome with regret. She knew she was about to get fired by the third Tucker Transportation owner. It was going to be a clean sweep.

"Yes," she said in a small voice.

"Did something happen between you and Tuck?"

She ignored the personal implication of the question. "I got to know him." It was an honest answer.

"You got to know him well?" Dixon was watching her carefully.

"Better than before. When he first showed up, I thought the same thing you obviously do—that he was a lazy playboy who was going to fall flat on his face and wouldn't even know it when he did. I wouldn't even help him. I mean, I helped him, of course. But I wasn't going the extra mile like I might have been. But then I saw how hard he worked. He truly was dedicated. And I started to understand that he hadn't chosen to stay away—your father had barred him entry."

"He has an office," said Dixon.

"That's what I said. And he does. But nobody wants him. He understands that full well."

"Amber?"

"What?"

Her fear was gone. Whatever was going to happen was going to happen. But she wasn't about to turn her back on Tuck. He'd worked hard and she wouldn't pretend that he hadn't, even to please Dixon.

"That wasn't my question."

She hesitated. "I know."

"What happened between the two of you?"

"Nothing."

Dixon waited, looking unconvinced.

"Okay, something," she said. "But it's over and done."

Silence settled thick in the air, but she refused to break it. She'd already said too much.

Dixon went first. "Are you in love with Tuck?"

She felt the world shift beneath her feet. "No."

She couldn't be. She wouldn't be. She'd made mistakes with Tuck, but she wouldn't make that one.

"I'm sorry," said Dixon.

"For what?" Was she about to be fired after all?

"That Tuck hurt you."

"He didn't hurt me."

And if he had, she'd get over it. She'd seen what falling for the wrong man could do, *would* do. She wasn't going to do that to herself.

Dixon gave a considered nod. "Okay. Tell me what else you know about Samuel."

"Why?"

"Because you just made an impassioned plea on his behalf. Do you want to drop the ball now?"

She didn't. "He works well with Hope. And I respect Hope. She has her finger on the pulse of social media."

"You think we need social media?"

"That's like asking if you need telephones or computers.

Yes, you need social media. Your father might not have seen it, but you need to think about the next twenty years, not the past twenty years."

"I'll give it some thought," he said.

She couldn't quite let it go. "*It* meaning social media, or keeping Samuel?"

Dixon coughed out a chuckle. "You know, Tuck went to great lengths to impress upon me how loyal you were to me. But what I'm seeing right now is how loyal you are to him."

"I'm not loyal to Tuck."

"Okay."

"I'm only being fair to him."

"Then, I'll be fair to you."

She swallowed. "You won't fire me?"

Dixon looked puzzled. "Fire you for what?"

"Insubordination."

"Is that a euphemism for offering your opinion?"

"In this case, it means offering my opinion forcefully and without provocation."

"That's not what I meant, but you're not fired, Amber. I'd hire fifty of you if I could."

She handed him the Blue Space file. "That was a nice thing to say."

"I'm hoping to win back your loyalty."

"You never lost it."

He glanced around the office. "Then, I can't help but wonder what exactly it was that Tuck gained."

She was about to say *nothing*, but Dixon turned and left her alone.

She stood for a moment, holding the atmosphere, remembering every little thing about Tuck until her heart throbbed and her chest ached, and she felt silent and alone and empty.

Tuck stared at his silent cell phone for a full minute before he slid it back inside his pocket. He was dressed to the nines, had a reservation at the Seaside, followed by tickets to a popular live comedy show, and he planned to end the evening at the Hollingsworth Lounge.

MaryAnn was a great date—bright, bubbly, lots of fun. But Tuck simply didn't have it in him right now. He didn't want to romance MaryAnn or anyone else. He didn't want to dine with them, dance with them or even sleep with them.

He was on the rebound from Amber. He got that, even though they'd barely dated. But the rebound had never hit him like this before.

The front door of the mansion opened and Dixon entered the foyer, doing a double take at the sight of Tuck.

"Hot date?" Dixon asked.

"Just got canceled."

"She get a better offer?"

"Something like that." Tuck wasn't about to tell Dixon that he was the one who'd canceled the date. He'd used a lame excuse of having a headache. As if a normal guy would give up a night with MaryAnn over a headache.

Trouble was, most normal guys hadn't fallen for Amber.

"Are you staying in?" asked Dixon.

"Might as well." Tuck loosened his tie.

"Drink?"

"Sure." Tuck followed his brother into the library.

He purposely sat down across from the chair where Amber had sat in her bare feet and sparkling dress. Then he smiled wistfully at the memory. She was so incredibly sexy with those luscious lips, simmering eyes, smooth shoulders and toned legs. He shifted in his chair.

Dixon handed him a crystal glass with two ice cubes and a shot of single malt. "What?"

"Nothing," said Tuck.

"You're smiling."

"I'm not sorry about the date." Tuck took a drink.

"That's an odd reaction." Dixon sat down.

Tuck gave a noncommittal shrug.

"I was talking to Zachary today," said Dixon.

"Why would you do that?" Tuck wouldn't have given the man the time of day.

"He's interested in coming back."

Tuck didn't bother responding. Dixon knew how he felt about Zachary.

Dixon seemed to give him a moment. "You got any thoughts on that?"

In response, Tuck scoffed. "You don't want to hear my thoughts on that."

"You don't think we should take him back?"

"I think we should drop him off the Michigan Avenue Bridge."

Dixon cracked a smile. "Let's call that plan B."

"Let's." Tuck drank again, pulling for plan B.

"Amber doesn't like him," said Dixon.

"Amber's not stupid."

"No, she's not."

Her image appeared once more in the chair across from Tuck.

"You're smiling again," said Dixon.

"Did she tell you her sister had a baby?"

"When did that happen?"

"Two weeks ago. Just before you got back."

"Is her sister in Chicago?"

Tuck nodded. "She is now." He found himself glancing around the library. "You ever give much thought to the way we grew up?"

"You mean with a controlling father and a distant mother?"

"I mean with gold-plated bathroom faucets."

"The faucets aren't gold-plated," said Dixon. "Though I'm honestly not sure about the dining room chandelier."

"We never worried about having enough to eat. Heck, we never worried about running low on gourmet ice cream."

"Rich people still have problems."

"I know that," said Tuck. "They never would buy me a pony."

He knew Amber's childhood challenges had been on a whole other level. Whenever he thought about that, it left him feeling petty.

"How about the fact that your father thought you were illegitimate?"

Tuck had given that revelation a lot of thought these past few days. It didn't change anything, but it did boost his confidence. He hadn't earned his father's disdain. It had been there all along.

"You said I knew," he said to Dixon. "Why did you think I knew?"

"Because of that night when we overheard."

"What night?"

"In the sitting room, listening at the air vent."

"We did that all the time."

Many nights, after their nanny had put them to bed, they'd sneak out of their room and listen to conversations going on downstairs. Usually they'd do it during parties, but they'd listened in on plenty of their parents' conversations, as well.

"They had a huge shouting match," said Dixon. "Dad accused her of fooling around. She denied it at first, but then admitted it. He said you had someone named Robert's hair and eyes."

Tuck sifted through his brain, but that particular fight didn't stand out. "I don't remember."

"You don't remember learning you might have a different father?"

"I must not have understood. How old was I?"

"Young," Dixon answered thoughtfully. "I said 'wow,' and you said 'wow' back. And I thought you got the meaning."

"I can only guess it went right over my head."

"Wow," said Dixon.

"I'm not going back to the way things were," said Tuck.

For some reason, the path forward crystalized inside his mind.

"Our father can like it or not," he continued. "But it's my company, too. I'm every bit as much his son as you are. I'm not going to be some token partner afraid of voicing my opinion. I'm going to fight you. I'm going to fight hard for what I know is right. Zachary is gone. He stays gone. Harvey, too. Amber…" He hadn't thought his way through what to do about Amber.

"Amber's great," said Dixon.

Tuck looked up sharply. He didn't like the tone of his brother's voice, and he didn't like the expression on Dixon's face. "You stay away from Amber."

"I will not. She's my assistant."

"And that's *all* she is."

"That's far from all she is."

Tuck found himself coming to his feet. "You better explain that statement."

"Explain it how?"

Tuck's voice rose. "What else is she? What is Amber to you? She won't date her boss. She can't date her boss. She would be supremely stupid to date her boss."

"Why?"

"Because it'll end badly for her. That sort of thing always does."

"So you didn't date her?"

"*No*, I didn't date her." Tuck would have dated her. But she'd said no. And she was right to say no.

"And you didn't sleep with her."

"*What?*" Tuck glared at his brother.

"You're acting pretty jealous for a guy who never dated her."

"I care about her, okay? Sure, I care about her. She's a nice woman. She's a fantastic woman. She's been through a lot, and now she's taking care of her sister. She does that. She takes care of people. She didn't like me, but she helped me anyway. And the whole time you were gone, she had *nothing* but your best interests at heart."

"She's loyal," said Dixon. "You've said that before."

"She is, to her detriment at times."

"Well, for a woman who's supposedly incredibly loyal to me, she sure talks a lot about you."

The statement took Tuck aback. "She does?"

"Almost as much as you talk about her."

"I don't—"

"Give it up, Tuck. You're obsessed with her."

"I like her. What's not to like?"

"You think she's pretty?"

Tuck could barely believe the stupidity of the question. "That's obvious to anybody with a set of eyes."

"You think she's hot?"

"Have you seen her shoes?"

"What shoes?"

"The… You know." Tuck pointed to his feet. "The straps and the heels and the rhinestones and things."

"Never noticed."

"There's something wrong with you, man."

"Why didn't you date her?" Dixon asked.

"Because I was her boss."

"Afterward—now—why don't you ask her out?"

Tuck sat back down and reached for the bottle on the table between them. He took off the cap and poured himself another drink.

"I did," he admitted. "She said no."

Dixon cocked his head. "Did she understand the question?"

"Yes, she understood the question."

"Did she give you a reason?"

"She doesn't trust me. She's got it in her head that I'm still an irresponsible playboy. She doesn't think she can count on me."

Tuck knew why she would feel that way. He also knew she deserved to feel that way. But she was wrong. If she'd give him half a chance, she'd find out she could count on him.

"So that's it? You're not going to fight?"

"How do I fight something like that?"

"How do you fight Dad? How do you fight his perception of you?"

"By standing up for myself. By taking my rightful place in this family."

Dixon cracked a smile. "And?" It was obvious he thought he had Tuck cornered.

"It's not the same thing. I have no rights to Amber at all."

"You do if she's in love with you."

"She's not—" Tuck froze. He gaped at his brother. "What makes you say that?"

"I asked her."

Tuck moved his jaw, struggling to voice the question, terrified to voice the question. "Did she say yes?"

"She said no."

Everything inside Tuck went flat. In that second, he realized he'd held out hope. He'd known it was impossible, but he couldn't seem to stop himself from dreaming.

"But she was lying," said Dixon.

Tuck blinked in bafflement.

"She's in love with you, bro."

"That can't be." Tuck didn't dare hope.

"I'm not saying she's smart or right. I'm just saying she is."

A million thoughts exploded inside Tuck's head. Was it possible? Should he give it another shot? Should he not take her refusal at face value?

"You need to fight," said Dixon. "You're tough, and you're smart and you know what you deserve. Fight Dad, fight Amber if she's being stubborn. Hell, fight me if you think I'm wrong."

Tuck tried but failed to temper his hope. "You are wrong. You're wrong about a lot of things."

"Then, fight me."

"But I hope you're right about this."

"You love her?"

"Yes," said Tuck, knowing it was completely and irrevocably true. He was in love with Amber and he was going to fight for her with everything he had.

Amber rocked Crystal in her arms while Jade worked on an English essay on her laptop. She told herself they were a family now. She had her job back, and the future was bright. Little Crystal was perfect, and she was going to grow up safe and happy, knowing she had a devoted mom and aunt to care for her.

Her gaze strayed to a glossy magazine on the coffee table. *Chicago About Town*. Jade had brought it home with the groceries. There was an inset photo on the bottom left, Tuck with a beautiful blonde woman. She didn't know who it was and it was impossible to know when the photo was taken. But Amber was jealous.

Tuck was back to his old life, while Dixon's words kept echoing inside her head. *Are you in love with Tuck?*

How could she have fallen in love with Tuck? How could she have been so foolish? She had so much going for her right now. Jade was working hard. She was going to pass her equivalency test. She was going to be a great mom.

Amber kissed the soft top of Crystal's head. The future was blindingly optimistic. All she had to do was get Tuck out of her head.

Her chest tightened and her throat seemed to clog.

"Amber?" Jade asked softly.

Amber swallowed. "Yes?"

"What's wrong?"

"Nothing."

Jade rose from her chair. "Is it too much?"

It was. It was far too much. Amber didn't know if she'd be able to get over him. She didn't want to keep fighting her feelings.

"Me and Crystal?" Jade continued. "Are we too much work?"

"What? No. No, honey. It's not you."

"You look so sad."

"I'm just tired."

"No, you're sad."

"I miss him," Amber admitted.

"Tuck?"

"How can I miss him? I know who he is. I know where it was going. But I couldn't seem to talk myself out of it."

Jade moved toward her, sympathy in her expression. "I know how you feel."

"Does it go away?"

A knock sounded on the door.

"Eventually, your head will overtake your heart," said Jade. "Though it can take a while."

Amber didn't like the sound of that. Her head was stronger than her heart, always. It was what had kept her safe and sane all these years. How could it be failing her now?

The knock sounded again and Jade brushed Amber's shoulder on the way to answer it.

Amber hugged her niece tight.

"I'm looking for Amber." Tuck's voice made Amber sit up straight. "Is she home?"

A buzzing started in the center of her brain, radiating to her chest then along her limbs. What was he doing here?

"What do you want?" asked Jade.

"To talk to her."

"Is it about work?"

"Yes."

Amber came slowly to her feet, careful not to disturb Crystal.

"It's okay," she said to Jade.

Jade sighed and opened the door wider.

Amber came forward. "Tuck?"

Jade gathered Crystal from her arms while Tuck smiled at the baby.

"She's beautiful," he said.

"What do you want?" Amber asked.

Tuck met her gaze. "I'm coming to work on Monday."

The words surprised her.

"Dixon's contemplating bringing Zachary back," said Tuck.

"He told me that, too," said Amber.

"It's a bad idea."

"I agree."

Tuck glanced behind her. "You mind if I come in?"

She hesitated, but she didn't want to be rude. "Okay."

"Did you tell him that's what you thought?" Tuck asked as she shut the door behind them.

"I did. Then I was afraid he might fire me."

"Dixon's not going to fire you."

"He didn't." But she'd made a mental note to keep her opinions to herself. She had grown used to being frank with Tuck, but her relationship with Dixon had always been more formal. She had to respect that.

Cooing to Crystal, Jade made her way down the hall, obviously deciding to give them some privacy.

"Are you planning to stop him?" Amber asked. "From rehiring Zachary."

"I'm going to try," said Tuck, moving to the middle of the room. "I'm going back, and I'm going to fight for what I want."

She was puzzled. "Why?"

"Because it's my company, too."

"It's a lot of work."

Right now, as he had in the past, Tuck had the best of all possible worlds.

"It is," he agreed.

"You don't need to do it."

"I disagree with that. Tucker Transportation can't run itself."

"But Dixon—"

"Dixon doesn't know everything."

"He knows a lot."

Tuck frowned. "What do you think of my brother?"

The question struck her as odd. "You know what I think of your brother. We spent weeks discussing what I thought of your brother."

"We spent weeks trying to keep our hands off each other."

Amber couldn't believe she'd heard right.

"Let me put that another way," he said.

"Good idea."

"What do you think of me?"

"Right this moment?"

"Right this moment."

Amber reached down and lifted the magazine, putting the cover in front of his face, reminding herself of exactly who he was.

"What?" He squinted.

"I think you're exactly what you seem."

"That's Kaitlyn."

"Nice that you remember her name."

"That's from last year. At the charity thing. The one for the animals. Pets, not the zoo."

"The humane society?"

"Yes."

"Did you have a nice time?"

"Why are you asking? What difference does that make now?"

"Because it's on the cover of a magazine."

He stared at her for a long moment. "I'm not dating anyone, Amber."

"I don't care."

But she was lying. She did care. She couldn't stand the thought of him with another woman. She wanted him for herself and she didn't know how to stop wanting that.

"You should care," he said. "You better care."

"I don't—"

"I asked you what you thought of me."

"And I told you."

He snapped the magazine from her hands and tossed it on the table. "Use words."

Her brain stumbled around. With him standing so close, she found she couldn't lie. "You're not good for me."

"Why not?"

"Don't do this, Tuck."

"Why not?"

"You know I'm attracted to you. You know we have chemistry. But we can't go there again."

"Why not?"

"Why *not*?" she all but shouted.

Why was he determined to make her say it?

"That's what I asked," he said.

"Because it's not enough."

"What would be enough?"

"Stop. Just stop." She wanted him to go away. Her heart was already shredded and he was making it worse.

"Me loving you?" he asked. "Would that be enough?"

His words penetrated and her brain screeched to a halt.

"Would it, Amber?" he asked. "Because I do. I love you. I'm *in* love with you. I want to work with you. I want to date you. I think I even want to marry you. Scratch that. I *know* I want to marry you. Now I'm asking again. What do you think of me?"

She worked her jaw, but no sound came out. "I…uh…"

He cocked his head. "I'm really not sure how to take that."

"You love me?" She couldn't wrap her head around it.

"I love you." He reached out and took her hands in his. "But I'm going to have to insist you answer the question. I swear, Amber, I don't know whether to kiss you or slink out the door."

"Kiss me," she said, joy blooming in her chest.

Tuck's face broke into a broad smile.

"I love you, Tuck. Kiss me, please."

He didn't wait another second. He kissed her deeply, wrapping his arms around her, drawing her close against his body.

"I'll be there for you," he whispered in her ear. "I promise I'll be there for you and for Crystal and for Jade. I'll protect you and fight for you. You can count on me now and forever."

"This doesn't seem real." She let the warmth of his body flow into hers.

"It's real, sweetheart. And it's definitely forever."

* * * * *

"I was ready to battle him for you."

Christian murmured the words, fingers grazing the wet streak on her cheek. "To demonstrate how committed I am to being your ardent husband and a zealous father to Marc."

Such beautiful words from such a challenging and unpredictable man. Noelle couldn't decide whether to laugh or cry. She was still debating when Christian cupped her face in his hands and brought his lips to hers.

The delicious pressure of his kiss held her immobile with shock for several frantic heartbeats.

She tunneled impatient fingers into Christian's hair and pushed her greedy body hard against his. She craved a man's hands on her. To feel a little helpless as he tore her clothes off and had his way with her. And Christian had a knack for that sort of thing.

His fingers bit into her hips as she rocked against him, the ache between her thighs building. When she could stand it no longer, she cried out as pleasure lanced downward.

Christian buried his face in her neck, lips gliding over her skin. "I knew you'd come around."

An icy chill swept through her at his words. Noelle clenched her teeth and cursed her impulsiveness. She tensed her muscles and twisted away.

"I haven't come around to anything."

* * *

Secret Child, Royal Scandal
is part of Cat Schield's Sherdana Royals trilogy

SECRET CHILD, ROYAL SCANDAL

BY
CAT SCHIELD

First Published in Great Britain 2016
By Mills & Boon, an imprint of HarperCollins*Publishers*
1 London Bridge Street, London, SE1 9GF

© 2016 Catherine Schield

ISBN: 978-0-263-91857-1

51-0416

Our policy is to use papers that are natural, renewable and recyclable products and made from wood grown in sustainable forests. The logging and manufacturing processes conform to the legal environmental regulations of the country of origin.

Printed and bound in Spain
by CPI, Barcelona

Cat Schield has been reading and writing romance since high school. Although she graduated from college with a BA in business, her idea of a perfect career was writing books for Mills & Boon. And now, after winning the Romance Writers of America 2010 Golden Heart® Award for Best Contemporary Series Romance, that dream has come true. Cat lives in Minnesota with her daughter, Emily, and their Burmese cat. When she's not writing sexy, romantic stories for Mills & Boon Desire, she can be found sailing with friends on the St. Croix River, or in more exotic locales, like the Caribbean and Europe. She loves to hear from readers. Find her at www.catschield.net. Follow her on Twitter, @catschield.

To Renee and Mary K.
Thanks for all the happy hours and the
conversations that have kept me sane.

One

Prince Christian Alessandro, third in line to the Sherdana throne, stood behind the current and future kings of Sherdana and glowered into the camera. No doubt he was ruining Nic and Brooke's fairy-tale wedding photos, but he didn't care. His last hope to remain a carefree bachelor for the rest of his life had been reduced to ashes the second his brother had gazed deep into his bride's starry eyes and pledged to love and honor her until the day he died.

Christian growled.

"Smiles everyone," the photographer cried, casting an anxious glance Christian's way. "This is our last photo of the complete wedding party. Let's make it count."

Despite his black mood, Christian shifted his features into less grim lines. He wasn't about to smile, but he could at least give his brother one decent photo. No matter how badly this marriage had disrupted his life, in the days to come he really would make an effort to be happy for Nic and Brooke. For today he'd simply don a mask.

"Let's set up over there." The photographer pointed to a small stone bridge that crossed a decorative creek.

The path beyond meandered toward the stables. Christian preferred his horsepower under the hood of a fast car, but he'd gladly take his twin nieces to visit their ponies just to get away. Bethany and Karina were old hands at being flower girls, this being their second royal wedding in four months, but being two-year-olds, they had a short attention span and were growing impatient with having to stand still for photos. Christian sympathized with them.

Since his accident five years earlier, he'd avoided cameras as much as possible. The burn scars that covered his right side—shoulder, neck and half of his cheek—had made him the least attractive Alessandro triplet. Not that it mattered much how he looked. His title, wealth and confirmed bachelor status made him a magnet for women.

Most women.

His gaze roamed over the multitude of assistants and palace staff required to keep the bridal party looking flawless and the photo shoot moving forward. Trailing the bride was a petite, slender woman with mink-brown hair and dual-toned brown eyes. Internationally renowned wedding dress designer Noelle Dubone had designed Brooke's dress as well as the one worn by Christian's sister-in-law, Princess Olivia Alessandro.

Born in Sherdana, Noelle had moved to Paris at twenty-two to follow her dream of becoming a fashion designer. She'd done moderately well until three years ago when she'd designed the wedding gown for the bride of Italian prince Paolo Gizzi. There'd been so much media coverage surrounding the nuptials that Noelle became an overnight success. Movie stars, European nobility and the very wealthy became eager for a Noelle Dubone original.

"Imagining your own wedding?" taunted a female voice from behind him.

Christian turned and shot his sister a sour look. Ariana was looking too smugly amused for Christian's taste.

"No." But the slim figure in blue-gray caught his eye again.

Noelle Dubone. The one woman in the world who'd come closest to taming the wildest Alessandro prince. He hadn't been worthy of her. She hadn't deserved to be treated badly by him. That he'd done it for her own good was what let him sleep at night.

"You should be," Ariana countered, looking stylish and carefree in a knee-length, full-skirted dress with puffy long sleeves. A fashion trendsetter, her wedding attire shimmered with gold embroidery and straddled the line between daring and demure with strategically placed sheer panels that showed off her delicate shoulders and hinted at more thigh than the formal occasion called for. "The future of the kingdom rests in your hands."

Christian grimaced. "Father's health has never been better and I don't see Gabriel dropping dead any time soon, so I suspect I will have time to choose a wife and get her pregnant."

Just the thought of it made him long for a drink. But as his mother had pointed out numerous times in the months since Nic had abdicated his responsibility to Sherdana by choosing to marry an American, Christian was no longer free to overindulge in liquor and women. The idea that he had to start walking the straight and narrow path after being the party prince all his life was daunting. He'd misstepped all his life. As youngest in the birth order, it was what he did.

Gabriel, as eldest, was the responsible one. The future king.

Nic, as middle son, was the forgotten one. He'd gone

off to America in his early twenties to become a rocket scientist.

Christian was the indulged youngest son. His antics had provided the paparazzi tabloid fodder since he was four-teen and got caught with one of the maids.

At twenty he'd been raising hell in London. He'd thrown the best parties. Drank too much. Spent money like it was being printed by elves, and when his parents cut off his funds, he'd started buying and flipping failing businesses. He didn't care about success. He just wanted to have fun.

At twenty-five several of his less prudent actions had blown up in his face, leaving him scarred and his heart shredded.

Now at thirty he was expected to give up his freedom for the crown.

"You only think you have time," Ariana countered. "Mother showed me the list of potential candidates. It's two-feet long."

"I do not need her help or anyone else's to find a wife."

"Neither did Gabriel and Nic and look how that turned out."

Gabriel had eloped five months earlier in a grand, ro-mantic gesture that had rendered him blissfully happy, but by marrying a woman who could never have children, he'd left his two brothers holding short straws.

As the last born of the triplets, Christian had made it clear to Nic that it was his duty to step up next. In order for the Alessandro family to stay in power, one of the three princes needed to produce a son. But before Nic could begin looking for a potential bride from among Europe's noble houses or Sherdana's female citizenry, the beautiful American, Brooke Davis, had stolen his heart.

And with their wedding today, it all came down to Christian.

"I can find my own bride without Mother's help."

Ariana made a noise unfit for a princess. "You've already been through half the suitable single women in Europe.

"Hardly half."

"Surely there was one woman among *all* those you've spent time with who appeals to you."

"Appeals, yes." Christian resisted the urge to search for Noelle again. "But not one I want to spend the rest of my life with."

"Well, you'd better find one."

Christian ground his teeth together and didn't answer. He knew Ariana was right. The price one paid as a royal was to not always get to do as one liked. Gabriel had been lucky to choose Olivia to marry before he understood that he was in love with her. But right up until he and Olivia eloped, Gabriel had grappled with his duty to Sherdana versus following his heart's desire.

Nic had the same issue with Brooke. He'd known he needed to put her aside and marry a woman whose children could one day be king.

But in the end both men had chosen love over duty.

Which left Christian to choose duty.

One of the photographer's assistants came to fetch them for more pictures, putting an end to the conversation for the moment. Christian endured another tedious hour of being posed with his brothers, his sister, the king and queen, and various members of the wedding party. By the time the session was finished, he was ready to get drunker than he'd been in the five years since the accident that left him with a disfigured body to match his tarnished soul.

What stopped him from making a beeline for the bar was Noelle.

It seemed perfectly right to walk up behind her and slip

his arm around her waist. Christian dropped a kiss on her cheek the way he had a hundred times, a habit from the old days that used to speak to his strong affection for her. For a microsecond Noelle relaxed against him, accepting his touch as if no time or hurt had passed between them. Then she tensed.

"You look beautiful," he murmured in her ear.

She didn't quite jerk away from him, but she lacked her usual grace in her quick sideways step. "Thank you, Your Royal Highness."

"Walk with me." It was more a command than an invitation.

"I really shouldn't leave the party." She glanced toward the bride and groom as if hoping to spot someone who needed her.

"The photos are done. The bride has no further need for her designer. I'd like to catch up with you. It's been a long time."

"As you wish, Your Highness." To his annoyance, she curtsied, gaze averted.

The gardens behind the palace were extensive and scrupulously maintained under the queen's watchful eye. The plantings closest to the I-shaped structure that housed Sherdana's royal family were arranged in terms of design and color that changed with the seasons. This was the most photographed section of the garden, with its formal walkways and dramatic fountains.

Toward the back of the extensive acreage that surrounded the palace, the garden gave way to a wooded area. Christian guided her to a small grove of trees that offered plenty of shade. There would be more privacy there.

"You've done very well for yourself as a designer."

Christian hated small talk, and it seemed idiotic to attempt any with Noelle. But how did you begin a cordial conversation with an ex-lover who you'd once deliberately hurt even as you told yourself it was for her own good?

"I've been fortunate." Her polite demeanor contrasted with the impatience running through her tone. "Luck and timing."

"You neglected to mention talent. I always knew you'd be successful."

"That's very kind."

"I've missed you." The words came out of nowhere and shocked him. He'd intended to ply her with flirtatious compliments and make her smile at him the way she used to, not pour his heart out.

For the first time she met his gaze directly. His heart gave a familiar bump as he took in the striking uniqueness of her eyes. From a distance they merely looked hazel, but up close the greenish-brown around the edges gave way to a bright chestnut near the pupil. In the past, he'd spent long hours studying those colors and reveling in the soft affection in her gaze as they lingered over dinner or spent a morning in bed.

She gave her head a shake. "I'm sure that's not true."

"I might not have been the man for you, but that doesn't mean I didn't care," he told her, fingertips itching to touch her warm skin.

"Don't try to flatter me." The words held no heat. "I was a convenient bed for you to fall into after you were done partying. You came to me when you grew tired of your superficial crowd and their thoughtless behavior. And in the end, you pushed me out of your life as if two years together meant nothing."

For your own good.

"And look how you thrived. You moved to Paris and became an internationally famous designer." He sounded defensive, and that wasn't the tone he wanted to take with her.

"Is that what you think I wanted?" Her breath huffed out in a short burst that he might have taken for laughter if she hadn't been frowning. "Fame and fortune?"

No, it's what he'd wanted for her. "Talent like yours shouldn't go to waste."

"Do you want me to thank you?" she asked, her voice dripping with sarcasm.

During the time they were together, he'd been more honest with her than anyone else before or since. Not even his brothers had known of the demons that drove him. Maybe he trusted Noelle because they'd been friends before they became lovers. Her openness and gentle spirit had offered him a safe place to unload all his fears and doubts. And because of that, she'd gotten the full weight of his darkness.

"No."

"Then why are we having this conversation after five years of silence?"

Because once again he needed her solace and support. The pressure of fathering the future heir to Sherdana's throne was dredging up his worst qualities. She'd talked him through bouts of melancholy in the past.

"I need you."

Her expression reflected dismay. "I'm no longer that girl." Her tone heated as she continued. "And even if I was, I have other things in my life that will always take priority over a…" As if realizing what she'd been about to say to her prince, Noelle sucked in a giant breath and pulled her lips between her teeth. Her next words were polite, her tone tempered. "I am no longer in a position to be your *friend*."

She twisted the word *friend* into something ugly. Christian read her message loud and clear. She wanted nothing more to do with him. Not as his confidante, his champion or as his lover.

Before he could argue, she dropped another one of

those annoying curtsies. "Excuse me, Your Highness, but I should get back to the party."

Christian watched her vanish back along the path and marveled at how thoroughly he'd mucked up his most important act of selflessness. She was right to shut him down. He'd repeatedly demonstrated that he was nothing but trouble for her.

But after talking to her, he knew if he was going to get through the next few months of finding a wife and settling down to the job of producing the next heir to the throne, he was going to need a friend in his corner. And once upon a time, Noelle had been the only one he talked to about his problems.

He desperately wanted her support. And although she might not be on board with the idea at the moment, he was going to persuade her to give it.

The evening air accompanied Noelle into the small, functional kitchen of her comfortable rural cottage, bringing the earthy scents of fall with her. As much as she'd enjoyed her years in Paris, she'd missed the slower pace and wide-open spaces of the countryside. And an energetic boy like her son needed room to run.

She placed the tomatoes she'd picked on the counter. Her garden was reaching the end of its growing season, and soon she would collect the last of the squash, tomatoes and herbs. Autumn was her favorite season. The rich burgundy, gold and vivid greens of the hills around her cottage inspired her most unique designs. One downside to her success as a wedding-dress designer was that her color palate was limited to shades of white and cream with an occasional pastel thrown in.

"Mama!"

Before Noelle could brace herself, her dark-haired

son barreled into her legs. Laughing, she bent down and wrapped her arms around his squirmy little body. Like most four-years-olds he was a bundle of energy, and Noelle got her hug in fast.

"Did you have a good afternoon with Nana?" Noelle's mother lived with them and watched Marc after school while Noelle worked. She glanced at her mother without waiting for her son's response.

"He was a good boy," Mara Dubone said, her tone emphatic.

Noelle hoped that was true. In the past six months, Marc had grown more rambunctious and wasn't good at listening to his grandmother. Mara loved her grandson very much and defended him always, but it worried Noelle that her son was getting to be too much for her mother to handle.

"I was good." Marc's bronze-gold eyes glowed with sincerity and Noelle sighed.

She framed his face, surveyed the features boldly stamped by his father and gave him a big smile. "I'm so glad."

He had his father's knack for mischief as well as his charm. The thought caused Noelle a small pang of anxiety. Her encounter with Christian this afternoon had been unsettling. After almost five years of no contact, he'd finally reached out to her. That it was five years too late hadn't stopped her heart from thumping wildly in her chest.

"Why don't you go upstairs and brush your teeth," Mara said. "Your mama will come read to you, but she can't do that until you're in your pajamas and in bed."

"Yeah." With typical enthusiasm, Marc raced upstairs, his stocking feet pounding on the wood steps that led to the second floor.

"Was he really okay today?" Noelle asked as soon as she was alone with her mother.

Mara sighed. "He is a wonderful boy, but he has a lot of energy and needs a firm hand." Noelle's mother gave her daughter a sly grin. "What he needs is a man in his life who can channel some of that energy into masculine pursuits."

It wasn't the first time her mother had made this observation. Noelle nodded the way she always did. "Marc's friends are going fishing with their fathers next week. Phillip's dad offered to take Marc, as well. Perhaps I should take him up on his offer."

"That's not what I meant and you know it." Noelle's mother set her hands on her hips and shook her head. "You are not getting any younger. It's time you stopped pining for that prince of yours. It's been almost five years. You need to move on."

"I am not pining for Christian. And I have moved on. I have a thriving business that takes up most of my energy and a small boy who deserves his mother's full attention."

With a disgusted snort, Noelle's mother headed for the stairs. From above their heads came a series of loud thumps as Marc worked off his energy before bedtime.

Noelle walked back into the kitchen to turn off the light and then repeated the process in the dining room and living room before heading up to the bedrooms. For a moment she paused at the bottom of the stairs and listened to the sounds of her family. Her mother's low voice, patient and firm. Her son's clear tones, happy and dynamic.

A firm knock on her front door snapped Noelle out of her musing. She glanced at the clock over the mantel. Eight forty-five. Who could be visiting her at this hour?

Although her farmhouse sat on an acre of land, Noelle had never worried about her isolation. She had neighbors on all sides and they kept an eye on her and her family. Perhaps one of her goats had escaped again. She'd been having problems with the fence on the east side of their pasture.

Flipping on the light in the foyer, Noelle pulled the door open. Her smile died as she spotted the man standing outside her front door.

"Christian?"

Determination lit his gold eyes. While at his brother's wedding, she'd found it easy to discourage the arrogant prince who'd put his arm around her waist and boldly kissed her cheek.

"Good evening, Noelle."

Anxiety gripped her. She'd worked hard to keep her personal life private. Having Prince Christian Alessandro show up like this threatened that.

"What are you doing here?"

"We didn't get a chance to finish our conversation earlier."

Why was she surprised that after five years of no contact he would think she'd welcome his popping around with no warning the way he used to when they were together?

"It's almost nine o'clock."

"I brought some wine." He held up a bottle of her favorite red. *Damn the man for remembering.* He gave her a coaxing half grin. His eyes softened with the seductive glow she'd never successfully resisted. "How about letting me in."

She crossed her arms over her chest, refusing his peace offering. "I already told you. I'm not the same girl I was when we were together." She had said the exact same thing earlier that afternoon, but obviously he hadn't been listening. "You can't just show up here unannounced and think that I'm going to let you in." To warm her bed for a few hours.

"You're mad because I haven't called."

He was apologizing for not contacting her? "It's been five years." Half a decade of living had happened to her.

It took all her willpower not to shove him off her stoop and slam the door in his face.

"I know how long it's been. And I wasn't kidding earlier when I said I missed you. I'd like to come in and find out what your life is like now."

"I've been back in Carone for two years. Why now?"

"Talking with you today brought up a lot of great memories. We had something."

"The operative word being 'had.'" A tremor went through her as she remembered the feel of his fingers against her skin, working magic unlike anything she'd known before or since. "My life is wonderful. I'm happy and complete. There's no room for you or your drama."

"I'm not the same man I used to be, either."

From what she'd read about him over the years, she believed he'd changed, but it wasn't enough to invite him in. "What we did or didn't have in the past needs to stay there." She knew immediately that her words had been a mistake.

"Did or didn't have?" The light of challenge flared in his eyes. "You mean to stand there and deny that we were friends?"

Friends?

Is that how he'd thought of her as he made love to her for hours? When he'd told her he didn't like her going out after close with the guys from the café where she worked part-time and demanded that she stop? Friends? When he'd treated her more like his embarrassing secret?

Noelle realized her hands had clenched into fists at his declaration and tried to focus on relaxing. He was no less infuriating than on the day he'd told her they had no future and she should go to Paris and take the job at Matteo Pizzaro Designs.

"What do you want, Christian?" She asked the question in a flat, unfriendly tone that was intended to annoy him. It didn't.

"I never could get anything past you." He straightened, putting aside all attempt to charm her. Determination radiated from him. "Can I come in? I really do want to talk to you."

"It's late." From the floor above came the pounding of feet. Marc had grown impatient and would be coming to look for her any second. "Perhaps later this week. We could meet for coffee."

"I'd rather have a private dinner. Just you and me like the old days. Perhaps you could come to my place in the city? I have some things I'd like to discuss with you and I don't want to do so in public."

Bitterness gripped her. He'd never wanted to be seen out and about with her. She scrutinized his expression. He'd obviously come to her with an agenda. But she sensed what he had to say wasn't about her son. So far, her secret remained safe. If he'd known about Marc, he would have led with that. So, what was he up to?

"I'm afraid my evenings are booked." Spending time with her son was her greatest joy, and he was growing up so fast. She cherished her evenings with him and resented any intrusion. "Perhaps I could come to your office?"

There was thumping on the stairs as Marc jumped down each step, one by one. Noelle's heart hammered in time. She had to conclude the conversation with Christian before her son appeared.

"Call me. We can discuss this next week. Right now, I need to go." She started to shut the door, but Christian put out his hand and stopped it. Marc's feet thundered across the wood floor; he was coming closer. "Fine. I'll have dinner with you."

"Mama, where are you?"

Christian's eyes widened at the sound of Marc's voice. "You have a child?"

She could not let this happen. Noelle shifted to put her full weight against the door and get it closed.

"You have to leave."

"Marc, where are you?" She heard her mother coming down the stairs now and prayed that Mara could get to Marc before he came to investigate. "I told you your mother wouldn't read you a story unless you were in bed."

"I had no idea," Christian mused, his expression strangely melancholy.

"And now you see why my evenings are busy. So if you don't mind, I need to get my son to bed."

"Can I meet him?" The prince stared past Noelle into the home's interior.

"No." Hearing the snap in her voice, she moderated her tone. "It's his bedtime, and meeting someone new will stir him up. It's already difficult to settle him down enough to sleep."

"He sounds like me."

It was a remark anyone might have made. Noelle knew there was no subtext beneath Christian's comment, but she was hyper-secretive regarding the paternity of her son.

"Not at all."

"Don't you remember how much trouble you had getting me to sleep on the nights I stayed over?"

She ignored the jump in her pulse brought on by his wicked smile. What she remembered were long, delicious hours of lovemaking that left her physically drained and emotionally invigorated.

"This is a conversation for another time."

"Mama, who are you talking to?" Marc plastered himself against her hip and peered up at Christian.

Too late. She'd let Christian distract her with bittersweet

memories, and now he was about to discover what she'd zealously kept hidden from him all these years.

"This is Prince Christian," she told her son, heart breaking. "Your Highness, this is my son, Marc."

"*Your* son?" The prince regarded the four-year-old boy in silence for several seconds, his mouth set in a hard line. At last his cold eyes lifted to Noelle. "Don't you mean *our* son?"

Two

Christian wanted to shove the door open and turn on the lights in the front entry so he could get a clearer look at the boy, but instinct told him it wouldn't change anything. This was his son.

"I don't have a father. Do I, Mama?" Marc glanced up at his mother, eyes worried as he took in her stricken expression.

"Of course you have a father," Noelle stated. "Everyone does. But not everyone's father is part of their life." She soothed a trembling hand over her son's dark head.

"And whose fault is that?" Christian's shock was fading, replaced with annoyance and grudging respect as he surveyed the boy—Noelle had called him Marc.

Tall for his age, which couldn't have been more than four and a half, he possessed the distinctive gold Alessandro eyes and wavy brown hair. Undaunted by Christian's keen scrutiny, the boy stared back, showing no apprehension, just unflinching hostility. And maybe a little curiosity, as well. Christian inclined his head in approval. A child of his would possess an inquisitive mind.

"We are not talking about this right now." Noelle glared at him. Motherhood had given her voice a sharp inflection that demanded immediate obedience. Almost immediately, however, her eyes widened as if she recalled that the man standing on her doorstep was a member of the royal family. Noelle modulated her tone. "Prince Christian, this is not a good time."

"I'm not leaving until I know what's going on."

"I'll make him go." Marc pushed past his mother and took up a fighter's stance, one foot back, fists up and ready to punch.

Christian didn't like how the situation was escalating, but he couldn't bring himself to back off. Too many questions bombarded him. Instead, he stared, belligerent and stubborn, into Noelle's lovely, troubled eyes until she sighed.

"Marc, please go upstairs with Nana." Noelle set her hands on the boy's shoulders and turned him until he faced her. When he looked up and met her gaze, she gave him a reassuring smile. "I need to speak with this man."

This man. This *man*? Christian fumed. He was the boy's *father*.

"Are you sure, Mama?" Marc demanded, not backing down for a second.

"Absolutely." Noelle ruffled her son's dark hair, doing an excellent job of disguising her tension. "Please go upstairs. I'll come talk to you in a few minutes."

With a guard dog's sullen disapproval, the boy leveled a fierce glare at Christian before turning away. Despite the outrage battering him, pride rose in Christian. His son was brave and protective. Good traits for a future king.

Noelle waited until her son was shepherded upstairs by a woman in her midfifties before she stepped out of the house and pulled the door shut behind her. Noelle's eyes blazed, the heat of her annoyance radiating from her in the cool night air. "How dare you come here and say something like that in front of my son. *My* son."

"You've kept a pretty big secret from me all these years."

She shook her head at him. "You need to go."

"You're mistaken. I need answers."

"You will not get them tonight." With her mouth set in a determined line and her hands set on her hips, she let her gaze drill into him.

"Noelle, I'm sorry for what happened between us in the past." He let his voice settle into the cajoling tone that always made women give in. "I know you think what I did to you was insensitive, but I deserve to know my son."

"Deserve?" Her chest heaved with each agitated breath she took. "Deserve? Do you remember telling me five years ago that I should move on with my life and forget I ever met you?"

His heart twisted as he recalled that gut wrenching speech. "At the time I was right."

"I loved you."

"It wasn't going to work between us."

"It still isn't." She glared at him.

Her anger told him she still resented the way he'd dismissed her five years ago, but she'd come back to Sherdana to live her life. A life he'd told her he wanted no part of. And she'd been doing great without him.

Better than he'd done without her.

"Don't you see," he began, regret a heavy weight on his shoulders. "For everyone's sake, we're going to have to make peace. I intend to be a part of Marc's life."

"I'll not have you put my son through the same heartache I endured."

Her words were meant to wound, but Christian barely felt their sting. He was completely distracted by the vibrant beauty of the woman standing up to him. Never before had Noelle's temper flared like this. He regarded her in mesmerized fascination. When they'd been together before, she'd been so agreeable, so accommodating. The sex between them had always been explosive, but outside the bedroom she'd never demonstrated a hint of rebellion.

Now, she was a mother protecting her child. Her fierceness enthralled him. Abruptly the idea of reigniting their friendship seemed far too bland a proposition. He wanted her back in his bed. That she'd produced a potential heir to the throne made the whole situation clear-cut. He intended to marry her, and one day his son would be Sherdana's king.

"He's not just your son, Noelle. He's an Alessandro. Sherdanian royalty." Christian let the statement hang in the air between them for several beats. "Are you planning on keeping that from him?"

"Yes." But despite her forceful declaration, her expression told him she'd asked herself the same question. "No." Noelle stalked over to where his car sat in her driveway. "Damn you, Christian. He was never supposed to know."

"Then why did you bring him back here?" He followed her, repressing the urge to snatch her into his arms and see if she'd yield beneath his kisses the way she used to. "You could have very easily lived the rest of your life in France or gone to the United States." Had she come back to be close to him?

"My stepfather died two-and a-half years ago, leaving my mother alone. I came back to be near her."

His heart twisted at her explanation. Noelle's mother

had remarried when Noelle was six. "I'm sorry to hear that. I know you two were very close. You must miss him very much."

"I do." Sorrow tempered her irritation. "It's been a hard time for all of us. Marc loved his papi."

Regret assaulted Christian. Marc had another papi that he'd never know if Noelle got her way. That wasn't fair to any of them.

"Why didn't you lie and deny that he's mine."

She regarded him in bemusement. "Even if he didn't have the Alessandro features, why would I do that? Have I ever been untruthful with you?"

No. He'd been the one who'd held tight to secrets. "You kept my son from me for over four years."

"And if you'd made an attempt to contact me, I would have told you he existed."

"What about tonight? You weren't particularly forthcoming. If Marc hadn't come to the door, you'd never have admitted he existed."

"You aren't interested in being a father."

"That's not true." But in reality, he hadn't thought much about fatherhood other than as a duty demanded of him by his position.

"The whole country is buzzing about Sherdana's need for an heir, and they look to you as the country's last hope to produce one." Her somber tone matched his own dour meditations on the subject. She was no more convinced of his worthiness for the task than he was. "And now here's my son. Your heir. A simple solution to your problems."

A solution perhaps, but not necessarily a simple one. He had a duty to the throne and his country. It was up to him to secure the line of succession with a son. His burden had grown lighter with the revelation that he had a son, but his troubles were far from over.

"He can't be my heir," Christian said, his heart hammering as he regarded Noelle, curious to see if she'd connect the dots.

She'd always had a knack for discerning the true intent behind his actions. Except for the last time they'd been together five years earlier. He'd hidden his heart too well when he'd broken off their relationship.

When she remained silent, he continued. "Unless I marry his mother."

"Marry?" Her voice hitched.

He should try to convince her that that's why he'd come by tonight. Suddenly he knew this was the exact right thing to do. Marrying her would solve all his problems. Now that he'd seen her again, he realized there was no other woman in the world he could imagine being married to. Five years earlier they'd built a relationship on friendship and passion. He'd been a spoiled prince, and she'd been a naïve commoner who adored him. Instead of appreciating the gift of her love, he'd taken her for granted. He'd never understood why her generous spirit had brought out the worst in him. She'd loved him, flaws and all, and he'd been self-destructive and stupid. It made no sense, but he couldn't stop punishing her for loving him too much.

"You'd make a terrific princess," he said, and meant it. "The country already loves you."

"I made two wedding dresses. That's not enough to make me *worthy* of anyone's love." She shook her head. "You have aristocratic women from all over Europe eager to become your wife."

"But I don't want anyone else."

"Are you saying you want me?" She shook her head and laughed bitterly. "You want Marc." A pause. "You can't have him."

Christian could see there would be no convincing her

tonight, and he needed some time to assimilate all that he'd learned. He had a son. The impact had only begun to register.

"We will talk tomorrow," he said. "I will pick you up at noon. Clear your schedule for a few hours."

"I could clear my schedule for a few months and you'd get the same answer. I'm not going to give you my son."

"I don't want to take him from you." He hated that this was her perception of him, but he'd made her believe he was a villain so what else could he expect? "But I intend to be in his life."

Noelle stared at Christian, the urge to shriek building in her. She pressed her lips together as her mind raced. The cat was out of the bag. No way it was going back in. Christian knew he had a son.

I don't want to take him from you.

She pondered his words, hearing the warning. He wasn't foolish enough to tell her outright that he planned to take Marc away, but what Sherdanian court would let her keep her son if Prince Christian fought her for custody? For a second Noelle had a hard time breathing. Then she remembered an illegitimate son was no use to him. Christian needed her help to legitimize Marc's claim to the crown.

Her son a king.

Her knees bumped together at the thought. Marc was only four. It wasn't fair to upend his life in this way. She'd seen what being a royal had done to Christian. He'd grown up resentful and reckless. The third heir, he'd had all the privileges and none of the responsibility. She'd lost count of how many times he'd complained that he wished everyone would just leave him alone.

But with Crown Prince Gabriel and Princess Olivia unable to have children, and second-in-line Prince Nicolas married to an American, Marc wouldn't be a spare heir. He'd be in direct line to the throne.

"Noelle." Christian reclaimed her attention by touching her arm. "Don't make this hard on everyone."

Even through her thin sweater his warmth seeped into her skin. She jerked free before the heat invaded her muscles, rendering her susceptible to his persuasion. Her heart quickened as she backed out of range. It was humiliating how quickly her body betrayed her. A poignant reminder to keep her distance lest physical desire influence her decisions.

Five years ago she hadn't any reason to guard herself against him. She'd belonged to him heart, mind and soul. That was before he'd demonstrated how little she meant to him. It still hurt how easily he'd cast her aside.

Fierce determination heated her blood. Her cheeks grew hot. She'd do everything in her power to make sure he didn't do the same thing to Marc.

"You mean don't make it hard on you." Her tone bitter, she noted the way his eyes flickered, betraying his surprise.

Through all his past selfish behavior, she'd reminded herself that as a commoner of passing prettiness and limited sophistication she was lucky he'd sought her out at all. Pliable as a willow tree, she'd demonstrated patience and understanding. But having her heart broken had given her a spine, and five years of training in the cutthroat world of fashion design had forged that spine into tempered steel. If he continued to push her, he would discover what she was made of.

"But you're right," she added, deciding that arguing would only make him more determined to get his way. In addition, while she might no longer be a doormat, she hadn't lost touch with what was fair. "You are Marc's father and deserve a chance to get to know him. Call me at my office tomorrow at ten. I will check my schedule, and we can figure out a time to meet and discuss a visitation schedule." Seeing Christian's dissatisfaction, Noelle added, "You will do this my way, or I will take Marc beyond your reach."

Christian was used to getting his way in all things. The way his eyebrows came together told Noelle she'd pushed too far. But she held her gaze steady, letting him see her stubbornness. In the end he nodded. From the glint in his eyes, she doubted his acquiescence would last long. In business he was known as a clever negotiator. She would have to watch for his tricks.

Glancing up at the house, she spied a small figure silhouetted in an upstairs window. Marc's bedroom overlooked the front yard. He wasn't going to go to bed without some sort of explanation from her. Sometimes he could be wiser than a child twice his years. It was partially her fault. She routinely gave him responsibilities, and Marc knew there would be consequences if he didn't keep his toys picked up, the garden watered and help shuffle his clothes to and from the laundry.

"I have to get my son to bed," Noelle said. "I'll speak with you tomorrow."

"Noelle." Christian spoke her name softly, halting her. "I meant what I said earlier. I really do miss you. I'd like for us to be friends again."

If he'd tried to cajole her regarding Marc, she might have softened toward him. Christian had a right to his son, whether she liked it or not, and his determination to have a relationship with Marc would eventually soothe her ferocious mama bear instincts. But the instant he tried to appeal to what had once been between them, all sympathy for him fled.

"I have a life filled with family, friends and purpose that I love. There's no room for you in it." She resumed walking toward the house without a backward glance. "Good night, Christian."

She didn't collapse after shutting the front door behind her, although she leaned back against the wood panel and breathed heavily for a few minutes until her heartbeat slowed. Had she really just faced down Christian and gotten the last word in? If her stomach wasn't pitching and rolling in reaction, she might have thrown a fist into the air.

Instead, Noelle headed upstairs. With each slow, deliberate step she regained the poise she'd learned in the stressful world of high fashion. The last thing she wanted was to upset her son and give him a reason to distrust Christian. Despite her measured pace, when she got to Marc's room, she still hadn't figured out a good way to explain the unexpected arrival of his father, a man she'd never talked about.

No surprise that Marc was jumping on his bed. On a regular day his small body contained enough energy to power a small village. After tonight's drama, he was a supernova.

"Mama. Mama. Mama."

"You know better than to jump on the bed," she scolded, stifling a heartfelt sigh. At least her mother had been able to get Marc into his pajamas. "Did you brush your teeth?" When her son showed no indication of answering her question, she glanced at her mother, who nodded. With deliberate firmness Noelle urged her son beneath the covers.

"Did you make the bad man go away?"

Time to correct her first mistake of the evening: letting Marc become aware of the tension between her and Christian.

"That wasn't a bad man, Marc. He was your prince."

Aversion twisted her son's features, amusing Noelle as she imagined the hit to Christian's ego at being so disparaged by one of his subjects.

"Don't like him."

Noelle wasn't feeling all that charitable toward Christian at the moment, either. She scooted her son into the middle of the double bed and seated herself beside him. Drawing in a breath, she braced herself to tell Marc that Christian was his father and then hesitated.

She couldn't bring herself to drop this bomb on her son until she figured out if having Christian in his life would benefit him. "Prince Christian would like to be your friend."

His little face screwed up in suspicion. "Does he like dinosaurs?"

"I don't know."

"Can he play football?"

"I'm not sure." Noelle suspected Marc had a list of activities he wanted to know about and smoothly redirected the conversation. "You'll have to ask him what he likes to do when you see him next."

"Will he get me a Komodo dragon?"

In addition to being obsessed with dinosaurs, Marc had a fascination with lizards and had received a twenty-gallon tank and a seven-inch leopard gecko from her dear friend Geoff for his fourth birthday. Since then, Marc had been lobbying for a bearded dragon, which would be twice the size of his current pet and require double the space.

"You know very well that a Komodo dragon is not a pet. They are seven feet long."

"But he could keep it at the palace, and I could visit it."

As wild a notion as this was, Noelle wouldn't put it past Christian to buy his son's love with a new pet. She would have to warn Christian against such a purchase.

The last thing she needed was a houseful of tanks containing lizards.

"That's not going to happen." She steered the conversation back on track. "Prince Christian might come to visit in the near future and if you have anything you want to know about that, I want you to ask me." She brushed a lock of hair off Marc's forehead and stared into his gold eyes. "Okay?"

The way her son was looking at her, Noelle suspected she'd bungled the conversation, but to her surprise she wasn't barraged by questions.

"Okay."

"Good. What do you want me to read tonight?"

Unsurprisingly he picked up a book on dinosaurs. Marc enjoyed looking at the pictures as she read the descriptions. Noelle knew he had the entire volume memorized. The cover was worn, and a few of the pages had minor tears. Her active son was hard on most things, and this book was one of his favorites.

It took half an hour to get through the book. Marc had forgotten all about Christian's visit by the time Noelle reached the last page. To her relief he settled down without a fight, his head on the pillow. A glance at the clock told her it was not long past his normal bedtime, and she congratulated herself on her minor victory.

Downstairs, her mother had opened a bottle of her favorite Gavi, a crisp Italian white with delicate notes of apples and honey. She handed Noelle a glass without asking if she wanted any.

"I thought you might be in the mood to celebrate," Mara said, eyeing her daughter over the rim of her glass.

Resentment burned at her mother's passive-aggressive remark. "Because Christian discovered I've been hiding his son all these years?" She snorted. "For the thousandth time, I'm not in love with him."

Mara didn't argue. "What are his intentions toward Marc?"

"He wants to get to know him."

"And that's all?"

"Of course. What else could there be?" Noelle had gone outside and shut the door before her conversation with Christian had gone too far, and knew her mother hadn't overheard anything. Still, she experienced a flash of despair as she recalled how Christian had raised the notion of legitimizing Marc by marrying her.

"The kingdom needs an heir. Now that both Prince Gabriel and Prince Nicolas are married, the media are obsessively speculating who your Prince Christian will choose to marry. The pressure is all on him to produce a son."

"He's not my Prince Christian," Noelle muttered, letting her irritation show.

"And now he knows he has a son."

"An illegitimate son." Noelle wanted to take back the reminder as soon as her mother's eyes lit with malicious delight.

"And here you are single and Sherdanian. Not to mention still harboring unrequited feelings for him."

"Don't be ridiculous. I'm not going to marry Christian so that he can claim Marc as his heir."

Her mother didn't look convinced. "Wouldn't it be your dream come true?"

"You were living in Italy when I met Christian, so you don't know what it was like between us. He's not husband material, and I'm not going to marry him because he needs an heir." Noelle heard heartbreak beneath the fervor in her voice. Five years had passed, but she hadn't fully recov-

ered from the hurt dealt to her when Christian pushed her
out of his life.

It wasn't something she intended to forgive or forget.

The café table on his cramped, third-floor balcony was
big enough for a cup of coffee and a small pot of hot pink
petunias. Christian sat on one of the two chairs, ignoring
the laptop balanced on his knee while he stared down the
narrow street whose details were lost to shadow at this
early hour. Thoughts on the encounter with Noelle the
night before, he watched the light seep into this old section of Sherdana's capital city of Carone.

Although Christian had rooms in the palace for his use,
he rarely stayed there, preferring the privacy of his own
space. He'd lost track of how many homes he owned. He
did business all over Europe and had apartments in the
major cities where he spent the most time. He owned two
homes in Sherdana: this cozy two-bedroom apartment in
the center of the capital where he could walk to bakeries,
cafés and restaurants, and a castle on a premier vineyard
two hours north of Carone.

After discovering he was a father, Christian had lain
in bed, staring at the ceiling while his thoughts churned.
Eventually he'd decided to give up on sleep and catch up
on his emails. Nic and Brooke had gotten married on a
Wednesday, which meant Christian had lost an entire day
of work. He usually worked from home until late morning. His active social life kept him out late most evenings,
and if he saw the sun come up, it was more likely that he
was coming home after a long night rather than getting
an early start on the day.

Despite his good intentions, he couldn't concentrate on
the reports that had been compiled by his CFO regarding
his purchase of a small Italian company that was devel-

oping intelligent robot technology. The columns of numbers blurred and ran together as his mind refused to focus.

Noelle had borne him a son and hidden the truth for five years, a pretty amazing feat in this age of social media. Last night, as he'd driven back to the apartment, he'd been furious with her. It shouldn't have mattered that he'd let her believe he wanted their relationship to end. She'd been pregnant with his child. She should have told him. And then what? He'd thought letting her go to pursue her dream of being a designer in Paris had been the best thing for her. What would he have done if he'd known she was pregnant? Marry her?

Christian shook his head.

It wouldn't have crossed his mind. She'd known him well. Better than he'd known himself. As the third son, he'd had little responsibility to the monarchy and could do what he wanted. So he'd partied to excess, made a name for himself as a playboy, indulged his every desire and thought no further than the moment.

The accident had changed all that. Changed him. He'd risked his life to save someone and had been permanently scarred in the process. But the fire that had ravaged his right side had wrought other changes. His selfless actions had impaired his hedonistic proclivities. Made him aware of others' needs. Before the accident he'd enjoyed being selfish and irresponsible. Losing the ability to act without recognizing the consequences to others had been almost as painful as the slow mending of his burns.

Thus, when he arranged for Noelle to train in Paris, he'd known that letting her think he no longer wanted her in his life would break her heart. Hurting her had pained him more than sending her away, but he'd known that if she stayed with him, he risked doing her far greater harm.

And now, thanks to his discovery of their son, she was back in his life. He ached with joy and dread.

Showing up on her doorstep last night had been a return to old patterns. When they'd been together before, he'd often popped by unannounced late at night after the clubs closed.

He'd met her at the café near his apartment where she waitressed. Unlike most of the women he flirted with, she hadn't been intrigued by his title or swayed by his charm. She'd treated him with such determined professionalism that he'd been compelled to pursue her relentlessly until she agreed to see him outside of work.

They didn't date. Not in a traditional sense. She was too serious to enjoy his frivolous lifestyle and too sensible to fit in with his superficial friends. But she was exactly what he needed. Her apartment became his refuge. When they finally became lovers, after being friends for six months, she was more familiar to him than any woman he'd ever known.

Not that this had stopped him from taking her for granted, first as a friend and confidante, and then as the woman who came alive in his arms.

Christian closed his eyes and settled his head back against the brick facade of his apartment. The breath he blew out didn't ease the tightness in his chest or relax the clenched muscles of his abdomen.

Last night he'd suggested that they should marry. The ease with which the words had slipped off his tongue betrayed the fact that his subconscious was already plotting. Speaking with her at the party had obviously started something brewing. Why not marry Noelle? The notion made sense even before he'd found out about Marc.

Years before they'd been good together. Or at least she'd been good for him. Sexually they'd been more than compatible. She'd been a drug in his system. One he'd tried numerous times to purge with no luck.

Discovering they'd created a child together, a much-needed potential heir to the throne, pretty much cemented his decision to make her his princess. He didn't need to scour Europe trying to find his future wife. She was right under his nose.

He should have felt as if an enormous weight had been lifted from his shoulders, but long ago he'd developed a conscience where Noelle was concerned. After the way he'd broken things off five years ago, she didn't want him anywhere near her. Persuading her to marry him would take time, and once the media got wind of his interest, they would interfere at every turn.

He'd have to work fast. She'd loved him once. A few intimate dinners to remind her of their crazy-hot chemistry and she'd be putty in his hands. Christian shoved aside a twinge of guilt. Being cavalier about seducing Noelle was not in keeping with the man he'd become these past few years. Scheming was something he reserved for business dealings.

Christian headed inside to shower and get dressed. For his country and his family, he had to convince Noelle to marry him. If it benefited him in the process, so much the better.

Three

An extravagant arrangement of two dozen long-stemmed red roses awaited Noelle in her office at the back of her small dress shop in Sherdana's historic city center. Coffee in hand, she stopped dead just inside the door and sucked in the rich, sweet scent of the enormous blossoms. She plucked a small white envelope from the bouquet, but didn't need to read the card to know the sender. The scarlet blooms signaled Christian's intent to stir up her quiet, perfectly ordered world.

Knowing she would get nothing accomplished with the roses dominating her efficient gold-and-cream space, Noelle called her assistant.

"Please get these out of here." Noelle waved her hand dismissively. When curiosity lit Jeanne's eyes, Noelle realized she'd let her irritation show.

Jeanne scooped the vase off the low coffee table. "Should I put them in the reception room?"

Noelle wanted to tell Jeanne to drop them into the trash out back. "Why don't you put them in the workroom? That way the seamstresses could enjoy the flowers."

"Are you sure you don't want me to leave them here? They're so beautiful."

Noelle's temper flared, sharp and acidic. Lack of sleep and frayed nerves were to blame for her reaction. She shook her head and strove to keep her voice calm as she tried to put a positive spin on her request. "Everyone has been working so hard. The flowers are for all of us," she lied, feeling only the mildest twinge of guilt at deceiving her employee.

Once the flowers were gone, Noelle opened her office window to the beautiful morning and let in the fresh air, but after an hour she could swear the scent of the roses remained. Restless and edgy, Noelle slid her sketchbook into her briefcase. She would go to her favorite café and work on the designs for next winter's collection.

The bell on the front door jangled, announcing a visitor. Because of her location among the quaint shops in the historic district, occasionally someone passing by would pop in, stirred by curiosity. Noelle's shop carried no ready to wear wedding dresses, but because her wealthy clientele could often be difficult to please, she had several bridal gowns on hand that had been rejected for one reason or another.

Jeanne's greeting carried down the hall as she approached whoever had entered the shop. Noelle gathered several pencils and froze in the act of dropping them into her briefcase. A deep voice rumbled in response to her assistant's inquiring tone. The pencils clattered as they fell from Noelle's nerveless fingers. Strong footsteps rang on the wood floor of the narrow hallway leading to her office.

Feeling much like a cornered cat, Noelle glanced up and saw Christian's imposing shoulders filling the doorway.

Cross that he'd followed up the flower delivery with a personal appearance, she spoke with unusual bluntness. "You were supposed to call me at ten not show up unannounced."

"I came to see if you liked the roses." He took in her pristine office and frowned. "Didn't you receive them?"

"Yes. I put them in the workroom for my employees to enjoy."

Not one muscle twitched in his face to betray his reaction, but she could tell her answer displeased him. She hated the way guilt rushed through her.

"I sent them to you."

All the time they'd been together, he'd never once given her flowers. She'd understood her role in his life. First as a sounding board for all his frustrations and woes. Eventually, she'd become his lover, a convenient one that he could drop in on whenever he was feeling lonely or in need of comfort. She'd made no demands, expected nothing, and he'd given her mind-blowing sex in return. To be fair, while they'd been physically intimate she'd also enjoyed a great deal of emotional intimacy, as well. But out of bed, Christian donned the charming persona he maintained to keep people at bay.

The roses had reminded her how susceptible she'd once been to his charm. What if nothing had changed in the past five years? She needed to determine if she could trust her head to guide her. He mustn't be allowed to think he could sway her with romantic gestures. For gestures were all they were.

"You're not going to make this easy for me, are you?" He crossed the threshold, crowding her office with his powerful presence.

"Why should I?" Noelle liked having her elegant desk as a buffer between them, but didn't want her entire staff hearing this conversation. Stepping out from behind the desk, she gestured Christian away from the door and closed it, trapping them together in the small space. "Five years ago you wanted nothing more to do with me. Now, you're desperate for an heir and you want my son."

"You forget that I came to see you last night knowing nothing about Marc," he grumbled in his deep, beguiling voice. His intent was clear. He intended to throw every trick in his abundant arsenal at her. "I saw you at the wedding and knew I'd made a mistake letting you go all those years ago."

His claim was so ridiculous she should have laughed in his face. But the words made her chest ache. How many nights had she lain awake, praying for his knock on her apartment door in Paris? Dreaming that he'd burst in, sweep her off her feet and declare he'd been a fool to let her go and that he couldn't live without her. Too many. In fact, she hadn't given up all hope until Marc's first birthday.

"I don't believe you."

"If you give me a chance, I'll prove it to you." His dark gold eyes glittered with sensual intent.

A hysterical laugh bubbled up in her chest. She clamped her teeth together and fought to appear unflustered. No easy task when the masculine scent of the man awakened buried memories. A tingle began between her thighs as she relived the joy of his hands on her body, his lips on hers.

Last night she'd stood up to him, an alarmed mama bear protecting her cub. Today she was a woman confronting a man who intended to persuade and seduce. Heat bloomed in her cheeks. She scowled, angry with herself and taking it out on him.

"If you want me to take your interest in Marc seriously,

you'd be better off demonstrating that you have what it takes to be a father."

"I agree." He nodded. "Which is why I sent a gift to Marc, as well."

Noelle bit back a groan. "What sort of gift?"

"A small thing."

"How small?"

"A child-sized electric car. My assistant said her son loves to drive his cousin's. He is about Marc's age."

She hissed out a breath. "You can't just do that."

"Of course I can."

Once upon a time she'd have teased him about his arrogance. Once upon a time she'd been madly in love with him.

"An electric car is an expensive toy. I want Marc to value art and stories and music. Not things."

"He's a four-year-old boy," Christian scoffed. "They want to get muddy and have adventures."

Noelle knew it was ridiculous, but she could feel Marc slipping away from her with each word Christian spoke. Her son would love this thrill-seeking prince and want to go live in a palace, and never once miss his mother. "And you're an expert on four-year-old boys?"

"I was one once. And he's a prince. He should always get the best."

Panic rose. Her voice dropped to a whisper. "That's not how I'm raising him."

"We need to be together for Marc's sake." Christian caught her hand and gave it a gentle squeeze. "He shouldn't have to grow up without a father."

Christian seemed sincere enough, but Noelle couldn't ignore that he needed an heir and knew just how stubborn Christian could be when he wanted something. She tugged her hand free and squared her shoulders.

"I can't possibly be with you," she said. "I'm involved with someone and we're quite serious."

Christian absorbed Noelle's statement with a slow eye-blink, his thoughts reeling. He'd come in too confident, certain that he could win over Noelle with a few roses and a bit of persuasion. She'd always been there any time he needed her. It had never once occurred to him that she might be in love with someone else. Acid burned in his gut at the thought of her with anyone besides him.

"You didn't mention anyone last night."

Her expression, once so transparent and open, betrayed none of her thoughts. "All I thought about was Marc and the effect your sudden appearance in his life would have on him."

"Who is this man you're seeing?" The question sounded more like an interrogation than a friendly inquiry.

"Someone I met shortly after I moved to Paris."

Five years. Had she run into his arms after Christian had sent her away? A knot formed in his chest.

"I'd love to meet him. Does he live in Sherdana?"

"Ah." Suddenly she looked very uncertain. "No. He splits his time between Paris and London."

Christian was liking this more and more. "Long distance affairs are so difficult," he purred. "As I'm sure you're finding out."

"Geoff loves Marc."

Christian saw resolve blazing in the depths of her chestnut-colored eyes.

"And Marc loves Geoff. They have a great time together. *We* are good together."

He wondered at her vehemence. Was she trying to convince him that this Geoff character was father material or convince herself that he was husband material? Either way,

Christian saw a foothold that would allow him to breach her defenses.

"When does he plan to come to Sherdana next?" A long unused oubliette beneath the castle on Christian's vineyard might be the perfect place to stash Geoff until Noelle came to her senses.

"Why?" Noelle regarded him with narrowed eyes.

"I'd like to meet him. Does he visit regularly?"

"Of course." But she didn't sound all that sure of her answer. "That is, when his cases permit. He's the managing partner of a very successful law firm specializing in human rights law and extradition." Pride softened her lips into a fond smile. "And of course, Marc and I travel to London and Paris quite often to visit him."

"How serious are you?" The more Christian heard, the less concerned he became that Geoff was going to prove a hindrance. If something of a permanent nature was going to happen between Noelle and her absent suitor, it should have occurred in the past five years. "Do you plan on marrying?"

She glanced down at her clasped hands. "We've discussed the possibility, but haven't made anything official."

What sort of man waited five years to claim a woman like Noelle? A very stupid one. And that was just fine with him. Christian had no qualms about stealing Noelle out from beneath the man's nose.

"Have dinner with me tonight."

Her eyes widened at his abrupt invitation, but she shook her head. "I can't. Geoff—"

"Isn't here and from the sound of things isn't likely to visit any time soon." A half step brought him close enough to hear her sharp intake of breath and feel the way her muscles tensed as he traced his knuckles along her jawline. The old, familiar chemistry sparked between them.

"You deserve a man who will appreciate you every minute of every day, not whenever his business dealings permit."

Noelle batted his hand away. "What would you know about how I deserve to be appreciated? When we were together, the only time you concerned yourself about my needs was when we were in bed."

"You make it sound like that's a bad thing." He spoke lightly, hiding his regret that he'd hurt her. He'd been a selfish bastard when they were together and hadn't grasped her worth. How ironic that finally understanding her value had compelled him to send her away.

Yet was he behaving any less selfishly now? After ignoring her for five years, he'd suddenly decided to drag her back into his life because he needed her once again. Was it fair to disrupt the tranquil, comfortable world she'd made for herself? Probably not, but now that he'd begun, Christian couldn't bring himself to stop. They'd made a child together. He had a son. That wasn't something he intended to walk away from.

"Christian, you weren't good for me five years ago, and you're not going to be good for me now. I was so madly in love with you I was happy with whatever scraps of your life you were willing to share with me. That's not enough for me anymore. I have a son who deserves to be loved and nurtured. He is my primary focus. Every decision I make is with his best interests foremost in my mind."

Christian's temper flared. "And you don't think his mother being married to his father is the best thing for him?"

"Not if the only reason his parents marry is so the Alessandro line continues to rule Sherdana."

Christian wasn't accustomed to cynicism coming from Noelle. She'd been sweet, innocent and as trusting as a kitten. His opposite in every way. It was why he hadn't been able to give her up even when he started to see shadows darken her eyes and her smiles become forced.

"Making Marc my heir is not the only reason I want to marry you." Although it was an important one to be sure. "I can't forget how good we were together."

Noelle shook her head. "I'm not sure you were good for me."

"I'm no longer the man I was." In so many ways that was true. He'd lost the ability to be frivolous and irresponsible. "The accident saw to that."

She flinched. "And I'm not the woman you once knew. Who's to say it would even work between us anymore?"

"Who's to say it wouldn't be better?"

As if to demonstrate his point, Christian slid his fingers around the back of her neck and drew her toward him. Without giving her a second to process his action, he lowered his lips to her and drank in her sweetness. A groan gathered in his chest at the way her mouth yielded to him. She gasped softly as her lips parted. He remembered all the times he'd held her in his arms and indulged his need for her with long, drugging kisses.

With other women he'd been quick to get to his pleasure. He liked his lovemaking hot and frenzied. Being with Noelle had brought out a different side of his personality. He'd never been in a rush with her. Her warm, silken skin and the gentle rise and fall of her slender curves had been worth appreciating in great detail. He'd adored her every gasp and shiver as he learned what pleased her. After a month he knew her body better than any woman he'd ever been with and yet she continued to surprise him.

Desire buzzed in his veins, the intensity rising as Noelle leaned into him. He freed her lips before longing made the kiss spiral out of control. Heart thumping madly, he inhaled her light floral perfume. The fragrance was more sophisticated than what she used to wear, reminding him that time and distance had made them strangers. His lids felt heavy as he lifted his lashes and regarded her flushed cheeks.

"You didn't stop me from kissing you," he murmured in satisfaction, wondering if it could really be this easy.

"I was curious how it would feel after five long years." Her neutral tone dampened his optimism.

"And?"

"Your technique hasn't diminished."

Christian stepped back and gave her a lopsided smile. "Nor has my desire for you."

"Yes…well." She didn't sound as if she believed him. "I'm sure you can find any number of women eager to distract you."

"It's not like that anymore."

"The tabloids say otherwise."

"The tabloids exaggerate. Any drama attributed to my love life is concocted to sell newspapers."

"So how do you explain the twin models from Milan photographed topless on your hotel balcony in Cannes?"

"They needed a place to crash and I spent the night on the phone to Hong Kong."

Noelle's lips thinned as she nodded. "And the Spanish heiress who ran away from her wedding with you?"

"It was an arranged marriage and she was in love with an architect from Brussels who happened to be doing some work on my apartment in London."

"You're asking me to believe you're in the habit of rescuing women these days?"

He understood her skepticism. Five years earlier his playboy reputation had been well earned. But the day he'd arranged for Noelle to study in Paris was the day he'd begun to change. She'd been the first woman he'd saved. And the only one who'd needed to be rescued from him.

"There's a long list of women I've helped. I could put you in touch with some of them if it would help improve your perception of me." She wasn't going to take his pursuit seriously if she thought he hadn't changed.

"I'm sure there are scads of women who would line up to sing your praises."

"Have dinner with me." He repeated his earlier invitation, determined to convince her this wasn't a ploy or a scam. "We have a great deal to talk about."

She shook her head. "The only thing that concerns me is your intentions for my son. We can talk about ground rules here or at your office. There's no reason for us to become more than civil acquaintances."

"That's where you're wrong. I can name several very good reasons why we should take our relationship to a close, personal level. Starting with the fact that I make you nervous." He caught her chin and turned her face so he could snare her gaze. "I think that means you still have feelings for me. I know I have feelings for you. We belong together."

"I'm with Geoff. Nothing you can say or do will change that."

Christian slid his thumb across her lower lip and watched her pupils dilate. No doubt she was counting on her words and actions to effectively put him off, but there was no hiding her body's reaction.

With a slow smile, his hand fell away. "We'll see."

Four

With her pulse hammering in her ears, Noelle spent a full minute staring at the empty hallway after Christian had gone. What had just happened? Knees shaking, she retreated to her desk and dropped into her comfortable chair with a hearty exhalation. To her dismay, her fingers trembled as she dialed a familiar number. When Geoff answered the phone, his deep voice acted like a sturdy net she could fall into and be safe.

"Geoff, thank goodness."

"Noelle, are you okay? You sound upset."

"I've just done a terrible, cowardly thing." Such drama wasn't like her, and she noticed that several beats passed while Geoff adjusted to her tumultuous state.

"I'm sure it's not as bad as all that."

She closed her eyes, and his steady tone calmed her. She'd met Geoff shortly after moving to Paris. He'd been at a party her boss was throwing and they'd hit it off immediately. Both had been grieving losses. Noelle was fresh from her breakup with Christian and Geoff had lost his wife of fifteen years to cancer six months earlier.

"It's really bad. I made up a serious relationship between you and me."

Amusement filled his voice as he asked, "Couldn't you just have told the guy you weren't interested? That's worked for you up to this point."

Normally Noelle blamed her lack of interest in men on the demands of her skyrocketing career and being focused on her son. The truth was she didn't find anyone as interesting or attractive as Christian. In the darkest hours of the night when she couldn't sleep and got up to sketch or visit her workshop, she suspected that the love she'd thought had died when Christian cast her aside was really only buried beneath a thick layer of pain and disappointment.

"It's not just a guy." In her agitation, she snapped one of her drawing pencils in two. "It's Christian, and he figured out Marc is his son."

"Ah." Geoff had been a shoulder to cry on when she'd first discovered she was pregnant. Seventeen years her senior, he'd been a combination of close friend and elder brother.

"I told you about the delicate political situation surrounding the Sherdanian throne. Yesterday Nicolas Alessandro married an American girl, leaving Christian the only brother capable of producing a future king. Last night he came to the house and met Marc. Now he's got it in his head that we should get married so Marc can be his legitimate heir."

"And he won't take no for an answer?"

"He's determined to win me over." Noelle trembled as her mind replayed the kiss. She hadn't forgotten the chemistry between them, but five years had dulled her memory of how susceptible she was to his touch. "I can't let that happen."

"So you told him we were dating?"

"I panicked. Which was stupid because he doesn't believe me. I need to show him that you exist and that we're very happy. Can you come spend the weekend with me? I'll call and invite him to have dinner with us." Silence greeted her announcement. "Geoff? I'm sorry, I know I'm putting you on the spot."

"Noelle, darling, you know I'm happy to help you any way I can, but are you sure this is the best tactic? I don't live in Sherdana. Even if I appear once and we give a great performance of being madly in love, he's not going to be dissuaded by an absent lover."

She thought back to Christian's remark about long distance relationships. "You're right. Call Jean-Pierre and ask him if I can borrow an engagement ring. A big one." The jeweler owed her several favors for sending business his way.

"Our relationship is moving awfully fast," Geoff teased, but concern shaded his lighthearted tone.

"I know and I'm sorry. I'm taking terrible advantage of our friendship, but I'm feeling rather desperate at the moment."

"There's no one I'd be happier to be fake-engaged to than you, but have you thought this through? Are you planning on staying engaged forever? What happens when we don't actually get married?"

"Hopefully he will be under enough pressure to marry someone suitable that he'll realize he can't wait around to change my mind."

"This plan of yours is full of holes."

Christian had a knack for shredding her customarily

sensible behavior. "We can talk about that when you get here."

"Very well. I'll see you Friday evening."

Noelle disconnected the call feeling marginally less anxious. Pretending to be engaged to Geoff was a ridiculous ploy, but hopefully one that would buy her enough space to get her emotions back under control. Christian had been on the offensive since Brooke and Nic's wedding. Every step he'd taken had backed Noelle into a corner. It was time she came out swinging.

Christian sat at his favorite table in Seillan's, one of Carone's finest restaurants featuring French cuisine. It was owned by a long-time friend of his, world-renowned chef Michel Seillan.

"Hello, P.C. Are you dining alone?" Michel gripped Christian's shoulder in an affectionate vise. The two men had gone to school together since they were seven years old and had spent a great deal of time tearing up the clubs of London and Paris in their early twenties. The nickname P.C. had evolved when Michel had complained that addressing Christian as Prince Christian took too long.

"No, I'm expecting a couple of friends."

"Female? And are you needing some help to entertain them?"

"Only one is a woman, and when have I ever needed help keeping women entertained?"

"Years ago, I might have agreed with you, but lately you've slowed down." Michel smirked.

"These days I'm more interested in quality than quantity."

With a laugh and another thump on Christian's shoulder, Michel departed. Minutes later a waiter appeared with a dry vodka martini. Christian resisted the urge to down the drink. For some reason, he wasn't feeling calm as the top of the hour approached.

Noelle might not be in love with the British barrister she was bringing to dinner, but that didn't mean the reverse was true. During the years when Christian and Noelle had been together, he'd never worried that another man might steal her away. She'd been devoted to him first as a friend and then as a lover. But that was before he'd sent her away. Before she'd had to raise their child on her own for four years.

Christian had never been one for settling down. No doubt Noelle continued to view him that way. The fact that he had to marry in order to produce an heir for the kingdom didn't exactly recommend his willingness or ability to be a good husband.

What if Noelle was ready to build a life with someone steady? To have more children? She'd want a man with a constant heart who'd devote unwavering attention to her needs.

The sip of the martini he'd taken stuck in Christian's suddenly tight throat. He coughed and coughed again as the liquor burned. Through watering eyes, he spotted Noelle entering the restaurant.

She was eye-catching in a fifties-inspired black dress with a bodice embroidered in gold flowers that hugged her torso and bared her arms. A wide band of black fabric made her waist look incredibly tiny, and the full skirt skimmed her knees. She wove between the tables with effortless grace, and Christian's heart twisted. The lively smile curving her full red lips was for the man who trailed after her. She'd always been pretty, but confidence and happiness had transformed her into a vivacious beauty. Desire stirred in Christian. But it wasn't his hormones that came to life. He wanted her, not just as a sexual partner, but as a supportive companion who lightened his bad moods and made his troubles fade away.

He'd forgotten how easily she aroused his emotions. How she made him ache for her laughter and long for the soothing caress of her fingers through his hair.

Christian stood as Noelle and her escort approached the table. The man was considerably older than Christian expected. Tall and lean, with blond hair and laugh lines around his gray eyes, he had close to two decades on Noelle. Seeing the level of fondness in her eyes, Christian was prepared to dislike the man intensely.

"Good evening, Noelle," Christian said, keeping his roiling emotions out of his tone.

"Good evening, Your Royal Highness. I would like to introduce you to Geoff Coomb. Geoff, this is Prince Christian Alessandro."

Noelle's companion had a firm handshake and returned Christian's assessing gaze with confidence that made Christian despise him even more. "It was kind of you to join us for dinner."

"Not at all."

Us.

The word on the man's lips bothered Christian more than he liked. It spoke of a familiarity that he no longer enjoyed with Noelle. He'd underestimated the threat her relationship with Coomb represented. While Christian had fully intended to convince Noelle to marry him through whatever means necessary, he'd presumed his methods would involve seduction and winning his son's love. He hadn't considered she might be perfectly happy with the affection and emotional support she received from Coomb.

Resisting the desire to scowl at the lawyer, Christian fixed a pleasant expression on his face and stepped forward to hold Noelle's chair out for her. To his annoyance,

Geoff was there a beat faster, and she flashed him another of her enchanting smiles as she sat. Christian waited until Coomb settled and then fell into the role of perfect host, all the while digging into the history between the two so he could figure out the best way to win Noelle back.

"Noelle told me you two met years ago in Paris."

"At a party," Geoff said, regarding Noelle with an intimate smile. "She was the most beautiful woman in the room."

Christian had little doubt of that. "And you've been together all these years?"

"We were friends awhile before we began to date," Noelle said, favoring Coomb with another of her glowing smiles. "Neither one of us was ready to jump into anything right away."

"I'd lost my wife a few months earlier to cancer." Geoff covered Noelle's right hand with his. "Noelle was a good friend to me. We grew very close."

Close was what Noelle and Christian had been until he'd ruined everything.

"Geoff kept me from quitting during that first year in Paris. Without his encouragement I would have run home at least once a week."

Despite the jealousy raging through him, Christian was glad Noelle had had someone to support her when he couldn't. He'd been too self-absorbed to appreciate what he had until it was too late. And then too stubborn to reach out and fix what he'd broken. After the accident, he'd reasoned Noelle had been better off without him. And he'd been right. She'd sacrificed too much to be with him.

But that was then. The noble part of him that had let her go five years earlier was no longer in charge of his actions. He was older and wiser these days. They had a son. She and Marc belonged with him.

The waiter brought Noelle a glass of red wine and a scotch for Coomb. As Noelle lifted her left hand to pick up her drink, the light from the chandelier overhead caught in the enormous diamond adorning her ring finger. Noelle noticed Christian's riveted attention, and her expression grew positively radiant.

"We're engaged."

"That's rather sudden." And convenient. The engagement had moved her beyond his grasp. Suspicious, Christian eyed the older man, hoping for some sign of subterfuge, but saw only fondness as the lawyer gazed at Noelle.

"Not sudden at all," Coomb replied. "We've been heading this way for years."

"You seemed content with the relationship as it was," Christian pointed out to Noelle. Had she been surprised by this turn of events, or was she guilty of deliberately misleading him? The Noelle he'd known had been free of guile. He didn't like to think she'd changed so much.

"I am content with our relationship in all its forms." Noelle gave Coomb a sweet smile. "I feel so very lucky to have such a wonderful man in my life."

Christian's gut ached as if he'd been kicked. Something ugly and dark formed inside him as he watched Noelle bask in Coomb's affection. Curses reverberated in Christian's thoughts. Being the uncomfortable third wheel wasn't how he'd expected the evening to go.

"But," she continued, fixing bright eyes on Christian. "I'm thrilled that we are going to be a family."

Was there a touch too much defiance in her delivery? Christian assessed her for a long moment before extending his arm to signal the attentive waiter. "We're celebrating," he told Antonio. "A bottle of champagne to toast the newly betrothed."

Inwardly seething, Christian waited while crystal flutes

were placed upon the table and filled, and then gave the newly engaged couple his most political smile. "May you enjoy a lifetime of happiness." She would assume that he meant her and Coomb.

Christian set the glass to his lips and drank the excellent vintage with little pleasure. While a part of him clamored to be the one she chose, more than anything he hoped she would be happy. *Idiot.* Why couldn't he stop doing the right thing where she was concerned? In all other aspects of his life he was a selfish bastard, but when it came to Noelle, he wanted what was best for her.

Of course, the solution was simple. He just needed to believe that the best thing for Noelle was for her to marry him.

In the days since he'd spoken to her at the latest royal wedding and discovered he was a father, Christian had lost numerous hours in daydreaming about his future with Noelle and Marc. Imagining long passion-filled nights in bed with her left him grinning in anticipation.

In contrast the thought of being a father distressed him. Nothing he'd done in his life had prepared him for such a daunting task. What part of buying troubled companies to tear apart and restructure gave him the skills to win the trust and affection of a four-year-old boy?

As a prince, he'd never had to work at making people like him. Those who didn't enjoy his company respected him because of his position. Foolish or ambitious women, who appreciated his money and position, vied for his attention. Sensible ones and those unsuitable for romancing he charmed without effort, but invested little of himself in the exchanges. His days and nights were consistently filled with an endless supply of business associates, social acquaintances or potential lovers. He cared little about any of them and his encounters blurred together in an indistinct gabble of memories.

Nothing about this shallow, drifting existence had bothered him until Noelle entered his life. She was a magnifying glass that sharpened his perceptions, making him see things as they were instead of as fuzzy renderings on the edges of his awareness. She'd provoked him to question why with all the money he made he wasn't using some of it to make a positive social impact. But when he'd donated to charities, he'd picked ones that would eventually provide a benefit to him and hadn't enjoyed the accolades heaped upon him.

Without meaning to she'd pushed him to do better. Be better. She'd never criticized his actions or made suggestions of things he should do, but as he discovered what was important to her, he'd begun to change. All his life he'd barely taken responsibility for himself, much less taken on the burden of anyone else's welfare. Suddenly he had this insignificant woman in his head all the time. In the morning he'd woken and wondered if she'd missed him in her bed. Throughout his day he noted things he wanted to share with her. She took up space in his narcissistic reality, and he resented her intrusion.

Realizing her effect on him had set off a chain reaction of bad behavior. She'd always forgive and forget, but that hadn't been the end of it for him.

He'd felt guilty.

And hated it.

Which had naturally led to even worse behavior and eventually the accident. Five years after the fact, that awful night continued to haunt him. He relived the pain and terror every time he caught a glimpse of his reflection or touched the puckered scars that marred his right arm and the right side of his chest, neck and face. The skin tingled in phantom pain. He could have undergone reconstructive surgery for the damage, but preferred to leave the scars as a reminder of his supreme failure.

Christian shook himself out of his dark thoughts and caught Noelle watching him. Worry, longing and regret raced across her face in rapid succession before she looked away. Christian stared at her as she laughed at something Coomb said to her. Was it possible that she still cared and was fighting desperately not to? Something inside Christian clicked into place like the resetting of a dislocated bone. He hadn't realized how out of whack his psyche had been until the pain vanished. In the peaceful aftermath, he began to plot.

Noelle might be engaged, but she wasn't married. The ring she wore represented a promise to wed, and he was notorious for making even the most stubborn, committed individuals change their minds.

Heart thumping in wild abandonment, Noelle gulped down the beginnings of panic. Despite the heartache and the half decade of separation, Christian continued to fascinate and disturb her like no other man. He'd been back in her life for three days, and her judgment was already lousy. She'd invented a fake fiancé and convinced Geoff to play along. All the while she fought against the longing to rake her fingers through Christian's thick, wavy hair and pull his mouth to hers.

Nothing good would come of getting caught up in the reckless desire that had hampered her innate common sense during the two years she'd loved him. He'd driven her to the highest peaks of ecstasy one day and left her wallowing in uncertainty and disappointment the next. Even accepting that she was responsible for her own happiness,

Noelle hadn't once barred her door or her heart against him. And in the end, he'd been the one to walk away.

Which was why she needed to be so careful now. There was more at stake than her foolish heart. She couldn't risk that Christian might hurt her son.

His son.

Noelle lifted her fork and held it suspended over the plate the waiter had placed before her. Her thoughts were too complex to sort out the ingredients of the elegantly plated meal. She saw her dinner as a mass of color: shades of brown from caramel to espresso, a range of greens and a golden sauce.

"Something wrong?" Christian prompted, his deep voice silky and sensual.

She made the mistake of meeting his burnished gold eyes. He looked as if he wanted to devour her right then and there. "It's too beautiful to eat."

His slow smile curled her toes. "I assure you it will taste even better."

Breathless in reaction to his dizzying charisma, Noelle jerked her attention back to the meal and admonished herself for letting him get to her. The cuisine that should have dazzled her palate tasted like sawdust in her dry mouth. When would Christian stop dominating her senses? She would have thought five years apart had dulled her body's reaction to him.

At least she maintained some control over her mind.

It probably helped that she had very little trouble resisting *Prince* Christian. Arrogant and confident, the royal persona represented everything that had broken her heart five years earlier. Especially when he'd shown up unannounced at her farmhouse after Nic and Brooke's wedding and presumed she'd marry him to legitimize Marc.

She gave her head a barely perceptible shake. Of course

he'd take the easy way out. Why go to the trouble to win a bride and get her pregnant when his former lover had already produced a potential heir. And then there were the two dozen red roses he'd had sent to her office. While grandly romantic, the gesture had barely aroused a twinge of temptation.

It was the vulnerability she'd infrequently glimpsed in him that destroyed all her self-preservation and led to repeated disappointments. During those moments, when his shoulders hunched and the cocky playboy vanished, her defenses crumbled. Whether or not he could accept it, Christian yearned for someone to believe in him, and until he pushed her out of his life, Noelle had naively thought that someone was her.

And now he was back. And making demands on her once more. Concern that Christian had appeared suspicious of her hasty engagement swept over her. Half acting the part of smitten fiancée, half because she needed reassurance, Noelle reached for Geoff's hand. He responded with a tender smile that would have made her heart flutter if she was actually in love with him.

Christian observed their exchange through half-lidded eyes and Noelle was convinced she and Geoff were successfully selling the fabrication. But when the stilted meal at long last concluded, it was Christian's hand, warm and too familiar, at the small of her back as they made their way from the restaurant. Geoff had deferred to Christian's rank, and she was now far too aware that her willpower wasn't as strong as she'd hoped. As she wove between the tables, a slowly expanding coil of heat threatened her peace of mind.

Christian's car and driver awaited him at the curb, but instead of bidding them good-night, he lingered while the valet brought Geoff's car around. They made an awkward trio.

When Geoff would have opened the car door and handed Noelle into the passenger seat, Christian used his height and broad shoulders as a not so subtle barrier to keep Geoff from reaching her.

"I've got this." Christian set his hand on the car door and lifted the corners of his lips, shooting Geoff a perfunctory smile that was quickly gone. When he shifted his gaze to Noelle, his eyes glowed with possessive intent.

"Thank you for a lovely evening," she said as Christian handed her into the passenger seat.

"I enjoyed meeting your fiancé, but we didn't get the chance to talk about Marc or our future. I'll call you tomorrow and we can discuss the best time for the three of us to get together."

Before Noelle could protest, Christian shut the door and with a brief, wicked grin at getting in the last word, backed away from the car.

Geoff glanced at her before pulling away from the curb. "Are you okay?"

"Sure," she lied, tearing her gaze away from Christian with effort. "Why wouldn't I be?"

"He's still watching us go."

Noelle's nerves were frayed by the tension. "How do you expect me to respond to that?" she snapped, her tone harsh. As soon as the words were out she hunched her shoulders. "I'm sorry. The man gets to me."

"From the way he was looking at you tonight, you get to him, as well."

Geoff probably meant for his words to reassure her. Instead, she just barely resisted the urge to drop her face into her hands and moan in misery. The last thing she needed was to speculate whether Christian's interest in marrying her was motivated by anything other than expediency.

"You're supposed to be the sensible voice that tells me

not to get involved with Christian." Noelle sighed, predicting a long sleepless night ahead. "I need to keep my head clear and my emotions on ice until he gives up on the idea of marrying me."

"You don't think he bought that we're madly in love and destined to live happily-ever-after?" Geoff's wry inflection had serious undertones. Earlier that day he'd tried to talk her out of her gambit, but she'd been too panicky to listen.

"Maybe at first."

"I thought I played the part of your ardent suitor very well."

"You did." The flaw in the plan lay solely at her doorstep. How could she pretend to be in love with Geoff if her heart still fluttered when Christian was near? With a woeful sigh she surrendered to the inevitable.

Noelle grasped the enormous diamond and slid the ring from her finger. It was a relief to take the clumsy thing off. She might have handled the weight better if she didn't feel so much regret about dragging Geoff into her schemes.

With one corner of his mouth lifted in a half smile, Geoff took the ring and popped it into his breast pocket. "And just like that I'm a single man again."

"It was my fault he saw through us. I shouldn't have attempted to trick him. He's far too astute for that. He's probably already had you checked out and knows we're not together."

Geoff's expression turned serious. "Your openness and honesty are what everyone loves about you. Don't let Christian turn you into someone you're not. Be honest with him about your fears for Marc."

At the moment Noelle wasn't feeling remotely honest or lovable. She was an anxious mother ready to defend her child through whatever devious or dirty means necessary.

"Are you sure the prince isn't sincere about wanting a relationship with Marc?"

"I don't know." Her heart had a different opinion, but Noelle couldn't trust the poor, misguided thing. "I'd feel better about it if he wasn't under pressure to produce an heir."

For five long years, a tiny, hopeful part of her had been waiting for Christian to appear on her doorstep the way he used to when they were together. Each year her optimism had dimmed until only a minute speck of it remained. Now he wanted back in her life. Not because he missed her or realized she was his soul mate, but because she'd given birth to his son, and Marc was a quick fix for his current predicament.

"You seem to have forgotten that you and Marc are a package deal." Geoff took his eyes off the road and shot her a somber glance. "The only way Marc becomes his heir is if he's legitimate. Which means Christian needs to marry you."

To her shame the thought sent a wanton burst of anticipation ripping through her. The way her stomach clenched was both familiar and unwelcome. She hated her body's involuntary reaction because that meant she was susceptible to the abundant tools in Christian's sexual arsenal.

She extended her hand, palm up. "You're right. Please return my ring. The engagement is back on."

Geoff shook his head, making no move to oblige her. "I'll not be jilted by you twice. You're going to have to sort out your issues with Christian without resorting to any more ill-advised schemes."

Five

Christian paced before the French doors that led from the green drawing room to the extensive garden at the back of the palace. He tugged his left sleeve down over his watch. During the past fifteen minutes, the movement had become a nervous tick as he'd checked the time every twenty seconds or so. Noelle and Marc were late to the meeting she'd finally agreed to. The waiting was eating away the last of Christian's calm.

He decided to take his agitation out on Gabriel. "I still can't believe you've known that I had a son and didn't tell me."

From his spot on the emerald-colored sofa in the center of the room, the crown prince of Sherdana glanced up from his smartphone, unruffled by his brother's aggressive tone. "Olivia and I suspected. We didn't know for sure. And until the DNA tests come back, you don't, either."

Christian snorted in reply as he continued his path

back and forth across the eighteenth-century carpet. The aimless movement wasn't improving his situation, so he stopped before his brother and scowled at him.

"He's my son. He has the Alessandro eyes and looks the way we did at four." Although the triplets weren't identical, as children they'd been enough alike in appearance to confuse strangers.

"So now you know." Gabriel's lips curved into a challenging smile. "What happens next?"

"I get to know my son."

From the speed with which his brother's attention returned to his phone, Gabriel hadn't approved of Christian's offhanded response. Irritation spread from his chest to his gut.

"What?" he demanded.

"You've always played it just a little too safe where relationships were concerned."

"And you haven't?"

It wasn't a fair criticism. Gabriel had fallen hard for Marissa Somme, the deceased mother of his twin two-year-old daughters. But unlike Christian, Gabriel was first in line to the Sherdanian throne and put duty above all else. From the moment he'd begun the affair with the half-French, half-American model, Gabriel had known it must end. Sherdana's constitution decreed that in order for his son to rule the country one day, the child's mother had to be either a European aristocrat or a Sherdanian citizen.

Marissa had been neither, and Gabriel had ended the relationship. At the time he hadn't known he was going to be a father. That bomb had been dropped on him weeks before he was to marry Lady Olivia Darcy. Her British ancestry made her an exceptional candidate for princess. Or that's the way it had appeared until her fertility issues had made her unsuitable to be Gabriel's wife.

When Gabriel didn't respond to his brother's ineffectual gibe, Christian continued. "What do you want from me?"

"An heir would be nice."

"Nice." Christian practically spit the word. *Nice* didn't describe the pressure his family had put upon him once Gabriel married a woman who could never bear children and Nic had announced his intention to make an American his wife. "You think I should marry Noelle."

That he'd already intended to do just that didn't lessen Christian's annoyance. He was sick of everyone telling him what to do.

"It's about time you put the needs of this family and this country above your own."

"What about Nic? He's been in America for ten years trying to build his damned rocket ship. Why does he get to keep doing what he wants?" Christian immediately regretted his petulant tone, but the resentment he'd kept bottled up for the past three months had a mind of its own.

"If you hadn't played the third-in-line-to-the-throne card like you always do, expecting me or Nic to be the responsible ones, you might have been able to marry the woman of your dreams, suitable or not. Then Nic would be the one ranting and raving about the unfairness of doing his *duty* to Sherdana."

Duty.

Christian was getting awfully sick of that word. Until four months ago, the only feeling Christian had about matrimony was utter relief that he'd never be forced down the aisle because the country required it. Producing an heir was Gabriel's obligation as firstborn. Christian enjoyed all the perks of a princely title without any of the demands. And he wasn't beleaguered by guilt over his freedom. If it was selfish of him, so be it.

"We all know I'm not marriage material," Christian

grumbled, casting a glance toward the doorway for the hundredth time. "I wonder what's keeping them."

He was eager to start bonding with his son. And convincing the child's mother that her life would be so much better as his princess. Princess Noelle had a nice ring to it. She might be resistant to the idea of marrying Christian the man, but once she saw how fast doors opened for her as his royal consort, she would realize that Christian the prince was a magnificent catch.

"They'll be here shortly," Gabriel said.

"Do you have some sort of tracking app on your phone that notifies you when guests arrive?" Christian's words were meant to irritate his brother, but the grim, uptight Gabriel of a year ago had been replaced by a relaxed, charming prince of the realm who was impossible to rile.

"No." Gabriel's lips curved in a private smile. "I'm texting with Olivia. She said Marc has finished his third cookie and Mother's ten-thirty appointment has arrived."

Adrenaline zinged through Christian. "Noelle and Marc are already here? How long?"

"About twenty minutes."

"Is that why you're in here with me? To keep me occupied while Olivia introduced Marc to our mother? Did it ever occur to you that I wanted to get to know my son a little before I sprang him on the family?"

"If that's the case, you shouldn't have arranged for him to come here today."

"Noelle suggested it. She didn't want me showing up at her home and bringing media attention with me, and I certainly couldn't spend time with them in public. The palace made sense, since she's been here several times." Christian massaged the back of his neck to ease the stiffness brought on by the stress of his brother's interference. "I thought we could have a quiet couple hours…"

Dammit.

He liked keeping his personal life as far from the palace as possible. While he didn't mind his romantic escapades making a splash in tabloids all over Europe, he'd never once gone out of his way to introduce any of the jet-setters to his family. His friends liked to party. So did he. End of story. Not one of them could have captured the heart of a nation the way Olivia and Brooke had. His women were flashy, spoiled and selfish. Not one wanted a deeper connection. That suited him just fine.

Noelle was the complete opposite. A timeless beauty, her meteoric rise in the world of bridal fashion had captured the media's attention. Every single article Christian had read about her in the past week had praised her vision and talent. They loved how she'd started as an assistant designer at Matteo Pizarro Designs and been mentored by the great man himself. Of course, Christian wasn't surprised by her success. He'd known five years ago that her gift for design would take her a long way. It was her lack of confidence that had held her back.

And her love for him.

"Did Olivia say anything about how the meeting with Mother went?"

With two royal weddings taking place within a couple months of each other, Christian had made himself scarce around the palace, but he was certain Noelle had met the queen during one of her dress fittings with Gabriel's twin girls who'd acted as flower girls for both Olivia and Brooke. Of course, on those occasions she'd been the talented fashion designer who'd crafted the fairy-tale wedding gowns worn by his brothers' brides. As the mother of what might just be the future monarch of Sherdana, she would undergo a vastly different scrutiny. What if the queen decided Noelle wasn't suitable to become a member of the royal family?

And what had the queen thought of her grandson? Would the child pass muster? Christian couldn't rein in his concern. "Did mother like Marc?"

From the way Gabriel's keen gaze rested on him, Christian had failed to sound casual.

"I'm sure Noelle will tell you all about it when she arrives. Olivia is bringing them now."

Christian would have preferred a briefing from an impartial third party like his brother's clever wife, but clamped down on his agitation. Instead, he focused on what he could recall of the boy. Their brief encounter had left him with little more than a series of impressions. Fierce Alessandro eyes. Protective stance. Disapproval of the man his mother had introduced as Prince Christian.

Had Noelle already explained to Marc who Christian truly was? Or did she plan to do so today with Christian at her side? It was a question he probably should have asked his former flame days ago, but Christian hadn't been thinking about how the news might rock the four-year-old's world. He'd been too caught up in how the discovery had impacted him.

"Do you and Olivia plan to stick around for a bit?"

Gabriel eyed him, his expression thoughtful. "We hadn't planned to."

"Would you?" Christian suspected the strain would be muted if he, Noelle and Marc weren't left alone right away. "Just for a bit. Marc might be a bit overwhelmed."

"Yes," Gabriel drawled. "I'm sure it's Marc that we need to worry about."

"If you're implying that I'm anxious…"

It wasn't like Christian to let anyone see him sweat, but maybe just this once it would be okay. If anyone would understand how he felt, it would be Gabriel. Several months ago, Sherdana's crown prince had been surprised in the same way when twin toddlers, Karina and Bethany, had arrived on his doorstep after their mother died. Christian had been impressed how well his brother had adapted to fatherhood. Of course, the girls were two years younger than Marc and probably hadn't yet missed having a father. But a boy was different. He needed a male influence in his life. Someone to look up to.

"I have a four-year-old son I've barely met," Christian murmured, overwhelmed with awe and dismay.

"It's terrifying." Gabriel clapped him on the back, the solid blow knocking Christian away from the brink of panic. "Can't wait to meet him."

As if on cue, a dark-haired boy streaked through the doorway and dodged around several carefully arranged chairs, making a beeline for the enormous fireplace at the opposite end of the room.

"Look, I can fit in this one, too." Dressed in navy pants and a pale blue shirt, Marc stood framed in the white marble surround, arms outstretched and wearing a precocious grin.

The boy's compelling enthusiasm drew and held every adult eye in the room. Christian was the first to look away. Noelle had entered on Olivia's heels, and he stole a moment to drink in her quiet beauty.

In manner and appearance, Noelle was more like Gabriel's graceful, elegant wife than Nic's bohemian spitfire. Today Noelle wore a textured brown sheath with black side panels that accentuated her slender curves. A two-inch ruffled flounce at the hemline boosted the design from simple to striking.

"Marc, come out of there," Noelle scolded with a quick

apologetic glance to where Gabriel stood with his arm wrapped around Olivia's waist.

After four months Christian still wasn't accustomed to his brother's easy affection with his new wife. Even as a child Gabriel had been somber and formal most of the time, as if his future crown already weighed heavily on his head. Christian marveled to see him now, relaxed and smiling as he kissed Olivia on the cheek and whispered something in her ear that brought rosy delight to her cheeks.

Christian tore his gaze from the happy couple in time to catch the wistfulness that softened Noelle's expression as she too regarded the royal pair. A realization tore at him: he wanted the same intimate connection with Noelle that Gabriel had with Olivia. A partnership that sizzled in the bedroom and worked everywhere else.

Pity he'd already betrayed the trust that would permit him to have, either.

Noelle couldn't think straight with Christian and her son in the same room. Given Marc's adverse reaction to Christian the night he'd shown up unannounced, she was worried that her son wouldn't want to have anything to do with his father.

And that was the least of her problems.

Having a meeting with Christian's mother sprung on her had been bad enough, but to then watch her transform from imperious queen to adoring grandmother in the space of ten minutes had made Noelle question her decision to keep Marc's paternity a secret. Now that the truth was out, she expected the pressure to legitimize Marc by marrying Christian would increase tenfold.

Nor did it appear as if she would have a single supporter in the palace if she decided against marriage. Olivia had already said the twins would be so excited when Marc came to live in the palace, and Gabriel was obviously enjoying his nephew's antics. The suspicion Noelle expected to encounter had been nonexistent. Everyone seemed to accept that Marc was Christian's son.

Which meant whatever Noelle chose for her son's future, she had no one to blame but herself for the consequences.

Her eyes hurt with the effort of keeping her gaze from devouring Christian. Whenever he was near, she had to fight to maintain a neutral demeanor. After a five-year drought, spending so much time with him was starting to eat into her willpower. It wasn't fair how easily she regressed into familiar patterns. Back when they were lovers, she used to spend hours beside him in bed, content to work on her designs or lapse into frivolous romanticism and doodle their names, connecting the letters with intricate loops and flourishes. Looking back on it now, Noelle couldn't believe she'd been that foolish.

"Marc," she called, putting aside her memories of past imprudence, "come meet Prince Gabriel."

The little boy gave a green sofa and several chairs a wide berth to avoid Christian before coming to stand at Noelle's side and fixing solemn, unblinking eyes on the handsome, regal man beside Olivia.

Prince Gabriel put his hand out. "Nice to meet you, Marc."

Most four-year-olds wouldn't have known to be awed by the man who would one day rule the country, but Marc had his father's confidence as well as his mercurial temperament.

"Nice to meet you, Prince Gabriel."

Noelle was torn between relief and pride at her son's exhibition of good manners, but she held her breath as he continued to speak.

"I like your palace. It's very large. Do you ever play hide and seek?"

Prince Gabriel's lips twitched at Marc's earnest question, but he gave him a grave reply. "Not for many years. But my daughters are big fans of the game. Perhaps one day you can play with them."

Marc didn't look to Noelle for confirmation before nodding. "I'd like that."

"Would you like to see the garden?" Olivia asked.

Christian stepped up beside his brother. "He might be interested in the stables, as well."

"Are there pumpkins in the garden?" Marc asked, acting as if he hadn't heard Christian. "We have three pumpkins at home, and they're this big." He demonstrated their size with his hands, adding about two feet to the actual diameter.

"No pumpkins, I'm afraid," Olivia said, glancing from Christian to Noelle. "But we have a pond with goldfish."

Noticing Christian's taut expression, Noelle said, "Marc, why don't you let Princess Olivia show you the pond and I'll be out in a little bit."

With an excited roar, Marc raced toward the French doors, Olivia and Gabriel trailing behind. As the trio exited the room, Noelle's tension ratcheted upward. A muscle bunched in Christian's jaw as he tracked Marc's rambunctious dash across the lush, verdant lawn until he was out of sight. At last his hard gaze swung to Noelle.

"What have you said to my son to make him hate me?"

She wasn't surprised by Christian's question. "I haven't told him anything at all about you."

"Not even that I'm his father?"

Noelle sighed. "No, not yet. I've always said that I never told his father about him because I liked our family just as it was."

"And he was satisfied with that?" Christian sounded skeptical.

"He's four. For the moment it's enough." Noelle knew her son's innate curiosity wouldn't allow him to let the matter drop indefinitely. "He doesn't hate you," she added.

"Then why is it he gives me a wide berth?"

"You weren't exactly charming when you showed up unannounced at my home."

"I was upset to discover you'd been hiding a son from me all these years."

"I wasn't hiding him." Noelle blinked in surprise as she took in Christian's bitterness. "You would have known about him if you'd ever bothered to contact me in the months following our breakup." She fumbled over the last word.

His dismissal of her hadn't felt like a true breakup. He hadn't said he was unhappy with their relationship or that he wanted to see other people. He'd just told her to take the job she'd been offered at Matteo Pizarro Designs in Paris. After she'd given him her heart and two years of her life, he'd not been the least bit regretful that she'd be moving so far away nor had he offered to keep in touch.

"See, you are still angry with me," he said, pointing a taunting finger at her. "And you're inferring I didn't want to be a part of his life."

Yes, she'd been hurt by his rejection, but that was five years ago. Granted, it still rankled her, but had she turned her son against his father without meaning to? Uncertainty put her on the defensive.

"You don't know me at all if you think that." The man was an insufferable egotist. "And may I point out that simply by your absence you've become alienated from Marc."

"Did you ever try to contact me?" Christian persisted. "To let me know you were pregnant?"

"To what end? You made it pretty clear you were finished with me." She shook her head, throat contracting in remembered pain. "And if I had, what would you have done? When would you have found time between work and play to be a father?" She was warming to her argument now. "Marc deserves someone who will be there for him all the time not when it fits into his schedule."

"Someone like Coomb?" Christian grabbed her bare right hand and held it up. "Where's your engagement ring, Noelle?"

His strong touch sent a burst of heat through her. She hesitated too long before attempting to tug free. "Geoff and I talked. Given the circumstances, he thinks it would be less confusing for Marc if he stepped out of the picture and gave you and Marc a chance to bond." Chest heaving, she stopped trying to make Christian let her go and stood glaring at him.

"It wasn't much of an engagement if he gave you up so easily." Soft and measured, Christian's remark cut her deep.

"He's concerned for Marc." Geoff had been right about her scheme being a bad idea. It had backfired mightily, and once again Christian perceived her as mundane and unable to inspire a man's passion. "My son loves Geoff. You should appreciate that he was willing to step aside and not complicate an already tricky situation."

Terrified that Christian would see the tears scalding her eyes, she spun away from him and took several steps toward the French doors and the safety of the garden. But she wasn't fast enough and he caught her before she could slip outside.

"I was ready to battle him for you," he murmured, fingers grazing the wet streak on her cheek. "To demonstrate how committed I am to being your ardent husband and a zealous father to Marc."

Such beautiful words from such a challenging and unpredictable man. Noelle couldn't decide whether to laugh or cry. She was still debating when Christian cupped her face in his hands and brought his lips to hers.

The delicious pressure of his kiss held her immobile with shock. She was transported back in time to their first kiss. It had started very differently than this one, in merriment not bitterness. They'd been laughing at something silly, a bit of urban slang she'd used wrong.

In the beginning of their unlikely friendship, Christian had come to her apartment when he was feeling low and out of sorts. He claimed she had a knack for chasing away his shadows, and she was flattered that a charismatic prince, one whose favor was sought by everyone, saw *her* as special.

Noelle tunneled impatient fingers into Christian's hair and pushed her greedy body hard against his. She was starving for physical affection. Being hugged by her son was wonderful, but sometimes she just craved a man's hands on her. To feel a little helpless as he tore off her clothes and had his way with her. And Christian had a knack for this sort of thing. His firm, masterful touch reduced her to quivering need.

His fingers bit into her hip as she rocked against him, the ache between her thighs building. She rubbed her breasts against his chest to ease her yearning, but the friction only caused her to burn hotter.

Men's voices, coming from the direction of the garden, awoke Noelle to the insanity of what she was doing. She broke off the kiss, but hadn't the strength to escape Christian's embrace. Had she lost all sense? Any second they could be discovered by the palace's staff, Christian's family. Her son.

Christian took advantage of her unsteadiness and buried his face in her neck. His lips glided over her skin, leaving a tingling sensation in his wake. "I knew you'd come around."

An icy chill swept through her at his words. Noelle clenched her teeth and cursed her impulsiveness. She tensed and twisted away.

"I haven't come around to anything."

"Ten seconds ago you were melted butter in my arms." He crossed said arms across his formidable chest and lobbed a wolfish grin in her direction. "I'd say that's a pretty good indication that you agree it's better for all of us if we marry."

With her heart pumping gallons of hot, sexually charged blood through her veins, it was a little hard to pretend she was unaffected by their steamy kiss. "Sex was always great between us," she admitted, "but it's not a reason to get married."

"Not the only reason obviously, but wouldn't you be happier with a man who can drive you wild in bed? I do that for you. Why are you fighting this?"

His arrogance left her momentarily speechless. She spent a silent few seconds studying his face. What she saw gave her reason to believe his confidence was at least partially contrived.

"I'm not fighting anything. I'm trying to make a sensible decision based on what's best for Marc and me." Her cheeks heated a little at the skeptical look in Christian's eyes. Okay, plastering herself all over him hadn't been sensible, but to be fair, he had a gift for jazzing her hormones and muddling her judgment. "And being kissed by you isn't making that any easier."

He stretched out his hand and cupped her cheek in his palm. Her wobbly knees hadn't let her move beyond his grasp, and she found herself held in place while he closed the narrow gap and dropped his lips to hers once again. Hard and brief, the kiss affirmed that he respected her admission and wasn't about to back off.

She sighed as his hand slid away. "I really need to go see what Marc is up to."

"Let's go."

Christian refrained from touching her as they exited the room and headed across the lawn in the direction of the koi pond. Longing knotted Noelle's muscles. Already she was too aware of the exact distance from his hand to hers. The expressive nuances of his gold eyes as he darted a glance her way. The heat pooling in her belly as she relived their kiss.

Marc was lying on one of the flat rocks surrounding the pool, his nose inches from the surface of the water as Noelle and Christian approached. Her son's enthusiastic chatter wasn't distracting enough for Noelle to miss the curiosity in Olivia's gaze as it bounced between her and Christian. Unable to stop the rush of heat that suffused her cheeks, Noelle wasn't sure whether she liked the princess's obvious approval. With so many people counting on Christian to produce an heir and Marc waiting in the wings to be legitimized, the pressure on Noelle was mounting.

Would anyone understand if she turned Christian down? Was she wrong to want her son to grow up without the responsibility of ruling a country looming over his head? And was it selfish to take her own feelings into consideration? Christian might be the sort of lover every woman dreamed of, but was he husband and father material? No, based on her past experience with him. But five years had changed her. Could the same be said for him? And how involved was she going to let herself get before she knew for sure?

Six

Christian stopped on the opposite side of the fishpond from his son and drank in the sights and sounds of the energetic boy from behind a polite mask. His heart continued to drive against his ribs following the encounter with Noelle in the green drawing room. An odd lightness had invaded his head as if he wasn't getting the proper amount of oxygen. Which was ridiculous because he was gathering huge lungsful of air laden with the scents of fresh-cut grass, newly turned earth and Noelle's light floral perfume. He suspected her scent was affecting his equilibrium.

Marc laughed as one of the big orange koi flipped its tail and sent water splashing onto his cheek. "Mama, did you see that? The fish waved at me."

"I saw. Why don't we take a walk to the barn?"

"It should be about time for Bethany and Karina's riding lesson," Gabriel added. "Maybe you'd like to see their ponies?"

"Sure." Marc got to his feet and went to slide his hand into Olivia's. "Will you take me?"

She exchanged a brief, poignant look with her husband and then shook her head. "I'm afraid Prince Gabriel and I have someplace we need to be, but Prince Christian knows the stables inside and out. He can take you."

Olivia and Gabriel said their goodbyes and headed for the palace. Marc watched them go before turning to his mother.

"Can't I just stay here with the fish? I don't care about ponies."

"A second ago you were ready to visit the barn," Noelle pointed out, the skin between her sable eyebrows puckering as she frowned. "And since when don't you like ponies?"

"I'll go if he doesn't come with us."

"That's impolite." Thunderclouds formed in her eyes. "Prince Christian is a very busy man. He is taking time away from his business to spend it with us."

"Can't he just go back to work?"

Noelle's lips firmed into a tight line, and she cast a mortified look Christian's way. Despite being frustrated that he was his son's least favorite person, Christian liked that she was concerned about his feelings.

"First the stables," Christian said, his tone shutting down further argument. "Then I'm going to take you and your mother to lunch at a really wonderful restaurant down by the river." Neither lunch nor being seen together in a public place had been a part of their original plan for the day, but Christian was feeling a little desperate at the moment.

"I'm not hungry." The boy had become sullen.

Christian was not going to give up. "That's too bad because this is a new American-style restaurant that has the best hamburgers and milkshakes in Sherdana." It didn't occur to him that Noelle might not want her son eating the less than healthy food until he noticed she was regarding the slim gold watch on her wrist. "It's okay if we go there, right?" he belatedly asked, giving her a winning grin.

"I wasn't planning on taking time for lunch. I have an appointment in an hour."

"Marc and I could go by ourselves." He smiled at the boy. "And I could drop him off after."

"I suppose that would work. How does that sound to you, Marc?"

The four-year-old dug the toe of his brown loafer into the ground and stared down. "I don't feel good."

Christian recognized a losing battle when he saw one. How was he supposed to get to know his son when the boy didn't want to have anything to do with him? "Perhaps another time then."

"Can we go home, Mama?"

"Of course." Noelle ruffled her son's dark wavy hair and mouthed an apology to Christian. "And straight into bed. That's where sick boys belong."

"But I was supposed to play with Dino this afternoon."

"I'm not sure you'll be feeling better that fast."

Marc aimed a surly glare in Christian's direction, obviously blaming him for the canceled play date, before taking the hand his mother put out to him.

"It was nice seeing you again, Marc." Christian sounded more like a prince and not at all like a father.

The boy said nothing. So, Christian tried a smile, but the muscles around his mouth didn't want to cooperate. His awkwardness around his son made him come off stilted and unfriendly. It wasn't at all like him. Gabriel's two girls adored Uncle Christian. He snuck them sweets and helped them play tricks on their nanny and the maids charged with caring for them. That he wasn't developing the same rapport with his son frustrated him.

"Please say goodbye to the prince," Noelle said.

Her firm prompting produced a grumbled response from Marc. Looking exasperated, Noelle tugged him in the direction of the palace. Christian watched their progress and waited until they'd reentered the building before heading back himself.

He was met halfway by his mother's private secretary. Gwen had been with the queen since the triplets had been born. Despite her sensible two-inch heels, her head barely came as high as Christian's shoulder. Her diminutive size sometimes caused her to be underestimated. No one made that mistake twice.

"The queen would like you to come to her office."

The summons wasn't unexpected. After meeting Marc, she was sure to have questions for Christian. "Right now?" His mother only sent her secretary when she expected immediate results, and the question would irritate Gwen, but he needed to release some steam.

Gwen's eyebrows arched. "You have somewhere more important to be?" So much for riling Gwen.

Christian shook his head. "Lead the way."

"I have things that require my attention. I'm sure you can find your way on your own."

Despite his foul mood, Christian grinned. Perhaps he'd gotten to her after all.

As much as he'd have liked to drag his feet on the way to his mother's first-floor office overlooking the meticulous gardens that were her passion, Christian figured the sooner she spoke her piece, the faster he could get back to the challenge of persuading Noelle and Marc that they should be a family.

"Good morning, Mother," he said as he entered her office and took a seat across from her. "Your gardens look lovely as always. I don't know how you do it."

The queen was not to be distracted by his flattery. "I'm surprised you noticed. It seemed as if your attention was focused on Noelle Dubone and that son of hers." The queen paused and tilted her head, prompting him to answer the unasked question. When Christian remained mum, she continued. "Or should I say that son of yours. You're planning to marry her, I presume. We simply cannot have any more illegitimate royal children running around Sherdana."

"I'm working on that."

"Good. I'd like you to have a ring on her finger before the media gets hold of this. We've had enough scandalous romance at the palace in the past year to last several generations of Alessandro rule. There aren't any other of your progeny running around Europe, are there?"

"Not that I know of." He didn't add that he hadn't known about Marc either, but if he was honest with himself, he hadn't always been as careful with Noelle as he'd been with other women.

His answer did not please his mother one bit. "Christian!"

"No. There aren't."

"How can you be sure?"

"I've been careful."

The queen's expression grew even more severe. "Not careful enough."

"Noelle was different." It was almost a relief to let himself think about her all the time. He'd spent five years pushing her out of his mind. When a bit of music reminded him of slow dancing in her apartment, her body languid against his as his palms coasted along her curves. Or when he'd catch a whiff of the perfume he'd bought her and remembered introducing her to several new places to wear the scent.

"Christian?" His mother's sharp voice jerked him back from those heady intoxicating days.

"Yes?"

"We need an heir for the throne." She didn't need to add that he was their last chance to make that happen.

He gave her a short nod. "I'll do whatever it takes to convince Noelle to marry me." He was more determined than ever because if Noelle refused him, he wasn't sure he could marry anyone else.

Noelle's shop was sized to cater to exclusive clients. Generally the brides arrived with a single assistant or an entourage of no more than six. Today's appointment was taxing the salon space. There were twenty opinionated family members and one browbeaten bride. The youngest daughter of a billionaire Greek shipping magnate, Daria was the last of her four sisters to marry, and they all had advice for their baby sister. Additional guidance was being provided by two grandmothers, the girl's mother, soon-to-be mother-in-law and several current and future sisters-in-law.

In advance of this appointment, Noelle had provided a dozen sketches in three rounds of correspondence over a period of two months. The bride or—as was looking more likely—the bride's family had chosen five of the twelve. Knowing she wasn't the only designer the bride was looking at, Noelle had pulled out all the stops. The gowns were elegant, fantasy creations perfect for a twenty-year-old bride. She looked gorgeous in each and every one.

While her family squabbled over every look, Noelle could see her designs had not yet resonated with Daria. The bride's bland expression grew more distant with each gown. She answered Noelle's questions in an unhelpful monotone. Rather than worrying that a two hundred thousand euro commission was slipping through her fingers, Noelle pondered what would make the young woman happy.

Noelle stood beside the door in the large dressing room while her assistant designer and head of alterations worked together to free her dissatisfied client from the latest frothy wedding dress.

"I have one last dress for you to try," Noelle stated, hoping the startled confusion on her assistant's face hadn't been noticed by the client.

"But I've already tried on the five gowns."

"I decided to make up an additional dress from the sketches I sent you." The gown was the first designed by Noelle based on a get-acquainted interview she'd had with the bride shortly after the engagement was announced. She'd been surprised that the design had been rejected during the first round and couldn't get it out of her head that the style was perfect for Daria. "Are you interested in seeing it?"

"Of course."

To Noelle's delight, a flicker of curiosity sparkled in the girl's dark doe-like eyes. "Wonderful. Calantha, could you please get Woodland Snow." Since each wedding dress had a personality all its own, Noelle named all her gowns.

"That sounds so pretty."

Noelle's spirits lifted at Daria's comment. It was the most animated the girl had been all day.

"I know it's not one of the designs you initially chose," Noelle said, taking over Calantha's role and helping Daria step out of the rejected gown. Handing the dress to the head of alterations, she made a surreptitious shooing gesture. The woman understood. Noelle wanted the bride's attention to be 100 percent on the new design. "But I think you'll find that the dress is much more striking in person than on paper."

The door opened, and Calantha entered with Woodland Snow. Daria's breath caught as she glimpsed the gown and her brown eyes brightened. This was the reaction Noelle had been hoping for.

"It's beautiful," Daria murmured, reaching out to finger one of the organza flowers sewn onto the sheer white overlay. "I remember this dress. It was my favorite."

Noelle bit the inside of her lip to keep from asking the girl why she hadn't fought for the design. She already knew the answer. Reports stated her father was spending upward of eleven million euro on the wedding. Daria was marrying the son of a very wealthy Italian count, and the event promised to make a huge media splash. The wedding dress Daria wore would have to be over-the-top to start tongues wagging, and this gown's beauty was in the details.

Working quickly, Noelle and Calantha slipped the gown over Daria's head and settled it into place. The young bride stood with her back to the three-way mirror to allow for the perfect reveal. First impressions were the strongest, and Noelle wanted the young woman to fall in love all at once.

"Okay, you may turn around."

Daria stared at her reflection. Tears filled her eyes. "It's perfect."

The gown was a single layer of white chiffon sewn with fluttering organza flowers and a scattering of pearls that mimicked clustered berries over a strapless nude liner. The simple boat neckline and capped sleeves drew the eye to Daria's striking bone structure and beautiful brown eyes. The other dresses had overpowered her, emphasizing her youth and inexperience. But as Noelle watched her consider her appearance, Daria's expression took on a look of proud determination.

"Do you want to show your family?"

Daria shook her head. "There is no reason. This is my wedding and I want this dress. They can see it on my wedding day."

Noelle nodded. "I'll send Yvonne in to see what alterations are needed. I'm thrilled we were able to find you the perfect wedding dress."

She excused herself and headed into the room that held Daria's family. With a smile that balanced diplomacy and firmness, Noelle announced that Daria had chosen a dress and was looking forward to surprising everyone with her choice on her wedding day. There was a mixture of surprise and annoyance on the women's faces.

An hour later, the exhausting group was gone, and Noelle dropped into a chair in her now-empty salon. To her delight, the young heiress had paid for the dress herself, declaring that by doing so the only opinion that mattered was her own. Noelle's staff joyously broke out the bottles of champagne reserved for occasions like these and joined their employer in celebrating.

Noelle was halfway through her third glass when the tinkle of a bell announced someone had entered the shop's reception room. Waving her staff back to their seats, she went to speak to their visitor. Two-and-a-half glasses of champagne consumed over an hour and a half were not enough to make Noelle tipsy, but the sight of Christian's imposing presence for the second time in one day made her head spin.

"Christian? What are you doing here?"

"I want you and Marc to join me at my vineyard this weekend."

She frowned as her body reacted positively to his invitation. "That's moving much too quick."

"I'm sorry, but I don't want to spend months and months tiptoeing around. I want to marry you and be Marc's father. He needs to know who I am and that you and I are serious about becoming a family."

Thanks to her nerve-racking encounter with the queen and the Greek bride's chaotic family, Noelle's diplomatic skills were in short supply. "But what if I'm not serious?"

"Come to the vineyard this weekend and let's talk."

"Just talk?" She suspected Christian would love nothing more than to get her horizontal to plead his case. "I'm not the susceptible girl I once was. You won't be able to seduce me into agreeing with you."

"How about if I just seduce you for the fun of it."

She was far more open to this suggestion but couldn't let him know it. "You should concentrate on your son. He is the one you need to win over."

"Are you saying if Marc comes around you'll marry me?"

Noelle shook her head. "It's just not that easy, Christian. I think you deserve a chance to be in your son's life, but I'm not convinced that what's best for him is to have his life turned upside down as the royal heir."

"What if we'd gotten married before Marc was conceived? Would you still feel the same way?"

He hadn't meant for his words to sting, but Noelle had once been very conscious that they came from vastly different worlds, and Christian was less than enthusiastic about inviting her into his.

"Since that was obviously never going to happen, the issue never crossed my mind." Her voice was stiff. Muscles rigid.

Five years ago, being his secret plaything had bothered her more and more the longer they were together. Then the tabloids began publishing pictures of him with the beautiful daughter of a Dutch viscount and speculation gathered momentum that they were on the brink of an engagement. She'd convinced herself to break things off. Christian had disputed the rumors and made love to her with such passion that she forgot all about the outside world for a while longer.

"Noelle." His deep growl of frustration sent a shiver through her. "I was young and foolish when we were together five years ago. I had no idea what I was losing when I let you walk out of my life."

"Let me walk?" Outrage flooded her with adrenaline. "You shoved me out."

Christian snorted. "Hardly. I told you to take a fantastic career opportunity."

"I wanted to stay with you." There, she'd admitted what had been in her heart five years ago. Spoken the words she'd been too afraid to declare the last time she'd seen him.

"You don't think I knew that? But I'd already taken too much from you, and you deserved better." His statement rang with conviction. "I cared about you more than I was willing to admit. Even to myself."

"I can't believe you." If she did, it would undo all the anger and resentment she'd built up over the years and leave her heart open to being hurt again. "You didn't want me around anymore."

"I know it's easy to blame me for the way things ended between us, but you can't truly tell me you were happy near the end."

Noelle shook her head. "No. I wanted what I couldn't have. To be the woman on your arm as well as the one in your bed."

"We tried that and it didn't work out very well, remember?" He was referring to the night of the accident, and the fact that her foolishness had almost gotten him killed.

"I remember. So, what makes you think it will be any better this time?"

"You'll just have to trust me that it will."

Seven

The luxurious town car slowed as it passed through the quaint village of Paderna, eight rolling miles from Christian's vineyard. Beside him, Noelle stared past her sleeping son at the shops lining the main street visible through the rear passenger window. With each mile they'd traveled, she'd relaxed a little more. And Christian's tension had grown.

"Just a little bit farther now," he murmured, his voice husky from disuse. They'd spoken little during the two-hour ride. After their contentious discussion three days ago, he was loath to bring up anything that might charge the atmosphere in the car and cause further damage to his relationship with either Noelle or their son.

"I forgot how beautiful the wine country is. And so close to Carone."

"Don't you have cousins up near Gallard that you visit?"

"Not in years, I'm afraid. Work keeps me too busy to

travel for fun." She probably wasn't aware of how wistful she sounded.

"Then I'm doubly glad you agreed to join me this weekend. Some time away will do you good."

She patted her briefcase. "This time is for you and Marc to get to know each other. I have several clients to prepare sketches for."

"You'll at least take an hour or so to tour the winery. I'm very proud of it." Although he made millions buying, fixing and selling corporations, his true passion was crafting the finest vintages in all the country.

He'd acquired Bracci Castle and surrounding vineyards six years earlier from Paulo Veneto, a Sherdanian count who had gambled his way deep into debt. As soon as the hospital had released Christian after the accident, he'd come here to hide and recover. At first the plodding country pace had pained him as much as his scorched flesh. Between his many business dealings and his numerous social engagements, he was used to operating at frenetic speed. Needing something to keep his thoughts occupied and off both the pain in his right side and the agony in his heart, he started learning what it took to produce wine.

At the time, the winery was barely breaking even and the wines were abysmal. Christian figured out that the general manager and winemaker were selling the grapes produced by the vineyard and buying inferior ones at half the cost, pocketing the difference. Within a week Christian had fired and replaced them with two men he'd wooed away from the competition. After sinking a ridiculous amount of money into desperately needed new equipment, he'd held his breath and hoped the grapes were as good as promised. The first harvest had gone well, and the wine produced that year won the winery its first award.

"These are all my fields," Christian said, indicating the rows of well-maintained grapevines.

"I remember when you mentioned buying the vineyard. You don't usually hold on to anything for long. Why keep it?"

"The place makes the finest wines in all Sherdana. Why would I want to give that up?"

"So it's a prestige thing." Her tone revealed that his answer had disappointed her. She wanted him to speak the truth not give her flippant responses.

"I have grown fond of the place."

She nodded. "I can't wait to see it."

And he couldn't wait to show it to her. The seven-hundred-year-old castle had a quirky charm so unlike his sleek, sophisticated apartments at the center of activity in Paris and London. His circle of friends thought he was mad to spend any time here. They couldn't figure out how he kept himself entertained without clubs or expensive restaurants. The isolation that had first bothered him was now like a balm to his soul. One he enjoyed too infrequently thanks to his business commitments.

The car rolled through the arch and beneath the portcullis that was the only way into the castle's outer courtyard. Where in medieval times this large area would have been cobbled, Christian had turned the space into a grassy lawn with paths. The car followed the circular driveway and stopped outside the keep's arched double doors. As the driver got out and opened Christian's door, several staff flowed out of the imposing stone building and headed toward the car. Christian hesitated before sliding out and turned to Noelle. Marc was starting to stir in his car seat.

"Why don't you let me carry him into the house," Christian offered, hoping the child would be less likely to protest since he was drowsy.

"Of course." Noelle exited the car behind him and stood looking up at the towering stone structure in front of her. "This really is a castle, isn't it?"

"What were you expecting?"

She wrinkled her nose. "Something more fairy-tale-like."

Christian chuckled. "It is a hulking brute of a thing, isn't it? Don't worry. You'll like what I've done to the inside. It has running water and electricity."

"No heated buckets of water hauled up from the kitchen and winding stairwells lit by torches?"

"You sound disappointed." It was good to banter with her. The repartee erased the years of separation and recalled why they'd once enjoyed each other's company so much.

"There's a part of me that is."

With his mood growing lighter by the second, Christian unbuckled his son from the car seat and lifted the boy in his arms. The weight of Marc's sleepy head on his shoulder filled Christian with blazing joy. Holding his child was such a simple thing. How many fathers didn't give it a second thought? For Christian the moment was precious, and he closed his eyes to imprint the memory, after which he followed Noelle inside.

The entry hall was a wide room that ran for twenty feet on either side of the front door with a fireplace on each wall. Here they were met by a handsome woman in her midfifties wearing a simple navy dress and a tasteful silver brooch in the shape of a lily.

"Noelle, this is Mrs. Francas, my housekeeper. Whatever you need, you may ask her."

The brunette smiled in welcome. "Ms. Dubone, how lovely to have you and your son staying with us. I will have your bags sent to your rooms. As Prince Christian stated, anything you need, please let me know. We look forward to making your stay extra special in the hopes you'll return."

When Noelle's eyes widened in surprise, Christian cocked his head at Francas's not-so-subtle hint. She'd been Christian's favorite nursemaid when he, Gabriel and Nic were growing up, and as such he gave her a little more latitude when she voiced her opinions than he might have with someone else.

"Thank you," Noelle murmured with a friendly smile.

They entered the great hall. In its heyday everyone in the castle would gather there for meals. The lower section of the thirty-foot walls was lined with dark wainscoting, and enormous paintings depicting hunt scenes were hung above.

"I feel a little bit like I've been transported back to the fourteenth century."

"When I bought the castle, it was in pretty bad shape. Veneto hated the country and rarely spent time at his estate. The stone floors were chipped and uneven. Plaster was crumbling everywhere. I decided to take some of the walls back to the original stone. Where the paneling was in better shape, it was restored."

"Oh!" she exclaimed, pointing at several suits of armor that stood at attention on one end of the room. "Marc is going to love those."

Hearing his name seemed to rouse him. Marc lifted his head from Christian's shoulder and blinked blearily. "Mama?"

"We're at Prince Christian's castle. Look at how big this room is."

Marc's eyes went wide as he gazed around. "Wow." He squirmed a little as he swiveled to check out the space in every direction, but made no attempt to get away from Christian.

Deciding to give up while he was ahead, Christian set down his son. "Go check out that armor over there." He pointed at a set with intricate gold filigree that looked too ornate to have ever been worn into battle.

"Is it yours?" For a couple seconds hero worship blazed in Marc's burnished gold eyes, and Christian reveled in his son's admiration. "Have you ever worn it?"

"No. It was made specially for one of my ancestors and only fit him," Christian explained.

"Did he wear it in battle with trolls?"

"Ah, no." He shot a questioning glance toward Noelle.

"One of his friends has an older brother who is into fantasy novels and likes to tell his brother and Marc all about them."

Christian nodded his understanding. "My great-great-great-great grandfather wore it to defend Sherdana's borders." He had no idea if that was true, but he suspected one of his ancestors had worn the armor, and the story had captured his son's interest.

"Neat."

To Christian's delight Marc was demonstrating none of his usual displeasure when his father was around. While the boy raced from the armor to the display of swords and battle-axes, Christian set his hand in the small of Noelle's back and guided her toward the salon. Here, carpet stretched the length of the stone floor, and paneling covered the rustic walls. Long windows, framed in royal blue velvet, overlooked the castle's inner courtyard. Late-afternoon sunshine fell upon the last of the summer roses. There was a cozy sitting area with wing chairs and a plush sofa before the large fireplace.

"This is where I spend most of my time when I'm here. The stairs—" he gestured to his right "—lead to the first floor and several guest rooms. I can have my housekeeper show you to your rooms now or…"

He hadn't thought much past getting Noelle and Marc here.

"Or?" Noelle prompted, fixing him with a curious stare.

Christian laughed. "I have no idea. How do you feel about exploring outside? There are some terrific views of the countryside from atop the walls."

"I think Marc would love that."

With their son racing ahead of them, Christian and Noelle strolled side by side through the courtyard and up a set of stairs that led to the battlements. The autumn sunshine heightened the greens and golds of the fields surrounding the castle. A light breeze blew Noelle's silky dark hair around her face and tugged at the floral scarf knotted about her slim neck. Christian stroked a strand of hair off her cheek and noticed the way her lashes fluttered at his touch.

Gripped by the desire to take her in his arms and kiss her soft, full lips, Christian trailed his fingertips down her neck and around to her nape. Her faint sigh was nearly his undoing. Only awareness of Marc running back and forth across the battlements, chattering about the height of the walls and pretending he was shooting arrows at the enemy below, kept Christian from acting on the impulses driving through his body. But it didn't keep him from talking about it.

"I think I'm going to go crazy waiting to taste you," he murmured close to her ear, near enough to feel the way her body started at the hot brush of his breath against her skin.

"I can't make any promises until I see how Marc settles down tonight." She peered at Christian from beneath long, sable lashes. "But I very much want to get my hands on you, as well."

His body reacted predictably to her bold remark. Heat poured into his groin while his muscles tightened in delicious anticipation. She left him breathless and off his game. He slid his fingers around her waist and drew her against his side while his lips grazed her temple.

"No one has ever gotten to me the way that you do." Before hunger overrode his willpower, he set her free and raked both hands through his hair. "What changed your mind?"

"I haven't."

"But you just said…" He regarded her, his brain blurry with confusion, wondering what to make of her secretive smile.

"That I've given up trying to fight the chemistry between us. I want to make love with you. It's all I thought about the entire trip here, but I long ago discovered, sex with you does not necessarily mean we have a future."

Noelle hadn't meant the remark to be cruel, but he had to understand where she was coming from. "I'm sorry if that sounded harsh."

"Don't be sorry. I had that coming. You're right. When we were together before, I had no intention of giving up my freedom. I lived in the moment and enjoyed being irresponsible and egocentric."

His words rang with regret, but Noelle wasn't sure he'd changed all that much. "And yet without the actions of your brothers putting you in the difficult position of being the only one who can produce an heir for the throne, you wouldn't be here with Marc and me this weekend."

The truth weighed heavy on her heart. But it didn't stop her from wishing he wanted her and Marc in his life simply because he cared about them. When she tried a smile, the corners of her mouth quivered with the effort of appearing poised and understanding.

"I'm not as bad as you think I am."

"You misunderstand me. I don't think you're bad. I just don't want you to think it's unreasonable for me to doubt your sincerity."

"What does that mean?"

"Be truthful. You want to have sex with me and hope that I will fall back in love with you so we can marry and you can fulfill your obligation to Sherdana."

"You make me sound like a coldhearted bastard." He glared down at her. "Yes, I want us to have sex. Making love to you remains the most inspiring, mind-blowing pleasure I've ever had with any woman. Was I a fool to push you out of my life and give that up? Of course. But I was stupid and afraid, and at the time it seemed like the best thing to do."

Noelle's breath lodged in her chest at his passionate declaration. She could believe that he valued their physical intimacy as much as she had. Although she'd been relatively inexperienced where men and sex were concerned, Christian had been as susceptible to her touch as she'd been to his.

"This is all so complicated," she murmured, her gaze trailing after Marc as she tried to remind herself where her priorities lay.

"It doesn't have to be."

Christian took her hand and squeezed with firm tenderness. Then he lifted it to his face and grazed the inside of her wrist with his lips. Noelle's full attention returned to Christian. Inside she shivered half in terror, half in delight. But when he gave her a smile of heartbreaking gravity, her heart skipped a beat.

Was he right? Should she just forget past disappointments and focus on the future? Once upon a time she would have given anything to marry Christian. Would she have cared if he only wanted her for the child she carried?

No.

She would have wanted her son to know his father and claim his birthright. Being afraid of getting hurt again was not a valid reason to keep Christian and Marc apart.

Noelle gathered a deep breath. "After dinner we should tell Marc you're his father. If we let this drag out much longer, he's going to be very confused that we didn't tell him sooner."

"I'd like that."

They completed the circuit of the battlements and headed back inside the castle to clean up before dinner. Marc was covered in dirt, but Noelle judged him too wound up to attempt a bath. Instead, she washed his hands and face and urged him into clean clothes before leaving him occupied with a game on her tablet so she could freshen up and change for dinner.

Noelle pulled out of her suitcase a simple black V-neck sheath made of rayon, with enough spandex to allow the material to mold to her modest curves. Diagonally placed black piping created interest on what could have been a forgettable dress. Over it she slipped a sheer black short-sleeve cropped jacket ornamented with clusters of downy black feathers. Peep-toe pumps completed the outfit. Noelle felt confident and sexy. Ready to match wits with Christian.

With her son racing down the corridor ahead of her, Noelle made her way back to the ground floor. Christian met her at the bottom of the stairs, looking dashing in a dark gray suit and a crisp white shirt. In a nod to country informality, he'd gone without a tie and left the top button of his shirt undone to expose the strong column of his throat.

Although she'd thought herself calm and sophisticated enough to take Christian to bed without succumbing to feverish, emotional drama, the man was so damned charismatic her heart fluttered wildly the instant their eyes met. Parts of her came to glorious life at his slow, deliberate grin. He would not let her withdraw her admission that she wanted them to make love. A heavy ache began low in her belly. She craved his hands on her. Judging from the heat blazing in his eyes, before the night was out he intended to make that happen.

But first, they had to get through a difficult conversation after dinner. Noelle knew by telling Marc the truth she was setting them on a path neither might be ready for. Never before had a meal dragged on the way dinner with Christian and Marc did. If Noelle's thoughts hadn't been in such turmoil, she might have been able to enjoy the excellent lamb chops and the decadent chocolate dessert. As it was, the food barely registered. She listened with half her attention to Christian's attempts to draw out Marc. He had regressed from his earlier friendliness on the battlements back to wariness.

After dinner Noelle guided her son into the salon where one of the maids had placed a pot of coffee. Christian's face showed none of the anxiety Noelle was feeling as she sat her son on the sofa before joining him on the soft cushions.

"Marc, I have something important to tell you about Prince Christian."

Her son squirmed as if fidgeting could somehow let him escape the sudden tension in the room. Noelle set her hand on his knees to stop him from kicking his feet against the sofa frame.

"What?" He slid down so his back was flat against the seat cushions and he was staring up at the coffered ceiling.

Noelle could tell she was losing her son and spoke

quickly. "I wanted to wait until you were old enough to understand."

As if paying no attention to her words, Marc let his body go limp and slid onto the floor. "Did you see that, Mama?"

"I did. Now please come sit on the sofa and listen to what I'm telling you." Her temper rarely flared with Marc, but the past ten days had left her emotions raw and her nerves frayed. She waited until Marc had flopped back into his original seat before setting her hands on his forearms and compelling him to look at her. "Prince Christian is your father."

"No." Marc shook his head hard enough to dislodge the controlled waves his mother had combed his hair into before dinner. "I don't have a father."

"You do. And he's Prince Christian."

Marc got to his knees and leaned close to whisper in her ear. "But I don't like him."

"Of course you do." She aimed a glance at Christian to see how he was reacting.

As if taking this as an invitation, he hunkered down beside his son and offered an engaging smile. Noelle's insides melted at his earnest warmth, but Marc wasn't swayed.

"I don't like him. I like Geoff."

"Just because you like Geoff doesn't mean you can't like your father, too."

"He's not my father. I don't know him."

"I'd like to change that," Christian said. "You and your mom can come stay at the palace, and we'll all get to know each other."

"I don't want to stay at the palace. I want to stay in my house." Marc's face grew red as his frustration grew. "Please, Mama. Can't we stay at our house?"

Noelle hated seeing her son upset and shook her head

at Christian. "It's a lot for him to absorb all at once. Why don't I take him up to bed? We can talk more tomorrow."

Christian ran his large hand over his son's dark hair, looking unsurprised but bleak when the boy flinched and pressed his face against his mother's chest.

"Of course." Christian got to his feet. "Given how we were doing earlier, I had hoped that would have gone better."

"As did I." Noelle dropped a kiss on Marc's head and stood. "Good night, Christian."

Heart heavy, she led her son upstairs to his bedroom where she urged him into his pajamas and found where the maid had put his favorite dragon when she'd unpacked his suitcase.

"Mama, you're not going to let Prince Christian make us live at the palace, are you?" Marc's plea carried less defiance than he'd shown downstairs.

"Not if you don't want to." She lifted the covers, indicated he should get into bed, and then fussed with the sheets and comforter while she sought for some way to convince her son it was all going to be okay. "But I think you might like the palace. You have grandparents, and an uncle and aunt and two cousins who will love spending time with you."

"I only want you and Nana."

What was really going on with Marc? He was usually excited to experience new things. He'd rushed into his first day of school without once glancing back at his mother. An extrovert like his father, he made friends easily.

"You know that Nana and I aren't going anywhere, right?"

Marc sat up and hugged his mother, his arms showing a desperate sort of strength. "Don't make me live with him."

"You don't like the prince?"

"He's okay." Marc sat back down and toyed with his dragon. "Do you like him?"

"Yes, of course." Noelle sensed there were more questions to come and wondered where her son's thoughts were taking him.

"Are you going to marry him?"

With all the time she and Geoff had spent together, Marc had not once asked her that question. Why did he think things were different between her and Christian? Had he overheard them talking, or was it just a logical progression because Christian was his father and in Marc's mind, parents were married?

"I don't know."

"Do you want to?"

Noelle chose her words carefully. "Not if you don't want me to."

Marc took a long time to think about his answer. At last he gave her a solemn nod. "I'll sleep on it." It's what his grandmother often said to him when he asked for something out of the ordinary.

Hiding a smile, Noelle leaned down and kissed her son on his brow. "I'll await your answer in the morning."

After reminding her son that she was right next door, Noelle departed Marc's room. She left the door cracked so the light from the hallway could flow across the soft carpet. They were in a strange place and occasionally he didn't sleep straight through until morning. She didn't want him to wake up to total darkness and get upset.

In her own room, she changed into her favorite ice-blue nightgown and picked up her sketchbook. Finding time to be creative these days was harder and harder as the practical needs of her growing business occupied her more every month. She had employees to supervise and financial data to keep track of. Fabric came in wrong or late. Equipment broke. Clients changed their minds. A hundred details demanded her attention every day.

With a weary sigh, she sat on the window seat that overlooked the inner courtyard and flipped to a blank sheet. For a long moment she stared at the empty page, her mind playing over the conversation she'd just had with her son.

Did she want to marry Christian? If she spoke with her heart, then the answer was a resounding yes. But she'd grown jaded in the past five years and more often chose to follow her head. It kept her from making mistakes and being hurt.

So if she was thinking and not feeling where Christian was concerned, why had she admitted to wanting to make love with him tonight? Heat flooded her core. She shifted on the comfortable cushion, but there was no escaping the pressure between her thighs. Her nightgown's cool silk caressed her flushed skin. Breath quickening, Noelle closed her eyes and let her thoughts drift from one erotic image to another.

A while later, Noelle glanced at the clock, surprised to see an hour had passed. She always lost track of time when Christian occupied her thoughts.

Noelle set aside her sketchbook. She pinned up her hair before slipping into the robe that matched her nightgown. She knew the way to Christian's room. He'd made certain of that when showing her which rooms she and Marc would use during the weekend. Feeling like the heroine in a gothic novel, Noelle moved swiftly along the forbidding stone corridors of the keep. Her light footsteps made little sound on the carpet, but to her sensitive ears, she could have been an entire marching band. By the time she reached Christian's door, her thudding heart and rapid breathing betrayed both nerves and excitement. She took a second to compose herself before knocking.

Wearing pajama bottoms and a scowl, Christian threw open the door as if he intended to shout at whoever had interrupted him. In an instant his annoyance vanished. "Noelle?"

"I'm sorry how Marc took the news that you're his father."

Christian's gaze flicked over her precarious updo, silk robe and bare feet. "You came here dressed like that to talk about Marc?"

"No." She put her hand on his bare chest, savoring the warmth and power of him for a split second before pushing forward. "I just thought it sounded like a more civilized opening than *I want you naked and inside of me before either of us knows what hit us.*"

Taking two steps backward, he gave way before her determined advance. Then his long fingers snagged in the belt that held her robe closed and he tugged her hard against him. She reveled in his passion, anticipation searing along her nerve endings. But as his lips neared hers, she turned her head aside. His breath stroked along her cheek.

"First we need a few ground rules," she murmured, fighting to keep her voice even as his fingers slipped her belt free and parted the robe.

"Ground rules?"

His hot breath against her ear made her shiver.

"This is about sex and nothing more. It doesn't mean I've changed my mind about doing what's best for my son, and it's not a promise that anything will happen between us in the future."

"You're pretty bossy for a half-naked woman."

Her robe fell to the ground, and Noelle gulped as his palms grazed over her silk-clad hips and up her spine. "Just sex," she repeated, her voice a hoarse rasp.

"So this is okay?" He cupped her breast, fingers playing over her rapidly hardening nipple while he watched her expression from beneath thick black lashes.

"Yes."

"And this?" His free hand dislodged the pins in her hair. He sank his fingers into the thick mass that fell around her shoulders and tugged to drag her head back and expose her throat.

Noelle forgot to breathe as he placed his mouth over the pulse in her neck and sucked. Her heartbeat shifted into an erratic rhythm. "Sure."

"So this isn't off-limits?" Moving with slow tormenting precision, his hand left her breast and glided down over her belly to cup her, the heel of his hand applying the perfect pressure to weaken her knees.

"Yes." She barely got the single syllable out before he began pulling his hand away. Frantic, she grasped his wrist and held him in place.

"But you said…"

"I meant no."

"Ah." The word sighed out of him. "I'm going to take you to bed now."

"Lovely."

She was off her feet an instant later.

Eight

Christian lowered Noelle onto the bed and stepped back to regard her. He'd seen her naked before. Made love to her too many times to count. But for some reason, every time held a special fascination for him. Bracing his hand on the mattress beside her, he trailed his fingers along her skin at the edge of the nightgown. When he reached one of the thin straps that held the gown up, he nudged it off her shoulder.

There was curiosity, not wariness, in Noelle's eyes as she watched him. Uneasiness tangled with desire in his gut. Did she have any idea how the glimpse of one pink nipple peeking above the neckline of her nightgown made him crazy? Her power over him was complete. He would do whatever she asked, give himself over to her pleasure and wait to take his own until she was thoroughly spent.

His erection pulsed as she slid the straps down her arms, taking the bodice with it. As if understanding his weakness, she shimmied the blue silk over her hips and kicked it off. Naked, she lay before him, her gaze confident and direct as she waited for his next move.

"Gorgeous." He ran shaking hands through his hair, savoring the moment. He'd waited five long years to make love to her again, and he'd be damned if he'd rush. "I've missed you."

She sat up and hooked her fingers in the waistband of his pajamas. "Then what's taking you so long to get started?"

The cool air against his naked flesh did little to reduce the heat pulsing through him. He stepped out of his pajama bottoms and caught Noelle's wrists before her fingers could close around him. Putting her hands around his neck where they'd be safely out of the way, he leaned down to take her lips in an explosive kiss.

Together they fell to the mattress. He lay on his back with her draped over him. His hands were free to roam her body at will. Skin like the smoothest satin slipped against his fingertips. Her body was perfect, not because she didn't have flaws but because he never viewed her with a critical eye. Long lean lines of sleek muscle balanced with graceful curves and small, round breasts. Too short to walk a runway, she was his ideal height. In heels, her forehead reached no higher than his lips.

He was kissing her when the need to have her beneath him struck. She gripped his hair as they rolled, laughing until he nipped at her exposed throat. Her back arched as he moved lower and pulled one hard nipple into his mouth.

"Christian." She panted his name as his fingers began their slow descent to the heat between her thighs.

"Yes, Noelle?"

Blood rushed to his groin as he found her wet and ready. Trembling at the effort of keeping his pace easy and unhurried, he slipped a finger around the knot of nerves and felt her shudder.

"Torture," she murmured, but the smile playing at the corners of her mouth told him she didn't mind.

He kissed his way toward her second breast, determined to give it equal and fair treatment. "You sound agitated. Do you wish me to stop?"

"No." She shook her head and lifted her hips as he trailed his fingers down the inside of her thigh to her knee. "I want more."

"More of this?" He swirled his tongue around her nipple and felt her fingers tighten in his hair. "Or...?"

Her head thrashed from side to side as he traced the seam between her thighs. Delighted to see he had her full attention, he slipped one, then two fingers inside her, touching the sensitive spot the way he knew she loved and watching her muscles tense with pleasure. Within seconds she came apart beneath his hands. He savored her every cry and quake, and was a little shocked at the speed and intensity of her orgasm.

As she lay with her eyes closed, her chest heaving with each uneven breath, he reached into his nightstand and pulled out a condom. When he turned back to her, he found her up on one elbow, watching him with glowing eyes. Her pale skin wore the rosy flush of climax, and she looked ready and eager for round two.

Happy to oblige her, Christian slid on the condom and leaned down to snag her gaze with his. "This time we'll come together," he promised and at her nod, positioned himself between her thighs.

Still not fully recovered from one orgasm, but eager to have Christian inside her, Noelle opened for him and felt him nudge against her. Anticipation tightened her nerves to bowstrings, and she told herself to let go. Instead, her body tensed still more. Panic grew as a myriad of half-hysterical what ifs bombarded her mind.

"Easy." Christian's soothing tone lessened her anxiety. "There's no rush."

That's where he was wrong. She needed the rush of passion to keep her brain disengaged. Thinking about what she was doing led to her questioning the wisdom of coming here tonight.

"I'm sorry. It's just…"

While Christian hadn't been her first lover, he'd been her last. For five years she'd concentrated on her son and her career, putting her personal life on ice.

Christian backed off and peered down at her. "Relax. It's fine." He caressed her disheveled hair back from her cheeks with gentle strokes of his fingers. "Talk to me."

"It's been awhile." The flush in her cheeks stopped being about passion and became embarrassment.

Wonder softened the aristocratic planes of his face. He cupped her face with his hands and forced her to meet his gaze. "Then we'll take it very slow."

His lips trailed over her cheek and found a corner of her mouth. She tipped her head to kiss him, but he'd already moved to nuzzle against the sensitive skin beneath her jawline. She closed her eyes and shifted position to offer him better access, shivering as the faintest brush of his lips tickled her skin.

"Touch me," he murmured. "You know what I like."

His words made her smile. She did indeed. She'd clutched his biceps when he'd moved between her thighs, but now, with his encouragement, she let her hands roam. Down his sides, across his tight abs. Her fingertips rode the ridges and valleys of his superb muscles. So much leashed power all hers.

He kissed her then, his lips moving over hers with mastery and controlled passion. He was letting her set the pace. Granting her the time to adjust to being loved by his hands and mouth. Almost immediately her body quickened. Uncertainty fell away. She wrapped her arms around his shoulders and tilted her hips to find his erection waiting for her.

"You know what I need," she whispered, rocking against him, feeling him slide through her slick folds and probe her entrance.

"Are you sure you're okay?"

"Never better."

He rocked forward, easing his way into her with smooth, gradually deepening thrusts. While her mind had blocked all awareness of her arousal, her body had its own agenda. She expanded to welcome Christian's possession and cried out in pleasure as he seated himself fully inside her. With barely a pause, he withdrew, and together they found a familiar rhythm.

How had she forgotten how perfectly they fit together? Bodies attuned, hands knowing exactly how and where to touch—their movements were so perfectly choreographed they could've made love the night before.

Christian's steady thrusts intensified the pleasure building in her body in the same way his rough, unsteady breathing and whispered words of encouragement and praise made her heart sing. Once again Noelle's climax claimed her fast and hard. As aware of her body's reactions as he was of his own, Christian timed his own orgasm so perfectly that they came at nearly the same moment.

In the aftermath, Noelle lay panting and dazed beneath Christian's weight, glad she'd been rational enough to be able to forget this bliss these past five years. Only by focusing on what had been bad about their relationship rather

than recalling the good had she learned to live without him.
And now he was back. And so were her memories of how
amazing his lovemaking had been.

As soon as Christian shifted to lie beside her, Noelle
scooted off the bed and made a beeline for her nightgown
and robe. She was almost to the door before Christian
spoke.

"You're leaving?" He'd levered himself onto his elbows
and stared at her in blank shock.

"I think it's best."

"But we haven't talked." He frowned. "And you used
to like to snuggle after we made love." He sounded so put
out that she had a hard time repressing a smile.

She reached behind her for the door handle. "Yes, well,
I don't want to give you the wrong impression."

That brought him to a sitting position. Looking adorable with his hair mussed and his strong, broad shoulders
slumped, he asked, "What sort of wrong impression?"

"Sex with you I can handle," she explained, echoing
what he'd once said to her. "But I can't do intimacy."

Then before he could rise from the bed to challenge her
bold declaration, she slipped out of the room.

Shortly after dawn the next morning, Noelle woke face-
down in her own bed, and her first emotion was relief. She
stretched her arms and legs, luxuriating in the cool sheets
and the unfettered peace of early morning. As amazing
as the previous night with Christian had been, she wasn't
prepared to dive back into the intimacy of sleeping in his
arms and being roused by his morning erection and sensual kisses.

Her skin prickled at the thought, and she smiled in
memory of his shocked and worried expression when she'd
blithely slipped out of bed after what had been the best

sex of her life. If he'd had any clue how shaky her legs had been, he might not have let her go without an encore. Instead, exhausted by her long and stress-filled work week and abundance of exercise both on the battlements yesterday afternoon and in Christian's bed last night, she'd enjoyed a blissful six-and-a-half hours of deep, restful sleep.

She'd barely finished heaving a deep, contented sigh when her bedroom door opened and the slap of four-year-old feet sped across the tile floor. A second later a small body landed on the mattress beside her, and Noelle rolled over to scoop her son into a snug embrace.

"Morning, dumpling," she cooed in his ear, savoring the squeeze of his strong arms around her neck. "Did you sleep well?"

"I dreamed I was a dragon who ate everyone in this castle."

"Even me?" She prodded him in the ribs and tickled him.

Marc writhed and giggled. When she let him gather a breath, he said, "No, Mama. I wouldn't eat you." He gave her a smug grin. "But I ate Prince Christian."

"Your father," she corrected, forcing a light note into her voice. "I don't know that it's polite to eat one of your parents."

"It's okay, Mama. He didn't mind."

Noelle decided not to belabor the point. "Are you hungry? What do you think they'll have for breakfast?"

"Waffles?" Marc asked, his eyes round with hope.

"I don't think they'll have those."

"I can make a special request to the cook," said a deep voice from the direction of the hall. Christian stood framed in the open doorway Marc had come through only moments before. "I'm sure she would be happy to whip up a batch."

Christian looked so handsome in khaki pants and a crisp white shirt with sleeves rolled up to expose his strong forearms. His unexpected appearance when her defenses were down sent her emotions flipping end over end. Somehow she managed a friendly smile. If she'd thought sex with Christian would simplify her feelings for the man, she was a fool.

"We wouldn't want her to go to any trouble."

"I'm sure she wouldn't mind." Christian surveyed her disheveled hair and bare shoulders and she blushed.

"Waffles." Marc crowed the word happily and tried tugging her off the bed. "Get up, Mama. I'm hungry."

"I'll go and arrange it. How long will it take you and Marc to get ready?"

"Half an hour?"

"Are you sure that's enough time?" Christian gave her a slow, complex smile that would take her hours to unravel. "I don't want you to feel rushed."

"It's fine."

With Christian lingering half in and half out of her room, Noelle wasn't inclined to ditch the covers and let him drink his fill of her in the clingy silk nightgown. That he'd seen it last night and much more besides didn't mean she wanted to parade before him in the light of day.

"Marc, why don't you go to your room and get dressed?" she said. "I put out your clothes last night. Don't forget to brush your teeth."

Her son scampered to do as she asked, but although Christian stepped aside to let him past, he showed no interest in withdrawing. In fact, he took a single step into the room. Having a man in her bedroom wasn't something Noelle was used to. Back when she and Christian had been lovers, she'd grown comfortable with being nude around him. But since Marc had come along, she'd fallen into the habit of conservative modesty. The only time she left her bedroom wearing just her nightclothes was in the middle of the night when Marc was a baby or if he had an infrequent nightmare.

"Shouldn't you be getting up, too?" Christian asked.

Noelle bit back a tart retort and slid out of bed. As the cool morning air found her bare skin, she shivered and reached for the silk robe that matched her nightgown. She moved with more haste than grace as she slipped her arms into the sleeves. Last night's confident vixen had been an illusion of shadow and lamplight.

"Don't you need to check with your cook about Marc's waffles?" She wanted him to go and take his penetrating gaze with him. The longer he stared at her, the more her poise suffered.

"As soon as you come here and give me a kiss."

She wrinkled her nose at him. "I haven't brushed my teeth, and I'm far from presentable."

"Do you think I care?" His velvet voice bore a trace of steel. "Come here."

Her muscles moved of their own accord, setting her on a direct path into his waiting arms. As she crossed to him, the glow of his smile thawed her chilled limbs. A second later, his warm hands slipped around her waist and the ardent pressure of his fingers pulled her snug against his unyielding torso. Abruptly impatient, she lifted up on her toes to bring her lips into contact with his sooner.

The kiss was hot and fast. Electricity arched between them, the voltage off the scale. Noelle's body came to instant life, and she moaned beneath Christian's mouth.

Almost as fast as she'd ridden desire upward, she was crashing back to earth. She couldn't let Marc see her and Christian locked in a passionate embrace, so she broke off the kiss and pushed her palms against the unyielding granite of his shoulders.

"Marc mustn't…" She sucked in much-needed air to clear her head.

"Damn." Christian stepped back. Chest heaving, he blinked several times before he managed to focus his gaze on her. "Noelle…"

She had no idea what he intended to say. Nor apparently did he because he merely stared at her for a long, silent moment and then shook his head as if to clear it.

"You said something about checking on breakfast," she prompted, overjoyed to see that the kiss had rattled him. Before last night he'd always been the one in control. His masterful seduction had swept her along. Past comfort zones and pride, reducing her every defense to ashes while he kept his thoughts private. "Waffles?"

"Waffles." With a brief nod he turned away, but before he left he spoke over his shoulder. "Take your time. I'll send one of the maids to check on Marc." And then he was off, striding down the hallway.

Noelle leaned against the heavy wood door, taking stock of the graceless lethargy in her limbs and the fanciful fluttering of her heart. She touched the tip of her tongue to her lips, noting they were still tender from last night's fervent kisses.

She closed her bedroom door and headed for the bathroom, determined to enjoy a long hot shower. Catching sight of her reflection, she noticed the invigorating start to her morning had put a smile on her face. The urge to hum surprised her, and she pushed aside the rational side of her brain that wanted to squash all her reckless joy. Monday morning would be soon enough for her return to cold reality. Until then she intended to see where this new beginning with Christian would take them.

* * *

Christian was still cursing his lack of control around Noelle as he reached the ground floor. As if summoned by his thoughts, Mrs. Francas popped into his line of sight and he stopped short.

"Is it possible for waffles to be served for breakfast?"

"Cook has a new recipe she will be happy to show off."

"And could you send one of the maids to check on Marc? I told Noelle we would take care of him this morning."

"Of course. I will send Elise." Mrs. Francas bowed. "There's coffee and this week's paper waiting for you in the salon."

"Thank you."

After his sleepless night, Christian was ready to consume an entire pot of the strong black stuff his cook brewed. The local paper awaited him beside the silver coffee service. When he came to Bracci Castle, he enjoyed immersing himself in the country life and unplugging from the world at large. Some trips he was more successful than others. Multimillion-dollar business deals rarely went smoothly. This weekend, however, he'd warned his assistant not to bother him with anything short of total bankruptcy.

He needed his complete focus on winning over Marc and demonstrating to Noelle that he was ready to be a father and a husband. Yesterday had been an emotional roller coaster for him. For a while during the afternoon, when Marc had abandoned his antagonism, Christian thought his troubles were over. He should have known it wouldn't be so easy. The boy was an Alessandro, after all. Maybe not in name, but certainly in personality and stubbornness.

Christian was on the sofa with a cup of coffee at his elbow, deep into an article about a northern Tuscany mudslide that swept away a house, injuring several people, when he heard a pair of voices coming down the stairs toward the salon. His composure took a hit as excitement and anxiety built. This weekend was a significant step toward the rest of his life. What happened here not only determined the future of his country's stability, but also any hope that Christian might have for happiness.

He pushed aside the thought that he didn't deserve Noelle or the joy she brought to his life. He'd lost her once because of his selfish stupidity. Screwing up a second time was not an option.

Christian was on his feet and moving to the stairs as his energetic son brushed past him in a mad dash to get to the dining room and the promised waffles. Chuckling, Christian held his hand out to Noelle as she completed her descent. His pulse bucked as she placed her elegant fingers against his palm and he found his lips curving into a foolish grin.

"Good morning," he said, his voice low and intimate. "You look beautiful."

Today's dress was a half sleeve, French blue sheath, paired with a whimsical pendant necklace. She'd donned flats instead of her usual pumps, which reminded Christian of her petite stature and inspired his protective instincts. Not that she needed his help. Her brown eyes sparkled with confidence above her cheerful smile.

"Thank you." To his surprise, she linked her arm with his as they headed out of the salon. "It was nice of you to send Elise to watch Marc. I was able to shower and dress without any interruption."

She gave a heartfelt sigh that made him long to pull her into a quiet corner and sink his fingers into the dark, wavy hair cascading over her shoulders. The lingering aftermath of the morning's fiery kiss continued to pulse through his veins like a potent cocktail consumed too quickly.

"You're welcome." Despite three cups of strong coffee, he felt sluggish and tongue-tied with her body pressed along his side.

"Will we be going to your winery today? I'm looking forward to seeing where Sherdana's finest vintages are made."

"I've arranged a tour and lunch with pairings of our best wines. Bracci Vineyards and Winery employs a world-class chef, and he's promised to amaze us with his cuisine."

"That sounds wonderful, but what about Marc?"

"My winemaker has several children near Marc's age who are eager to meet him. I assure you he will not be bored."

"Sounds like you have it all figured out."

Christian smiled at her, wishing that was true. His heart and mind were on the same page. He wanted to marry Noelle and make Marc his legitimate son, but instinct told him what might happen for appearance's sake wouldn't bring him the fulfillment he craved. There were those in-between moments when she didn't notice his attention, her smile faded and the sparkle left her eyes. She was putting on a good show for both Marc and him, but Christian sensed she had doubts.

After breakfast Christian spent an hour throwing a ball with Marc in the outer courtyard while Noelle looked on. The boy was crazy about American baseball and had brought a ball and his mitt with him. Christian didn't spend a lot of time in the US, but had several business colleagues he spoke to regularly who had introduced him to the sport. Given his son's fascination with the game, Christian decided he'd better get up to speed quickly.

On the five-mile drive to the winery, Marc rattled on about fastballs and curveballs from the backseat of the blue convertible Maserati Christian kept at the castle. Since the autumn day was sunny and mild, he drove with the top down, his attention split between the empty country road and Noelle's flawless profile as she lifted her face to the sun.

"What a glorious day," she said, stretching her arm across the seat to rake her nails through his hair. "Did you plan this, too?"

Something about her tone made him think she was mocking him. "I ordered it specially for you." He dropped a kiss in her palm. "I only want the best for you."

She withdrew her hand and made a fist as if to capture his kiss. "It's nice to hear."

"You don't believe me." It wasn't a question, but an accusation.

From the backseat, Marc interjected his own question. "When we get there, will I get to stomp grapes?"

Christian's mood brightened at yet another chance to curry favor with his son. "Sure." Although the grape harvest wasn't set to happen for another week, there would likely be a way to pick a few grapes and let Marc and the other kids participate in the ritual.

"No." Noelle shook her head, adamantly opposed.

"Mama, please."

"I think your mother is worried that it will stain your feet purple."

"Will it? That's great."

He shot Noelle a triumphant look, not the least bit daunted by her scowl. Christian intended to do whatever it took to win his son's love. Even if it meant siding with him against his mother from time to time."

"Christian, I don't think that's a great idea."

"It'll be fun. Something he can show off at school and make the other kids jealous."

"Wine-colored feet?" She shook her head in a maternal show of disgust. "Okay, you can stomp grapes."

While Marc whooped in the backseat, Christian reached over and squeezed Noelle's hand in thanks. Her lips softened into a smile at the gesture, and she put her hand atop his.

The car rolled down a long driveway flanked by fields of grapevines and came to rest near the low building that housed the tasting room and an intimate space available for private parties and lunches such as the one Christian had planned today with Noelle.

Almost before Christian turned off the engine, Marc had unbuckled his seat belt and was keyed for the instant his mother opened the passenger door and tipped her seat forward. He wiggled through the door and was off across the lawn in a flash, heading for the tasting-room door. Noelle called after him, but Marc was too excited to slow down. By the time she and Christian reached the building, Marc had disappeared inside.

"I love his enthusiasm," Christian commented as he held the door open for Noelle. "Everything is an adventure. You've done a good job raising him."

"Thank you, but the job's not over yet." She paused in the doorway and touched Christian's arm. "I know I haven't done much to improve your relationship with Marc, but I want you to know that watching you with him this weekend has made me realize how important it is that you two bond." She paused. "No matter what happens between us, I want you and Marc to have as much time together as possible."

"I appreciate that." While he was grateful for her approval, he was less than pleased that she continued to doubt whether they had a future as a family.

"Mama, is this where I get to stomp grapes?" Marc tugged at her hand. "Can I do it now?"

Christian chuckled. "Let me talk to Louis and get it all set up," he told his impatient son. "Why don't you see if Daphne has some fresh grape juice for you to try." He indicated a pretty blonde girl behind the bar. While Marc raced toward the bar and climbed up onto the tall stool, Christian turned to Noelle. "Give me a couple minutes to get Marc settled. Then we can go on our tour."

Nine

Noelle waited until Christian disappeared through a door in the back of the tasting room before joining her son. Even without a single sip of wine, she was suffering the effects of intoxication. Not that she could be blamed for feeling giddy and light-headed when Christian turned on the charm. The man had convinced her to let her son stomp grapes. Noelle shook her head, contemplating the reactions of Marc's teachers and his classmates' parents after he broadcast his weekend's activities at school. No doubt she would have some explaining to do.

But to see her son so happy was worth it. Noelle sighed. Watching Marc's wariness toward his father fade made her question her decision to not tell Christian that she was pregnant. At the time she'd been afraid he'd reject her again. No. That wasn't the whole truth. She'd also been angry.

She was still angry.

Last night she hadn't gone to Christian's room motivated solely by desire. She'd had something to prove to herself and to him. She needed to prove that she could surrender her body to the passion he aroused without giving over her heart at the same time. Leaving as abruptly as she had was meant to demonstrate that this time around she wasn't going to lead with her heart but her head. The woman she was today never would have taken the little Christian had offered her five years earlier.

But she would never be truly happy keeping her emotions bottled up, either. There had to be a happy medium between giving too much and not giving enough.

At Marc's insistence, she sat beside him and tasted his grape juice, pronouncing it delicious. He gave her a huge grin and then went back to telling Daphne all about the armor he'd seen at Bracci Castle. Noelle ran her fingers through his thick, dark hair and considered how many times a day he reminded her of Christian.

As if summoned by her thoughts, he appeared at her side. "Ready for the tour? Louis's son is going to take Marc to where the other children are. They'll play for a while and have lunch. Afterward Louis is going to set up the grape-stomp contest to see who is the best stomper."

"Me!" Marc exclaimed, jumping down from his stool, fists in the air.

Noelle laughed at his enthusiasm. "Well, you certainly have the energy for it." She ruffled his hair and watched him run toward a tall boy who was gesturing for him to follow.

Half an hour later, she and Christian came to the end of the tour, and Noelle was eager to sample some of the wines she'd learned about. "I'll never take wine for granted ever again," she promised Christian before thanking their guide, Bracci Vineyard and Winery's exceptional wine-maker, Louis Beauchon.

"I'm glad to hear it." Louis was a handsome man in his early forties with prematurely gray hair and striking blue eyes. He had a ready smile and an abundance of hilarious stories about people he'd worked with during his twenty-five years of winemaking. "You'll have to let me know what you think of our wines after lunch."

"I'm afraid my palate is nowhere near as experienced as Prince Christian's, but I look forward to sharing my impressions."

"That's all I need. I'll see you later at the grape stomp."

Christian steered her along a curving path that wound through the garden at the back of the tasting room and through a set of French doors that led into an intimate dining room. At the center of the space was a single table set for two and covered with a white tablecloth and fine china. Two servers, dressed in black and white, stood to one side of the room, welcoming smiles on their faces.

Once Christian had assisted her into her seat and joined her at the table, the servers stepped forward and poured the first wine. Noelle lost herself in Christian's deep voice as he described the wine being served and commented on the meal to come. One course followed another, each being served with a different wine. Despite the small portions, Noelle was beginning to feel overcome by all the rich, fla-vorful dishes by the time dessert arrived.

"Chef Cheval is a genius, but I don't think I could eat another bite," she protested, as a delicate chocolate basket filled with white chocolate mousse and a single raspberry was placed before her. As with each course, the gorgeous plating made the food irresistible. How could she resist dessert? "Maybe just a bite."

Noelle didn't notice Christian's intense regard until

she'd scraped the plate clean and set her spoon aside. She cocked her head at him but had no opportunity to ask why he was staring. A short, round man in chef's whites entered the room, his toque set at a jaunty angle.

"Prince Christian!" the man exclaimed in a deep baritone. "How wonderful to have you back."

"Chef Cheval." Christian gestured in Noelle's direction. "This is Noelle Dubone."

"Chef, this was the most amazing meal I've ever had. Thank you."

The chef bowed to her. "I'm so glad you enjoyed it. Prince Christian said I must prepare only the best for you."

"He did?" She shot Christian a wry look, wondering how many other women had been given such royal treatment. "Well, you've both made my visit to Bracci memorable."

"You will come back? I appreciate a woman who likes to eat."

Noelle laughed. "Of course," she said, growing more and more accustomed to the idea of becoming a permanent fixture in Christian's life. "I appreciate a man who cooks with your flair."

"Well, good." The chef gave Christian an audacious wink before taking his leave.

The servers cleared the dessert plates and topped off both water and wineglasses before taking their leave. Noelle swirled her wine, soothed by the excellent food, the early fall scents and the distant sound of children at play. Relaxed to the point of sleepiness, she wondered if there might be time for a nap when they returned to Christian's castle.

"Did you mean what you said about coming back?" Christian's abrupt question cut through her lethargy.

"I did." She stumbled a little over the words, wondering why he'd grown so serious. "Why?"

"I didn't want to pressure you this weekend by talking about the future, but after last night, I think I have a right to ask about your intentions."

"My intentions?" Noelle wondered when the world had turned upside down. "Since when does a man ask a woman about her intentions regarding their relationship?"

"Since the man has stated his desire to marry the woman, and she comes to his room with seduction on her mind and leaves the man feeling as if he's been nothing more than her plaything."

Noelle pressed her lips together to hide a smile, but couldn't stop her eyes from dancing. Christian growled at her in mock severity.

She replied with an equally insincere apology. "I didn't mean to take you or your body for granted. As for my intentions, I plan to continue as I did last evening, exploring our mutual chemistry and seeing where things lead."

To her surprise Christian sat back and crossed his arms over his chest. "Not good enough."

"No?"

"I'm serious about you. This isn't going to be a casual affair where we play it by ear or take it one day at a time."

"Because your family is pressuring you to marry and produce an heir who can rule one day." Noelle tensed at the unwelcome reminder of why she and Marc were here this weekend. "I'm not going to decide the rest of my life or Marc's in a few short days no matter how wonderful they've been. I need time to decide what's right for him."

"And you're not yet sure I am?"

"It's not about you. It's the responsibility he'll face one day. You once told me how Gabriel changed when he realized he was destined to be king. I don't know if I want that for Marc."

Christian reached across the table and took her hand in his. "With my father in perfect health and Gabriel so young, Marc will be more than ready when the time comes for him to rule."

While Noelle appreciated Christian's logic, she wasn't ready to lose her baby to the country of Sherdana. "I just wish he was old enough to help me with this decision."

"Mama." Marc skidded through the doorway, flushed and disheveled. "We're going to stomp grapes. Come on." Without waiting for her, he ran back out of the room.

Laughing, she got to her feet. "You heard your son," she said, tugging on Christian's hand. "Let's go."

"He certainly has the imperious demeanor of a future monarch." Grinning, Christian threw his napkin onto the table and stood.

"Don't you mean tyrant?"

"He must get his bossy nature from his mother." Christian's arm snaked around her waist before she reached the French doors. "I find that an unexpected turn on."

He spun her into his arms and captured her lips in a sizzling kiss. Noelle sagged against him, admiring his knack for turning a lighthearted jab into a sincere compliment. Even knowing they could be caught at any second, Noelle darted out her tongue to taste the smooth chocolate and heady wine lingering on Christian's lips. His fingers tightened almost painfully against her ribs before he pushed her to arm's length.

"You are bad for my willpower," he told her, his voice a husky rasp. "First this morning and now…"

"Mama, are you coming?" Marc's plaintive wail came from across the yard.

Noelle gathered a shaky breath. "If we hold up the grape stomp much longer, my son will never forgive me."

Hand in hand they walked around the corner of the building where the bulk of the wine process happened and came upon a gathering of children and workers. Although the official start to the harvest was a week away, enough grapes had been gathered to fill three half wine barrels for the children to stomp.

In addition to Marc, Louis's youngest son and the vineyard manager's daughter were barefoot and ready to begin. The half casks had been set on a platform. Below each stomping container sat collecting jars for the juice. The children would pulverize the grapes with their feet, and the first one to produce the required amount of liquid would win. Seeing her son's grim determination, she knew Marc would give it his all.

"He has my competitive spirit," Christian murmured near her ear a second before Louis's wife signaled the start of the contest.

Noelle relaxed against the arm Christian slipped around her waist, enjoying his solidness against her back. "Yes. Some days that gets to be a problem."

Despite her words, she rooted for her son. Not that Marc needed the encouragement. Displaying the abundant energy that exhausted both Noelle and her mother on a daily basis, he ran in place, his concentration riveted on the grapes beneath his feet. Watching him, Noelle realized that while he was her baby and she wanted to protect him from harm, Marc was more resilient than she gave him credit for. He wouldn't suffer beneath the extreme media attention on the horizon. Nor would he be pushed into uncomfortable circumstances by Christian's family. There was too much of his father in him for him to take on the weight of rule until he was damn good and ready. And she hoped he had enough of her common sense to know when that moment was.

Beside her, Christian cheered as Marc was the first to accumulate the requisite amount of juice. After planting a firm, enthusiastic kiss on her cheek, Christian strode to the platform and swung his triumphant son out of the half cask. Noelle winced as vivid purple juice dripped from her son's feet and stained Christian's khaki pants. Heedless of the damage to his clothes, Christian set Marc on his hip and each threw a celebratory fist in the air.

Noelle felt the tiniest prick of sadness. Where once she'd been everything to Marc, she recognized that his father would soon be occupying more and more of his attention. Noelle couldn't help the panic that welled up. She'd built such a comfortable, safe life for herself and Marc, but so many changes were looming on the horizon.

Louis's wife came to her side. "Try lemon juice to get the grape stains off his feet."

"That works?"

The woman grinned. "It will help."

While Noelle chatted with Louis's wife, Christian cleaned off Marc's feet and wrangled him back into his socks and shoes. Hand in hand they then walked in her direction.

"Did you see how good I stomped, Mama?" Marc ran in place, demonstrating his winning technique. He gripped a bottle of sparkling grape juice, his prize for winning.

"I did." She noticed Marc hadn't released Christian's hand. Her chest tightened, but she offered her son a proud smile. "You are the best grape stomper in all Sherdana."

"He certainly is," Christian said, his gaze fond as it rested on Marc. "Are you ready to head back to the castle?"

"I think I've had enough excitement for one day. And someone needs a bath." She gazed pointedly at her son's feet.

"No, Mama. I want to show everyone at school that I stomped grapes."

"You can tell them about it," Noelle countered.

To her surprise, Marc didn't argue further. Instead, he waved goodbye to his new friends and trotted ahead of his parents to the lot where Christian's car waited.

On the way back to Bracci Castle, Marc's excited chatter gave way to silence.

Christian glanced over his shoulder. "He's out."

"Not surprising." Noelle felt a yawn coming on. The slow country pace combined with the delicious, filling lunch was making her sleepy. "I guess his bath will have to wait until later."

"I could use a nap myself," Christian said. "I didn't get a lot of sleep last night."

Noelle ignored the pointed look he shot her way. "That's odd. You were in bed by eleven."

"Yes, but I had a very eventful evening and couldn't figure out why it came to such an abrupt end."

"Perhaps because it wouldn't do for the eventfulness to become common knowledge."

"Why not when it's only a matter of time before we make our relationship official?"

"You seem very sure that's how things will go."

"I'm not so much confident as determined. Now that Marc is getting more accustomed to me, I expect to spend a lot more time with him. Which means you'll also be seeing more of me. You can't resist me forever."

Noelle sighed. Truth was, she couldn't resist him at all.

Christian slid into a charcoal-gray suit coat and straightened his blue-gray tie. The full-length mirror in his Carone apartment dressing room reflected back a somber aristocrat with chiseled features and wary eyes. It was not the face of a man about to propose to the mother of his son.

Since returning from the weekend at Bracci Castle five days ago, Christian had spent every evening with Noelle and Marc. They'd dined at her farmhouse, the palace and the restaurant that served American burgers. Tonight, however, he'd arranged for a private yacht to take Noelle and him on a romantic cruise down the river. During dinner, he planned to officially ask her to be his wife. On his nightstand sat the five-carat princess-cut diamond she would be wearing three hours from now.

As his driver wove through Carone's streets on the way out of the city, Christian reflected that he wasn't giving Noelle the time she'd asked for to decide if this was the right future for her and Marc. Last weekend it had been easy to promise her space. They'd reconnected both physically and emotionally. But these past five days had been hell.

He wanted to wake up with Noelle and have breakfast with Marc. To throw the ball with his son in the evenings and read him a bedtime story before taking Noelle in his arms and spending the night making love to her. A chaste good-night kiss at eight o'clock was completely unsatisfying.

When the car stopped in Noelle's driveway, Christian didn't wait for the driver to open his door. He was impatient to see Noelle and get their evening started. Before he could knock, Noelle's front door whipped open and Marc grinned at him from the foyer.

"Mama," he called, whirling on stocking feet and racing back into the house. "Prince Papa is here."

The blending of his two titles continued to amuse Christian. He suspected that the "prince" half would eventually go away. Until then, he was satisfied that his son had accepted Christian's role in his life.

"Marc, I'm right here," his mother admonished as she emerged from the main living room. "There's no reason to shout."

Christian stepped into the house and shut the door behind him. Word was out that he and Noelle had been spending time together, and he didn't want any telescopic lenses capturing the kiss he was about to give her.

Tonight's dress was a retro-style teal silk with a matching long-sleeve coat. The hemline was a bit shorter than usual and displayed a tantalizing amount of shapely leg. She wore her hair in an elegant topknot that he couldn't wait to dishevel. Simple pearls adorned her delicate earlobes, and a matching strand encircled her neck. She gave him a welcoming smile, and he stepped forward to draw her firmly into his embrace.

The warm feminine scent of her made his head spin as he claimed her mouth in a tender, poignant kiss. He kept a ruthless hold on his libido. This was not the time nor the place to show her how five days of abstinence had driven him mad with longing. They had all evening and much of the night for him to demonstrate how fully beneath her spell he'd fallen.

"Shall we go?" he purred beside her ear, feeling the shiver that passed through her muscles. "I have a full night planned."

She pulled back and regarded him with alarm. "I can't stay out all night. Marc gets up early and will expect me to be here."

"I will have you back before the roosters start to crow." For most people this would only be a saying, but in fact Noelle kept several chickens on her acre of land, and Marc had mentioned the rooster's predawn bugling several times.

"Thank you."

Christian held her hand as the town car wove through Carone to where the yacht was moored. Earlier that day, he'd prepared a speech. It ran through his mind like a hamster on a wheel and he found himself oddly tongue-tied. Thankfully, Noelle had never been bothered by silence between them, but tonight her tranquil acceptance offered him no solace.

After boarding the yacht, Christian led her to the salon. The September warm spell would enable them to enjoy a romantic dinner on deck where they could observe the lights of the city reflecting off the water as dusk became night. But that would come later. He had something he needed to get out of the way first.

A bottle of champagne was chilling in a silver bucket on the bar. Two tall flutes stood beside it, waiting to be filled. Christian had asked for privacy during this cruise except while dinner was being served. He wanted no audience this evening. Since the champagne had been opened, all Christian had to do was pour the sparkling liquid and hand Noelle a glass. He was happy to see that his hands didn't shake as he clinked his flute with hers.

"To us." He felt rather than heard his voice break awkwardly and swallowed far too much of the fizzy wine. The bubbles burned as they went down, and he coughed.

Noelle peered at him over her flute and cleared her own throat. "I think we should get married."

A racing speedboat passed recklessly close to the yacht, almost drowning out her words. Wondering if he'd heard her properly, Christian searched Noelle's expression.

"Did you say we should get married?" The noise of the speedboat was receding, but Christian continued to hear buzzing.

"Why do you sound so surprised? I thought that's what

you wanted." Anxiety flitted across her delicate features. "Have you changed your mind?"

"No." Explaining to her that he'd planned out the romantic evening with the sole intent of proposing seemed a little anticlimactic. "You've just caught me by surprise."

"I said I needed some time to think about it." Her gaze was fixed on the passing shore. "After watching you with Marc this week, I realized just how much he's missed not having his father in his life."

"So, this is about Marc and me." He'd been thinking in terms of finding the sort of marital bliss and perfect little family that Gabriel and Olivia enjoyed with the twins.

"Well, yes. Isn't that what you've wanted all along? To become Marc's father and to legitimize him as your heir?" Her obvious confusion proved she had no clue how his feelings for her had grown over the past couple of weeks.

And now he had no reason to tell her. She was happy with her decision to marry him. They would have a good partnership, and the sex between them was fantastic. Why muddy things with sentimental declarations of romantic love?

"It's exactly what I want," he told her, pulling the small jewelry box out of his pocket and opening the lid so she could see the ring. "And I've had this waiting for the moment you agreed."

Christian was happy to let her think he hadn't planned for anything out of the ordinary tonight. He lifted her left hand and slipped the ring onto her finger. As eager as he'd been all day to present this token of his commitment, the way the moment had played out left him with a hollow feeling in his gut.

"It's beautiful," she breathed, sounding more emotional than she had while suggesting they get married. She lifted onto her tiptoes and kissed him.

For once desire didn't consume him at the slightest brush of her lips. He tasted the champagne she'd sipped and inwardly grimaced at the bitterness of his disappointment. Calling himself every sort of fool, Christian plunged his tongue into her mouth and feasted on her surrender. She was his. That was all that mattered.

"We should tell my family tomorrow," he said, sweeping kisses across her forehead. He drew back and gave her his best smile.

"Marc first," she replied. "I don't want him hearing it from someone at school. Can you come by in the morning?"

"Of course."

They carried their champagne outside and sat at the beautifully set table. Around them white lights had been strung to provide a romantic atmosphere. Servers brought the first course and, by mutual agreement, Christian and Noelle spoke no more about their plans for the future until they could be safely alone again.

"The timing on this is quite good," Christian said. "Ariana returned from Paris yesterday, and Nic and Brooke aren't set to leave for Los Angeles until the end of the week. We can tell my whole family at once."

"That's wonderful news. Have you thought when you'd like the wedding to take place?"

"We could elope to Ithaca the way Gabriel and Olivia did."

Noelle shook her head. "I don't think your mother would approve. Perhaps we could have a Christmas wedding?"

He didn't like the idea of waiting three months to make her his wife, but having been on the sidelines for his brothers' weddings, he understood a great deal went into organizing a royal affair.

"Whatever you desire."

She gave him a funny little smile. "Just don't bother you with any of the details?"

"I'm sure between you, Olivia and my mother, any opinion I might have would be shot down in an instant."

The large diamond on her left hand winked at him as she lifted the champagne flute to her lips. "I promise you can have a voice in the arrangements if you tell me the one thing you always pictured having at your wedding."

"I never imagined getting married." Christian saw no reason to avoid the truth.

"No, I suppose you didn't."

Her smile wasn't as bright as some he'd seen, and he felt compelled to change that.

"It took the right woman to change my mind."

"The right circumstances."

Christian wanted to argue. To convince her that he had other reasons for marrying her besides legitimizing Marc and securing the throne for his family. Five years ago, knowing she'd never choose success over love, he'd manipulated the circumstances that swept her out of his life. She'd never believe he did it for her own good. Or that his actions had been noble even if on the surface they appeared selfish.

So, instead of creating conflict on the heels of a great victory, he did what any sane man would. He said to hell with dinner, took her in his arms and carried her to the master cabin.

Noelle rolled onto her side in the yacht's roomy master bedroom to watch the play of muscles in Christian's back and the delectable curve of his bare butt as he crossed the cabin to open a window and let in some cool evening air.

"The crew is going to wonder what happened to us,"

Noelle commented, her breath catching as Christian turned in her direction and shot her a wicked grin.

From his lustrous mahogany hair to his absurdly long toes and every magnificent line, dip and rise in between, he was hers. The jubilant thought lightened her heart and weighed on her mind.

"You don't think they heard us and know exactly what we're up to?"

Fresh air spilled across her overheated flesh and she broke out in goose bumps. She should feel embarrassed that her impassioned cries and his climactic shouts had penetrated the stateroom's thin walls. Instead, she found herself grinning.

"Too bad we didn't open the window beforehand. We could have given the entire riverbank something to talk about tomorrow."

Christian dropped onto the mattress and reached for her. "We could go for an encore."

Laughing, Noelle batted his hands away from her breast and thigh before snuggling against his left side and dropping her head onto his chest. His fingers traced soothing patterns on her hip as they lay together in silence.

It was hard to be this close to such a superb example of masculinity and not let herself go exploring. He sighed as she traced his collarbone and worked her way across his pectoral muscles. Glancing at his face, she noted his thick lashes lying against his cheeks. This gave her the chance to survey the right side of his upper body, where the worst of the scars were gathered. Moving with care, she grazed the tips of her fingers over the damaged flesh. Christian flinched.

She jerked her hand away. "Did I hurt you?"

"No." His chest expanded as he sucked in a ragged

breath. He stared at the ceiling, gold eyes dull. "The scars are ugly." His voice rang with self-disgust.

Noelle doubted many people saw this darker side of Christian. In public he exuded capability and confidence that she knew took a great deal of energy to maintain. Only with those he truly trusted could he let down his guard. Noelle had been happy to lend him what strength she could.

"You got them rescuing Talia after Andre lost control of his car," she reminded him. "They're your badge of courage."

"You know what happened?" His muscles tensed. "How? That was never public knowledge."

"You forget that I spent a great deal of time with Olivia in the days leading up to her wedding. For some reason she wanted to impress upon me what a brave, honorable man you were." Noelle suspected the princess had known Marc was Christian's son for some time. She kissed his damaged shoulder and felt a shudder rage through his body. "I don't understand why you kept the truth about the accident a secret. You were a hero."

He shook his head. "I blame myself for the crash. If I hadn't been chasing after Andre's car, he never would have driven so recklessly and lost control."

He'd raced into the night after Talia, his ex-lover, abandoning Noelle at a party to do so. Getting ready for the party that night, slipping on the bracelet Christian had given her for her birthday, she'd been giddy with anticipation of their first public appearance as a couple. But after that night, it was a long, long time before she was happy again.

Noelle wasn't sure why she'd picked the evening of her engagement to dredge up the past. Maybe her subconscious wanted to remind her that Christian held too much power over her happiness. Message received. This was going to be a marriage built on respect and passion. Friendship and sex. No reason she needed to yield her heart and risk being hurt again.

Christian's long fingers swept into her hair as he brought his lips to hers for a long, searing kiss. Noelle melted beneath his hot mouth and caressing hands. As her blood raced through her veins and pooled in her loins, she smiled. Her body she could give him without reservation.

She would be his wife, his princess and the mother of his children. Noelle hoped it would be enough.

Ten

Noelle sat on her office sofa, her bare feet tucked beneath her, and tapped her pencil against the sketchbook on her lap. The enormous diamond on her left hand felt awkward and strange. She caught herself staring at it a dozen times in the past hour as her mind struggled to assimilate the dramatic changes taking place. She was engaged to a prince. And not just any prince, but the prince of her dreams. It didn't seem possible.

Of course, it wasn't a fairy-tale engagement. Last night she'd been the one to suggest that they marry. She had merely formalized what Christian had already proposed, but it wasn't as if he'd dropped to one knee and pledged his undying love. At least he'd been ready with a ring.

She spun the diamond so it wasn't visible and turned her attention back to the sketchbook. To no avail. In two hours she and Christian would be breaking the news to his family. She'd already told her mother, but Marc didn't yet know. He'd woken before dawn with a stomachache and she'd kept him home from school. With him sick it hadn't seemed the best time to divulge that she and Christian were getting married, despite the fact that he and his father were getting along very well these days.

Her cell phone buzzed, and Noelle abandoned her work with a relieved sigh. The number on the screen caused a spike in her pulse. She sat up straight and slipped her shoes back on.

"Noelle Dubone," she said in a crisp voice, wondering if it was good or bad news to hear back so soon on a business venture.

"Noelle, it's Victor. I hope I'm reaching you at a good time."

"Yes. Fine." She sounded a trifle breathless and told herself to calm down. "How are you?"

"Good. Good. I'm calling to let you know that I just spoke with Jim Shae, and he is very interested in backing you with a ready-to-wear line of bridal fashions here in the States."

Victor Chamberlain was a friend of Geoff's who she'd met in London several years ago. An American businessman whose daughter had been looking for something fresh and unique in a wedding dress, he'd become Noelle's first big client. Last February during New York Fashion Week, he'd introduced her to several venture capitalists and suggested she should consider expanding into ready-to-wear.

Creating one-of-a-kind wedding dresses was vastly different from mass-producing an entire collection, so she'd teamed up with Victor to create a business plan that he'd pitched to investors.

"That's wonderful news." With joy dancing across her nerve endings, it took a few seconds for reality to strike. What was she thinking? She was engaged to a Sherdanian prince and needed to start planning now in order to make a royal wedding happen by Christmas. Keeping up with her current clients would be stressful enough. She didn't have time to start a new business venture.

"Can you be in New York next week? Jim would like to meet with you and discuss details."

Next week? Noelle worried her lower lip as she went to check her schedule. "How many days would I need to be there?"

Victor hesitated before answering. "At least three. Besides Jim, I want to set up meetings with buyers from the top bridal shops and media interviews. You should start planning for New York Fashion Week in February. You'll need a terrific venue. I know someone who can help with that."

"Three days..." Noelle's mind worked furiously.

Perhaps she and Christian should postpone the announcement of their engagement until after her New York trip. With a start she realized there was no question in her mind that she intended to embark on this business venture. Was splitting her attention between Sherdana and New York a wise move at the beginning of her marriage? On the other hand, did Christian plan to stop all business travel? Not likely.

"Let me know as soon as possible when you'll be flying in," Victor continued.

"I'll make all my arrangements and be in touch later today."

First of all, she needed to tell Christian what had just happened. But as she scrolled through her contacts for his number, she faltered. How would he view her decision to jump into a major business venture without talking to him about it first? He should be happy for her. But would he question her priorities? Her commitment to this marriage?

Or was she the one questioning her commitment?

Noelle sank into her office chair and stared out the window overlooking the alley behind her salon. In two hours she would be announcing her intention to marry Christian. She spun the ring on her finger. Once word got out, she'd better be ready to go forward. Not only would a broken engagement create a scandal the country didn't need, but her actions would confuse Marc and set a bad example for him.

Conflict churned Noelle's insides. Christian deserved to be a full-time father to Marc, and that would be better accomplished if Noelle honored her engagement and married Christian. Marc benefited. Christian benefited. The country benefited. Three wins. Noelle didn't have to feel guilty about focusing on her business instead of playing the part of dutiful wife. Christian was getting the heir he wanted.

Despite arriving at a reasonable conclusion, Noelle wasn't convinced Christian would agree. She keyed his number and heard the call going through.

"Noelle." He purred in her ear. "I was just thinking about you."

Her toes curled in her pink, superfine Louboutin stilettos. With his warm brandy voice flowing from the phone's speaker, she was hard-pressed to summon all her earlier doubts. Of course, she wanted to marry Christian. No other man could make her come alive just by breathing her name.

"I've been thinking about you, as well." Was that her coming across all sexy and mysterious? She curved her body sideways in the chair, any trace of the capable businesswoman lost beneath a rush of feminine pleasure at hearing her lover's voice.

"I'm heading into a conference call in a moment. Is everything okay with Marc?"

Suddenly Noelle couldn't find the words to share her

confusion and doubts. "He's better. Turns out it wasn't the flu but an entire bag of cookies that caused his stomach-ache. I just wondered if you wanted to have dinner at my house tonight."

"Absolutely. If you think Marc will be well enough, we can tell him about our engagement."

"That's what I planned. The sooner the better." And she would also tell him about her new venture. Together they would figure out the best way forward.

"I have back-to-back meetings between now and when I'm supposed to pick you up for our meeting with my family, and I don't want to be late so I've arranged for a car to take you to the palace."

"That's not necessary. I've made my own way to the palace a dozen times. I'll be fine."

"It's what I want. You are no longer visiting as a de-signer or a guest."

Hearing his determination, Noelle conceded. "Very well. Just don't leave me facing your family alone."

"Never fear." Rich amusement filled his tone. "I'll see you at three."

Noelle disconnected the call and sat with the phone in her lap, preparing herself to do the right thing for all concerned.

Christian stared at the slow-moving traffic ahead of him, about to break the promise he'd made to Noelle two hours earlier. He had ten minutes to get to the palace and fifteen minutes of driving ahead of him. He should have anticipated that his meeting with Gaston would run late. The man was a savvy politician in the perfect position to block Christian from securing land he needed outside Carone to develop his next project. The negotiations had been difficult.

With Sherdana's economic troubles easing thanks to an influx of technology businesses, Christian had decided to focus more of his attention on investing close to home. This would mean less travel and more time spent with Noelle and Marc. It was important as a new husband and father to put his family first.

Drumming his thumbs against the steering wheel, Christian willed the cars in front of him to move. His impatience wasn't just about the traffic. He was eager to see Noelle again. Having to postpone telling Marc this morning had been disappointing, but sharing their news with his family was the next best thing.

When Christian arrived in the family's private living room, Noelle was already there with his parents, Nic, Brooke and Ariana. Standing at ease beside his sister, Noelle looked stunning in a richly embroidered pale pink coat over a simple ivory dress. Before making his way to Noelle's side, Christian swung by to greet his parents.

"You're late," the king scolded.

"Traffic," Christian explained. "Besides, Gabriel and Olivia aren't here yet."

The queen offered her cheek for his kiss. "You'd better have good news for us."

"The best." He smiled his most confident grin.

Obligations satisfied, he headed toward Noelle. As he took his place beside her, Gabriel and Olivia rushed hand-in-hand into the room. Their exuberant smiles drew everyone's attention. Christian experienced an uncomfortable stab of envy at the strength of their connection. They were surrounded by family and yet so in tune with each other. Would he and Noelle ever get to a point where they enjoyed that sort of intimacy?

"We have wonderful news," Gabriel began, his unrestrained delight making him seem far younger than thirty. "We are going to be parents."

For a moment the room was deathly quiet as Christian's family absorbed this impossible announcement. Olivia had undergone a hysterectomy four months earlier, rendering her incapable of having children.

The queen was the first to recover her voice. "How?"

"My eggs were viable for a month after my operations. The doctors were able to harvest several. We found a surrogate and just came from her first doctor's appointment. Everything looks good." Olivia turned a radiant smile on Gabriel.

He bent his head and gave her a quick kiss. Then he glanced around the room. "And we're having twins."

Ariana ran to Olivia and threw her arms around her sister-in-law. Nic and Brooke stepped up next. While a part of Christian was thrilled for his older brother, most of him was numb. He glanced at Noelle to gauge her reaction. She watched the happy couple through eyes that shone brightly with tears. Christian felt his throat lock up and could only stare, mind blank, as his parents stepped up for their turn to congratulate their son and daughter-in-law.

Noelle poked him in the ribs and whispered, "Go congratulate them. This is amazing news."

"What about our news?" He sounded like a grumpy old man. "It's pretty amazing, too."

"This is their moment. I don't want to ruin it." She placed the flat of her hand against his back and gave him a shove. While she didn't have the strength to move him, her recommendation was clear.

Was there some other reason why she didn't want to announce their engagement? Was she thinking of backing out now that Gabriel and Olivia had figured out a way to supply an heir for the throne?

Christian pushed aside concern and caught Noelle's hand in his. Together they joined the circle of well-wishers.

"You seem to have a knack for producing twins," Christian told his brother, smiling despite his heavy heart.

"At least these two won't be identical," Gabriel replied.

Several members of the staff brought the champagne that Christian had made sure was on ice to toast his engagement, and everyone except Brooke—who was pregnant—enjoyed a glass. No one seemed to recall that Christian had organized the family meeting or wonder what his announcement might have been.

The frustration he'd begun feeling the instant Noelle suggested they put off sharing the news of their engagement began to grow. He'd put all his energy into convincing Noelle that they belonged together as a family and now his brother had to come along at the absolute moment that Christian was the happiest he'd ever been and spoil everything.

Thirty minutes into the celebration, he pulled her aside. "I really think we should announce our engagement."

Noelle glanced at Gabriel and Olivia. "Now isn't a good time. And I need to get back to my shop."

His dismay expanded. "I thought we'd have the afternoon to celebrate making our engagement official."

"Something came up earlier that I need to take care of."

Considering that he'd arrived at the palace almost twenty minutes late because of his own meeting schedule, Christian forced down his irritation.

"What time should I come by tonight?"

She pressed her lips together and didn't meet his eyes. "About that. Why don't we wait a little while before we tell Marc."

"Why don't I take you back to your shop, and we can discuss that on the way there."

"Christian—"

"You owe me an explanation for your sudden turn-around."

She ducked her head and nodded. "I know."

Without drawing attention to themselves, they slipped out of the room and headed to the side entrance nearest the family quarters where Christian had left his car.

After assisting Noelle into the passenger seat, he slipped behind the wheel and started the powerful engine. Wasting no time on preliminaries, he stomped on the gas and, as the car shot forward, demanded, "What's going on?"

"Gabriel and Olivia are going to be parents. This changes everything."

It did, and he hated them for it. "It changes nothing. I'm still Marc's father. I deserve to be in his life."

"Of course you do, but now we don't need to rush into anything." Both her words and her tone betrayed her relief.

Christian ground his teeth together, using only half his attention to negotiate past slower-moving vehicles. "I didn't realize we were rushing."

"Didn't you? We were planning for a Christmas wedding." She was spinning her engagement ring around and around. "You wanted to make Marc your legal heir as soon as possible so that your family would continue to enjoy political stability."

"I want to be a family with you and Marc," he corrected.

"And we still can, but it's nothing that has to happen right away."

The problem with her argument was that each day Christian grew more impatient to live under the same roof as her and Marc. His bachelor lifestyle no longer interested him.

"My brother has already demonstrated that he only

knows how to produce girls," Christian argued. "What makes you think this time will be different?"

"In a month or so they'll be able to tell the sex of the babies. In the meantime…" Noelle slipped the ring from her finger and held it out to Christian.

"You're breaking off our engagement already." A statement, not a question.

His heartbeat slowed to a near standstill. This couldn't be happening to him.

"It isn't a real engagement." Clearly her perception of their relationship differed from his. "I mean, we aren't in love or anything, so it's just an arrangement."

She wasn't wrong. He'd used legitimizing their son as an excuse for marriage. As always, taking what appeared to be the easiest path had led him into a bramble hedge. Now he was stuck with the consequences.

"I care about you. I don't want to lose you."

She smiled. "And I care about you, but as you often used to remind me, you aren't cut out for marriage. You were marrying me out of duty. Now you don't have to."

"Keep the ring." He tightened his grip on the steering wheel. "We'll postpone announcing our engagement for a month."

Noelle closed her fist around the diamond and set both hands in her lap. "I don't feel right keeping it."

"It's yours. I bought it for you." He didn't want the damned thing back. "We'll proceed as we've been for a few weeks longer. You're right that we rushed. Circumstances pushed us too fast. Now we have all the time in the world."

When she didn't respond, he glanced over at her. His stomach twisted at her obvious discomfort.

"What?" he prompted.

"See, the thing is…" She hesitated, and stared out the passenger window for so long he thought she might have forgotten he was beside her. "I called you earlier today to tell you about something that just came up."

He did not like the sound of this. "What sort of something?"

"A business opportunity. I have a meeting with an investor next week. He's interested in backing a line of ready-to-wear bridal gowns."

"That's fantastic."

She smiled at his enthusiasm. "I'm very excited."

"You don't seem to be."

"It's just that the potential investor wants me to expand my business in the US, specifically New York City. That's where my meetings are next week."

He was starting to see why she was so subdued. "That's a long commute."

"I was worried about it."

"And now you're not?"

"I think Gabriel and Olivia's news might have allowed us to dodge a bullet."

"How so?"

"You didn't really want to get married, and now you don't have to. Marc is your son. As he gets a little older, we can figure out a visitation schedule that enables you to see as much of him as makes sense."

"And in the meantime?" Christian was having a hard time keeping his rising anger out of his tone. "Am I supposed to just let you take Marc to New York and not see my son?"

"No, of course not. I'll have to travel back and forth between New York and Europe. I have many clients on this side of the Atlantic whom I can't afford to neglect. But I'll be creating a collection to show at New York Fashion Week in February that will kick off my ready-to-wear line and

I'll probably be spending the bulk of my time in America leading up to it."

"Marc should stay here with me." It's not what Christian had intended to suggest. He couldn't imagine living without Noelle or his son, but once again he'd used Marc as a decoy to distract her from the full scope of his emotions.

"I can't leave him in Sherdana. I'm all he's known his whole life. He's too young to understand why his mother is leaving him."

"You don't take him with you every time you travel for business. We'll start small. How long are you going to be in New York next week?"

"A few days."

"That's perfect."

"No."

"You go to New York and meet with your investor while I stay here and take care of Marc. If we'd gotten married, it's what would have eventually happened. The only difference is the lack of a legal document."

She gave a soft gasp. "A custody agreement?"

"A marriage license." Christian stopped the car in front of Noelle's shop and put it in Park. Turning in his seat, he took her hand that held the ring and opened her fingers. "I'm not giving up on the idea of marrying you," he said, slipping the diamond onto her right hand. "Take this ring as a sign of my faith in us as a couple and as a family."

"I'll wear it until I return from New York. At that point we will sit down and discuss what's best for Marc and for you and me."

Which meant he had a little more than a week to convince her to go forward with their plans to get married. If he hoped to convince her they belonged together, he'd better pull out all the stops. He wasn't going to make the mistake of letting her go a second time.

* * *

The morning she was scheduled to leave for New York, Noelle woke with her stomach twisted into knots. She was about to embark on the most ambitious project of her career. To fail would mean she'd not only risked damaging her reputation as a designer and a businesswoman, but had created a rift between Christian and her for nothing.

She'd decided not to leave Marc at home with either his father or her mother. This wasn't a two-day hop to Paris or Milan. This was a ten-hour plane ride and an ocean between them. Her son didn't share her anxiety about their separation. Taking him with her meant Marc would be missing a field trip to the zoo. He'd protested vehemently, and reminding him that they'd visited less than a month ago had only made things worse.

"Marc, please go upstairs and brush your teeth. You must get dressed. The car will be here any moment to take us to the airport." She turned to her mother. "Why is he being like this?"

"He doesn't want to go. Why don't you leave him with me? He shouldn't be stuck in a hotel room in New York while you're working."

While a part of Noelle knew her mother was right, she couldn't quell her uneasiness at the thought of leaving him behind. She'd made arrangements for a nanny to stay with Marc while she conducted business, but didn't know if she was comfortable letting the woman roam around the city alone with him.

A knock sounded on the door. The car she'd arranged to take her and Marc to the airport had finally arrived.

"Marc, the car is here. There is no more time for games." She experienced an uncharacteristic longing to bury her face in her hands and cry. "Mama, can you get him upstairs to change?"

Still in his pajamas, Marc was running the circle from the kitchen, through the dining room, into the living room and back to the kitchen, arms held out, pretending he was an airplane. Noelle glanced at the clock. She wore no makeup, had thrown her hair into a damp updo because tussling with Marc had robbed her of the time to dry it, and her blouse was stained with syrup.

Noelle went to answer the door and discovered not a driver, but Christian standing on her steps. His eyes narrowed when he caught sight of her, and she realized he'd never seen her in such disarray.

She gestured him in. "Good morning, Christian. Please come in. There's coffee in the kitchen." Behind her came Marc's protesting wail and her mother's warning tone. "As you can tell, my household is in chaos and I'm running late. I thought you were the driver I hired to take us to the airport. He was supposed to be here twenty minutes ago."

Rather than walk past her, Christian backed her against the entry wall and cupped her face in gentle hands. Her muscles went limp as his lips covered hers. The kiss was tender and full of longing. She opened to him, sliding her hands into his hair to keep their mouths fused together.

A low groan built in her chest. It was the first time he'd touched her like this since she'd broken off their engagement, and she felt like a spring flower coming to life after a long, harsh winter.

"Prince Papa." Marc's slippered feet thudded down the hall toward them.

Christian broke off the kiss and surveyed Noelle with enigmatic eyes before turning to scoop his son off the floor and lift him high above his head.

While her son shrieked in delight, Noelle put a hand to her chest and snatched several seconds to recover. In the long years apart from him, she'd forgotten that being kissed by Christian was an excellent way to begin her day.

As Christian set Marc back on his feet, Noelle nudged her son toward Mara. "Marc, please go upstairs with Nana and get dressed so we can be ready to leave if the car ever gets here."

"Noooo." And before Noelle could stop him, he'd bolted out the still-open front door, his howl fading as he raced away.

She started for the door, but Christian caught her arm. "I'll get him. Why don't you take a couple minutes and have some of that coffee you mentioned earlier."

"We're already running late. If we don't get going now, we'll miss the plane." She thought of the appointments set up for later that day and bit her lower lip in frustration.

"I'll get you there."

She shook her head. "I have a car coming."

"I mean to New York."

Behind him, Marc flashed by on the front lawn. Noelle was so focused on her annoyance with Marc that it took a moment for Christian's words to penetrate.

"How are you going to do that?"

His slow smile sent goose bumps racing over Noelle's skin. "I have a very luxurious private plane gassed up and waiting for us at the airport."

"Us?" What was he saying?

"I've cleared my schedule for the next few days so I could accompany you and Marc to New York. I thought that while you worked, Marc and I could play."

Instantly Noelle knew her son would love that. Spending time with his father had become something he now looked forward to, and it would ease Noelle's mind knowing Marc wouldn't be cooped up in a hotel room with a stranger their entire stay.

"I can't ask you to do that."

"You didn't. I volunteered."

Her mind flashed to the kiss a moment earlier. "I hope you understand I'm going on business. What just happened…" She made a vague gesture toward the spot where he'd pinned her to the wall and kissed her senseless. "I hope you don't think…"

The glow in his eyes told her that's exactly what he was thinking, but he shook his head. "I'm going to spend time with Marc. You don't need to worry that I'll distract you from any of your plans."

Oh, he'd distract her, all right. The craving to make love with him purred in her body like a contented cat. It would only be a matter of time before it woke and dug in its sharp claws.

"I guess then I can send the driver on his way."

"Already done."

Before she could protest his high-handedness, Christian was out the door.

"You'd better put on some makeup and fix your hair," Mara said, rich amusement in her voice. "Not that Prince Christian will care one way or another. He seems to approve of you no matter what."

Cheeks burning at her mother's teasing, Noelle raced upstairs to change out of her stained blouse and finish packing. If a couple new pieces of lingerie found their way into her suitcase as well as a sexy black lace nightgown, that didn't mean she had changed her mind about staying focused on business.

Since Christian was dressed casually in jeans and a gray sweater over a white collared shirt, Noelle decided against her original choice of a tailored burgundy suit and slipped into black skinny pants, a denim shirt and her favorite pair of black flats.

To show her mother that she didn't intend to go all out for Christian, Noelle applied black liner on her upper lids and enhanced her lips with a brilliant red. By the time she emerged from her bedroom with her suitcase, Christian had Marc dressed, his hair combed and teeth brushed. Noelle didn't marvel at how he'd accomplished so much in such a short period of time. She merely sent him a grateful look and headed downstairs.

Christian's driver fetched their suitcases while she settled Marc in the backseat and slid in after him. A moment later Christian joined them, his body solid and reassuring at her side. The worry and doubts that had plagued her these past few days abruptly lost their power. As the car began rolling down her driveway, Noelle sighed and squeezed Christian's arm.

"Thank you for coming with us."

He covered her hand and smiled. "No thanks necessary. I'm happy to be with you and Marc."

It wasn't a calculated line to impress her, but the unadorned truth. Noelle's heart expanded. Suddenly her decision to break off their engagement appeared like the worst one she'd ever made. Christian loved Marc. And she loved Christian. The truth flashed in her mind like a neon sign. Of course she loved him. She'd never stopped. For five years she'd ignored the truth by focusing on maintaining a balance between her career and being the best mom she could.

But her realization came too late. She'd already agreed to marry him and then called it off, freeing Christian from any moral obligation he might have felt toward her and Marc.

Christian tugged on the dark green scarf she'd knotted around her neck. "Where'd you go? You're a long way off."

"Sorry."

"Marc and I were just discussing our plans for New York. He's very excited to go to his first baseball game."

"I packed my glove," the boy announced. "So I can catch a home-run ball."

"Actually, we'll be sitting behind home plate so you'll have to catch a foul ball instead."

"Foul balls!" Marc exclaimed, kicking his feet. "And the zoo."

"Bronx or Central Park?" Christian asked.

"Both."

Noelle laughed. "You're going to be busy."

"It'll be fun. I've never had much opportunity to sight-see in New York. Every time I've been there it's been for business."

"I think I'm a little envious of you two," Noelle said and meant it. Ever since finding out she had an investor for her ready-to-wear line, she'd been caught up in all the deal's details. Now, she wished someone else could take care of business while she hung out with her two favorite men.

"Mama has to work." Marc grinned past her toward his father, and the two shared a special moment that excluded Noelle.

"Mama has to work," she agreed, so glad her son had this wonderful man in his life to love him.

Eleven

When the pressure changed in the jet's cabin, Christian stretched his legs and glanced toward his son. Despite his excitement at visiting New York, Marc was a good traveler. Considering the boy's abundant energy, Christian had worried that Marc would be a restless terror. At the beginning of the flight, he'd settled right down with crayons and a coloring book. Later, Noelle and Christian had taken turns reading to him for an hour after which he'd had lunch, napped and was now quietly enjoying a Disney movie.

This had offered plenty of time for Noelle and Christian to talk. By mutual consent, they'd not strayed into any tricky personal topics while their son sat nearby. Instead, Noelle had laid out her business plan and asked Christian for feedback.

"Your third-year numbers seem a little conservative. Are you really convinced your business will grow at only seven percent?"

"Seven is a little above average and a safe estimate."

"You've never struck me as the sort who goes for safe." He hadn't imbued the comment with subtext, but Noelle's eyes narrowed.

"I have Marc to think about now. I can't jump into something if there seems to be some inherent risk involved." Although her tone was mild enough, tension formed little lines around her mouth.

"I understand." But Christian wasn't sure he did.

"Do you? Because doing what's best for him is my top priority."

Somehow they'd strayed from discussing business, and Christian had no idea what she was trying to tell him. "I understand." Repeating the words didn't have the effect he'd hoped.

Noelle grew even more agitated. "I know I've been hard on you. And I've been selfish."

Since it was obvious she had something to get off her chest, Christian kept his mouth shut and let her vent. She was beautiful, with her tantalizing lips painted bright red and the green of her scarf heightening the chestnut tones in her eyes. She'd kicked off her pointed black flats and sat with her feet tucked beneath her. The pen she'd been using to make notes was jabbed into her topknot for easy access. He wanted very badly to haul her onto his lap and kiss her silly.

"I want Marc to see you as a permanent fixture in his life."

All day she'd been swapping the engagement ring back and forth between her right and left hands. He doubted she was even aware that she was toying with the ring or that at the moment it rested on her left hand exactly where Christian wanted it.

"I thought that's what we've been doing with the dinners and outings."

"Yes." She kept her gaze trained on his shoulder. "But I think we should have something formal in place."

"A custody agreement?"

Her shoulders stiffened for a moment as if she were wincing from a blow. Christian could tell the offer wasn't easy for her. A second later she nodded.

"I think Marc will benefit from more time with his father."

"Not as much as his father will benefit." Christian kept his tone light to conceal his heavy heart. Always impatient, he wanted to claim both Noelle and Marc as his.

Noelle gave him a tremulous smile. "You always know just what to say."

"What sort of time did you have in mind for Marc to spend with me?"

"Obviously it will depend on your travel schedule. I thought maybe when we get back you could take him overnight and see how it goes."

"I didn't get a chance to tell you last week, but I've restructured some of my business dealings to keep me in Sherdana more. I'd like as much time with Marc as you're willing to give me." And with Noelle, but that didn't seem as likely now.

"That's wonderful. Seeing more of each other will only strengthen your relationship with Marc."

"And what are you planning to do with all your free time?"

Giving him partial custody would offer her a break from motherhood. An opportunity to date. Although he was convinced she wasn't in love with Geoff, he couldn't claim to know how the lawyer felt about Noelle. Suddenly Christian wasn't so sure he liked where things were heading.

She laughed. "I suspect for the next year or so, I'll be working around the clock to launch my ready-to-wear line and continue expanding my couture business. While he's with you, I won't have to worry that Marc is being neglected."

Christian considered what she'd said. It hadn't occurred to him that she'd feel guilty for working hard at her thriving business. "It will be good to have both of us there for him."

"You're right." She leaned forward, her expression earnest. "I didn't realize how much Marc needed a father until these past few weeks. I'm sorry I didn't tell you about him sooner."

Christian was touched by her apology but knew he couldn't let her take all the blame. "I never gave you any reason to think I would be there for Marc." He regretted missing Marc's first four years, but also for failing Noelle even as he thought he was trying to help her. "I wish I could take back the past five years."

Noelle shook her head. "I don't. If you hadn't broken things off I never would have gone to Paris and had a chance to learn under Matteo."

"And become an internationally famous wedding gown designer."

"You see. It all worked out perfectly in the end." But her smile wasn't as bright as her voice. "In the end you did me a huge favor."

Maybe he had, but Christian acknowledged that he'd also done himself a disservice by letting her go.

An exhausted Noelle returned to her suite at the Four Seasons after a grueling second day of meetings and interviews to find her son wearing a Yankees jersey and cap and carrying an autographed baseball in his mitt.

"And then he swung like this." Marc demonstrated a dramatic swing that spun him in a circle. "The ball went like…gone…gone…gone. Home run!" He threw his arms into the air and ran around the suite's living room as if running the bases.

"Goodness." Noelle looked to Christian, who stood with his hands in the back pockets of his jeans, watching his son with such fondness a lump formed in Noelle's throat. "Sounds like it was a fun game."

"It was grrreat." Marc charged toward Christian, who absorbed his son's enthusiastic hug with a grin. "And tomorrow we're going on a boat ride to the Statue of Liberty."

"You two are certainly taking advantage of all New York has to offer." Once again Noelle found herself regretting all the quality time she was missing with her son.

Christian picked up on the source of her melancholy as he swung Marc into his arms. "You could cancel your meetings and join us."

"Tempting." She smiled through her weariness. "But I only have tomorrow morning to get the last of the details hammered out."

"You're running yourself ragged."

"I know, but it will be worth it in the end." Satisfaction suffused her. As grinding as the pace had been since the jet's wheels had touched down on the New York runway, her ready-to-wear line was getting the right backing and garnering the perfect buzz.

"I'm really proud of you." While Noelle had been lost in thought, Christian had set down Marc and stepped close. "I want you to know that whatever you need I'll be here to help."

When his arm slid around her waist, drawing her against his body for a friendly hug, Noelle's pulse bucked. The man smelled like sunshine and soap. She longed to rest her cheek against the cotton stretched across his broad chest and let the world fade away. Her hunger for him flared. It had been a week since they'd made love, but with all that had happened in the meantime, it felt more like months.

Noelle leaned back and gazed up into Christian's molten gold eyes. Her knees weakened at the heat of his desire, and her lips parted as he lowered his head. A small body crashed against them, reminding Noelle that she and Christian weren't alone. She set her hand on Marc's head, frustration making the ache of longing that much more intense.

"What sort of plans do you have for dinner?" Christian asked, his arm sliding away from her body. He'd booked a suite at the Four Seasons in order to be close to his son. "Marc had a hot dog, popcorn and cotton candy at the ballpark, so I thought it would be a good idea to feed him a healthy dinner and we hoped you'd be able to join us."

As hard as it was to turn down the offer with two pairs of matching gold eyes trained on her, Noelle shook her head. "I'm having dinner with some designer friends of mine, and then there's a gala I'm attending afterward."

Marc showed less disappointment at this news than Christian. Their son was having far too much fun with his father to notice his mother's absence. As Marc dashed over to retrieve his mitt and autographed baseball from the coffee table, Christian's deep voice rumbled through her.

"I'm sorry you can't join us."

"So am I." And she meant it. "If it wasn't business…"

He nodded in understanding, his hands sliding into his pockets once more. "That's why you're here."

While part of Noelle appreciated his support, she couldn't stop wishing he'd ask her to cut her night short so she could tuck Marc into bed and maybe invite Chris-

tian to linger for some private time with her. Instead, he
headed to his son, leaving her free to get ready for her
evening out.

Three hours later, Noelle stood beside Victor, her mind
far from business and the well-dressed crowd gathered
to support a local food pantry. She was wondering if she
could plead a headache and get back to the hotel in time
to put her son to bed.

And the other thing…

All night long her heart and body had been wrestling
with her mind regarding Christian. She longed to spend
the night in his arms. To pretend she hadn't broken off
their engagement in a foolish rush because she'd thought
to beat him to the punch. But could she have married him
thinking that he was merely following through on a con-
tract he'd made with her? It had been one thing to marry
him knowing he didn't love her when they were both taking steps to secure the future of the country.

"This has been a fantastic couple of days," Victor said,
his enthusiasm dragging Noelle's attention back to the
ballroom. "I think your line is going to be a huge success."

"Have I told you how much I appreciate all you've
done?"

"I've just started things rolling."

"You've done more than that. You've created a tsunami
of media interest and made sure that I'm meeting all the
right people to make this line a success."

"I believe in you." Victor's shrewd brown eyes softened.
"I wouldn't have partnered with you if I didn't. You're
talented and business-savvy. It's been a pleasure working with you."

"It's been wonderful working with you, as well." Throat
tight, she gave him a smile as she squeezed his hand.
"Now, if you don't mind, I'm going to go back to the hotel

and tuck my son into bed. I've neglected him terribly these past two days."

"I understand perfectly."

Noelle turned down Victor's offer of his car and left him to make her way out of the ballroom. It was nine-thirty, but she doubted Marc was in bed yet. She was in the process of sending Christian a text letting him know she was on her way back when someone behind her called her name. With a weary sigh, Noelle turned and spied a tall, bone-thin woman in her early thirties coming toward her, recognizing her as the *Charme* magazine editor who'd been overheard making disparaging remarks about her most recent fall couture collection. Not surprising, since she and Giselle had been rivals at Matteo Pizarro Designs and Giselle knew how to hold a grudge.

"Giselle, how lovely to see you." Noelle gave her former coworker a polite smile.

"I understand you and Prince Christian Alessandro are hot and heavy once more."

In the old days, before she'd realized what a snake Giselle could be, Noelle had told the seemingly sympathetic woman all about her two-year relationship with Christian. "We are friends." There was no way Noelle was going to tell the woman anything.

"Friendly enough that he accompanied you and your son to New York."

Although there had been speculation, the media hadn't yet discovered Christian's true relationship to Marc, and Noelle had no intention of sharing anything with Giselle.

"He's a friend," Noelle repeated, keeping her tone bland. "Now, if you'll excuse me, it's been a long couple of days." She turned to go, but Giselle's next words stopped her.

"I hear you're launching a ready-to-wear line."

Reminding herself that despite the animosity between

them, Giselle had an influential position in the industry, Noelle put on her interview face. "That's why I'm in New York. To meet with my backer and start making arrangements for manufacturing."

"Oh, Prince Christian isn't backing you?" Giselle's surprise didn't ring true. "I thought with you two being so close…and since he's helped you out before."

What was Giselle trying to get at?

"Prince Christian has never helped me."

When triumph flashed in Giselle's eyes, Noelle felt her uneasiness rise. Giselle had sabotaged her efforts several times when Noelle had first joined Matteo Pizarro Designs. Naively believing Giselle had been her friend had enabled the older woman to take credit for Noelle's ideas and ruin an entire week's worth of sketches before they were set to present their designs to Matteo as part of a special runway collection he was to exhibit at the Louvre. When, in the hour before they were to meet with Matteo, Noelle had crafted five sketches and Matteo had selected one of those, Giselle had been livid.

"You can tell the rest of the world such lies, but I know the truth."

"What truth?" Noelle knew better than to ask, but Giselle's absolute confidence had rattled her.

"That you never would have gotten the job with Matteo Pizarro without your prince's help."

"That's a lie."

"I heard Matteo speaking to Claudia about it. He said you were too inexperienced to hire, and he never would have considered you except that he was doing a favor for Prince Christian."

Noelle awakened to the truth as if she'd been slapped in the face. She'd been so shocked that she'd landed a position with such a prestigious designer. Her work was acceptable, but not outstanding. Only after she started working for Matteo Pizzaro and been inspired firsthand by the man's brilliance had she begun to gain confidence as a designer and take chances.

"It might be true," Noelle conceded, "but that's because Prince Christian believed in my talent before I did." And he'd see it as a great way to end their relationship.

But did that really make sense? Surely Christian had ended things with dozens of women without finding them a dream job that sent them five hundred miles away.

Giselle must have perceived Noelle's confusion as vulnerability because she stepped closer. "You'd be nothing if he hadn't used his influence to get Matteo to hire you."

"Maybe I wouldn't be a wedding gown designer to the wealthy and famous," Noelle agreed, no longer the naïve twenty-five-year-old girl Giselle had been able to take advantage of. "But I would still be the mother of an amazing little boy. And I'd be all the better for never having met you."

So much for playing nice with the media. Noelle turned on her heel and slipped from the ballroom, her heart racing after the ugly encounter. Her thoughts were a chaotic jumble as she slid into a cab for the two-mile trek back to the Four Seasons. She didn't doubt Giselle spoke the truth about Christian arranging for her to get the job with Matteo. What she couldn't sort out was how she felt about it.

Fifteen minutes later she let herself into her hotel suite, surprised to find Christian watching TV in her living room. There was no sign of Marc.

"You're back early," he said, using the remote to turn off the TV. He got to his feet as she crossed the room.

"I wanted to tuck Marc in, but it looks like I'm too late."

"He fell asleep on the couch around nine. The last two days have been pretty busy."

"You didn't have to stay. What happened to the nanny?"

"I sent her home. I have a couple things on my mind to talk to you about."

"I have something on my mind, as well."

Christian regarded her curiously as he gestured toward the sofa. When they were both seated, he said, "Do you want to begin?"

"I found out something tonight that I'd like you to confirm."

"Go ahead."

"Did you get me the job at Matteo Pizarro Designs?"

He looked startled, but whether by her question or the lack of accusation in her tone, Noelle couldn't guess.

"Yes."

"Why?"

"Because you were talented, and I knew you wanted it."

She shook her head. "And so you could break things off and not feel guilty?"

"I broke things off so you'd take the job." .

Such altruism was not in keeping with his character, and Noelle wasn't sure she believed him. "You broke things off because you wanted to be with Talia."

He took Noelle's hand and lifted it to his right cheek. She touched the puckered skin of his scars. "How much do you remember about the night of my accident?"

Her first impulse was to pull away, but he held her fast. Christian wore his scars from that night on his skin. She wore hers inside. "We went to a party and I drank too much and got out of control because I thought you and Talia took off together."

"You didn't drink too much." Christian's expression hardened. "You were drugged."

"What?" The night had been unusually fuzzy, and she didn't remember more than one drink. But drugged? Why would he have kept something like this from her? "By whom?"

"Someone I thought was my friend." The anger in his voice was very real.

"Why?"

"You know how wild the crowd I ran with was. We treated the world like it was our playground, and we could do whatever we wanted without consequences. In contrast, you were sensible and worked hard at your career. The more involved I became with you, the less I saw them. They didn't like it very much, especially when I tried to bring you into our circle. They decided to go after you."

"By drugging me?" Noelle shivered as she realized just how vulnerable she'd been that night. She'd woken the next morning in her own bed with no idea how she'd gotten there. There'd been a video of her on the internet. She'd been dancing like a drunken fool. Because she couldn't remember any of it, she wasn't sure if she'd acted out because Christian had left with Talia or if he'd taken off because of how she'd been acting. "I thought you broke up with me because of how I behaved that night."

"I did. When I realized how much danger being with me had put you in." He shook his head. "They wanted you out of my life. It worked."

"But you left the party." She remembered being told that he was gone. Well, that wasn't quite true. Memories of the evening's events grew very indistinct after the first hour or so. The next morning the internet had lit up about the horrific car accident. There'd been no mention of a passenger, but she assumed the royal family simply covered that up.

"Because I thought you did. Talia used your phone to text me, saying that if I couldn't treat you any better then maybe one of your friends would. I chased after you and thought that you were leaving with Andre. At the time I didn't realize it was Talia. I followed them."

She couldn't grasp how his mind had been working that night. "You thought I left with Andre?" The skeptical laughter bubbling in her chest died beneath Christian's somber gaze. "How could you believe I would do that?"

"You'd been unhappy for a while. I thought perhaps you'd had enough."

"But to leave in the middle of a party after sending you a text? And with one of your friends?" It stung that he'd understood her so little. "You knew how I felt about you."

"Yes. But I let you think I wasn't exclusive even when I knew you weren't seeing anyone else."

His phrasing caught her attention. "You let me think? What does that mean? That you weren't seeing Talia and all the others you'd been photographed with?" Christian had never made excuses for his freewheeling lifestyle or said the sorts of things a girlfriend wanted to hear. Social media had buzzed with his exploits, and while that had hurt, Noelle had recognized that if she wanted him in her life, she had to share him.

"Not after the first few months. I didn't want to be with anyone but you." He rubbed his temples. "I hated that."

"Because I wasn't beautiful and exciting like all the other women you partied with?"

"You were both beautiful and exciting. But I didn't like having anyone relying on me for anything. And the way you looked at me…" He sighed. "Things were happening to me that I didn't like."

"Things?" she echoed, half afraid of what he might tell her. She'd mostly succeeded at never reading between the lines with Christian, knowing that way led to madness. But then he'd never been particularly vague. Voice light, she prompted, "What sort of things?"

A fissure formed in his granite expression. "Feelings."

"I can see why that upset you." She couldn't resist some faint mockery. It helped hide the pain his words caused.

Why had caring about her been something he'd been so unhappy about? At the time, she would have been thrilled beyond belief to think that she'd meant something more to him than just a tranquil pit stop in his eventful social life.

"I knew from the first that I wasn't good for you." He caressed her cheek with his knuckles. "Instead of taking your talent to Paris or London, you stayed in your tiny Carone flat, working for a man who claimed your designs as his own. Being with me kept you stuck. That's why I encouraged you to send off your résumé and portfolio."

"It wasn't your fault that I was afraid." Of taking a chance with her career and finding out she couldn't compete. Of losing the man she loved. "I just wasn't ready to leave Sherdana."

"But once you thought we'd broken up, you jumped at the chance to interview for a position at Matteo Pizarro."

"That's not fair. When I thought you'd chosen Talia, I knew I had to get away from Sherdana." It wasn't until she'd settled in Paris months later and discovered Christian and Talia weren't together that Noelle recognized her insecurities had worked against her.

"Exactly my point. Even after you got the job with Matteo Pizarro, you hesitated."

She'd paused in the middle of packing and visited him in the hospital, hoping he would ask her to stay. He'd been so cold. "You told me you'd moved on."

"Would you have left if I hadn't?"

She couldn't meet his eyes. "I wanted to be with you."

"And being with me caused you to be in danger. For your own good I sent you away."

"What would you have done if I'd told you I was pregnant?"

Christian shook his head. "I'd like to believe I would've done the right thing, but I honestly don't know."

"What would have been the right thing?"

"Marry you. Settle down. Become a good husband and father."

Noelle couldn't stop the wry smile that curved her lips. "Neither one of us was ready for that."

The way his eyebrows shot up said she'd surprised him. "You were."

"I was happy in Paris. I loved what I was doing. It was hard to manage my career and being a new mom, but I discovered such satisfaction in my ability to do both."

"See, breaking up with me was the best thing that could have happened to you."

"That's not true." But she couldn't deny that in many ways he'd done her a favor.

"So what happens now?"

"Now?"

"I'm no longer a young, irresponsible cad. You are thriving in your career and as a mother. We've demonstrated that the chemistry between us is hotter than ever. I have a son that I love, and want to be a full-time father. Marry me."

She saw what he was offering and spun the large diamond ring on her finger. He'd always been what she wanted. So, why couldn't she just say yes?

Twelve

Christian saw Noelle's hesitation and felt his heart tear.

"Victor convinced me to move to New York for the next six months so I can focus on the ready-to-wear line."

"Victor convinced you?" Christian probed her expression. "Or did you have this in mind before you left Sherdana?"

"A little of both," she admitted. "Thanks to you Marc loves it here, and I don't know how I'm supposed to take care of all the manufacturing issues and marketing details if I'm in Europe."

"You let me believe that I would have partial custody of Marc. Have you changed your mind?"

"No. We will figure something out about that."

"But you and I won't be together."

She stared at her hands and shook her head. "Being Marc's parents and having great sexual chemistry aren't strong enough reasons to get married. I don't want to get divorced in a few years because the only time we're compatible is in bed."

"I don't plan to divorce." Just the thought made his chest ache. "I intend to spend the rest of my life with you."

Again she didn't answer right away. If her goal was to convince him that she didn't share his commitment, he refused to let her succeed. Pushed to fight for the woman he wanted, Christian stood and scooped Noelle into his arms. He silenced her protests with a fierce glare and marched toward her bedroom. Setting her on her feet near the bed, he shut the door and stripped off his shirt before turning to face her.

"Christian, this isn't going to change my mind about staying in New York." So she said, but her gaze roamed his bare torso in hungry desperation.

"I have no intention of talking you out of moving to New York." He eliminated the distance between them with deliberate strides, letting passion incinerate his fear of losing her. "I only want what's best for you."

He hadn't meant for his words to upset her, but suddenly she looked stricken. Moving with slow tenderness, he slipped the dress from her body and worshipped her soft skin with his fingers and lips. The catch on her strapless bra popped free, no match for his expertise, and she sucked in a sharp breath as he took one breast in his hand.

With his desire spiraling in ever tightening circles, Christian dropped to his knees before Noelle and hooked his fingers in her white, lacy panties, pulling them down her thighs. The vibration in her muscles increased, threatening her stability. To keep her upright, he framed her slender hips with his hands. Her flat stomach quivered as he trailed kisses across it.

He'd missed the chance to watch her belly grow round with his son. He set his forehead against her, overwhelmed by how much more he stood to lose if he couldn't win her love. His sudden stillness prompted her to ride her palms across his bare shoulders and dragged her nails through his hair. He wrapped his arms around her and set his cheek against her abdomen.

"Christian?"

He'd never fully appreciated the power of her soothing touch. How her quiet voice and fervent embrace created a sanctuary that let his worries slip away.

"I wasn't completely truthful when I said I only wanted what was best for you. What I really want is what's best for me. And that's you."

"Make love to me."

Not needing to be asked twice, Christian lifted her off her feet and set her on the mattress. Together they stripped the comforter away, exposing the cool sheets. Noelle knelt on the bed and snagged the waistband of his trousers, drawing him toward her. Moving with confidence, she unfastened his belt and slid down his zipper until she'd freed him.

He had the package open and the condom ready, but when she began to slide it down his erection, the heaven of her strong fingers closed around him ripped a groan from his lips. Rolling her fingers over his sensitive tip, she gave a half smile as his hips bucked forward. Shuddering, too aroused to withstand her ministrations for long, Christian sucked in a sharp breath and freed himself from her grasp.

"You drive me crazy," he growled a second before claiming her lips in a hot, fiery kiss.

Tenderness vanished beneath the onslaught of her answering passion as she pushed her breasts against his chest and drove him crazy with the seductive sway of her hips. Filling his hands with her adorable butt, he shifted her off the mattress and coaxed her thighs around his waist. With his erection hardened to the point of pain, he laid her on the crisp sheets and moved between her thighs.

But he didn't enter her as she'd expected. Instead, his lips grazed over her mound, causing her head to lift off the bed and her gaze to sharpen. Enjoying the play of emotion on her face, he dipped his tongue into her sizzling heat and tasted her arousal. With a groan, her head fell back and her hips strained forward. Christian grinned as he began again, finding the rhythm that she liked and coaxing her toward climax.

She came against his mouth, her back arching, his name on her lips. In the aftermath, she lay with her eyes closed, her chest rising and falling with each unsteady breath. Smiling, Christian kissed his way back up her body. He settled between her thighs and kissed her with all the longing that filled his heart. Then, at her urging, he eased into her tight heat. She burrowed her fingers in his hair and set the soles of her feet on the mattress, tipping her hips to meet his slow, deep thrust.

Now it was his turn to cry out. Burying his face in her neck, he began to move. Pleasure swept over him in a stormy rush. He set his teeth against the glorious friction, fighting against the orgasm that threatened to claim him. By slowing his movements, he was able to regain some control, but the provocative sweep of Noelle's hands over his hot skin wasn't making things any easier.

"Faster," she murmured, her teeth catching at his earlobe. "I want you to come hard." Her throaty voice and the flick of her tongue over the tender spot where she'd nipped him caused him to shudder and almost lose control.

"Damn it, stop that," he growled, cupping one butt cheek and adjusting his angle just a bit to allow his pelvis to rub her just so.

With her eyes closed and her lips curled into a satisfied grin, she yielded to his pace. Content to watch her, Christian barely noticed the heat building in his groin until it threatened to engulf him.

"Come with me," Christian said. It was a plea rather than a command.

He thrust more powerfully. Her lashes lifted and her eyes met his. This is what they were good at. Connecting at this intimate level. Her vulnerability had taught him openness. Her strength had made it safe for him to let go. She'd never judged or demanded. Just given. It had made him want to give in return.

Fighting against his orgasm until she started to go over the edge, Christian felt something inside him struggling to get free. Noelle's beautiful eyes widened as the first spasms of her climax began. Wild with relief, Christian drove forward into his own release, the force of it ripping a harsh cry from him. Blackness snatched at him as stars exploded behind his eyes. Dimly he heard Noelle call his name.

For what felt like an eternity, wave after wave of pleasure pounded him. At last there was only peace and ragged breathing. Weak and shaky, Christian shifted his weight off Noelle and gathered her into his arms. She returned his hearty embrace with matching energy. They lay entwined for several minutes before Christian went to the bathroom and came back with a towel and her nightgown.

She'd never liked sleeping naked, which was fine with him because he enjoyed gliding his hands over her silk covered curves and stripping her bare each time they made love. Once her glorious breasts, tiny waist and slender hips were concealed beneath the pale green fabric, Christian set the alarm on his phone to wake them at 5:00 a.m. and pulled the covers up over them both.

This would be the first time they spent the night together since reconnecting, and Noelle's lack of protest made Christian wonder if she'd changed her mind about his proposal. If he could spend the rest of his life with Noelle, he would be happier than he deserved to be.

He stopped resisting the pull of exhaustion. Keeping up with Marc's boundless energy had taken its toll. Content in a way he hadn't been for a long time, Christian buried his nose in Noelle's fragrant hair and sighed.

"I love you," he murmured and drifted off to sleep.

Christian's words lanced through Noelle, shocking her to complete wakefulness. Before the echo of his voice faded, his deep breathing told her he was unconscious. Her first impulse was to shake him awake and force him to repeat the words. Had he meant them? Had he even realized what he said? Why was it the man couldn't speak his heart unless he was semiconscious?

Noelle lay awake for a long time, her cheek on Christian's bare chest, listening to the steady thump of his heart. She pondered the impact her expanding business was about to have on her son and her love life. Was it wrong to want it all? Success with her ready-to-wear line? The family she'd longed for with Christian? The thought of reaching out and grabbing nothing but air worried her, but she wouldn't see stars without overcoming a fear of the dark.

No solutions revealed themselves that night. She awoke to an empty bed and a brief note on hotel stationery from Christian, letting her know he had taken Marc to his suite so she could get ready in peace. The note was brisk and informative, lacking the romantic overtones left over from the previous night.

Heaving a sigh, Noelle got up and went to shower. Had all her what-ifs and how-tos from the previous night been a waste of time? Perhaps in the hazy aftermath of some spectacular lovemaking she'd only imagined what she longed to hear Christian say.

No. Noelle refused to believe that. She knew what she'd heard. Christian loved her. Based on how he'd protected her from his friends and pulled strings to get her on the path to a fabulous career, he'd loved her for a long time. That he had a hard time being vulnerable didn't surprise her.

Not only had he run with a condescending group of entitled troublemakers who tormented anyone who showed weakness, he'd also been the youngest of three princes, far from the throne with no expectations placed on him. Christian had once shared that he often felt like an afterthought. Noelle suspected this was what had led him to act out.

On the way to her first meeting, Noelle called her assistant back in Sherdana to check on her appointment for later in the week and was delighted to learn that the bride had postponed until the following month. This opened up the rest of the week, and more than anything Noelle wanted a quiet dinner with Christian and to spend a day roaming New York City with him and their son.

Knowing that Christian had cleared his entire schedule so he could be there for Marc, she sent him a text asking if they could postpone returning to Sherdana. He responded with a photo of him and Marc cheek to cheek, both giving a thumbs-up. Warmth spread through her, and she clutched the screen to her chest. Loosing a ragged sigh, she sent back a smiley face and spent the rest of the ride organizing a romantic dinner for two.

At a little after four in the afternoon, Christian carried his sleeping son across the Four Seasons lobby and into an elevator. Along the way he caught several women watching him, their expressions reading *isn't that sweet*. He resisted smiling until the elevator doors closed. He wasn't accustomed to women approving of his deeds and found he rather liked it.

Noelle was working at the desk in her suite when he let himself in. She started to rise, but he waved her back. In the past couple of days, he'd grown accustomed to caring for Marc and enjoyed it a great deal.

After taking his son's shoes off and tucking him beneath a light blanket with his favorite stuffed dinosaur, Christian returned to the living room. Noelle had put away her laptop and was standing near the wide windows staring out over the city. As Christian drew near, she smiled at him over her shoulder.

"Another hectic day?"

"I don't think there's a single question about the Statue of Liberty that Marc didn't ask."

"I'm sure." She leaned her head back against Christian's shoulder as he slipped his arms around her. He felt more than heard her sigh. "I love you."

Unsure if he'd heard her correctly, Christian held perfectly still, afraid to say anything and ruin the moment.

"But I think you already know that," she continued.

"I don't. I didn't." Chest aching, he turned her to face him. "I love you, too. You know that, right?"

She smiled at his earnest tone. "I didn't until you told me just before you fell asleep last night."

"I'm sorry it took me so long to say it. Those three words have played through my mind a hundred times over the past week. A thousand times since we first met. I guess I've avoided the truth for so long that it became a habit to hide it from you, as well."

"You're not the only one who has trouble breaking old patterns of behavior. I ended our engagement because I didn't believe you could possibly want me as something other than the mother of your son."

Cupping her face in his hands, heart racing to the point where he was light-headed, Christian searched her expression. "Does that mean you've changed your mind about wanting to marry me?" He sounded neither calm nor casual as he asked the question. To his relief she didn't leave him in suspense for long.

"I've always wanted to marry you," she teased. "Nothing could change that."

No longer capable of holding back his impatience, Christian put his hands on her shoulders and gave her a little shake. "Are you going to marry me?"

"Yes!" She threw her arms around his waist and lifted her lips to receive his kiss.

Christian wasted no time letting her know how delighted he was by her decision. One ravenous, joyful kiss followed another until a weight struck their legs. Setting Noelle's lips free, Christian glanced down at his son. Noelle's hand was already smoothing the sleep-tossed waves of Marc's dark brown hair.

"Mama, I'm hungry."

Snatching breath back into his lungs, Christian chuckled. "How is that possible after everything he's eaten today?"

"He has a lot of growing to do before he'll be as big as his father, and that takes fuel."

Christian bent and hoisted his son into his arms. Marc wrapped one arm around each of his parents as they stood close together.

"Your mother and I are getting married so the three of us can be a family," he said, catching a glimpse of Noelle's nod. "What do you think about that?" It was risky to ask a four-year-old such an important question when his stomach was empty, but Christian refused to wait another minute before making the engagement official. And telling Marc was as official as it got.

"Yeah. Will I get to live at the palace?" A couple weeks earlier it was the last place he'd wanted to visit, but now that he'd met his cousins and explored some of the rooms, he'd become much more interested in making it his home.

"Sometimes we can spend time there..." Noelle began, shooting Christian a quick frown.

Marc squirmed in Christian's grasp, his hunger once again snagging his attention. "May I have some cheese?"

Noelle made Marc a snack out of supplies stocked in the small refrigerator. When her son was content, she turned to Christian once more.

"Where are we going to live? The farmhouse is too small. Your apartment in Old Town has no outside space for Marc to play."

"I am in negotiations for an estate about twelve miles from the center of Carone. When I first learned about Marc, I decided he'd need more space than I currently have. If you approve of it, we can live there." He paused, wondering if she'd forgotten last night's decision to live in New York for six months. "As for the time you're planning to spend here, we can always rent an apartment near Central Park."

"We?" She looked hopeful.

"Before my brothers chose love over duty to the Sherdanian throne, I'd been considering expanding my ventures into the US. This seems like an excellent time to explore new territory."

Almost before he finished speaking, Noelle wrapped her arms tightly around his waist and pressed her cheek to his chest. "I'm so relieved to hear you say that. I didn't know how I was going to live apart from you these next six months."

Christian hugged her in return. "You didn't seriously think I was going to let you get away a second time, did you?"

She tipped back her head and gave him a wry smile. "Get away?"

"You have no idea what it cost me to let you go."

The torment in his voice made her shiver. She pulled him down for a kiss. Mindful of Marc's presence, they kept it affectionate and light. There would be plenty of time for passion later when they were alone.

As soon as Marc finished his snack, Christian lifted him into his arms and pulled out his cell phone. Earlier that day he'd realized that as many pictures as he'd taken with his son these past few days, not one of them had included Noelle. As the three of them clustered together in front of the window overlooking the New York skyline, Christian snapped their photo and sent it to his parents and brothers with the message that he and Noelle were engaged. Despite the time difference, he received immediate congratulations from everyone.

"It's official," he warned her. "There's no backing out now."

She regarded him with sparkling eyes. "You almost sound worried that I might."

"I learned the hard way never to take you for granted." He kissed her temple. "That will not happen again."

"We've both made mistakes and learned from them. I can see us making more."

"But as long as we don't let doubts come between us, we'll be just fine."

"Better than fine," she said, resting her head against his

shoulder and watching Marc put together a puzzle of the Statue of Liberty. "We're going to be gloriously happy."

Christian's arm tightened around Noelle. "That, my dazzling wife-to-be, sounds just about perfect."

* * * * *